# Praise for Mel

## *The Wings of P*

"On an atmospheric island with a ruined castle, a page-turning mystery unfolds. . . . Melanie Dobson writes with a heart bent toward healing, and again she delivers an intriguing story of the bonds of family, the mystery of time, and the power of love."

**PATTI CALLAHAN HENRY,** *New York Times* bestselling author

"This captivating tale seamlessly weaves past and present for a layered tapestry you won't want to miss. From the first page, I was hooked on this story of identities lost and found, of hearts broken and made new. I fell in love with the haunting setting, complex characters, and the ultimate redemption in *The Wings of Poppy Pendleton.*"

**JOCELYN GREEN,** Christy Award–winning author of *The Metropolitan Affair*

"Mystery at every turn threads *The Wings of Poppy Pendleton*, Melanie Dobson's captivating family saga set amid the Thousand Islands in the St. Lawrence River. . . . Absolutely fascinating and beautifully written—I could not put this book down!"

**CATHY GOHLKE,** Christy Award Hall of Fame author of *Ladies of the Lake* and *Night Bird Calling*

"*The Wings of Poppy Pendleton* is a hauntingly beautiful time-slip mystery overflowing with hidden secrets that impact multiple generations. Dobson's skillful artistry of words brings the Thousand Islands setting to life, weaving complex characters, page-turning intrigue, hints of romance, and inspiring faith-filled hope into both past and present."

**DARLENE PANZERA,** award-winning author of *The Groom She Thought She'd Left Behind* (part of the Runaway Brides collection)

"Melanie Dobson creates a timeless time-slip mystery that bounces between the stories of two little girls and two troubled women, two different historical periods, and the mysteries surrounding their lives. Intriguing, and powerful, this is novel to experience, ponder, and share, where the twist and turns of beautiful phrases abound."

**SUSAN G. MATHIS,** award-winning Thousand Islands Gilded Age author

## *The Winter Rose*

"Dobson is quickly establishing herself as a new powerhouse in dual-timeline Christian fiction. This is a potent examination of redemption after scars, and, more simply, a good story, told well."

*LIBRARY JOURNAL*, starred review

"Melanie Dobson is a master at time-slip stories, and *The Winter Rose* is no exception. With skillful prose, impeccable research, heart-tugging characters, and a plot full of intrigue, Dobson keeps readers turning pages until the very end."

JODY HEDLUND, author of the Bride Ships series

"*The Winter Rose* is a blossom of hope in a broken and hurting world. From the snowy Pyrénées to the lush forests of Oregon, from the scars of war to the solace of family, Melanie Dobson weaves a story of how God can transform the pain of the past into a loving plan for the future. This book will remain in your heart long after you turn the final page."

STEPHANIE LANDSEM, author of *In a Far-Off Land*

"A magnificent novel set in the midst of WWII in France with ripples that continue to the present day. Dobson's beautiful descriptions, well-drawn characters, and deep insights pull the reader into this story and won't let go until long after the last page. Altogether brilliant and breathtaking."

LIZ TOLSMA, bestselling author of *A Picture of Hope*

## *The Curator's Daughter*

"Fans of Kristy Cambron and Rachel Hauck will devour this split-time tale with two equally strong story lines."

*LIBRARY JOURNAL*

"Drawing from historical events and modern-day issues, Dobson creates a story that transcends the years and combines multiple themes—resilience, faith, and forgiveness—and is filled with vivid historical details and emotional twists. . . . A great book for fans of WWII inspirational stories."

HISTORICAL NOVELS REVIEW

"Fans of WWII inspirationals will love this."

*PUBLISHERS WEEKLY*

"Set in a world coming apart at the seams, this story will sweep you up in life-and-death struggles but ultimately fill you with love and hope. A haunting, totally immersive novel."

**CHRIS FABRY**, bestselling author of *Under a Cloudless Sky*

## *Memories of Glass*

"*Memories of Glass* is a remarkable, multilayered novel that weaves stories of friendship and faith in wartime Holland together with a modern-day orphanage in Africa. Memorable characters portray the complexity of human relationships and reveal the lasting consequences of our choices, whether cowardly or courageous, and the mysteries kept me turning pages, leaving me with much to ponder."

**LYNN AUSTIN**, bestselling author of *If I Were You* and *Legacy of Mercy*

"Like colored shards in sunlight, Melanie Dobson once again shines her light of truth in this elegantly complex and gripping tale of the hidden terrors of the Netherlands during WWII. *Memories of Glass* is a remarkable story and one that will linger in the hearts of readers long after the last page."

**KATE BRESLIN**, bestselling author of *For Such a Time*

"Breathtaking, heartbreaking, and ultimately uplifting, *Memories of Glass* shows the beauty of helping others, the ugliness of people helping only themselves, and the destructive power of secrets through the generations. Melanie Dobson's memorable characters and fine eye for detail bring the danger of the Netherlands under Nazi occupation to life. This novel will stay with you."

**SARAH SUNDIN**, award-winning, bestselling author of *The Sky Above Us*

## *Hidden Among the Stars*

"This exciting tale will please fans of time-jump inspirational fiction."

*PUBLISHERS WEEKLY*

"A romantic tale of castles, lost dreams, and hidden treasures wrapped inside a captivating and suspenseful mystery complete with an unpredictable, unforeseen, and unexpected ending. Not a book to miss!"

MIDWEST BOOK REVIEWS

"Star-crossed, forbidden love and the disappearance of family members and hidden treasure make a compelling WWII story and set the stage for modern-day detective work in Dobson's latest time-slip novel. . . . *Hidden Among the Stars* is Dobson at her best."

CATHY GOHLKE, Christy Award Hall of Fame author of *Ladies of the Lake* and *Night Bird Calling*

"*Hidden Among the Stars* is a glorious treasure hunt, uniting past and present with each delightful revelation. It's must-read historical fiction that left me pondering well-crafted twists for days."

MESU ANDREWS, award-winning author of *Isaiah's Daughter*

## *Catching the Wind*

"Dobson creates a labyrinth of intrigue, expertly weaving a World War II drama with a present-day mystery to create an unforgettable story. This is a must-read for fans of historical time-slip fiction."

*PUBLISHERS WEEKLY*, starred review

"Dobson skillfully interweaves three separate lives as she joins the past and present in an uplifting tale of courage, love, and enduring hope."

*LIBRARY JOURNAL*

"A beautiful and captivating novel with compelling characters, intriguing mystery, and true friendship. The story slips flawlessly between present day and WWII, the author's sense of timing and place contributing to the reader's urge to devour the book in one sitting yet simultaneously savor its poignancy."

*ROMANTIC TIMES*

"Readers will delight in this story that illustrates how the past can change the present."

LISA WINGATE, national bestselling author of *Before We Were Yours*

# The Wings of Poppy Pendleton

## Also by Melanie Dobson

*Chateau of Secrets*
*Shadows of Ladenbrooke Manor*
*Beneath a Golden Veil*
*Catching the Wind*
*Enchanted Isle*
*Hidden Among the Stars*
*Memories of Glass*
*The Curator's Daughter*
*The Winter Rose*

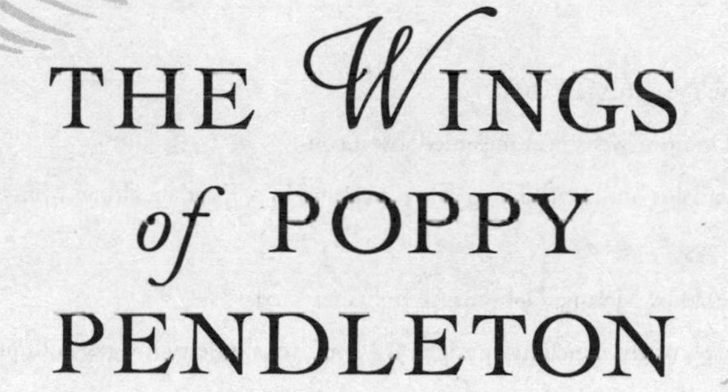


MELANIE DOBSON

Tyndale House Publishers
Carol Stream, Illinois

Visit Tyndale online at tyndale.com.

Visit Melanie Dobson's website at melaniedobson.com.



*The Wings of Poppy Pendleton*



Cover designed by Libby Dykstra

Edited by Kathryn S. Olson

Published in association with the literary agency of Natasha Kern Literary Agency, Inc., P.O. Box 1069, White Salmon, WA 98672.



For information about special discounts for bulk purchases, please contact Tyndale House Publishers at csresponse@tyndale.com, or call 1-855-277-9400.

**Library of Congress Cataloging-in-Publication Data**

A catalog record for this book is available from the Library of Congress.

ISBN 978-1-4964-7456-8 (HC)
ISBN 978-1-4964-7457-5 (SC)

Printed in the United States of America

29 28 27 26 25 24 23
7 6 5 4 3 2 1

*Marjorie Wacker MacKim*

*1923–2005*

*I may never know your full story,*

*but your life inspired this one.*

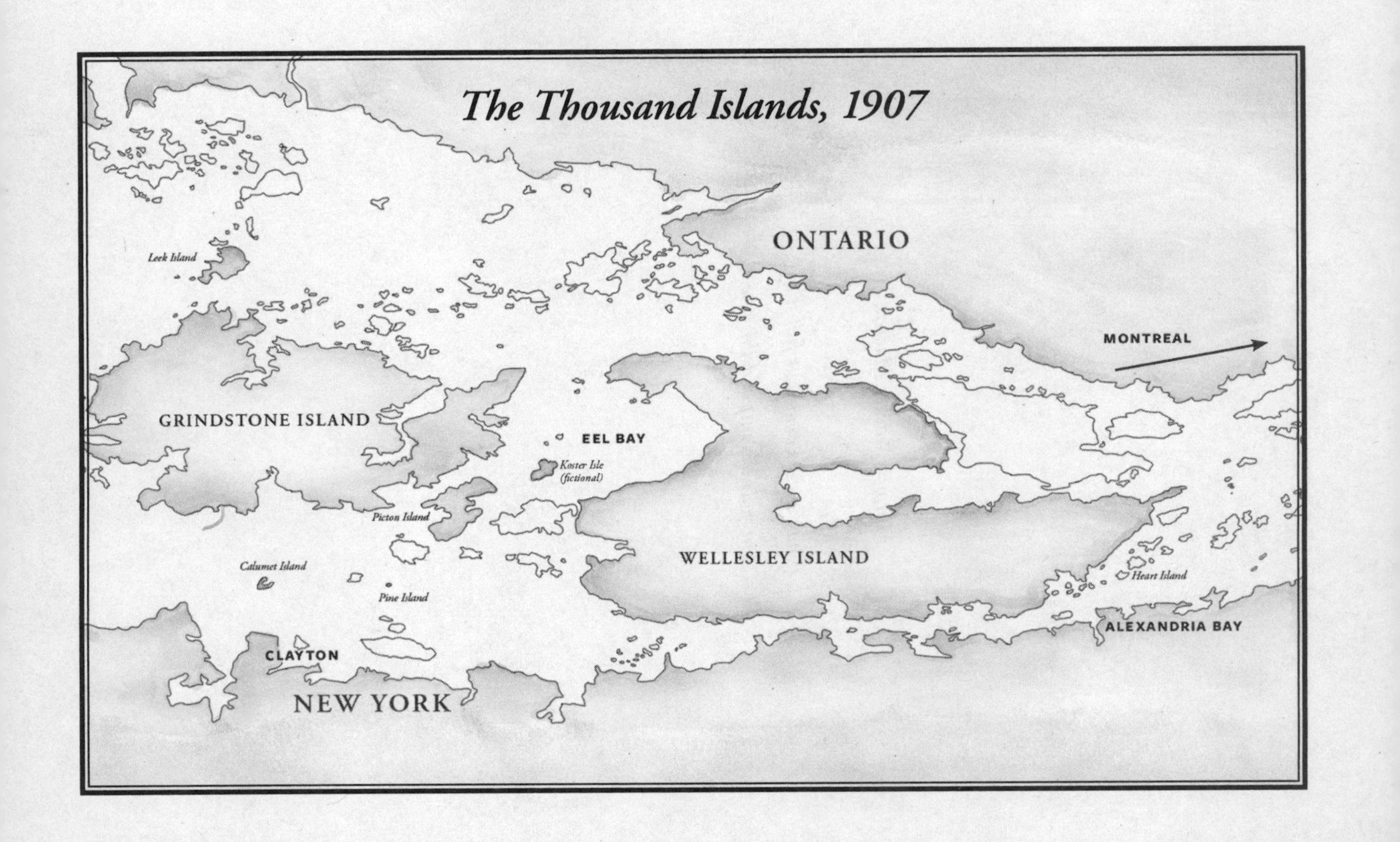
The Thousand Islands, 1907
ONTARIO
MONTREAL
Leek Island
GRINDSTONE ISLAND
EEL BAY
Koster Isle
(fictional)
Picton Island
WELLESLEY ISLAND
Calumet Island
Pine Island
Heart Island
ALEXANDRIA BAY
CLAYTON
NEW YORK

# PROLOGUE

"ARE YOU COLD, MADAME?"

Her hands shook like the tremors from the ship's bell, clattering against the shreds of wet fabric that hung at her sides, but she didn't answer his question. Truth was, she felt neither hot nor cold. In fact, she felt nothing at all.

The man draped a blanket over what remained of her nightclothes and the weight of it anchored her to the ground.

"What's your name?" he asked, a pocket notebook and pencil in hand. As if her answer might somehow capture the horror when no words would suffice.

"I need something . . ." She tugged the blanket taut across her chest, covering the purse that hung around her neck, but even then, the shaking wouldn't stop. "Something to drink."

A fur-cloaked woman poured tea from a thermos, the tin cup steaming in the night air.

A handful of skiffs had unloaded on this remote shore along the St. Lawrence, dozens of passengers now scattered on the crags, a crush of debris littering the rocks. Surely more people had been rescued. Hundreds had been on the ship. A thousand even.

She squinted into the fog, thick as paste, searching, but not even the burning kerosene in the lighthouses could be seen. How many more would still arrive on this dark shore? How many names for this man to collect?

Only one name mattered to her.

The tea melted away the ice in her mind, and then grief sprang from a fresh well, threatening to drown her heart and mind, stealing her breath.

She should have stayed frozen.

"Your name?" the man repeated, tapping his lead on paper as tea spilled over her cup.

*Her name.*

If only she could rid herself of it. Dump every letter overboard and let them sink to the bottom of this wretched river. "I don't remember—"

"I only want to help you find your family," he said.

"I have no family."

"Your husband," he persisted. "Children."

"I had neither before the wreck."

He lowered his pencil. "Then I suppose you can be glad of that."

She felt the cold now, stealing up from her fingers, reminding her she was still alive. "I am glad of no such thing."

His gaze wandered to the fog-laden river as if he could see the sunken ship. "The court will find out who caused this," he said. "You'll get money."

He was trying to comfort her, she knew, but everything was wrecked, not just the steamer. "I don't want their money."

His eyes narrowed as if questioning the soundness of her mind. "You'll be the only one who doesn't."

She stepped carefully on another rock, her feet bare. Had she been wearing her slippers when the steamer began to list? She still couldn't feel her toes.

Another rowboat arrived at the water's edge, its steel bow flashing in the lantern light. And something else. A shimmer of gold on the stony shore.

She picked up the watch case and traced her fingers across the flowers engraved on the front. The gilded stamp on the back with the Pendleton name.

"Where are you going?" the man called as she shuffled over the stones, rushing toward the rowboat.

"I have to find someone."

"But you said—"

She waded into the icy water, searching the faces of those who'd survived, hoping for a miracle on one hand but afraid of who she might find.

She didn't recognize anyone on board.

The survivors were escorted into a church basement and buried under shells of blankets as they awaited news of their loved ones. And they continued waiting as dozens of coffins were brought through the door.

Hours later, another man appeared at her side, one with a ledger, inquiring again of her name.

"Sister," she finally said.

He looked up, and she could see a glimmer of compassion on his hardened face.

"You're a nun?"

She didn't know who she was anymore.

"I have to record everyone's name." His forehead crested with wrinkles as he contemplated the gravity of his work. "So we can account for the missing."

She dug through the attic of her mind, searching for names in the dusty travel trunks that she'd long forgotten. He needed a name, but she couldn't give him the one inscribed in the ship's manifest.

A picture emerged in her head of a woman immortalized in stained glass, her story woven through the Scriptures. A deceived woman who became the deceiver. A woman who received a new name after her servant bore her a son.

"Sarah," she told him, and he scribbled her new name into the ledger. "Sister Sarah."

From a dark corner, she watched as more survivors stepped into the cramped basement, all of them drenched in river water. Watched the wooden coffins pile up at the side of the room, no respecter of age or class. Watched and waited even as her heart longed for the impossible.

In spite of Sarah's doubt, in spite of her deception, God had redeemed her life.

Perhaps it wasn't too late for her.

Perhaps He'd still give her a miracle.

A girl clung to one of the coffins until the man with the registration book guided the child to the shadows. "Sister Sarah can pray with you."

But she wasn't qualified to pray for anyone.

"She needs you," he begged, and with those words, she did what she once thought foolish.

Sarah cradled the girl's hand and begged for God's mercy on her.

In the morning hours, Sarah wandered along the shore again as dawn finally broke through the haze. Then she dug the Pendleton timepiece out of her pocket, and with a loud cry, she hurled it back into the St. Lawrence.

The shifting river sands, she hoped, would forever bury its curse.

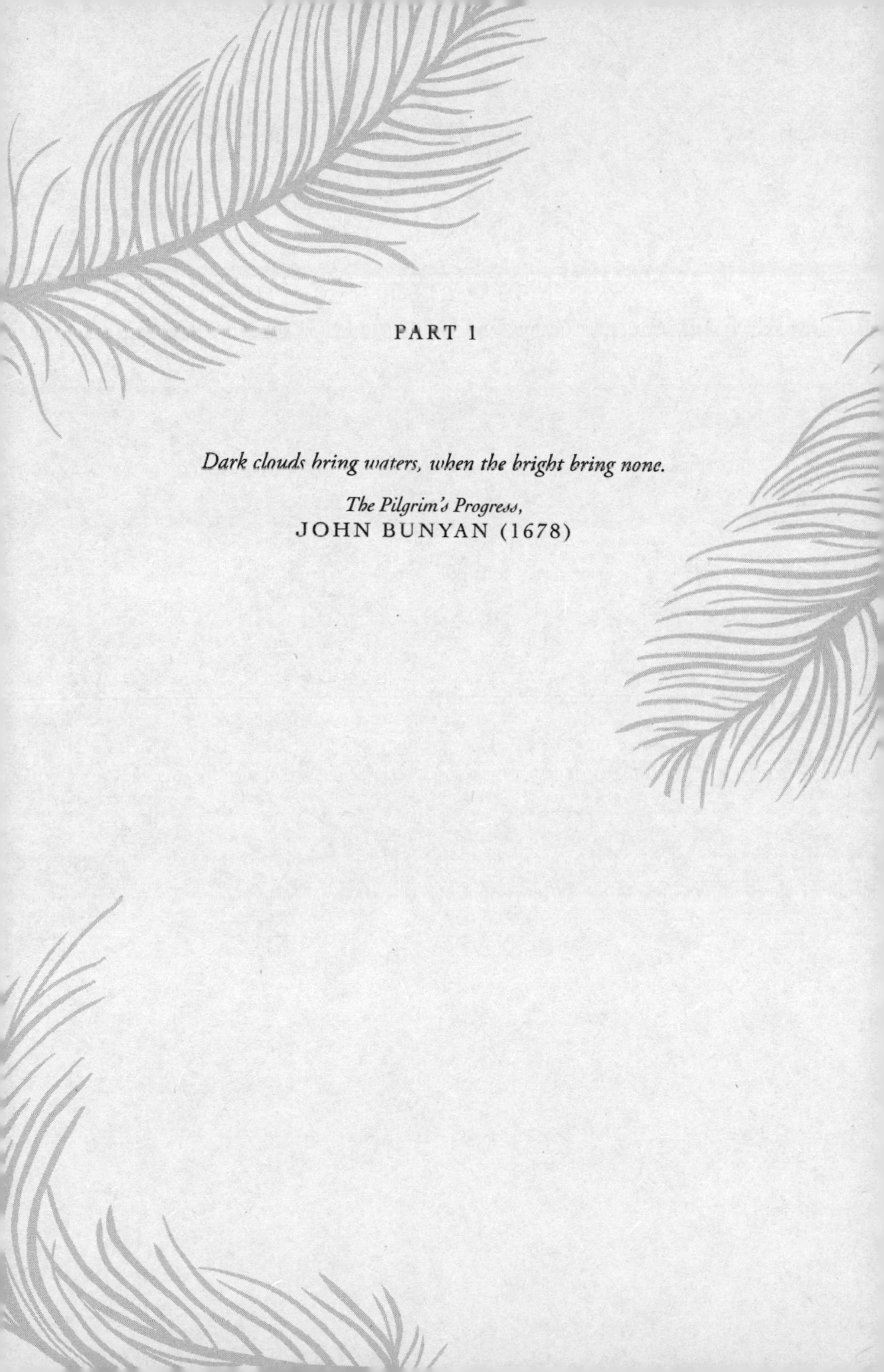

# PART 1

*Dark clouds bring waters, when the bright bring none.*

*The Pilgrim's Progress,*
JOHN BUNYAN (1678)

1

# CHLOE

KOSTER ISLE, NEW YORK
APRIL 1992

Waves battered Chloe Ridell's motorboat as she steered around the imposing ruins on Koster Isle, the roof of the old boathouse draped precariously low. The castle above it had been built on granite, withstanding almost a century of storms, but one swift uppercut of wind could overturn her and *Lolli*, the mahogany runabout that her grandfather had built forty years ago.

In good weather, it only took fifteen minutes to cross from the village of Clayton to her island, but she'd already been battling the river for a half hour. Soon, she hoped, she'd be tucked away in her cottage with a mug of hot chocolate and a crackling fire and two sweet dogs who slept on her bedroom floor. Even if they lost electricity, her home was a safe place in a gale.

But the river wasn't safe, especially on a night like this. The St. Lawrence threw punches on all sides as its steel-blue waters curled and snaked between island pods. While river rats like her had learned to respect the whims of its fists, it still took every bit of concentration to duck its nasty hooks and the jabs aimed at *Lolli*'s hull.

If she fell tonight, Grandpa Cade's runabout would join the vast graveyard of ships below the surface, buried in the St. Lawrence sand, and it would take everything within her to climb the rocks on the shoreline. Like a musk turtle, she thought, shimmying up to sun.

Jenna, her best friend and business partner, had begged her to spend the night in the apartment that Chloe kept over Cade's Candy Shop, but in spite of the dark clouds, the rumble of thunder downstream, she'd needed to return to her cottage on the island. While she couldn't explain the urgency, she'd learned over the past thirty years to follow the whispers inside her head.

*God whispers*, Nana had called them. But she hadn't expected His whisper to lead her straight into a storm.

Chloe throttled back to surf over an icy wave as it battered her slicker, soaking her face and hands. Neither the voices nor this gale would take her down tonight. "C'mon, *Lolli*," she shouted as they rode another wave.

Locals liked to name their boats for the whimsical, perhaps in an effort to ward off fear. *The Good Ship Lollipop* was what Grandpa Cade had christened his prized speedboat with the red candy-striped vinyl seats, named for a trip to the candy shop that Shirley Temple sang about on the silver screen.

Decades ago, when custom boats were prized as works of art as well as modes of transportation, Ridell Boats had constructed scores of beautifully crafted and varnished runabouts in Clayton. But most people wanted fiberglass now or aluminum or even inflatable boats. Easy to maintain. Reliable. Quick to sell for a good price. People didn't care like they used to about craftsmanship. Before her grandfather had died, he wanted to build one last boat to call his own. Then he'd passed ole *Lolli* on to her.

A shudder quaked across her chest as another hulking wave roiled toward her, black water sparking green in the sidelight. One hand clutching the wheel, the other on her throttle, she and *Lolli* had been flung back into the ring.

As the storm pressed against her, trying to corner them against the island's rocky shoreline, Chloe shoved the throttle so the wind wouldn't pin her against the rocks or plunge her into the frigid bay or push her into Canadian waters. With winds blowing northeast toward the Atlantic, a thousand miles upriver, she'd be halfway to Montreal by morning if she didn't fight back with a fury.

The gale frothed around the bow and whipped off the hood of her slicker, unfurling it like a sail. Her drenched hair wrapped around her head like a turban, but she wouldn't release the wheel or throttle to untangle it. Only a few more minutes now, and she'd be home.

Another bend ahead, and she swept around the island before throttling down. Ducking, she glided under the elbow of a beech tree and then she guided the boat between a curtain of vines that covered the entrance to her lagoon.

Here, in the shelter of trees, stormy waves tempered back into a slow boil.

Here she didn't have to be afraid.

With a deep breath, Chloe wiped the soaked strands of hair off her face, and the frantic pounding in her chest began to calm as she skirted a garden of marsh grass that swayed with the current. Grandpa Cade had built a shingled boathouse along this shore many years ago. A home for *Lolli* with its open front and narrow dock and a workshop for him overhead.

As *Lolli* nudged the bumpers with her nose, Chloe killed the motor and reached for the dock. "Steady now," she said as if the boat had ears. Then she unraveled the line.

*Docking's a lot like sewing,* her grandpa used to say. Chloe was no good as a seamstress, but her grandma had taught her the basics of stitching.

*Lasso the piling,* that's what Grandpa Cade always said. *Lasso, loop, and then thread the needle twice.* With a firm tug, no storm in these islands could detach her bowline from the wooden anchor.

The boat secure, Chloe unlatched the chipped hold and removed her leather tote, wrapping it quickly in a plastic bag to protect the shop's ledger and her foil-wrapped burger that she'd picked up from Jake's BBQ. Everything else could remain in the boat until morning.

On a night like this, no one would be scrounging around in her lagoon.

At the end of the boathouse was a narrow path that her grandfather had paved to his cottage when he was the caretaker of Koster Isle—or Ghost Island, as locals called it. The celebrity guests back at the turn of the century would arrive at the grand boathouse with its towering ceilings and intricate fretwork on the other side of the island and cross over a stone bridge before a member of the family or staff would escort them up through a covered passage to Poppy's Castle.

The official castle name was Pendleton, but Grandpa Cade had always referred to it as Poppy's. As if the girl who disappeared almost a hundred years ago might still be hiding inside.

Grandpa Cade passed away back in 1977, and her grandma died just two months ago, stepping into heaven almost fifteen years after he was gone. Nana never talked with her about the old castle or mystery that shrouded it. It was as if she'd carved a line across this small island in her mind and set the port side adrift. In Nana's mind, the castle and its stories were gladly buried in the sands of time.

As Chloe climbed the stone path, passing by the old icehouse and an abandoned chapel and a dilapidated powerhouse filled with rusty switches and dials, she longed to set several things in her own mind adrift, but the pieces always seemed to float back, often in glass bottles that shattered when they crashed into shore. Sometimes she felt like a fraud, living on an island built by another family, living in the shadow of their castle that had been abandoned since the early 1900s. But this was her grandparents' home—her home now—and she desperately wanted to keep the memories that they'd cultivated here alive.

The rain had stopped, and as darkness settled over the island, Chloe's flashlight cut through the haze. A few years after Grandpa Cade had died, she and *Lolli* had gotten lost in one of those creeper fogs that snuck up behind her and tossed a gray blanket over her head. The floodlight had glared back at her that night, reflecting her stupidity like a mirror. For hours she'd dodged shoals, trying to find her way back to Clayton, until the tank ran dry. Marsh grass had trapped her and *Lolli* near Toothpick Island until another river rat delivered a can of gasoline and a tumbler of coffee in the light of morning, along with a memorable scolding to keep Chloe off the water in a storm.

The path rose steeply up the side of the cliff, water slapping against the sandstone below, a tangled wall of branches and vines that protected the island and fifty thousand square feet of castle to her left. Raindrops clung to the braids of ivy, glistening in the light beam. Only in the winter, after the leaves were swept away in the winds, was Poppy's Castle visible from this trail.

Pine needles showered down as Chloe neared the end of the path. Her cottage was cocooned in a dip on the north shore, wreathed in sumac and balsam fir. The house had been built in the early 1900s like the castle on the hill, and with her grandparents' tender care, the cottage had ridden out the storms, just like they'd loved her through the emotional storms of adolescence and protected her from the many storms that raged through the North Country. How she missed her grandpa's laughter, her grandma's open arms and mugs of hot chocolate whenever Chloe came home.

They had spent their lives protecting and caring for this island, and now she was the only one left in the Ridell family to continue their legacy. She'd promised herself that she would care well for their home and candy shop after they passed on, but now that they were both gone, she didn't have nearly enough money to do either. The store brought so many people joy, but it was floundering financially and she didn't have enough income even to renovate what remained.

It was hard enough to think of selling the candy store, but it would wreck her heart if someone tore down the castle and cottage on her island and built a shiny mansion in their place. She'd keep fighting to preserve this small island and all its stories. Drop an anchor in the only place that she'd ever called home.

Then she'd never be swept away in life's storms again.

Strands of brown hair stuck to Chloe's cheeks in the wind, framing her lips as she whistled for her dogs tonight, watching for the two Labradors who always raced out from their shed to greet her. Stopping for a moment, she listened for their barks, the cracking of sticks and scattering of stones under paws, but she didn't hear anything except the shudder of branches along the path.

"Maple?" she called first to the older dog. Then she shouted for Sugar.

Moonlight slipped between a crease in the clouds as she waited, spilling over her island. Then a bolt shot straight up her spine.

Where were her dogs?

A hundred scenarios smashed into her brain, none of them good. A slip off a cliff. A broken floorboard in the boathouse. Bald eagles hunting for food.

*No sense pondering the possibilities.*

Nana's voice smoothed over some of the worry tethering her, and she tried to set her fears adrift with mental scissors that had grown rusty from use.

There were no dangerous animals or snakes on her island—the only animals besides her dogs were the hare and skunk and red squirrel who crossed over the ice in the winter and became stranded in the thaw. No guests would visit without an invitation. No intruders, to her knowledge, had trespassed in years. And no ghosts haunted the walls except those kept alive by tour boat guides to entertain their guests.

It was the immaterial that brought tourists by her island in droves. All the stories about the tragic death of Mr. Pendleton and the disappearance of his only daughter.

The only telephone on the island was in her cottage, and Jenna had told her to call this evening. But her best friend knew that service would be spotty in a gale. Chloe would meet up with her first thing tomorrow.

She turned off the main path, into a narrow corridor between trees as the rain poured again, the front light of her cottage glowing ahead. Boughs brushed her slicker and bag as she yelled one more time for her dogs, but all she heard was the crash of a falling branch, the rattle of her front door.

Perhaps she'd forgotten to let Sugar and Maple out this morning. If so, her home would be foamed and frothed and muddied by eight rowdy paws in search of trouble.

Swinging the leather bag to her other shoulder, Chloe unlocked the aluminum storm door and turned the knob for the wooden door behind it. With a flip of a switch, electric light flooded the pine floor and mint-green walls in the entryway.

The submerged cables that connected her to the mainland were something she'd never stopped being thankful for, but her thankfulness was short-lived tonight. When neither Maple nor Sugar greeted her inside, she quickly extinguished the overhead.

If someone else was on her island, it made no sense to announce she was home.

She dropped the tote on the dining table and tiptoed through the kitchen and living room. On the other side of the back door was a covered patio with two chairs chained to the cement floor beside a half cord of wood. Instead of opening the door, she sidestepped to glance through the picture window that framed Eel Bay in the daylight, the Canadian shore shimmering in the distance.

But all Chloe saw tonight was a dark mound on the floor.

# 2
# *AMELIA*

JULY 1907

A wave of indigo and pink swirled across Pendleton Castle, flower petals cresting in the sunlight. *Papaver somniferum* was the Latin name for the elegant blossoms beaded with pearls, but her husband preferred to call them poppies. A common name, Amelia thought, for a man who typically snubbed commonality.

Leslie Pendleton was known for his grandiosity. The gilded walls of their mansion on Fifth Avenue. The opulence of their new summer castle in the Thousand Islands. The diamond watches that he distributed to the upper crust and the pricey tonic that he sold as a miracle cure for children in pain. All of it made him, made them, just as wealthy as the Astors or any of the New York elite, but the Pendleton money was unfashionably new. The crumbling pillars of society would rather dust off their dwindling assets, wallow together in what they had left, than embrace the nouveau riche.

Amelia ran her hand across the stone balustrade as servants raced between the veranda and the manicured gardens and terrace below. The old guard of New York might snub the Pendletons, but most politicians and poets and businessmen orbited like planets around Leslie, basking in the light, and she was quite willing to accommodate her husband's need to shine. Happy to live in the safety of his shadow.

As long as Leslie was firmly in the center of her world, the Pendleton sun would continue to shine.

The carpet of poppies lay beyond the clothed dinner tables, the platform for a magnificent view of the bay. Amelia had thought it irresponsible to flaunt what many considered a vice. She'd even warned Leslie that poppies would never root in soil frozen solid from the winter snows or flower in the winds that battered their cliff. But she'd been wrong about the growing. The flowers decided to bloom right where they were planted, just in time for their daughter's fifth birthday.

Everything was going exactly as Leslie had planned.

A hundred guests from across New York would crowd the veranda and lawn tonight, but when the guests and family were gone for the season, when only the caretaker remained, a row of marble statues watched over the flowers and waterfront as if they were guarding the island from pirates of old.

While she'd envisioned an island retreat for privacy, her husband had wanted to populate it with the masses ready to unfurl their sails in hopes of riding the Pendleton wind. And he was planning to ride these same winds to the Senate first and then on to the White House.

Leslie had been raised in a moderate family, but these days he ranked moderation up there with commonality. Neither was a good means to his end.

"It's the perfect afternoon for our soiree!" Leslie had stolen up behind her, already dressed in a swallowtail coat, his black hair and mustache tamed by a shiny pomade.

With a quick glance, he critiqued Amelia's silk kimono and bare toes that soaked in the warmth of the tile. "You look like you're about to retire for the night."

"I haven't had time yet to prepare myself."

"The guests will start arriving by five."

"I'll be ready." All she needed was an hour with her lady's maid, and they still had at least two. Enough time to make sure the tables were set to Pendleton standards.

"A reporter from the *Post-Standard* is coming."

"You already told me—"

"Fool of a man," Leslie spat. "Hearst should have sent someone from the *Journal*."

It wouldn't benefit her to disagree, but she was certain that Hearst's men were more concerned with scooping Pulitzer in the tangled politics of New York City than covering a party eight hours north via train even if President Theodore and Edith Roosevelt were the honored guests.

Leslie and the president had been friends for almost two decades, starting back when Teddy—as his friends called him—began exposing the corruption in New York. Both men were in their early twenties at the time, just beginning to lay the foundation for their future careers. These days, Teddy preferred wilderness to New York or Washington, and Leslie planned to take his old friend fishing on their grand schooner in the morning. He'd thought that alone newsworthy.

But the reason for the invitation ran much deeper than fishing and friendship. Last year Teddy had worked to pass the Pure Food and Drug Act, which called out opium as a dangerous drug. Leslie needed to make sure their loyalty to each other remained stronger than the law.

"Will you give the reporter a tour?" Leslie asked. "His name's Harry."

"If I must." She preferred entertaining their guests, but she'd do everything in her power to make this evening a success.

"Just keep him away from—"

"Mr. Pendleton!"

They both turned to see Cade, the island's caretaker, jogging toward them. When he stopped, Cade swiped back his unruly bangs and caged them in a cap.

Leslie stepped forward, brushing down wrinkles in both sleeves. "What is it?"

"A boat has arrived."

"A yacht?"

"No, sir." Cade glanced across the veranda as if he could see the boathouse through the curtain of trees. "A sailing skiff."

Leslie stepped up beside the man who had breathed life into Koster Isle. "It's too early for guests."

Cade straightened the sleeves of his work shirt. He was more than a decade younger than Leslie but equally as smart, Amelia thought. Without his knowledge of everything from carpentry and boat maintenance to horticulture and the electric dials in their powerhouse, the Pendleton family wouldn't be able to live on this island. Cade was a magician, really, fixing all the broken things. And he didn't orbit around Leslie. Whether or not her husband recognized it, Cade had his own galaxy.

"Should I ask them to wait in the boathouse?" Cade asked.

"No." Pivoting on his toes, Leslie pointed Amelia toward the French doors. "Go get dressed!"

Cade had the courtesy to look away, but the servants scurrying below stopped to watch, their heads tilted back like baby birds ready to feed. Blast all of them, Leslie included. They'd have to fill their bellies with gossip from someplace else.

Her head high, Amelia moved with the elegance of Princess Beatrice toward the doors, minding her own pace. Royalty never rushed, that's what her mother used to say. No matter the chaos in the world around them, royalty breathed calm.

Inside the grand hall, Amelia's shoulders caved as she moved swiftly up the carpeted staircase that rose like an elephant's sturdy trunk and then bridged out on the second level before climbing three more floors. A corridor on the second floor of their castle ribbed together the private rooms of the Pendleton family, and along every wall, from the grand hall to the family quarters, were Pendleton clocks. Dozens of them in various colors and sizes, an orchestra of ticking and chimes. A reminder that nothing could stop time from moving forward.

Her sanctuary overlooked the aviary and a forest of trees. In the distance, from the window near her vanity, she could see the roof of Cade's house and the river beyond. Once the guests were gone, she planned to sit on the davenport for hours, rest her feet and sketch her birds. No one except Penelope and Leslie would disturb her here.

Rose, a woman barely eighteen, waited inside Amelia's dressing room with an ivory gown in hand. The lacework puffed like clouds on the shoulders and then flowed down each arm, an emerald ribbon cinching the midsection. Amelia's corset would have to be wound tighter than a spool of thread for her to fit inside.

Rose hung the dress beside the vanity as Amelia fixed herself in a small velvet chair, the door behind cracked open so she could hear the passing conversations and any word from below. Clusters of tinted colors and creams crowded the vanity, beaded combs, hairbrushes, and a vase with flowers from the gardens. Amelia had purchased the ivory brush, made with the smoothest of horsehair, in London. The silver hairbrush, stubbled with boar bristles, had been imported from India.

Like Cade fixing every broken thing on their property, Rose could work magic with these tools.

"I won't let you down, Mrs. Pendleton," Rose said with a British accent that matched Amelia's. While she was barely out of her youth, Rose had been reared in London and was a master of all the latest fashions.

"I should hope not."

"We could roll and sweep your hair up like this." Rose demonstrated in the mirror. "Then braid it around the top like a crown."

Rose twisted and tugged at the raven-colored strands until they circled the top of Amelia's head. After she critiqued the new style in the glass, Amelia pointed at the bouquet that decorated her vanity. "We should weave a few of the summer flowers into the braid."

"Of course," Rose said. "You'll be on the front page of all the papers when we're done. The belle of this ball."

Amelia eyed the door's reflection in her mirror. Some days she wanted nothing more than to challenge the formidable Astor and Vanderbilt families, the crème de la crème of New York's decadent crop, but other days, she wanted to slip away with Penelope and hide from all those who were trying to take down the Pendletons.

How long would it take Leslie to find her if she ran away?

The house was full of winding passageways hidden behind the walls. Leslie had designed them so the servants could move secretly between rooms like elves who toiled through the night hours, and the family, he'd said, could use the tunnels to sneak down to the boathouse. Escape, if necessary.

Leslie had plenty of friends in his world, but he'd also accumulated a fleet of enemies along the way. Pendleton Castle was more fortress than retreat, and in that moment, she wondered who Leslie was hiding from here.

She'd never leave her husband, of course. He'd divorce her in days if she disappeared, and she was nothing without the Pendleton name.

In the mirror, she caught a glimpse of her daughter's jade eyes peeking around the doorpost, watching Rose with her brush and mouthful of hairpins. Penelope needed no iron to curl her locks. The blonde spirals bounced over her thin shoulders like rays of sun at first light, the choice shades reserved for dawn. Amelia had to send Penelope's nursemaid away before they came to the island, but her daughter would have a tutor and governess when they returned to the city. Leslie spared no expense when it came to their only child.

"Would you like me to take Poppy back to the nursery?" Rose asked.

"No." Amelia waved her hand to Penelope. "Come join us."

Penelope tiptoed over the rug, her pink dress fluttering like petals in the breeze. Timid when Amelia so wanted her to be strong. She'd need it in a few years when it was time for her to swim upstream with all the heirs and heiresses who saw her as competition instead of as a friend.

How Amelia longed for a friend for both of them.

"Mummy," Penelope whispered as she studied the colorful jars. Then she looked up at the four members of the Koster family framed together on the wall. Amelia was only four when her father commissioned the portrait, her sister six. A few years before, he had begun searching for a replacement for his wife. He'd never divorced their mum in England, but he might as well have when he decided a mistress was more in vogue.

The mistress was quite agreeable to the arrangement until Lord Koster lost his fortune and the Koster family manor home and all that wonderful land where Amelia had ridden horses as a child. When all he had left was the lordship title, a wife residing at the Holloway Sanatorium in Surrey, and two daughters in his care, the mistress took a carriage back to London.

Cade had thought Amelia would want her family's portrait featured in her private space, but she would have preferred to hide it in the basement. Burn it, for that matter, or throw it off their fancy boat and let the sturgeon nibble away.

When Penelope's eyes lingered on the portrait, Amelia tapped her shoulder. "What is it, love?"

Her gaze fell to the floor, hiding in the shadows too. "I'm scared of the party."

Penelope loved to watch from afar, but she hated it when adults critiqued her clothing and hair. Finding fault with Mr. Pendleton's daughter made his opposition feel as if they had power over the entire Pendleton family.

"You'll win all of them over," Amelia said.

"I want to hide."

"Look at me, Penelope."

The girl slowly raised her head.

"Don't ever let anyone force you to attend a party," Amelia said, "or stay anywhere, for that matter, when you know it's time to leave."

A shift behind them, and when Amelia looked up at the vanity, Leslie had stepped into the reflection, a sheer wall of black and white across the frame. His cheeks were patched with pink, his hair still glued in its perfect state, as if nothing could ever ruffle it. And Rose blushed when Leslie glanced at her in the mirror.

Penelope scrambled across the dressing room, her arms outstretched until Leslie lifted her with one arm and swung her around before setting her stockinged feet back on the tile floor.

"Of course you're going to the party," he said.

"But Papa—"

"I'll take good care of you, Poppy," he said as if she were a flower instead of a child. Amelia had pleaded with him to call their daughter by her given name, but he refused. "We must respect our guests by greeting them, but then you can tuck yourself away in the nursery."

"Yes, Papa."

"And you have to join us because I have a grand surprise planned for your birthday."

Her eyes widened as if she needed extra space to take it in. "What is it?"

Leslie held up a magazine with the Roosevelts on the cover. "How would you like to meet the president of the United States?"

He wanted her to be impressed—Amelia could see the expectation on his face—but Penelope didn't care about a president. She'd rather go fishing with her father.

"Is Teddy here?" Amelia asked as Penelope's eyes narrowed to shut out this unwanted surprise.

"He should arrive soon."

"The president has a son about your age," Amelia told her. "I bet he'd like to see your baby warbler."

A smile began to warm her face again. "What's his name?"

"Quentin."

Penelope pressed herself up on her toes as if she might fly. "I hope he likes birds."

"I'm sure he will like yours." Hopefully she and the Roosevelt boy would play well together. Penelope needed someone her age to celebrate with her.

"He will like every one of your little flock," Leslie pronounced.

"Who was on the skiff?" Amelia asked.

"The reporter from Syracuse. He wanted to look around the island before anyone else arrived."

Amelia winced when Rose stabbed her scalp with one of the pins. "And you're letting him roam freely?"

His gaze flitted toward Rose. "I don't have anything to hide."

Amelia's chin rose slowly until she met the gray critic in Leslie's gaze. And she knew he was lying. They'd become quite adept at hiding things from each other.

"Take her to the nursery," he told Rose, his eyes lingering on the maid as she guided Penelope out of the room.

"What is happening to us, Leslie?" Amelia's voice sounded like leather, tanned and hardened over the years.

He focused back on her. "This is not the time to discuss it."

"I'm right here and yet you can't keep your eyes off my maid."

Laughter lodged in his throat. "Of course my eyes are wandering. You can barely get yourself dressed, Amelia, before the event of the summer, and now you're wearing a strange assortment of foliage in your hair."

She plucked out the flowers and tossed them on the ground. "That's a pitiful excuse."

"Ever since Poppy—"

She interrupted him. "Your wandering started long before Penelope was born."

"Poppy," he growled. "Why do you insist on calling her that blasted British name?"

"Because poppies represent all that is bad in our lives."

She thought he'd storm out then, leave her alone, but he didn't move. "Opium has provided for your every need."

"The clock company has provided—"

"Clocks don't provide enough income for a house filled with fancy birds that are costing me a fortune in food and electric heat. I had to negotiate an alternate source."

She would not allow him to blame her for their financial situation. He was the one who bought an entire island without discussing it with her and then built them a castle to host extravagant parties. Never once had he confided their financial obligations.

"What do you want to tell me?" she asked.

"Everyone knows our marriage is a sham. The women whisper and the men—"

"I don't care what anyone says about us."

"They mock me, Amelia."

"That's what happens when a husband is philandering with the women of society and their servants alike. But we are not a sham. I am your wife and will be for the rest of your life. All I've ever wanted was for us to be a family."

"That's a lie you tell yourself." He wiped a hand over his stiff hair. "You love your birds more than you ever loved me."

"I love you and our daughter."

"You love no one but yourself, Amelia."

She wanted to reach out and slap him like he was one of the servants. "You don't know anything about me."

A knock on the door, and he turned toward it. "We'll finish talking after the party."

He wouldn't really divorce her, would he? Not with the White House in sight.

"I don't want to discuss it anymore," she said. "For Penelope's sake."

"Sometimes I wonder if Poppy is even my daughter."

"Leslie—"

"Is she?"

At her silence, he whirled on his heels, gone before she could reply. And her heart broke like a wave against the craggy shore.

3

# CHLOE

Both Sugar and Maple lifted their heads when Chloe flipped on the porch light, but the dogs didn't stand. Her heart pounding, Chloe yanked open the back door and squinted in the burst of light.

Protected by the aluminum roof, sandwiched between her two dogs, was a girl.

Chloe's mouth gaped open as she studied the child. Eight . . . maybe nine years old? Her lion's mane of hair rested against Maple, a perfect match on the dark-brown pillow of fur. One of her hands was stretched out to Sugar's neck, and balled up on the chair beside her was a plastic trash bag.

Had she been wearing the bag for a raincoat? With her thin shirt and damp jeans, she must be freezing.

"Well done," Chloe whispered to her dogs. They couldn't do anything about the blowing rain, but they had circled themselves around their guest to protect her from the wind.

Kneeling on the wood, Chloe felt the girl's forehead. Instead of warmth, her skin felt as cool as the raindrops that were pecking at the roof, soaking the banister. She needed a doctor, but they'd never make it back through the dark maze of islands in this storm.

Chloe rushed back inside and retrieved one of Nana's hand-knitted blankets. The door rattled behind her as she draped the blanket over the child, branches beating on the other side of the railing like they were trying to put out the storm.

When the girl's eyes finally opened, the dogs parted like the Red Sea, and she rose slowly to rest against the wicker chair, brushing damp curls away from her eyes.

"Are you okay?" Chloe asked, grateful for Nana's blanket to help revive her unexpected visitor.

The girl stared back. "You're the candy lady."

Most everyone in Clayton knew her and her grandmother, but she didn't remember seeing this child before. "Have you visited my shop?"

The girl's voice grew stronger. "Cade's Candy."

"That's right," Chloe said. "What's your name?"

She swept her hand across Sugar's back. "Emma."

Chloe waited for her last name or some sort of clue as to how she ended up on Koster Isle. When she didn't expound, Chloe brushed a puddle of water off the second chair and sat on the wicker. "Did the winds bring you here?"

"No," Emma said. "A friend has a boat."

"Must be a good friend." Or a really bad one. Who would drop a child off on an island and leave without checking to see if the island's one resident was home?

Chloe hadn't noticed the shoebox tucked under the chair until Emma slipped it out. Nor had she seen the second bag filled with clothes. "We have to get you inside."

Chloe reached for the bag, but Emma tugged it away. "That's mine."

"I'll help you carry your things."

"I can carry them myself."

When Chloe dropped her hand, she heard a strange noise, almost a squeak, under Emma's other arm.

Head cocked, Chloe studied the damp cardboard with a tiny hole punctured in the side. "What's in your box?"

The cardboard shifted under the protective bridge of Emma's arm. "I can't say."

Any child was welcome in her home, but Chloe wasn't certain about the unidentified creature that accompanied this one. "Perhaps we should leave your box outside."

Emma plopped into one of the chairs, balling herself over the box and plastic bag, cemented to the wicker like the chair legs chained to the patio floor.

"Please." Chloe nodded back to the door. "Let's talk in the living room."

The girl didn't move, and Chloe knew that stance. She'd done the same thing when she'd first arrived on the island more than twenty years ago, the summer of 1969, except she'd remained balled up in Grandpa's boat. *Lolli*, she'd already known, was a friend.

Nana had to trek all the way down to the boat and offer her hot chocolate and a warm bed before her stubbornness began to subside. Chloe had been more interested in the dogs that accompanied her grandma than the bed, but hot chocolate had sweetened the deal.

Grandpa Cade would tell Chloe to be strong with this girl, build respect. Nana would say to give her a peppermint stick and a hug.

Then again, if nothing else worked, her grandpa would bribe Emma with his maple sugar candies. No one could resist the soft, sweet concoction that had made his shop famous with locals and tourists alike.

"You can bring your things inside," Chloe finally said to calm the storm building between them. "Including the box."

When Emma shook her head, Chloe sank back into the damp seat. Was this how her grandparents felt when they brought her home? They'd seemed confident in their care, but they must have been sad about what happened. Scared, even, like her. Adults, she'd learned early on, could be like smoke and mirrors, hiding the parts they didn't want their children to see.

"Please . . . ?"

Emma squirmed but didn't leave the seat.

Chloe had vowed to herself to bring joy into the life of every child she met, give them a reason to smile, but she wasn't sure how to help Emma now.

"I have hot cocoa," she announced as she stood, sounding a lot like Nana. "Made from scratch."

When Chloe reached inside the door and flipped on the kitchen lamp, light spilled onto the patio. The warmth of it beckoned Emma forward, but she still hesitated until Sugar scurried into the cottage.

The four of them formed a little parade through the back door. Sugar and Emma. Chloe and Maple. A victory march.

Emma placed her shoebox on the counter, its pine surface chipped and dented like everything else in this old kitchen. Like everything on Koster Isle, really. Time had seemed to stop the night Poppy disappeared, and the life that remained here had wrapped itself up in a preserver and opted to float through the storms instead of swim away.

The warped shoebox shuddered, then the smallest shuffle of sound followed from inside.

"Is it a mouse?" Chloe eyed the box as if it might burrow down in the gap between the counter and fridge. She had enough mice to warrant two traps in the basement and one out in the shed. Children and dogs were welcome, but she didn't need any extra rodents in her cottage.

"No." Emma hugged the plastic bag filled with clothing to her chest.

"A gerbil?"

Another noise, the softest meow, slipped under the fold of the lid.

"Ah . . ."

Emma propped open the lid and scooped out a tiny mass of fur and whiskers that wiggled in her hands. Chloe eyed the two dogs lounging in the living room that shared space with her kitchen. Maple had stretched out across the couch, exactly where he wasn't supposed to be, and Sugar curved around the edge of the hearth. Sugar seemed mildly curious, nudging up her head for a glance, but sleep trumped her interest.

Emma hugged the kitten to her chest. "His name is Fraidy."

Chloe took a deep breath, her voice barely a whisper when she spoke again. "What's he afraid of?"

"Everything." Emma brushed her fingers over the gray fur as if she could smooth away every fear. "Mitch named him Spider, but I changed it."

"Who is Mitch?"

Emma brushed a curl away from her eyes when she shook her head. "He's a nobody."

Chloe quietly pulled a bowl out of the cupboard. If Emma had good parents, they must be worried sick. Perhaps Chloe could call them tonight, if she proceeded carefully, to let them know where their daughter was. Then she'd take the girl home in the morning.

"Why would a nobody bring you to my island?"

Instead of answering her question, Emma nuzzled her head into the kitten's side as if she could disappear deep inside its fur.

Chloe filled the electric kettle with water and flipped it on, grateful for underwater cables that defied wind. "What's your phone number?"

"I don't have a phone."

"You don't have one personally or there's no telephone in your home?"

"I don't have a house or a telephone."

"What about your parents?" Chloe asked.

"Don't have those either."

Something was terribly wrong with this girl's story. Just like something had been wrong with her own story at that age. But that didn't mean Emma had been neglected. Perhaps she'd gotten lost or run away. Perhaps . . . well, she couldn't think of a single good reason as to how this girl had ended up on a private island at this hour, in weather that kept most adults home.

Chloe picked up the portable telephone to call Gavin McLean, a high school friend who was now a deputy with the Clayton police, and report a missing child, but silence met her ear instead of a dial tone. The gale must have taken down the lines again on the mainland.

She slipped onto a barstool beside Emma. "Who do you live with?"

The girl cradled the kitten close to her chest, her gaze on the kitchen window. Everything beyond the patio looked gray in the wash of porch light. "Adults ask lots of questions."

"Because the answers can be really important."

With the kitten secured in one hand, Emma scooped the plastic bag off the counter and dumped it onto the pine chair that Chloe's grandpa had hewn and polished almost a century ago. "Or scary."

She couldn't argue with that. In the morning, Gavin would help her find Emma's family.

As she waited for the water to heat, Chloe removed a box of dried milk from the pantry. Grocery space was limited in *Lolli*'s hold, so fresh milk was a rare commodity in her kitchen, but with a quick stir of the white powder into warm water, Fraidy seemed quite pleased with Chloe's culinary skills.

Emma opened her plastic bag as the cat drank powdered milk, and she removed each item carefully. A sweatshirt. Pair of jeans. Three T-shirts. Socks. A Strawberry Shortcake nightgown. She refolded each piece before stacking them on the only cushion that Maple hadn't occupied and then pulled a scrapbook out of the bag, placing it on top of the stack.

With the brisk saw of a knife, Chloe split the soggy takeout burger and served it up on two plates like it was the finest of dining. Then she scooped homemade chocolate mix made with cocoa, rock sugar, powdered milk, vanilla, and a crushed candy cane into two mugs. The aroma of peppermint and chocolate filled the house, and it was the most wonderful smell in the world, Chloe thought. Rich with the best kind of memories.

Sweets were her happy place, and the happy place of many others, she'd discovered over the past eight years of helping manage her grandparents' candy store. Locals liked to tell her stories about Cade. Her grandfather had been like a modern-day St. Nick, bringing gifts to people wherever he went. Bits of driftwood he'd fashioned into a duck or squirrel. Freshly picked flowers. Tins of Nana's hot chocolate and bags of homemade candies.

There was something really special about candy, Chloe had discovered when she started working at the store. The bright colors and shapes and sugary flavors. For some of her older customers, it took them on a journey back to their childhood. To all the sweet goodness of being a kid. For others, candy was an opportunity to regain a small taste of a childhood missed.

Her grandparents weren't here any longer, but Chloe wanted nothing more than to carry on their legacy. Gift people of all ages with kindness. Make life a little happier.

The mug of hot chocolate in her hands might not allow Emma the freedom to be a kid, but Chloe hoped that she would embrace the sweet. The hope of good things for her life ahead.

When the kitten finished his milk, Emma placed him back onto a rag in the box that they'd deemed his bed. Then she engulfed her half of the burger and took one of the steaming mugs from Chloe.

"It's good," Emma said after a long sip. "Thank you."

"My nana used to make hot chocolate for me after a particularly hard day."

"What about your mom?" Emma asked.

Chloe paused, surprised by the question. If only she had a better answer. "My mother wasn't the kind to make treats." Or dinner, for that matter. Other substances, she'd learned over the years, had grounded her parents' food pyramid. "How old are you?"

"Ten."

Another gust shook the cottage, raining pine on the roof. Chloe had occupied the same room at the back of this house since she was six, leaving only for college, but she'd kept her grandparents' bedroom in good order.

"I have an extra room where you can sleep tonight," she said. "Would you like to shower?"

Emma brushed her hand over the kitten's back before looking at her. "Will you watch Fraidy?"

"Of course."

The girl placed the box on the hearth and moved a chair between the cat and Sugar. Then she slipped into the bathroom, leaving the scrapbook on top of her clothes. While she didn't touch Emma's book, Chloe eyed the mosaic of brightly colored paper glued to the cover. Someone had decoupaged every inch of it with paper birds.

After she cleaned the kitchen, Chloe collapsed on the chair between cat and dog. Holes riddled the pink nightgown Emma was wearing when she returned to the living room, and Chloe wished she'd paid better attention to her grandma's sewing lessons. She might have been able to make this one thing better.

"I'm not going home." Emma lifted the scrapbook and tucked it under her loose curtain of a sleeve.

"That's not up to either of us, I'm afraid."

The girl eyed the dark window as if she might try to flee in the storm.

"This is the only safe place to sleep on the island," Chloe said.

Emma lifted the kitten from his box, and Chloe didn't protest when she escorted the tiny creature into the bedroom.

Two dogs, a girl, and a kitten, all packed into the cottage with her.

In the morning, they'd sort it out.

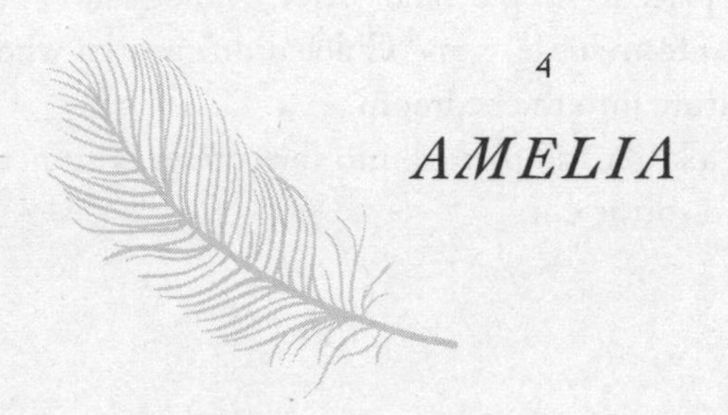

# 4

# *AMELIA*

Guests arrived in waves on Koster Isle, cruising into the harbor on yachts built to impress, wooden hulls to protect, looming sails to play in the winds. All the boats lined up like boxcars on the shore below.

Instead of greeting their guests on the veranda, Amelia had escorted the reporter toward the beautiful iron and glass aviary, built to equal the ornate birdhouses across England, that her husband abhorred.

"Mr. Pendleton is quite the celebrity tonight," Harry Baden said as she unlocked the door, a notebook gripped in one of his hands and a pencil in the other as if this was the story of the century.

He might not be Hearst's reporter, but Leslie would still revel in those words.

When they stepped into the glass house, Amelia opened a canvas bag with birdseed and sprinkled it on the ground. "He's celebrated wherever he goes."

"Poppy!" One of the birds called out Penelope's nickname before a cloud of blue feathers swept over Amelia's path, wings spread wide like he was preparing to cross the rainforest that had once been home.

"What was that?" Harry asked as he scribbled a note on his tablet.

"A macaw," she replied. "Mr. Pendleton imported him with several other birds from Paraguay."

Fred was always looking for Penelope. Her daughter didn't speak much in the house, but she spent hours singing and talking to the birds.

"This is an extraordinary place," the reporter said, his gaze following the trail under the glass. "I've never seen anything like it."

"We have several unique species." Harry hadn't been interested in seeing the aviary, but this was her favorite place on the island. And it was her tour. All the guests, she speculated, would want to see their exotic birds before the night was over. "Minnie is over on the bamboo. Fred is her beau."

Harry's gaze followed hers to the macaw perched on a tree that Leslie had imported along with the birds. Her scarlet head turned to watch them, the hem of her blue and yellow wings dusting the smooth branch. Fred swept up beside his mate, and she began preening his feathers.

"Macaws pair for life, you know."

Harry fixed the knot on his tie. "I don't know much about birds."

"They are social and intensely devoted creatures." What she'd wanted for her marriage. She and Leslie might not like each other much anymore, but devotion must eclipse their feelings.

Harry wrote another note on his tablet. "Why did you decide to build an aviary?"

"Our daughter loves birds." When Amelia held out her hand, a lorikeet flew to her finger. "And I'm rather fond of them myself."

She had collected almost twenty species, and the architect said if they could keep the building warm during the winter, this structure could house at least fifty birds. Leslie had an electric boiler installed in the aviary when he wired the castle so their birds would bask in warmth year-round.

"What is your daughter's name?"

"Poppy." The word squawked again out of the macaw's lips, but the reporter didn't seem to notice this time.

"She's not yet five." Amelia glanced back at the castle, at the oriel window that jutted out from the third floor and overlooked the river. "We're keeping her name out of the papers until she's older."

Except the *Evening Post*. They'd run a story about Leslie's famous tonic last year, and Leslie had expounded on the talents of his only child. He'd even referred to her as Penelope instead of Poppy for the more distinguished readers although it wouldn't be hard to determine the namesake of Poppy's Tip-Top Tonic.

When Amelia saw the newspaper, she was quick to remind him of what one of his growing list of enemies might do to convince a doting father to side with them. Leslie hadn't mentioned Penelope's name to the papers since. And even though his ads touted that it was the best tonic for babies, he had never allowed Amelia to give even a drop of the tonic to their daughter.

Harry looked up. "It would be easy for me to find her name."

"And it would be easy for Mr. Pendleton to rescind his invitation to join our gala."

One of his thin eyebrows slid up as he studied her. "Ava Astor is in all the papers."

Amelia bristled at the name. "What the Astor family does is none of my business."

He smiled. "What the Astors do seems to be everybody's business."

"Poppy," the macaw yapped.

Amelia glanced back at the creature. "Hush."

"I'll do my best to keep your daughter's name out of my article, but I can't make any promises about my editor," Harry said, scribbling another note. "What about your story?"

One of her eyebrows slipped up. "What of it?"

"You're from England . . ."

Amelia whisked a fallen leaf off one of the benches but didn't sit. "You've done some digging."

"Not much, I'm afraid. Your accent betrays you."

She tugged at her lacy sleeves. "I have no secrets."

"Except your daughter."

She shrugged. "The world will know all about her soon enough."

"Tell you what." Harry propped up a foot on the bench. "What if we make a deal?"

She eyed the man curiously. "What sort of deal?"

"I won't report your daughter's name, and you contact me before the other papers when you're ready to introduce her."

The latch on the aviary door clicked open, and she turned to see Cade. The caretaker removed his denim cap before releasing a low whistle that seemed to curl through the leaves. The scarlet macaw flew to a branch near him, nuzzling Cade's outstretched arm, the bird's admiration split between Fred and this man who fed her.

While Leslie had purchased these birds, the aviary was Cade's domain. He cared for them like he cared for the home and their island when the Pendleton family and staff were in New York.

"Poppy," the bird said one more time as if he could make her appear.

Cade laughed. "Sorry, old girl. She's not with me today."

"Poppy?" Harry eyed Amelia, his pencil poised above the paper. "Like the name of your husband's drug."

"I'll contact you when I'm ready to disclose the name of our daughter."

Cade glanced between her and the reporter. "Someone is asking for you in the nursery."

"I must go then." She lifted her dress and stepped away from the reporter as he scribbled on his paper. She groaned inwardly but didn't scold him. Harry was right—he could easily inquire about Penelope and print her full name with his article—but if he kept his word, she would telephone him first when she was ready to talk about Penelope.

"If you like birds—" Cade stepped toward Harry—"you must see the ones on the shore. We have canvasbacks and herons congregating down there."

"I don't particularly like birds."

"The boats, then." Cade nodded toward the glass on his left, to the sails that spiked over the trees. "An Elco just dropped anchor."

"A what?"

"Motor yacht," Cade said. "It's like a floating home with a mahogany hull and sleeping berths."

"I'm not really intrigued by boats either."

"Mr. Pendleton has all different kinds of boats," Cade persisted. "Electric. Sailing. A gasoline-powered motorboat. You'll be intrigued by the time you leave."

Harry looked reluctant to follow the caretaker, and Amelia feared for a moment that he and his questions might follow her up to Penelope's room.

"Cade will take good care of you," she said before turning away. She'd thank him later for rescuing her.

"I'd like a tour of the house," Harry said.

Cade opened the door for her, and she swept outside before she heard his response.

Had Penelope really been asking for her or was this Cade's escape plan? Rose was doubling as a nursemaid until they could find a new one, but either way, Amelia would check in before Penelope took her nap.

If Leslie continued flirting with Rose, she would have to release her like she'd done with the governess. Older women weren't inclined to take direction well from her, but it was becoming increasingly impossible to keep young women on their staff. She had to rid him of distractions and remind him that she—that their marriage—was indispensable.

She couldn't bear to think what might happen if Leslie cut the rope that tied them together, let her float away like her father had done with her mum when he admitted her at the sanatorium. Lady Koster had escaped completely into a place of her own making after a few months at Holloway.

Staff members scrambled by Amelia as she ascended the flights of stairs slowly in her elegant dress, the tick of Pendleton clocks keeping time. When she reached the top floor, only Penelope was inside the nursery, asleep on one of the two beds.

Where had her maid gone? They'd hired about twenty people in addition to the eighteen servants they'd brought with them from the city to help with the rooms and food. Rose was supposed to watch over Penelope while Amelia was greeting guests downstairs.

Painted across the nursery wall, towering over Penelope's bed, was a jungle of vines and leaves and colorful birds perched on different branches. And scattered on the floor were dozens of toys that Leslie had handpicked from FAO Schwarz.

But even in the city, Penelope preferred to play outside rather than in the nursery. She would circle the lawn, arms lifted, as if she might be able to fly with the birds.

Amelia tiptoed across the carpet and surveyed the river like an archer of old, searching for an enemy. At times, the nursery felt more like a watchtower than a room for Penelope to sleep and play in. A fortress of sorts from those who wanted to harm their family.

While it was Leslie's job to keep them safe, Amelia fought relentlessly to protect their reputation.

Tonight was her debut as queen of Pendleton Castle. Lady Koster, her mother, had always wanted her daughters to marry royals, and if Lady Koster were still alive, she would be whispering in Amelia's ear, reminding her to mingle among the elite as if she was their equal. Impress the guests with her wit and a glimpse of the Pendleton wealth. Not even Mrs. Astor, her mum would say, should dare cross her.

Tonight Amelia would make her mum proud. When the evening ended, the guests would admire her hospitality and charm, and perhaps the staff would finally respect her as well.

Silver clouds funneled up from the west like prongs on a trident, but she and Leslie would defy lightning and thunder and the gods of the sea. Nothing was going to stop their Independence Day gala or the celebration of Penelope's birthday. Not the tardiness of the president or the incessant questioning of the reporter or a bit of rain. Even if Neptune dipped his trident into the river, swelled the middling waves around them, their party would continue.

Between the Koster family's noble tradition and the wealth and ingenuity of her husband, they would continue building their kingdom together, billowing out like a summer storm.

"Mummy."

Amelia turned from the window to see Penelope peeking over the string of white bows that had been embroidered around the edges of her linen sheets.

"You're supposed to be asleep." Amelia's hem swished across the carpet like a broom as she moved toward the bed.

"Not a wink will come."

"Then you'll have to go searching for one." Amelia sat on the bed beside her. "And you'll only be able to find sleep when your eyes are closed."

Penelope scrunched her eyes together, calming the stormy pools. Her daughter was always quick to respond. A heart ready to obey.

A flaw from her Koster roots.

Amelia pushed back one of Penelope's curls, but unlike their owner, the curls were quite independent.

Leslie might be the sun in the Pendleton galaxy, Amelia the moon, but Penelope was the brightest star. He'd never been happier with Amelia than the day she'd brought their daughter home. Everything had seemed to come together for her husband in those hours. His purpose reborn, his life renewed. Now he had an heir on whom to bestow an inheritance. A daughter who wanted nothing more than to be at his side.

He'd been elated, but Amelia had been terrified of losing it all.

While some people allowed life to happen to them, Amelia had spent the past decade mortaring together the opulent bricks of society in their Fifth Avenue mansion. She'd tried to stay coy with the reporter, but in the coming months, her neighbors along Fifth Avenue would be begging for an invitation to Koster Isle. And she'd already resolved to do the same thing that had been done to her. No one who'd snubbed her in the city, not even an Astor or Vanderbilt, would be welcome here. And no government leader or corrupt smuggler or distraught mistress would bring her family down.

"Will you stay with me?" Penelope begged. "Just until I wake up. I won't sleep long."

Voices drifted through the open window, and she knew Leslie would be looking for her downstairs.

"Rose will stay with you."

"But she's not here."

"Papa must have had a job for her." The corset poked Amelia's ribs as she perched like a bird on Penelope's bed. She didn't want to leave her daughter in the tower alone. "I'll stay until she returns."

A smile lit the girl's face. "Maybe tomorrow night, you can sleep there." Penelope pointed at the second bed in the room, closer to the window. "For my birthday."

"I'll spend the night after all our guests return home."

Penelope's smile fell. "When are they leaving?"

"Some will be leaving in the morning, but most of our guests will stay through the weekend." She smoothed her fingers over the lace that lined Penelope's sheet. "Why don't you like having company?"

"I like children company," she said, her nose crinkled. "Nice ones."

"President Roosevelt's son should be nice."

Penelope folded her hands on the bedcover. "We can play in the birdhouse tomorrow."

"After your nap, Rose will bring you dinner in the library. You can watch the guests from the window," Amelia said. "Which means you must fall asleep right away so you're not too tired."

"But I'm still not sleepy . . ."

"It's going to be a lovely party." The words flowed from her lips like a song. "Beautiful dresses and mountains of food and the most splendid ices. And then fireworks after dark."

"Have I ever seen fireworks?"

"When you were younger," Amelia said. "Much too young to remember. But you'll never forget them now. It's like a thousand fireflies spiraling across the sky, all of them celebrating the eve of your birth."

Penelope closed her eyes. "I'm never going to be able to sleep."

"Just a short nap." She kissed her cheek. "Rose will wake you when it's time."

The girl grabbed her hand. "Please don't leave."

"I'll wait by the door until she returns," Amelia said as she stepped toward the door.

"Mummy?"

She turned back. "What is it?"

"You're the best mummy in the world."

She smoothed her hand over the taffeta on her gown to brush away the wrinkles. "Rest well, Penelope."

"Poppy," the girl whispered before Amelia shut the nursery door.

She waited outside for another minute, but Rose still didn't arrive. And Leslie's anger would only mount if she didn't join him soon.

As she began to descend the staircase, she found her maid scrambling up the steps, strands of golden hair escaping out of her white cap and scattering across her shoulders.

"I'm terribly sorry," Rose said, her breath breaking like waves against the cliffs. "Mr. Pendleton asked me to—"

Amelia lifted her hand, stopping her. She didn't want to know what

Leslie had asked her to do. "Your first priority tonight is to take care of Penelope."

The maid nodded even though both of them knew Leslie superseded any other direction. "I'll watch over her, Mrs. Pendleton."

"I know you will."

"Won't let her out of my sight."

"She's out of your sight right now."

"When she wakes," Rose blurted, quite flustered as she rushed up the remaining stairs.

Amelia called up to the maid before she reached the fourth floor. "Penelope should, under no circumstances, be left alone again."

"Yes, ma'am."

"After she rests, she'll take dinner in the library and then join the guests outside for fireworks."

Penelope wouldn't feel so overwhelmed with the guests when they were all focused on the light display.

After Amelia descended the staircase, she straightened the emerald ribbon on her gown and stepped onto the marble floor.

Leslie was wrong. She wasn't just thinking of herself. She was thinking about him and Penelope. About the people they'd invited to the party and the whole of society across New York.

If she had her way, none of their guests would ever forget this night.

5

# CHLOE

"She won't tell me where she's from," Gavin McLean said, his polished badge ornamenting a chest that had broadened with age. He would turn thirty in July, almost six weeks before Chloe. After nearly a decade on the force—and a lifetime along the river—he was one of the best officers in Jefferson County.

If anyone could unravel Emma's story, Chloe was confident that he could.

"I'm not sure that she knows." Chloe glanced out the plexiglass window at the girl sitting on a bench in the concrete hallway, her legs dangling over the side, a shiny white shoebox in her lap. She'd washed Emma's clothes this morning and helped tame her curly hair back into a ponytail. At the moment, she looked like any other fourth or fifth grader in Clayton.

In the hours after breakfast, Chloe had asked Emma about her family, but she wouldn't expound on her vague answers. Instead they'd worked together to clean off the storm debris from the patio and then the boathouse floor and seats of *Lolli*.

Chloe didn't bother to check the castle. That place had been damaged many years ago.

Gavin turned away from the window, his fingers drumming the metal desk. "She doesn't seem to have amnesia."

"No . . ."

Gavin met her gaze again. "Then she can tell us how she arrived on Koster Isle."

Chloe leaned back against the edge of a whiteboard and folded the soft cable sleeves of her fisherman's sweater across her chest, thinking back over bits of conversation with Emma, wondering what she'd missed. "She's scared of something."

Gavin flipped again through a stack of notifications on his desk as if he might have missed Emma's picture. "I won't return her to a place that's not safe."

"She mentioned a man named Mitch but wouldn't tell me anything else about him."

One of Gavin's eyebrows edged up. "She didn't tell me about this man."

"I don't think she trusts adults."

"I'm afraid there might be a good reason for that," he said.

"But she's extremely smart."

"I agree." Gavin picked up a pen and clicked it. "Certainly smarter than I was at her age."

Chloe smiled as he scribbled a note. She and Gavin had dated in high school for about a half second. It became quickly apparent to both of them that romance was not in their future, and they'd been faithful friends ever since.

Gavin had married a lovely girl from Alexandria Bay after college, someone they'd both known from youth group. Chloe had volunteered to help with the wedding, and as she and Belle bagged up mints from Cade's Candy Shop in white toile, tying them together with yellow ribbons, she'd begun to dream about her own future. Not about her own wedding—she could never imagine herself married—but she wondered what it would be like to make commemorative candy to mark a couple's special day. Candy monogrammed with the new couple's initials, glittering like royalty, a perfect color match with the décor and gowns.

Gavin and Belle's wedding had planted a new dream inside her, but she never told her grandma. They didn't have enough income or the time, for that matter, to design specialty candy beyond the treats that Nana and Grandpa Cade had developed when they first opened the store.

"Your kids will be smarter than you too," she quipped.

"They already are."

She laughed. "They're only like two and three!"

"Four and five now," he said.

"A blink, Gavin, and another two years are gone."

He slipped a yellow form out of a desk drawer. "Anything else I should know about Emma?"

"She brought some sort of scrapbook with her. A collage of bird pictures pasted on the cover."

The wooden chair creaked when Gavin leaned back. "What's inside her book?"

"No idea," she said. "I didn't want to snoop."

"Snooping is a parent's job."

"I'm not her parent." She stepped away from the whiteboard and sat on a chair across from his desk.

"No, but a bit of snooping could help us reunite her with one of her family members." He rolled the yellow form into his typewriter. "Maybe you can take a look inside the scrapbook tonight."

Chloe glanced again at the girl outside the office glass, waiting for her in the lobby. Most kids, at least in her experience, would be lying on the bench by now or swinging their legs over the edge or even skipping or sliding across the shiny floor.

Then again, her experience usually involved children who either wanted candy or had already consumed too much. "She reminds me of . . ."

Gavin looked up. "What?"

She brushed a hand in front of her as if she could erase the memory. "Nothing."

Gavin clicked a few keys on the typewriter. "I'll have to call Children's Services."

"Of course."

"You staying in town this afternoon?"

She reached for her tote bag and draped it over her shoulder. "I'll be at the shop until about four, as long as the weather holds. I'm not crossing the river again if it storms."

"I hope not. Most people wouldn't go near the river in a squall like that. Lost a half dozen boats at the marina last night and a gentleman up near Ogdensburg who was trying to bail his fishing boat."

They both paused to remember another life lost to the St. Lawrence.

"I can't explain it," she said. "Except I knew I was supposed to go home."

"Your dogs would have been fine sleeping in the shed."

"But she wouldn't have been okay." Emma had curled over the shoebox in her lap, whispering to her kitten.

"You have a sixth sense, Chloe. You sure you don't want a job on the force?"

"It's a rather long road from selling candy to fighting crime."

"The sergeant and I could help you shorten that path."

She smiled. "I think I'll stick with Cade's Candy."

"You really should name your shop Chloe's Candy."

"It's not mine."

"It is now," he said, but every customer who came through that door, every corner of the store, reminded her of her grandparents. Every local who visited, it seemed, had been their friend.

With a quick glance at the clock, she realized it was almost noon. Jenna was probably worried sick about her. "Speaking of candy . . ."

"I'll stop by after I hear from the social worker."

"Thank you," she said. "I just got a new shipment for the summer crowd. Gummy sharks. Seashell mints. Chocolate turtles. I'll put together a box for you."

"Then I might show up before the social worker returns my call."

"The candy is for your kids."

"Right," he said before returning to his typewriter.

Chloe stepped into the hall, and Emma hopped up from the bench. "Are they going to arrest me?"

"Of course not," Chloe said as they moved toward the door. "But why didn't you tell Officer McLean about Mitch?"

"He doesn't need to know about him."

"Every single piece of your story is important."

"I told you, he's a no—"

"A nobody," Chloe repeated. "I get it. But he might help us find your parents."

When Emma snorted, Chloe stopped walking. "What's wrong with Mitch?"

The girl shook her head.

"Did he hurt you?"

Emma pulled the shoebox closer to her ribs, but she didn't answer. Instead she walked right out the station's front door.

Gavin would find this man, Chloe hoped, and if he had harmed Emma in any way, Gavin would arrest him.

She rushed to the girl's side so they could walk the three blocks over to the riverfront, past the village park and the church she'd attended for most of her life. The sun was warm on this Saturday morning, the only trace of last night's storm puddled along the fence, and ahead of them, the river was calm, an acid-sweet mixture of taffy and diesel flooding her nose. The whirling pools from a Sea-Doo reminded her of a confectioner whisking up peaks of blue meringue and piping them onto a steel tray. Between the winds and rain and all manner of watercraft, the river view transformed with each new day, but the aroma in town rarely changed.

While the official name for this region was Thousand Islands, almost two thousand parcels of land breached the surface like the beluga whales upstream, the pods skipping between Ontario and New York. An invisible borderline split the seam of the St. Lawrence—the United States behind them, Canada straight ahead. By the middle of May, tourists would flood this area to ride the ribbons of summer waves. Locals enjoyed the summer weather, but they liked their iceboats and sailing skates just as much, skirting across the channel after winter smoothed it into a rink between nations.

When the water froze, her dogs spent their nights on Jenna's maple farm and Chloe and Nana had stayed in the apartment above their shop. Until last August, at least, when her grandma had to be moved to a memory care facility in Watertown.

Turning onto Riverside Drive, Chloe ducked under a display of kites that hooded the Swim & Sail window. Cade's Candy Shop stood across the boardwalk from the old train depot.

She and Jenna were beginning a new rhythm this summer. In the mornings, Jenna and their summer staff would work at the store while Chloe and her dogs were on the island. Then she'd cross the channel to manage the afternoon crowds.

Sadly it would be their last summer working together, Chloe guessed, based on the balance left in her business account. After Nana's lawyer informed Chloe that her grandma had been living primarily off Social Security in her last years, she understood there would be little left beyond the island and candy store. She didn't want to sell either, but her personal account had dwindled almost as low as the business one in the past month. She'd already decided to forgo a salary this summer, living on the little that remained of her own savings, so she could keep the shop afloat.

She wanted to ignore the realities, pretend all was well, but no matter how much she deposited in the reservoir of her imagination, her dreams wouldn't pay taxes or staff salaries or the bill to keep their lights on.

Emma leaned like the Tower of Pisa toward the shop's window display as if the chocolate truffles and vintage peppermint sticks and maple sugar seashells tucked into caramel sand might catch her fall.

Chloe tapped the glass. "Would you like a bag of sour cherries?"

Emma's eyes narrowed as if the vintage concoction was more trick than treat.

"Or maybe something chocolatey. We have the best fudge in the entire North Country."

Emma's gaze broke away from the display. "Do you have lemon drops?"

"Of course."

"I'd like one of those, please."

"I just might be able to find a few lemon drops for you and Fraidy to share."

Emma shook her head. "He doesn't like lemon."

"Then you'll have to eat the extras for him."

A brass bell chimed when Chloe opened the door, and Jenna glanced up from behind the front counter, an oak-brown ponytail resting across her shoulder, a pile of receipts in her hand. No matter how busy their shop, Jenna handled every customer and situation with perfect ease.

The dwindling funds in Chloe's account paid for the continued operation of their candy store, but without her best friend's management magic, there'd be no shop. Jenna's stellar skills had kept the shelves stocked, the business afloat, and their income mostly black for the past five years.

"I'm glad to see you," Jenna said as pushed the receipts aside to begin wrapping a box of candy. "I thought the storm might have blown you and *Lolli* all the way to the Atlantic."

"It was an adventure, for sure."

"Next time, please stay in the apartment. I'm going to lose my mind worrying."

Chloe waved Emma into the store. "You shouldn't worry about me."

Jenna's scissors sliced through a strand of red ribbon before she curled it into a licorice-like roll. "I was more worried about *Lolli*."

"Very funny."

"But someone really should worry about you!"

As Emma hovered near the front door, Chloe scanned the shop. It was a bit worn around the edges these days, but the vintage décor from the 1960s still brought locals and visitors alike bucketloads of joy. And the candy, of course. The team filled bags and boxes to spec and then wrapped them in the prettiest of paper.

On the left was a birch counter, this one displaying dozens of candy-filled canisters and one hefty espresso machine. While most everything in the shop remained the same from when her grandfather opened the business, cappuccino was the latest fad for her older clients, and Chloe aimed to please both kids and their parents. The machine hadn't paid for itself yet, but she hoped the crowd this summer would want lattes or cappuccinos on the cooler days.

In the center of the shop was a wooden sculpture commissioned from a local artist, the polished wood base worn from all the hands that brushed over the sapphire waves and their stormy crests. The tallest children could run their fingers over the hull of the old schooner, its bow pointed toward the ceiling, the sculpted sails rippling in a fierce wind as it rode over imaginary waves.

In lieu of glass, the artist had designed each porthole with the rainbow swirls of a lollipop. *The Good Ship* was engraved on the side, and while kids often called it a pirate ship, it reminded her of everything good about this place.

Her gaze wandered up to the black-and-white photograph framed behind the register, and her grandparents smiled back as if pleased with her and Jenna and all the children who continued to visit their shop.

"Your lawyer called." Jenna waved a pink slip in one hand as she tore off a piece of Scotch tape with the other. "Said she really wants to wrap things up with your grandmother's estate."

"The only thing I want to wrap at the moment are bags of candy."

"Eventually you're going to have to settle it, Chloe."

"I plan to." Twice now, she'd walked right past the Seaway Credit Union door instead of stopping to close this final account. Maybe no one else would understand, but she wasn't ready to sever that final tie with the grandparents who had given up most of their twilight years to raise and care for her. Settling the estate. Shuttering the shop. Maybe even selling the island. She'd just lost Nana, and now all these other pieces . . . it was like stripping away layer after layer of insulation when she wanted to preserve the warmth.

"And that reporter called again from Syracuse." Jenna tossed her a second note with a phone number. "He really wants to talk to you."

"I don't talk to reporters about the Pendletons."

"Maybe he just wants a tour of the castle," Jenna said.

"Him and everyone else."

She'd like nothing more than to solve the castle's almost century-old mystery that had ballooned into epic lore for the tourists and cured into legend among locals. But she didn't want the investigation to be public. No matter what the Syracuse paper uncovered, a stream of boaters would find their way into her private lagoon, and then the swarms would climb the rickety steps on Koster Isle like they'd been designed by Walt Disney and machete their way through the thicket.

But Poppy's Castle was no Haunted Mansion with safety precautions in place. Someone was bound to get hurt on her island . . . or worse.

The few dollars left in her bank account would be flushed right down the toilet of litigation, and she would lose everything. While she was as curious as anyone about Poppy's disappearance, it was almost a century too late to help the girl. There was no good reason for the *Post-Standard* to exhume this story.

"You should still call him back." Jenna's gaze dropped like an anchor to Chloe's side. "Well, hello. Who are you?"

"Emma." The girl thumbed toward Chloe. "I'm with her."

Jenna looked back and forth between them, waiting for an explanation as to why her partner was being shadowed by a ten-year-old.

Chloe closed the door. "It's a long story."

"Short version, please. People have been drifting in all morning like they caught a ride on the winds of that storm."

Emma pulled out a stool at the front counter and placed her shoebox on top. "We're her guests."

"Guests?" Jenna asked, clearly surprised at the concept that Chloe might welcome someone into her home.

Chloe shrugged. "I have company sometimes."

"Like squirrels, maybe."

Chloe stepped behind the counter and glanced at the list of orders beside the register. She grabbed one of their signature boxes—tackle boxes, they called them—to fulfill the next purchase, the plastic frame designed with twelve different compartments for a variety of treats. The lid was clearly stamped *Cade's Candy*, the blue-and-silver logo with a bright purple balloon. The old-timers in the islands loved the candy boxes and so did the tourists.

Chloe filled one of the bottom compartments with the requested malt balls. Then she reached for the glass jar on the top shelf and scooped a handful of lemon drops into a paper cup for Emma before slipping the rest into a cube beside the chocolate and malt.

"Emma is staying with me for a couple of days."

"On the island?"

"I'm not sure," Chloe said, glancing at Emma. "That's a conversation best tabled for later."

Jenna slipped onto a stool near Emma and crossed her legs. "Do you have an extra pair of shoes in your box?"

"Fraidy is inside."

Jenna looked back at Chloe.

"Her kitten." Chloe opened a canister of Nerds and filled another compartment with the pellets. Technically, they didn't allow animals in their shop, but this was an exception. "He's a good cat."

Emma propped the shoebox beside the espresso machine and cracked the lid until the kitten's head peeked out.

Jenna glanced at Chloe. "What do your dogs think?"

"That he needs a canine aunt and uncle to keep him out of trouble."

"If only your dogs could do that for you . . ."

Chloe flicked a Nerd at her friend, and it clipped the tip of Jenna's nose before shooting across the floor. Jenna would have hurled something in return, but the front door chimed and two harried moms marched the local Brownie troop inside. A swarm of brown beanies and yellow shirts rushed the counters, buzzing about their favorite treats.

Behind the troop, a flash of gray bounded out of the shoebox and bolted to the espresso machine, hiding between it and a canister of vanilla powder. The troop leaders, Chloe hoped, wouldn't ask for a coffee drink.

Jenna turned her back to conceal the kitten's hiding place while Chloe quickly scooped candy into bags for the girls, hoping none of them would notice Fraidy. She could only imagine the mad scramble to catch the animal and the resulting shatter of glass, candy flying everywhere. Not even Willy Wonka would be able to rescue them.

"You're a saint," Chloe whispered to Darlene, the troop leader whose yellow uniform blouse and khaki-colored skirt looked quite elegant above wedge heels.

A grin pressed up Darlene's face. "St. Nicholas, maybe."

"Santa Claus?" Chloe asked as she slipped a few extra peanut butter cups into a bag for her friend.

Darlene toasted the air with the treats. "The patron saint of all things chocolate. How much do I owe you for these gems?"

"Those are on the house."

"No—"

"Let me gift the ultimate gift giver."

Darlene held the peanut butter cups to her heart. "You're gonna make me cry."

Chloe smiled back. "No tears allowed in my shop."

"Then we better head out."

Emma ducked under the counter, Fraidy now secured in his owner's arms as the Brownies giggled over their paper candy bags. When Darlene saw the kitten, she quickly shuffled her troops out the door. Chloe almost followed her, not to run away but to beg for advice. Candy was the only resolution she knew for a child's woes, and Emma had already eaten lemon drops.

The phone rang, and after Jenna answered it, she held the receiver out to Chloe, covering the mouthpiece with her hand. "It's Logan Danford again, from the *Post-Standard*."

"I'm not talking to him."

"Chloe—"

"I'm really not."

"He seems like a nice enough person," Jenna whispered. "Not like that last reporter."

*"Ridell owns a washed-up little shop,"* Chloe quoted from memory, *"the candy on her worn shelves scattered like flotsam along a forgotten shore. More like bait and tackle than a candy and coffee store."*

"That writer was trying to be clever."

"It was stupid."

"The rest of his review was better," Jenna said.

Chloe snorted. *"With a little work, she could turn her sweet shack into a toothsome trove."*

"Immature maybe, but he took some nice pictures."

"That man has no idea how hard we work." Maybe the building needed maintenance, the candy selection a bit of a makeover, but supply costs had skyrocketed and most people spent less than five bucks whenever they walked through the door. No one could amass a treasure trove of sweets on a bankroll comprised mainly of nickels and dimes.

Jenna lowered the phone, her hand still wrapped around the mouthpiece. "You are going to have to get that review out of your head."

"I'm afraid it's stuck there."

"Lots of customers have mentioned wanting to visit our washed-up little shop. It means quaint or something in their minds."

"If only *quaint* paid the bills . . ." Chloe heard a sound from the other side of the counter. One that sounded an awful lot like tears.

As she rounded the corner, Emma curled like a mama cat over her kitten.

Chloe sank down beside her. "Is Fraidy hurt?"

Emma wiped away her tears. "I don't think so."

"Are you?"

"No."

The girls must have scared her.

"The rule about no crying doesn't apply to children," Chloe said as Jenna spoke to the reporter, her voice muffled. Nothing beneficial would come from digging up the past. She needed to focus on the lost girl with her today, not one lost almost a century ago. "You can cry as long as you'd like in here."

Emma shook her head. "Tears are for wusses."

"Whoever told you that straight-up lied," she said, wishing she could ease the girl's pain.

Emma ran her hand down the kitten's back as if she could find a bit of comfort there, and Chloe tentatively, awkwardly, opened one of her arms. Emma leaned like she'd done with the display window until her head was pillowed on Chloe's shoulder.

"Who told you not to cry?" Chloe asked, but Emma didn't answer.

Chloe loved to laugh with the kids who came into her shop, fill their bags with treats, but she didn't really know how to just be with a child. Or be a child, for that matter. By the time she was Emma's age, she was practically an adult.

Unsure of what else to say, she waited quietly as fresh tears fell from Emma's eyes, and when she looked back at the counter, Jenna was watching them.

Sadness broke through her friend's gaze before she mouthed, "Good job."

Chloe didn't feel like she was doing much good, but she would be there for this girl until Gavin found either her family or someone to foster her.

And she stood by what she'd told Gavin this morning. While Emma was strong, she was scared of something or someone in her world. Scared, it seemed, into a cavern of silence.

## 6

# *AMELIA*

Silver clattered against porcelain as the Pendleton guests savored their lobster salads, vermicelli soup, and tender beef Wellington wrapped in flaky pastry and drenched with Madeira wine. Conversation volleyed across elaborate centerpieces made of summer flowers and seashells and gold-plated mirrors to reflect the evening light. While the sky had begun to darken over the veranda, Amelia was relieved that not a single raindrop had fallen.

Dessert would be served inside, and the parade of ices, all of them shaped like birds, was the grand finale. A local blacksmith had fired the ice molds from Amelia's sketches, and then their cook, a woman trained at the Marshall's School of Cookery, had filled them with an assortment of custards and sorbets before freezing them in the icehouse.

The cold sweets, Amelia hoped, would help cinch the political aspirations for her husband. He'd told no one else, to her knowledge, about his ultimate goal to obtain the White House, but several people around their dining table, she suspected, would do just about anything to stop him. Leslie had been prepared to convince them otherwise until he disappeared from the table about twenty minutes ago. If he didn't return soon, she would send James, their butler, to locate him.

At least the reporter was nowhere to be seen. Perhaps Cade had worn him out with the tour.

While a servant filled her and Leslie's glasses with wine, Amelia glanced back at James, trying to signal that her husband had enough to drink, but he was watching the French doors.

So much hinged on tonight. Not just Leslie's political aspirations, but their marriage and future as esteemed members in New York's gilded society. She wouldn't let it fall apart.

"Is everything in order?" she whispered when Leslie finally returned to his seat, his tailored coat askew.

"I went to check on the boats," he said. "Where is that man?"

At first, she thought he was looking for one of the staff but quickly realized that he was speaking about President Roosevelt.

"I'm sure he and Edith are on their way." And, hopefully, their son to help celebrate Penelope's birthday. "Something must have demanded their attention this afternoon."

Leslie took another sip of wine. "They should have been here an hour ago."

"They're coming, darling," she said as if she was privy to the president's calendar.

It didn't matter if the Roosevelts appeared. As long as Leslie curbed his drinking, the evening would be a success. He would be pleased with her work, and they could forget the ugly words that had ricocheted between them earlier. Perhaps he would even put aside his philandering for a season, and they could truly be a family.

But even as conversation flitted around them, Leslie was so distracted by Teddy's absence that he was failing as a host.

"What do you think about the Food and Drug Act?" Arnold Ingram, a millionaire from Rochester, asked from across the table. After winning a seat in the House of Representatives, Mr. Ingram had built his own castle in the Thousand Islands, his fortune originally mined from silver and gold.

Leslie wanted the man's support before he announced his own campaign, but this congressional act to regulate the content in food and drugs was a tricky one. Leslie's response would ripple far into their future.

"I believe people are entitled to know what they are eating and drinking." To punctuate his claim, Leslie took another sip of wine.

"Of course." Mr. Ingram eyed the blossoms that graced their table runner. "Just as the government is entitled to a portion of anything that, shall we say, brings people an extra measure of joy."

Amelia cringed at his inference. Opium and its ability to bring what some referred to as joy was the last thing she wanted her guests to discuss tonight. "You must tell us about the river races," she said, desperate to change the subject. "We've heard they were—"

Leslie didn't let her finish. "President Roosevelt is opposed to the consumption of any opium product."

Mr. Ingram soaked a piece of beef in the wine sauce. "Which is exactly why Roosevelt won't win another election."

Teddy had been moved into the presidency in 1901 after President William McKinley was shot at an exposition in Buffalo, but the people—Leslie included—had officially elected him in 1904. Now he was fighting against all manner of corruption in the United States.

Leslie had stood beside his friend's progressive Square Deal reforms to protect farmers and coal miners from unfair business practices, but he wasn't nearly as fond of the president's proposals to regulate drugs and inform the public of the ingredients inside their food and medications. While he might say otherwise to the politicians at their table, the truth was, her husband didn't think the mothers who bought his profitable tonic needed to know the name of every item they spoon-fed their children.

"Perhaps the government should reconsider taxing opium," Leslie said as if the idea had just occurred to him. "Expand business even further in this nation."

"And encourage the revelry?" Mr. Ingram asked, chewing with his mouth partially open.

"Our government is profiting plenty from other revelry," Leslie said slowly. "Perhaps lifting the tax would discourage the current conflict."

Mr. Ingram choked on his piece of meat.

"Opium doesn't lead to revelry," Mrs. Ingram stated with the greatest of confidence. "Pure debauchery is its consequence."

Leslie's laugh was patronizing. "I don't believe any debauchery could be defined as pure."

"Then simple debauchery," Mrs. Ingram acquiesced. "All opium, in my opinion, should be banned."

Amelia placed her hand ever so gently on Leslie's pant leg, willing him to curb his opinions. No good would come out of his banter, no matter how witty, with Mr. Ingram's wife.

"My good woman," Leslie continued, shooing Amelia away. "Why should we ban the simplest of pleasures—nature's remedy really—from those who need it most?"

Mrs. Ingram's forehead divided into rivulets as pronounced as the waterways between their islands. "Modern remedies offer a cure and allow the faculties of one's mind."

"But not, perhaps, the merriment of one's spirit," Leslie continued. "Why regulate, as your husband stated so eloquently, what brings joy to those who have so little or a measure of relief to those in pain?"

Mrs. Ingram glared at her husband as if she'd just realized that she had married a fiend.

"Mr. Pendleton and I are fully confident," Amelia said, "that the Congress and president will find a reasonable compromise between vital cures and a vice."

The squeeze on Leslie's leg wasn't gentle this time—more like clawing with her fingernails—but he still didn't pay heed to her cue.

"My dear wife." Leslie slipped an arm around the back of her chair, but his narrowed eyes held no endearment. Then he lifted his wineglass with his opposite hand in a salute. "There's nothing wrong with a vice or two."

Blasted wine. Leslie already polarized with his words when he was sober, making some people think he was a champion while others, like Mrs. Ingram, were becoming increasingly convinced of his demonic state. This particular vice, rarely consumed in their house, would be the ruin of him and his political ambitions.

That would bring none of them joy.

"Mr. Pendleton."

She and Leslie both turned to see Cade with a crisp envelope in his hand. How handsome he looked in his borrowed cloak, like he'd just stepped away from one of the estates in Yorkshire or the Hamptons. And how proud her mother would have been of this very English world that Amelia had re-created between a former and present British colony.

"This just arrived." Cade held out a telegram. "I thought it might be important."

Leslie ripped open the seal and dug out a slip of paper. Then the envelope sailed to the ground.

"The president sends his regrets," Leslie announced.

Amelia held her breath for a moment, silencing a gasp. "He's not coming?"

"Not until morning." Leslie tore up the telegram, its pieces snowing the sandstone.

Amelia glanced up at the tower where their daughter still slept. "At least he'll arrive before Penelope's party."

"The messenger is waiting in the boathouse," Cade said. "Shall I send a reply?"

Amelia glanced at Leslie before she spoke. "Tell him we understand his inevitable delay and eagerly await his arrival."

Cade nodded briskly and turned toward the waterfront. Even though he was only a few years past twenty, he would be much better suited to replace James as their butler or perhaps work as a secretary to her husband instead of a caretaker. Then again, they needed Cade to fix the intricate electrical wiring in this house and all the workings on their assortment of boats. The man was a marvel really. Koster Isle couldn't flourish without him, and she suspected he would feel out of place in the confines of their city home.

A single raindrop changed the course of their evening when it blew across the balcony, splashing off one of the mirrors. Guests sprang from their chairs and streamed through the open doors before the storm began to funnel from the sky.

"Dessert is in the dining hall," Amelia called.

The women followed her, but Leslie countered her plan. At his invitation, the men swarmed to the gilded smoking room like honeybees to their hive.

James reached for the antique platter that held a decanter of their finest Scotch and a box of Spanish cigars. The cigar would balance Leslie, but the last thing he needed was another drink. If he started his foolish talk again about opium, he'd shatter the entire hive.

"Don't fill Leslie's glass," she ordered, but the butler looked confused as if he couldn't imagine refusing Mr. Pendleton's request.

Clearly he couldn't be trusted.

"Here," she said, reaching for the Scotch. "I will serve them."

If Leslie stung her, so be it. It was better than him ruining this night.

A sweet cloud drifted into the hall, and she prayed it was only smoke from their cigars, not the opium that he touted as merriment.

Leslie sprang up from his seat when he saw her and the decanter in her hands. Then he motioned her outside the room and closed the door, returning the Scotch to the butler's silver tray.

She stared at the amber drink, wondering what Leslie would do if she tried to wrestle it away, but a public brawl would benefit no one.

Leslie opened the door just wide enough for James and his decanter to slip into the smoke, and when they were alone, Leslie turned back to her. "We don't need your interference, Amelia."

She straightened the ribbon around her waist. "Quell your drinking, and you won't need anyone to interfere."

"You are going to ruin this evening," he spat.

"I'm not the one ruining it!"

Mrs. Ingram strolled into the hall, her opal gown shimmering in the light.

"Are you looking for dessert?" Amelia asked.

"I'd like to rest for an hour before the fireworks begin." Mrs. Ingram reached for the wainscotting, seeming to balance herself against the strip of wood. "If this storm stops, of course."

Leslie nudged Amelia's elbow. "My lovely wife will escort you to one of the guest rooms."

Fireworks were already exploding inside Amelia's chest, but she nodded with all the grace that she could muster. "Of course."

"And you can check on Poppy while you're up there." Leslie stepped back into the smoking room. Then she heard brass scrape across the newly polished wood. Her husband had locked her out of his sacred space.

Mrs. Ingram cleared her throat. "Should I find it on my own?"

"No." Amelia stepped forward. "I will take you."

"In my house, we have a matron to guide our guests."

Amelia bristled at the criticism. "We're still acquiring our summer staff."

"I'm glad to offer recommendations," the older woman said.

Amelia directed her toward the main staircase. "I would welcome any recommendations that you have."

"Do you not have a lady's maid either?" Mrs. Ingram asked.

"I have a fine maid, but she is caring for our daughter tonight." No reason to explain that she hadn't hired a new nursemaid for Penelope.

"I didn't realize you had a child."

"I'm trying to keep her name out of the papers," Amelia explained. "So she can enjoy a bit of privacy during her early years."

"A gift, to be sure."

Amelia opened a door on the second floor that led into one of eight rooms prepared for the guests who weren't sleeping on their boats or at a hotel on the mainland. Then she switched on an electric lamp. Light flooded the lavender walls and towering headboard with curtains draped from the ceiling. While the Ingrams would be returning to their island tonight, Mrs. Ingram could rest here.

"Please let me know if you need anything else," Amelia said.

"If you could save me a bowl of custard—"

"Of course."

They all had their vices.

When she left the room, Amelia glanced up the flight of steps. Penelope should be awake soon, dressing for her dinner meal and ice cream and then fireworks if the storm subsided.

A noise startled her from behind, and she jumped. All of the staff and other guests, to her knowledge, were downstairs. Who was inside this bedroom?

The door was ajar a few inches, the interior dark. Was the reporter sniffing around the upper floors? If so, what had the *Post-Standard* uncovered that propelled him into their private rooms? She shivered at the thought.

Harry Baden's story about the Pendletons' island gala might be a ruse.

"Hello?" she whispered as she pushed open the door, but no one answered.

Turning on the light, she scanned the velvet furnishings, the ivory vanity and upholstered bench at the end of the bed. Rain pounded against the windows, streaking and shaking the glass. She must have heard the storm. Harry was probably buzzing among the bees below, molding his story from the bits of gossip that mixed with the smoke before he returned to a hotel in Clayton.

She'd check on Penelope and then return to the party. Instead of battling for temperance, she'd make sure that James had plenty of nectar for the bees. If all the men were as tipsy as Leslie, perhaps none of them would remember precisely what her husband did this evening.

7

# CHLOE

The night was still as Chloe sipped hot cocoa on the back patio, her shoulders wrapped in one of the cozy blankets Nana had knitted for her more than twenty years ago, not long after Chloe came to live on the island.

Grandpa Cade had spent decades building luxury boats by hand, and her grandparents had invested well over the years, buying this island and purchasing the candy shop, but instead of upgrading their home or flying south when the westerly winds escorted frigid temps from Lake Ontario, freezing the river and land, they'd lived frugally in the coziness of this cottage. Grandpa Cade had knitted the walls around them with the greatest of care and Koster Isle provided everything they needed. Why would they go anyplace else? It wasn't until Grandpa Cade passed away that her grandma turned the upper floors of the candy shop into an apartment for the harsh winter months.

The island had been named Koster to honor Mrs. Pendleton's family, but sometimes Chloe thought of it as Ridell Isle since her grandparents had lived here decades longer than the Pendletons. Now that Chloe was the last Ridell, she wanted to plant her roots on this island.

Sighing, she set her cocoa on the table. As a breeze blew up the cliff from the river, she snuggled into the warm blanket that still smelled just a bit like Grandpa Cade. In her mind, he embodied everything about this island—the smells, the rugged strength, the courage to weather the storms. And, it seemed, a few of the island's secrets.

The shop, she'd already resolved in her heart, would have to be sold, but how was she ever going to let go of Koster Isle? More than anything, she wanted to keep it, but she didn't have the income to maintain the land or cottage. Her father had depleted his accounts long ago on booze and drugs and gas for his VW Bus, and her grandparents had spent any inheritance on Chloe's education and then memory care and medical bills.

Was it selfish of her to preserve this place?

Koster Isle embodied all that was good in her life, experienced through two people who loved God and all those around them. Chloe had learned from them what it meant to lay down one's life, as Jesus had done long ago. How His sacrifice had the remarkable power to wash away sin. The mistakes in one's past, Nana had said, could be fired and sculpted and repurposed for something good.

Her grandma firmly believed that God had a plan for every man and woman who followed Him. Chloe wanted to follow, but sometimes she didn't know which direction to go. What did God want next for her? Or did He have anything planned at all?

It seemed rather lofty to think that God might have something planned for her life, but she would continue listening, intently, to the whispers in her mind. And she'd fight with everything inside her to preserve the remarkable work of her grandparents and share their legacy, whenever she could, with others.

Like the girl spending another night in their home.

She glanced back at the window. Perhaps God did have something planned for her right now. Tonight, it seemed, He wanted her to care well for a lost, or perhaps runaway, child.

Chloe stood carefully so she wouldn't startle the dog who slept on a flannel bed beside her. Then she tiptoed back into the house and gently opened the cracked door into Emma's room. In the soft glow of a night-light, she could see the girl resting peacefully on the bed, Sugar rolled like a snowball on the floor.

Maple spent most of his nights on the patio, but Sugar had taken to sleeping in their guest's bedroom, seeming to watch over the kitten and his owner. Chloe had relaxed any house rules—okay, totally dumped them—since Emma arrived. The dogs that her grandparents had kept always slept in the shed, but Chloe liked having Maple and Sugar in the house. And she liked having Emma as her guest.

A bit of sadness crept inside Chloe at the thought of the girl leaving. It had been a full week since Emma had seemed to wash up with the storm. Children's Services was searching for a foster family along with her biological one, but until they found a home, Chloe had volunteered to care for her. Emma was good company for all of them.

With only three weeks left until summer break, the social worker said Emma could wait to return to school. Emma said there'd be no return. She'd never been to school in the first place.

Chloe almost stepped back into the hallway, but then she saw Emma's scrapbook on top of the dresser and she inched closer, curious. Pasted on the scrapbook cover was a brilliantly colored bird with blue wings and haunting eyes that seemed to be staring back at her. Chloe didn't know much about birds, but it looked like one found on a tropical island, photographed by *National Geographic*.

She ran her hands across the ripples of dried paste. Then her fingers hovered over the cover before curling around the edge. Gavin had told her to look inside for more information, but guilt still plagued her. Was it right to plow into Emma's private world without permission?

*For her own good.*

Those were the words that kept rolling through her head. The same words she'd heard from another social worker when Chloe was young.

She wasn't certain this was for Emma's good. The girl was plenty smart and her fears were probably justified. And she'd asked so little of Chloe—only that Fraidy could stay with her and that Chloe would respect this book.

"It doesn't feel right," she said as if Sugar might be listening. In fact, it felt very wrong. Like finding a lost child alone on her island, in a raging storm.

If Chloe could stack up what she valued for herself, privacy would be close to the top. And violating this value for her guest felt like epic proportions of wrong.

She moved back to the door.

"You can look at it," Emma whispered.

She turned slowly, afraid to startle her. "Are you certain?"

Silence.

"Would you like to show it to me?" Chloe asked.

"No."

Chloe reached for it then. She understood well Emma's conflict of the heart, afraid to share her past even as she wanted others to know.

Carrying the book under one arm, Chloe returned to the patio. Maple's chin was on the edge of his flannel bed, his ears tucked back, as if he was equally intrigued by Emma's book. Leaning down, she petted her old friend behind the ears.

With Maple at her side, an accountability of sorts, Chloe slowly opened it.

Inside was a bigger photograph of the bird on the cover, labeled *Scarlet Macaw*. Someone had secured the picture from a magazine and tucked it with a poem, handwritten in a fancy script, behind a plastic sleeve.

Words she couldn't read in the dim light.

Turning, Chloe opened a storage box and pushed aside her garden gloves and rain boots before pulling out a flashlight. The bird gleamed under the plastic, the faded writing legible.

*Flames whip in fury, royal embers caged in brass.*
*Soaring, searching, wandering, beating against glass.*
*Secrets, she whispers in the storm.*
*Secrets, she boldly sings.*
*But no one hears her voice, they only see her wings.*

Strange and beautiful mixed into . . . Chloe wasn't sure what. The fury of the scarlet macaw. The blue and yellow of its wings.

Why was it beating against the glass?

No one had titled the poem or added a byline, the words unanchored to any author.

Emma could have cut out the pictures, but she hadn't compiled the book. The pages had been worn from years of use, amassed long before Emma was born. And the poem had been written by an adult who seemed to crave freedom like the birds.

Chloe stared out at the hemlock and oak trees that propagated with reckless abandon across her island. Even if the porch light was off, she wouldn't be able to glimpse the water beyond their branches tonight. Clouds blocked any light trying to rain down on the river.

Perhaps the poem stemmed from a much deeper place than the writer's obsession with flames or birds. Perhaps she was beating herself against the glass, trying to break free from her caged world.

Who had put these words to paper? And how did Emma end up with the book?

Chloe had stopped trying, for the most part, to search for impossible answers in her life, focusing on problems that she could solve, like the day-to-day operations at the candy store. The shop had brought her just as much joy—and probably more—as her customers.

Birds, it seemed, brought the same joy to whoever had compiled this scrapbook of pictures and poetry. Perhaps the royal embers and wings helped the author understand the world around her.

The pages to follow were filled with pictures and sketches of a variety of birds, each one clearly labeled. *Flowerpeckers. Stellar Jays. Lorikeet. The Blue-Grey Flycatcher.*

The artist had drawn a flycatcher posed on a tree, its slender face slanted toward the sky. Below was a description by John James Audubon in 1840 when he sketched and wrote *Birds of America*.

*This diminutive lively bird is rendered peculiarly conspicuous by its being frequently the nurse or foster-parent of the young Cow Bunting, the real mother of which drops her egg in its nest.*

Why would a mother leave her chick with another bird? The flycatcher, she thought, was a hero to raise another bird's hatchling as her own.

Then again, what if the flycatcher didn't know the egg had landed in her nest? Maybe she thought the abandoned bird was hers.

Chloe carefully turned the page again, and the next sleeve displayed a pair of lovebirds, their wide orange eyes gazing at each other as if they really were in love.

Under the photo was a handwritten description.

*One of the smallest parrots, lovebirds are quite loyal, bonding with their mate for a lifetime. Small but social, the birds feed each other, preen each other, and fly in the wild with their flocks. They don't like to be alone.*

Some of the sleeves held more poems; others contained detailed descriptions of the birds. Fascinating . . . but none of it would help them find Emma's family.

Chloe kept turning the pages, reading the various descriptions, until she reached the end. In a sleeve on the last page was a newspaper photograph of a building instead of a bird, but the plastic was creased, making it impossible to view in the flashlight beam.

"What is this?" she whispered as if Maple could respond.

She angled the page to ward off some of the glare, and it looked like a glass house with trees inside, a stone wall towering behind the glass. At the bottom was a caption, and she rotated the book again to read the words.

*Pendleton Birdhouse.*

Only a slender portion of the article was displayed on the page, the words chopped and diced. Whoever had cut this out was clearly more interested in the black-and-white photograph than the words flushed, at one time, to its left.

The only words that she could read were the name of the paper—the *Post-Standard*—and the date.

*July 6, 1907.*

Chloe blinked several times, her brain buzzing. That was a year she knew well from local history. The year that Poppy Pendleton disappeared and everything changed for the Pendleton family.

Looking down at Maple, a new series of pictures circled through her head, each of them threaded together like a reel of film tumbling out of its canister, a movie shot in her mind almost twenty years ago.

Chloe had been about Emma's age when Bucky—her grandpa's springer spaniel—had led her and Grandpa Cade to the castle. Nana didn't want them to visit, but she'd taken *Lolli* to the market that day and her grandpa needed to check on the old place—that's what he'd told Chloe. She'd followed right along, of course. She'd walk a hundred miles on the coldest of days, if she must, to be with him.

The castle was daunting enough as an adult. As a kid, it felt like Dracula's castle with its stone tower perched high on the cliff and beveled windows on the upper floors. Full of secrets, she was sure. And she hadn't even known back then about Poppy.

"Can we go inside?" she'd asked, wanting to explore.

Grandpa Cade had stooped to pull out a handful of weeds sprouting through the terrace seams. "Nope."

"Why not?" She squinted at a window, but all she saw were shadows.

Her grandpa threw the weeds to the side of the terrace and pushed his denim cap away from his eyes. "I'm afraid to say, I've lost the key."

She'd clapped her hands together. "I'll help you find it!"

"I fear it's gone for good."

With those words, her heart seemed to cave. She'd understood better than most at that age about things being gone.

He grinned at her. "But if anyone could find the key to this place, Chloe, you could."

She hadn't thought to ask about a locksmith or suggest that her jack-of-all-trades grandfather simply pick the old lock. Her focus shifted, clinging to his confidence in her. Cade—the much-loved caretaker of this island—thought she could find the key. Those simple words, the courage he'd set in her heart, had carried her through many a storm.

"We'll find a way together," she said, her faith in his skills boundless.

"It's not safe," he told her then.

"Why not?"

Chloe closed her eyes, struggling tonight to retrieve the answer to her question long ago, but this memory, like so many of her childhood memories, evaded her. Surely she would have remembered if her grandpa had answered.

Instead they'd quietly walked around the perimeter of the castle, checking the doors, making sure everything was secure. Even then, she'd known the property was falling apart, bits of rock mounded around the sides, tree limbs dusting the ground. And she'd been afraid.

But her grandpa didn't seem to notice the crumbling pieces or her fear. He'd told her that it was his job to care for the place, long after the Pendletons were gone. And she wondered, even then, how he could care for it without going inside.

Leaning back in her chair, Chloe remembered the smell of flowers that morning, a bird's song in the trees. And then the crunch of something under her sandals.

She'd been walking near the cliff, staring down at the boats, wondering when Nana was going to return.

"Come along," Grandpa Cade said as he took her hand.

"Did you hear that?"

"What?" he asked.

She scanned the ground. "It sounded like glass."

But if there were any shards, they were hidden by a carpet of leaves and stems.

"Must be from a broken window," he said. "Watch your step."

She'd looked up at the wall of windows, evenly spaced like portholes on a ship, but she hadn't seen a broken one. Was the glass from the birdhouse?

He'd steered her away from the cliff, and then they'd hiked the half mile around the island to the cottage on the other side. A world away from Pendleton Castle.

Maple placed his head on her lap, and she rubbed his ears. In hindsight, she should have asked her grandparents a lot more questions about the house and the Pendleton family and why Nana didn't want them visiting the castle.

When she was a child, Chloe had vowed to find the key and open the front door, but even after Grandpa Cade passed on, Nana's warnings kept her away. Something about the castle frightened her grandma, and the thought of breaking into it had always felt like disrespect to the woman who'd loved Chloe well. Even now that Nana was gone, her gut twisted at the thought of going inside.

She glanced down at the last page of the scrapbook again and saw a tiny piece of stained paper, something scribbled across it.

*For Penelope.*

Chloe stared down at the words as if they might take flight.

Penelope. Poppy.

Although old-timers in this region remembered the Pendleton family, they rarely talked about them. It was the tourist boats that told extravagant stories about a Gilded Age child who'd disappeared.

How did a scrapbook for Penelope end up with Emma?

Even as she closed the book, her curiosity piqued, her mind wandering back to the castle. Were the doors still locked, the windows unbroken? Was there glass hidden among the weeds?

And was it possible that Emma's arrival wasn't a coincidence after all?

If Gavin and the social worker could figure out who gave Emma the scrapbook, maybe they could find the connection between the scrapbook owner and Koster Isle.

Soon she would climb up that hill and remember what happened there, but for now she would focus on helping Emma.

No matter how they arrived in the nest, every chick needed a mother bird watching over them.

And every child needed a safe place to call home.

# 8

# *AMELIA*

The crackle of fireworks rippled and then faded over the St. Lawrence as the smell of gunpowder drifted across Koster Isle. Amelia scanned the crowded terrace and aviary beyond. Her poor birds. They were used to the rain beating on their glass house, but not fire in the sky. The lights would have them all aflutter tonight.

She'd ask Cade to check on them before he retired. His presence alone would coax them back to sleep.

The clouds had wrung themselves out an hour ago, and the guests were enjoying the coolness pooled outside. Amelia thought the storm might deter the pyrotechnics, but the men had created a spectacular display to commemorate their independence from England. And the eve of Penelope's birthday.

She glanced up at the tower, wondering if the fireworks had coaxed her daughter to the window. If she'd finally fallen asleep, was it better to awaken her at this late hour or let her rest? Leslie had wanted Penelope to greet their guests and she'd wanted her to watch the firelight in the sky, but now she was vacillating. Penelope would need her sleep before the festivities tomorrow.

On the other hand, Amelia had promised that her daughter could see the fireworks, and no good mum broke her word.

She desperately wanted to be a good mother, but motherhood had proved to be more daunting than she'd imagined. While she wanted to care well for Penelope, she couldn't imagine the senior Mrs. Astor checking regularly on her children when they had a governess employed. And they'd grown up just fine. Amelia's mother, on the other hand, was constantly doting on her and her sister and look what happened.

Perhaps a little distance was healthy for all of them.

"Where is Poppy?" Leslie asked when he stepped up beside her. Scotch radiated from his warm breath, a rift of greased hair stranded between his eyebrows. Fighting, she realized, was futile. Her husband would be lucky to wake before noon to greet the Roosevelts.

She smoothed the ribbon on her dress, wishing she could loosen her corset. Air was in short enough supply, but with her ribs imprisoned by satin and steel, it barely coated her lungs. "She's asleep."

"The grand finale is coming." Scotch splashed out of Leslie's glass as he listed like a ship that had taken on too much water. She caught his arm, trying to balance his large frame. This was why her husband rarely drank alcohol or smoked the opium whose virtues he liked to extol. Some men grew more steely under the influence, focused even, but Leslie became sloppy.

Why did he have to consume so much tonight? It was like he wanted to bring their family down.

Or maybe he just wanted to take her out. Now that he had an heir in Penelope, he didn't need a wife. Or at least, he didn't need her. Another woman might be ready to take her place.

Leslie tried to pull away from her grasp, but she didn't let go. He was already too curious about her maid, and she didn't need him, especially in this state, wandering upstairs.

"Where are you going?" she demanded.

"To fetch my daughter."

"Our daughter," she said loud enough for those around them to hear.

He reached out as if the banister might have followed him into the house, but his hand banged against one of his clocks instead.

"I'll help you to your bedroom." Maybe if he went to sleep now, he would be in decent shape after breakfast, before Penelope's party and the arrival of the Roosevelts.

At least Harry Baden had left to submit his article. Not that he would report Leslie's behavior, but it might sway his thinking.

"I'm not going—"

"You can't make it up to the nursery." Amelia's words slithered off her tongue, and she hated this person she'd become. But there was no turning back. If she began to unravel, if her secrets were exposed, Leslie would be more than angry. He would destroy her.

"The smoking room," he slurred.

*So be it,* Amelia thought. At least that would contain him until morning. At this late hour, most of their guests wouldn't notice he was gone.

Two lamps glowed in the room, the others turned off so they wouldn't distract from the firework display. She helped navigate the floundering ship he'd become, between leather chairs and onto a velvet-topped sofa. Then he collapsed back on the pillows and closed his eyes.

"You're pretty, Am—" He stumbled over her name.

At least he had the presence of mind to know it was her.

"Amelia," she said as she switched off another lamp.

He didn't stop. "Lady Amelia—pretty as pie and mean as a rattler."

"Only when someone steps on me."

"Rattle, rattle, rattle." He laughed at himself.

She glanced around the golden room again, its cushions and rugs askew. "What were you smoking in here?"

"Rattle, rattle . . ."

"Go to sleep, Leslie."

"You're not my mother."

"Sometimes I wonder . . ."

Sometimes she wondered what would happen if Leslie was gone. She wouldn't have to mother him anymore.

Before she turned off the second lamp, Amelia saw a woman standing in the shadows, trying to blend in with gilded panels that glittered in the light. Or perhaps she was trying to escape into the skeleton of staircases and tunnels that fused the castle together.

Amelia shivered even before she knew who it was. Someone else was witness now to her humiliation. "Rose?" she whispered, not wanting Leslie to wake.

The maid stepped forward, her gaze on the carpeted floor, her gray cap crooked. "Yes, Mrs. Pendleton."

"Why are you here?"

The younger woman's lips pinched together as if she was in pain, her hands tucked in the pockets of her apron.

Amelia moved forward until she stood almost eye to eye with her maid. Even with her heels, Rose was an inch taller than her, but her maid would slip through a crack tonight if she shriveled any further into herself.

"Why are you here, Rose?"

"I'm—"

Amelia slapped her across the face. "Speak up!"

"Leslie sent word for me to meet him."

A snore from the couch shook the fireplace pokers near her husband's side. "He clearly doesn't need your service now."

"I should wait."

"I told you to watch Penelope!" The tremor in her voice was almost as dreadful as Leslie's snore.

Rose's chin trailed back and forth as if she was dusting off her collar. "But he told me—"

"I am telling you to return to your post." Amelia studied her maid's face. What did Leslie see in this girl who looked like a prickly piece of straw, her hair bundled in a dust-ridden bale? He was using her, Amelia suspected, to taunt his wife.

Rose looked between her and the inept man on the couch.

"He asked me to run an errand."

"Don't lie to me, Rose."

"I'm not lying," she cried. "I need this job."

"Then you better hurry upstairs." Amelia brushed her gloved hands together. "Mr. Pendleton won't even know you were here."

After Rose disappeared through the panel, Amelia walked slowly over to her husband. His mouth hung open, the bitter words silenced on his drug-numbed tongue, the blazing light extinguished by opium and Scotch.

Leslie's vices, she feared, were going to destroy the Pendleton name along with his political ambitions. And they would destroy her and Penelope alike.

How were they supposed to live like this for the rest of their lives?

She turned off the final lamp and locked the door from the inside so none of their guests would find Leslie in this state. Then she slipped like Rose had done through the golden panel. No electricity had been installed in the corridors, but she followed the hanging lanterns through the hall before the last of the fireworks exploded in the sky.

9

# CHLOE

"Have you ever seen Poppy's Castle?" Chloe asked Emma as they trekked around the island on the path her grandfather had carved.

Emma shifted the upgraded cat carrier to her other arm. "Yes."

Chloe formed her next words carefully, proceeding with caution. "Have you seen it often?"

The girl shrugged. "Every time we go to Clayton."

"Of course." Stupid question. It was impossible to miss the turret when they sped away from the lagoon, its stone walls rising above the trees.

Copper tints in Emma's unruly hair gleamed in the sunlight as she batted a branch away from the carrier and then ducked under the swing of leaves. In just a week, Emma had gained enough weight to look more like the stalk of a sunflower than a reed, a healthy gain with the meat and veggies she gobbled up in Chloe's cottage along with a few treats from the shop. Fraidy had been eating a fair share of tuna and salmon as well.

The trail veered left, streaking down the side of the cliff like a lone raindrop on glass. Waves brushed against the cliff below, the river calm this morning. On the right, barely noticeable between the trees, was another path that Grandpa Cade had paved years ago, this one leading up to the castle.

Chloe and her dogs always descended together toward the lagoon. Then Maple and Sugar would spend their day guarding Koster Isle.

*"Gie it laldy,"* she shouted as she tossed a smooth stick into the trees. It was what Grandpa Cade used to say, feigning a Scottish accent.

Sugar raced after the stick, and when she retrieved it, Chloe tossed it again. But instead of continuing down the path, Chloe stopped in front of a tangled wall to her right made from scraggly juniper bushes and pitch pine.

The newspaper photo of the birdhouse floated into her mind, the memory of glass when she'd visited the castle as a girl, the conversation with Grandpa Cade about a broken window. It seemed odd to construct a birdhouse here with the frigid winters, but oddities abounded during the Gilded Age.

Had her grandpa known about the Pendleton birdhouse?

And why was she so afraid now to return to the castle on her own?

She'd spent much of the night racking her brain, unsuccessful in trying to explain the fear. Then she'd tried to rationalize it. The stories, she'd told herself, were why she was afraid. Not the rumored ghosts.

Chloe turned slowly to Emma. "Thank you for letting me look through your scrapbook last night."

Emma's gaze dropped to her new tennis shoes, their fabric a robin's-egg blue. "You're welcome."

"It's a beautiful book," she said. "Could you tell me where you found it?"

Emma didn't reply.

"I'm trying to help you find your way back home."

The dogs stopped on the path below, their tongues lolling, probably wondering at their delay.

"I don't want to go back to that place," Emma said, hugging Fraidy's carrier to her chest.

"Why not?" Chloe asked as a yellow warbler perched on a branch nearby, cheeping a warning, it seemed.

"The pages were beautiful," she continued, trying to engage the girl beside her. "Whoever put that together seemed to be mesmerized by birds."

Chloe brushed her hands over her sleeves as a breeze swept up from the water, a hawk circling in a thermal above the cliffs. "Will you tell me who compiled the book?"

"I don't know," Emma said.

"Did you live with her?"

Emma shook her head.

"Tell you what." Chloe eyed the overgrown path that separated them from the castle, then she checked her watch. She'd promised to be at the shop by noon so Jenna could leave for an appointment. Then she and Emma would meet with Kaitlyn, their social worker, after lunch. But it wasn't even ten o'clock yet. An hour's delay wouldn't affect Jenna's plans. "The last picture in your album was of a birdhouse. I think I know where it used to stand."

Emma's green eyes swelled like a wave. If nothing else, she was finally interested.

"Would you like to see if we can find it?" Chloe asked.

Emma hesitated. "I've never been to a castle before."

"I haven't been to this one in a long time."

"But you live on the island."

"Weird, huh?" Chloe said. "My grandfather brought me here a few times when I was younger. It was his special place, and . . ."

Instead of finishing, Chloe whistled for her dogs, and they trotted back up the path, confused at this break in their normal routine. Then she turned back to Emma. "It makes me a little sad to visit without him."

The girl nodded solemnly as if she understood the deep sadness of missing a loved one.

Chloe had been fifteen when her grandfather died. He had fallen asleep in the cottage and angels, Nana liked to say, whisked him away. So many questions she wished she had asked him. So many stories, she feared, slipped away with him that night.

The dogs sniffed the ground while Chloe peeled back the wall of brush. Clusters of white serviceberry blooms dangled over the muddy trail before them, veiled in weeds.

Every once in a while a group of teens would embark on a late-night expedition to search the island for ghosts, but long ago, the winds had taken the steps that linked guests from the Pendletons' boathouse to the castle. It was impossible to scale the granite cliff without climbing gear, and as far as Chloe knew, none of the kids had ever found this overgrown path or the entrance to the tunnel, now hidden in the trees, that staff once used to transport goods between the river and house.

She motioned Emma forward. "Let's see if we can get through."

"Are you sure we're allowed back here?" Emma asked as she stepped onto the path, bringing up the rear.

Chloe smiled. "Yes, we're allowed."

She'd taken over the care of her grandparents' cottage and the lagoon, and maybe one day soon, she would bring a shovel and trimmer here as well. Only when you cleared away the weeds, Nana once said, could a heart heal.

It still felt like she was betraying the woman she loved by visiting this place, but now that her grandma was gone, maybe it was finally time for her to clear this path on the island and the one inside her alike.

The castle wasn't far from the cliff, about two hundred feet. Weeds circled the medieval-looking house like a moat or fortress wall, and then the pathway opened to a stone terrace and marble steps curling up to a veranda with imposing French doors and curtained windows.

The dogs took off ahead of them, but Chloe stopped walking when she realized she was alone. Turning, she looked back at Emma.

The girl's gaze was on the house, her eyes wide again. "It really is a castle."

"Yes, it is."

"It's so big."

"I said the same thing when I was about your age."

Emma lowered the cat carrier, securing Fraidy by a pillar. "Can we go inside?"

"Unfortunately not," she said. "I don't have the key."

Emma tilted her head as if trying to sort through Chloe's refusal. "I thought this was your island."

"It belonged to my grandparents."

"But—"

"No one has been inside the house for many years." Decades probably.

Emma didn't press her, but Chloe suspected she knew about locksmiths.

"I wonder what's in the tower," Emma said.

Chloe leaned back, following Emma's gaze to the top of the stone turret. "I don't know."

"Don't you want to go inside?"

"I do, but—" she took a deep breath, fear simmering inside her—"it's complicated."

They climbed the moss-stained steps together, and the view from the stone balcony, between the clips of trees, was extraordinary. A snapshot of river and the shoreline of New York. While they couldn't see Clayton, the town was to their right. On a clear night, the lights of passing boats would streak across the surface even as the stars rained down.

When she was younger, Chloe thought often about Poppy Pendleton, wondering what had happened to the girl, and standing on the veranda, looking down at the water, she couldn't help but wonder again—where had Poppy gone?

Leslie Pendleton, Poppy's father, died the same night his daughter disappeared. Grandpa Cade thought the girl had fallen off one of the cliffs, into the river, and couldn't make it back to shore. Even if Poppy could swim, even if the air was moderately warm on a summer night, even if no child should ever drown, the St. Lawrence didn't play favorites. All ages and abilities from avid young swimmers to the elderly had lost their lives in the cold currents and craggy shoals.

Mr. Pendleton, some thought, had died in his grief. And Mrs. Pendleton's heart must have ripped in two when she lost her husband and her daughter. No amount of money could mend a broken heart.

Then again, the river almost always returned its victims, and Poppy's body was never found. There was always the possibility that someone took her or she ran away, pure coincidence that it happened the same night as her father's death. It wasn't like a five-year-old, living on an island, could run far, but if she had stowed away on someone's boat, why had she left home? And why hadn't anyone returned her to the island?

The lingering mystery of Poppy's disappearance was what kept people like the reporter at the Syracuse paper intrigued. But it didn't really matter what happened exactly, all these years later. Life had moved on in the islands without the Pendleton family.

Wind rustled the leaves around them as Emma pressed her nose against a window coated in dirt, peering through a slit between the curtains.

"What do you see?" Chloe asked, remembering when she'd tried to peer through the weathered glass as a child.

"Everything is dark."

"Maybe we can figure out where the birdhouse was located."

Wind swept up the cliff as the two of them moved to the side of the house, and Chloe pointed at the edge. "Don't step too close."

"I know."

"It's a straight shot down."

Emma turned back, her hands clasped together. "I'm not stupid."

"Of course not." The girl had been pushed into adulthood too early in life. Any direction, no matter how important, seemed to be viewed as opposition. As if she wasn't capable of taking care of herself.

Chloe understood.

"You are the smartest kid I know," she said before stomping on the rocks.

Emma dropped her defense, her arms falling to her sides. "What are you doing?"

"I thought there was glass here." She searched through the weeds, about fifteen feet away from the cliff, but she didn't feel any shards beneath her shoes. Perhaps she had imagined it when she was younger.

Another picture appeared in her mind, one of her and Grandpa Cade together as they'd looked up at the old castle. She remembered it clearly now, the odd thing he'd said. No creature could live in a glass house for long, he'd told her. Both were bound to shatter.

Had he been here when the birdhouse shattered?

"Look at this," Emma said.

Turning away from the cliff, Chloe followed the girl's voice into the trees. She was holding a tarnished metal sign, the top arched like a rainbow. *Aviary*, it read.

"What does it mean?" Emma asked.

"It's another word for a birdhouse." Chloe glanced across the weedy platform. As the caretaker, Grandpa Cade would have been responsible for cleaning up the glass. Why would he tell her the shards were from a window?

And if he hadn't been honest about the birdhouse, what else had he kept from her?

None of it made sense.

"It seems that the Pendleton birdhouse was located near here," she said slowly, the thud of her heart knocking into her chest.

Emma looked back up at the tower and then scanned the open cliff. "I wonder what happened to it."

"Maybe a storm blew it away."

A chickadee whistled in the trees, and Chloe closed her eyes, pretending for a moment that she was in the old aviary, a flock of birds fluttering around her. It must have been magical to stand here among them. Poppy probably loved the birds.

With a glance at her watch, she saw it was almost eleven. Time for *Lolli* to carry them over to Clayton. In a few hours, they would meet with the social worker to hear news, she hoped, about Emma's family.

"What's that?" Emma asked, staring into the trees.

"I don't see anything."

But Emma was already walking into the forest, and Chloe hurried after her. Moments later, she found Emma kneeling by a brown-winged bird. A downed sparrow.

"Something's wrong," Emma said as she scooped up the sparrow.

Chloe didn't touch the trembling bird. "It has a broken wing."

Tears rushed into Emma's eyes. "We have to fix it."

"I'm afraid it's too fragile."

Emma straightened her back, her voice strong. "Even a fragile wing can fly again."

Chloe thought of the numbers dropping rapidly in her bank account.

She barely had enough to pay her regular bills. But if she could help the bird and Emma alike . . .

"Perhaps it can fly again," Chloe said as she directed Emma toward the path. "We'll stop at the vet to see if he can fix it."

Emma picked up Fraidy's carrier with her free hand. "She'd like that."

"I thought your kitten was a boy."

"Not Fraidy," Emma said. "My neighbor on the island. She can fix broken wings."

Chloe slowed her walk. "Was this woman a friend to you?"

Emma simply nodded as she moved down the path, the bird carefully cradled in her hand.

The world had been searching for Poppy almost a century ago, but there were layers upon layers to unravel for this girl right now.

Someone had to be missing Emma today.

And Chloe prayed it was someone good.

## 10

# *POPPY*

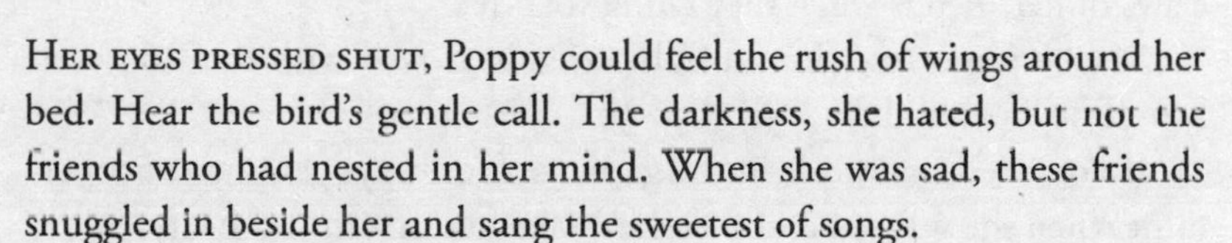

HER EYES PRESSED SHUT, Poppy could feel the rush of wings around her bed. Hear the bird's gentle call. The darkness, she hated, but not the friends who had nested in her mind. When she was sad, these friends snuggled in beside her and sang the sweetest of songs.

Papa worried about her being alone, but she was never really alone. The birds were always with her.

Stretching her legs under her bedcovers, scrunching her toes, Poppy wondered again what it would be like to fly. Then she giggled quietly before whispering to herself, "Silly girl."

Birds didn't fly with their feet. They spread their arms wide and sailed with the wind. No matter where they flew, the wind always blew them back home.

She lifted her arms and breathed deep the jasmine breeze, layers upon layers of it, that flooded through her window. The tang of river. The sweetness of grass.

Voices rose into the tower with the wind. Then laughter and the clink of silver. She'd heard it plenty of times in their city house. After Francine, her old nursemaid, fell asleep, Poppy would sneak down the hall and listen to dinner parties through the grate. Sounds mesmerized her, all the colors and smells, but people did not. They patted her head and commented on her dress and asked too many questions. Then she wished that she had wings.

No one ever patted a bird's head.

Now Francine was gone, and when Mummy was busy, Rose was supposed to watch over her in this strange new house. Rose told Poppy to pretend to be asleep until the party was over. Mummy wouldn't want to wake her, and Papa, she hoped, would be too busy to visit the nursery. She could stay right here with her birds.

The door squeaked open, and she clamped her eyes shut again. Then she stilled her breath.

Only Papa would awaken her so she could meet his friends. He was worried about her not having any of her own.

She'd told him over and over that she had plenty of friends. Fred and Minnie and Little Sue, the parakeet. She'd whispered all the names to him, but instead of smiling, his forehead had pinched tighter than the claws of her friends when they clung to a tree.

Maybe tomorrow she could be friends as well with the Roosevelt boy. If he liked birds.

If not, she'd find Cade in the gardens. He always gave her a peppermint when she was sad and then he'd take her to visit the aviary.

"Holler for me anytime," he told her when she had first arrived on the island. "I'll help you with whatever you need."

According to her mum, Cade could fix anything.

"Penelope," a voice whispered.

Her naughty eyes sprang open, and she squinted in the shadows. "Mummy?"

"Yes, sweetheart."

Her heart fluttered like the wings in her mind. Mummy was always kind, but she'd never called her anything sweet before.

"I don't want to go downstairs." Poppy grasped the covers in her wings, digging her toes into the branch of her bed frame.

Mummy kissed the top of her head, the ribbons from her hat dangling over the pillow, the scent of lavender on her skin.

"We don't have to go on the veranda," she whispered. "Let's sneak away instead."

"But where will we go?" she asked. Mummy never snuck away.

"We'll have an adventure. Just the two of us."

Poppy wiggled her fingers again. What would they do on an adventure? She'd never been on one before.

Mummy must be trying to surprise her for her birthday. Maybe Cade had found another bird for the house. This one she'd name after him.

"Where is your most favorite place in the world?" Mummy asked.

Poppy squinted in the light that funneled up from the party, but Mummy's hat hung so low that Poppy couldn't even see her eyes.

Perhaps this wasn't a surprise at all. Perhaps something was wrong. Mummy never went on adventures, and she should know Poppy's favorite place. It was her favorite place too.

How could Mummy have forgotten?

Poppy sighed, trying not to feel disappointed. Sometimes she felt lost in this new house. Alone. "You know my favorite place."

"But it might have changed."

"The birdhouse, Mummy. It will always be my favorite."

"Of course," she said in her royal voice. That's what Papa called it when Mama spoke British. "Perhaps we can spend the night in there, just the two of us. To celebrate your birthday."

"Rose will worry about me."

"Oh, I've already told her about our adventure. She thinks it's a lovely idea." Mummy unwrapped a bundle under her arm. "But we can't have you traipsing around in your nightgown."

Poppy giggled at the thought, the birds fluttering inside her chest. What if she traipsed through all the fancy people just like this, a pillow in one arm, her teddy in the other? Even Papa would have to smile.

"We will slip on this special dress." Mummy sounded more urgent now. Worried, even. Sometimes Mummy worried more than Papa.

The dress was warm on this summer night and prickly, but Poppy was too curious to be disagreeable. What would it be like to really hear the flapping of wings when she closed her eyes? She could fly with the birds all night in her dreams.

It would be the best birthday.

Mummy held out a bottle. "Take a sip of this."

Sometimes Rose gave her a tonic to help her sleep, but Mummy never did. In fact, both her parents said it would make her ill.

"I don't want to sleep anymore." A grand adventure awaited them. She didn't want to miss a single moment.

"This is for flying, not sleeping," Mummy said. "It will give you wings."

Poppy swallowed the syrup.

"Quickly now." Mummy tucked the glass bottle into her pocket, and they tiptoed down the hall, their skirts lifted as if the carpet might splash their hems.

She heard music below, the string of the harps. Could her birds hear the music? Did they know how to dance? She could imagine them swirling in circles to the melody. Swirling and swirling . . .

Mummy hushed her when she laughed again.

Poppy collapsed on the ground, listening to the music, tapping her shoulders to see if her wings had grown, but Mummy lifted her off the carpet. "We've no time to waste."

They weren't tiptoeing anymore. Nor did they travel down the front stairs. Instead, Mummy opened one of the panels where the servants hid and lifted a flickering lantern from its hook.

Poppy hesitated, but only for a moment. It was an adventure, after all. Mummy knew the way.

The tunnel curved like a wave through the house, and she didn't like it much. One could get lost behind these walls, trapped like a fish or seal. Away from the breeze, she might never fly again.

"Mummy?" she started, wondering how long it would take before they were outside.

"We'll talk soon, sweetheart. Just not in here."

Her heart warmed again. Mummy thought she was as sweet as Cade's peppermints.

Finally they pushed through a small door and onto the grass, far from the party. Poppy took a breath of river air in the darkness. How she wished that both she and Mummy could adventure together in the sky.

"We're almost there," Mummy said, holding the brim of her hat in the breeze.

Poppy glanced around them until she saw the path. Then she pulled on Mummy's other hand. "The birdhouse is this way."

"Later," Mummy said in a voice that didn't sound royal.

An explosion overhead made Poppy jump, and then trails of white fell from the sky, sprinkling like salt into the river.

"Fireworks," she whispered, mesmerized. Mummy must have brought her this way to see the parade of lights.

Her head started feeling funny. Dizzy. Perhaps it was almost time to fly.

She could fly all the way to the stars.

But Mummy stole her away from the light. "Hurry up, Poppy."

A gust swept up the side of the cliff, stealing Mummy's hat, and Poppy's eyes grew wide.

"Cade!" she shouted into the night.

But the man who could fix anything never found her.

# 11
# *AMELIA*

"Mrs. Pendleton." Someone nudged her side, and she rolled over. "Please wake up."

Was it morning already? She wasn't ready to continue the festivities, especially if it meant waking Leslie.

The guests had lingered on the veranda until well past midnight, and she'd met briefly with the staff after their guests were gone. Some of them would be up all night to prepare for the arrival of the Roosevelt family and then a special birthday luncheon with stewed lamb and snow custard for Penelope since she refused to eat fish or chicken or any kind of bird.

Rose stripped back the bedcover. "Please, Mrs. Pendleton."

"Another hour," she murmured, her entire body blanketed with exhaustion.

A rash of whispers outside her door, but she couldn't understand what was said. Not that it mattered. She was the mistress of this castle.

Queen. And she couldn't possibly be regal without a few more hours of sleep.

A creak on the wooden floor, and someone else stepped into her room.

"Is Poppy with you?"

Her eyes sprang open at their caretaker's voice even as she pulled the covers over her nightdress. What was Cade doing in her room?

"Penelope is in the nursery." They knew where to find her.

"She's not in her bed," Cade said.

Amelia lifted her head. "Rose?"

"I've looked everywhere for her." The maid reached for the bedpost to steady herself. "She can't be far."

Amelia tossed back the covers and sprang from her mattress, blood gushing through every vein as Rose handed her the kimono that had been draped over the vanity chair. Cade had the decency to look away while she dressed, but propriety be hanged. She had to find her daughter.

Up the stairs she raced, straight into the nursery. A mound of blankets had replaced Penelope in the bed.

She turned to Rose. "How long has she been gone?"

"I don't know."

Heat drained out of Amelia's skin as she collapsed on the blankets, the chill of the early morning settling like ice in her bones. How could they have lost Penelope? She'd been here in her bed just hours ago. She had seen her asleep . . . hadn't she?

With a start, she realized that she hadn't actually seen Poppy when she'd returned. She'd only seen a lump under her covers, this same mound that she assumed was her daughter. And Rose—the covers were flat now over the nursemaid's bed, but Amelia was certain they'd been drawn over her earlier. At the time, she'd been relieved that Rose had returned.

She pointed at the maid. "You were sleeping when I came before."

"I haven't slept a wink tonight."

Amelia bundled a blanket in her arms. Was it possible that Penelope had already been gone when she checked? It wasn't like Penelope to leave her room alone, but the sound of the fireworks . . . she would have been worried, like Amelia, about her birds.

She'd probably fallen asleep in the aviary with Minnie or Little Sue beside her. Surely they'd find her there.

"What time is it?" she asked Cade.

"A few minutes past two. Perhaps Mr. Pendleton knows where she went."

"Don't waken him." Leslie was in no condition to be bothered. If he was coherent enough to understand, he would only deter their search.

"But—"

"We have to find Penelope first," she said.

Then they would fetch Leslie hours from now, in time for a late breakfast.

Amelia was the first to arrive at the aviary. Looking back, she didn't remember climbing down the veranda stairs or running across the lawn, just unlatching the aviary door and flinging it open as she called her daughter's name. Rose and Cade rushed in behind her, scouring the path and the branches on both sides, but Penelope wasn't there.

She checked the smoking room next, in case Penelope had found her way through the walls, taking care not to disturb her husband's sleep, but Penelope wasn't there either.

The staff was roused, Amelia lighting a lamp for each member. Then they fanned out across the island, combing the forest and cliffs, scanning the surface of the river.

Amelia swept down the tunnel to the boathouse and searched the moonlit channels between moored yachts. The current that slapped against their monstrous boathouse and the cliff on the other side. She called Penelope's name again, but all she heard in return was the cry of a mockingbird.

Bile rose in the narrow cavity of her chest, burning her throat, lungs begging for air.

A nightmare. That's what this was. And she was trapped inside.

Surely she'd awaken soon to find her daughter padding up beside her bed, asking if they could visit the birds. Then she'd fire Rose and hire an elderly nursemaid, one who wouldn't distract her husband.

Amelia rubbed her hands together, trying to break free from the darkness that was smothering her. The blanket of fear. She should keep moving, searching, but her feet were frozen in this place.

"Penelope!" she shouted from the landing outside the boathouse. "Poppy!"

Her shouts traveled over the waves, up the river, filtering into the night like the wake of a dream. Did a sound ever die or did it keep traveling in the wind? Somewhere, perhaps, Penelope would hear her.

Amelia listened as the breeze swept across the platform again, but no one answered her call.

This was no dream. Her daughter was gone.

No matter how hard she'd worked to make something of herself, build up Leslie and their wretched kingdom, care for Penelope, she was useless. Now their daughter was gone, and when Leslie awoke, he'd send Amelia away too.

Worthless. Just like her mother.

Amelia pushed back her loose hair that had been raked by the wind. The staff had been searching for hours now. *Hours.* And the island wasn't very big. Smaller than Manhattan's Central Park.

Where was she supposed to look now?

No one had asked her again about Leslie. They probably thought he was walking the perimeter, searching along the cliffs. The jagged edge. The long drop. What if her daughter had fallen into the river? Amelia could see it clearly in her mind. Penelope wandering outside alone, a flash of her life burning as she fell, its flame doused by the river.

Amelia shivered again. Neither she nor Penelope could swim. Even if she heard her daughter's voice in the water, pleading for help, what could she do? The river would swallow them both.

"I'm here with a delivery," a man called from the other side of a steam yacht.

Amelia jumped at the interruption, startled by the unknown voice. Multiple yachts and houseboats had moored here for the night, the guests asleep at this late hour. Perhaps this man was one of the crew. Perhaps he had seen Penelope.

She stepped forward to ask, her toes inches from the surface, but then she heard another voice.

"You won't be visiting Leslie tonight," a woman whispered.

Amelia stopped. Was that Rose?

And who was waiting to visit her husband?

"He's preoccupied." The woman said something else, but her words were muffled by the hull between them.

Amelia froze on the platform, listening for other voices.

"I don't care how many people are on the island," the man said.

"You will when you get caught," another man replied. "A houseful of witnesses who would like nothing more than to put us in prison."

"Just get me the money," the first one spouted.

And the woman answered him. "I'll get it."

Her fool of a husband. One of the most important evenings of their lives, and it seemed he had invited other guests to deliver his vile drug.

Amelia heard a rush behind her as lantern light splashed across her robe, any instinct to run buried under shock. Too many strange things were happening on this island. Things she couldn't control.

"Mrs. Pendleton?" Cade called from the steps.

An oar plunged into the water, paddling the opposite direction, and she shivered one more time. Opium, she feared, would be the death of them all.

12

# CHLOE

"We found a family for you," Kaitlyn said, like Emma had won the state lotto.

"I don't need a family."

The caseworker had agreed to meet with Chloe and Emma in the Clayton police station. Not the most cheery of environments, but Kaitlyn brought plenty of cheer with her. Most kids probably appreciated her enthusiasm, but Emma sat on a chair in Gavin's office between Kaitlyn and Chloe with the sleeves of her new polka-dotted parka crossed over the cat carrier, her eyebrows scrunched together.

If they weren't careful, Emma would bolt straight out of this conference room.

"Everyone needs a family," Kaitlyn explained with a smile, her fiery red hair piled in a loose bun. "And you'll love the family that we found for you. They live in the prettiest house outside Watertown, right next door to a playground, with three kids about your age and a Siamese cat."

Emma hugged the carrier to her chest. "I have my own cat."

"Unfortunately—" Kaitlyn stopped, but it was too late.

Emma scooted to the edge of her seat. "I'm not leaving Fraidy!"

Chloe leaned toward Emma, her fingers brushing over the sleeve of the parka they'd picked out together. "I'll take good care of her," she promised. "Just until you settle."

"And I'll take good care of you," Kaitlyn told Emma as she pulled a stack of papers from her briefcase, placing them on the round table. While her hair was messy, she was the consummate professional with her tidy leather case, dove-gray dress suit, and matching gray pumps.

Emma refused to look at either of them. Her eyes were on a bulletin board with at least a dozen shady-looking men and women wanted by police. "I'm not going."

"I'm afraid you don't have a choice," Kaitlyn said, an ounce of cheer sifting away. "But you won't be alone. I'll drive you to Watertown."

Emma's heels burrowed into the concrete as if she might be able to tunnel right through it.

Chloe motioned to the social worker. "Can I speak with you outside?"

"Of course." She patted Emma's stiff shoulder. "We'll be right back."

The women stepped into the hallway before closing the door behind them. What would happen if Emma refused to leave? The thought of Gavin and another deputy escorting her out . . .

Chloe shook her head. She couldn't process that right now. "This family—are they good people?"

"I believe so."

"But you're not a hundred percent sure."

"It's impossible to be a hundred percent certain, but I'm as sure as I can be. They've attended all our classes and passed the background checks, and even more important than the logistics, they seem excited about welcoming Emma into their home."

Chloe watched Emma on the other side of the glass. "She's not going to leave here without her kitten."

Kaitlyn sighed. "The family is ready to care for her, but they don't want another animal. The most important thing is for Emma to be in a safe place."

The words tangled inside Chloe, and she quickly tried to unravel them. Kaitlyn was right. Emma needed a good home, a safe one, with qualified parents. If this family was willing and able to care for her, she'd have to help Kaitlyn convince Emma.

"I just need her clothes," Kaitlyn said. "I'll take her to Watertown in an hour."

*An hour.*

The social worker should take her to a waiting family today, but Chloe wasn't quite ready to let go.

"Can you bring her things to the station?" Kaitlyn asked.

"Of course." But she wasn't about to pack the girl's clothing and album in a plastic bag. She'd stop by the market and buy a bona fide suitcase on her way home. "Perhaps Emma can go with me so she can say goodbye to the dogs. We can meet you back here in an hour."

"I'm afraid that would only make it harder for her to leave."

Kaitlyn was right. It was a terrible idea.

Chloe checked her watch. It was almost two. "I'll get her things right now."

"Thank you," the social worker said. "That'll give me time to make sure my paperwork is in order. I'll pick up dinner for her on the way, and we'll have her all settled into her new home before bed."

"I'm sure she'll be fine once she's there."

Kaitlyn glanced toward the door before lowering her voice. "Emma told me earlier that you were her aunt."

Chloe blinked. "That doesn't make any sense."

"I wanted to clarify with you."

"I don't have any nieces or nephews." Any living relatives, for that matter.

"I knew you weren't related," Kaitlyn said, "but I thought you should know what she was saying."

"Why would she tell you that?"

"It's not that unusual." Kaitlyn brushed her hands over her sleeves. "Kids from traumatic situations often create stories about their family. They're trying to survive in a confusing world where things don't make sense."

Kaitlyn was still talking but her words swirled together in a wind that swept through Chloe's mind. She no longer saw Emma behind the glass.

Instead it was herself as a child, walking up the path on Koster Isle, hand in hand with her father.

Strange—she hardly ever thought about him—and didn't remember ever being on the island together.

Her father was laughing, and even though her little-girl self was trying hard to understand, she couldn't figure out what was so funny. She wanted him to be happy. Wanted to laugh with him. But all she'd felt at his strange laughter was fear.

Instead of taking her to visit the castle, like Grandpa Cade had done when she was older, her father had directed her to the cliff. And they'd stood together on the edge, rocks balancing their heels, air under their toes, the river ready to catch them if they fell. She couldn't have been more than three or four. Only a few years before . . .

A pain bulldozed through her mind, and she pressed her hand against her head, trying to push back the memory, but she couldn't force it away.

What had her father been thinking?

He'd grabbed her hand again, squeezing it even tighter as they turned toward the castle tower. They'd stared at it together, the wind ruffling their sweaters, their backs.

"Ghosts," he'd finally whispered. "There are ghosts everywhere."

She'd studied the windows above, searching the dark glass. "I don't see anything."

"They're here. Just waiting until dark. Then they'll come out."

A shiver had raced up her spine. No wonder, looking back, why she didn't want to visit the castle. Her father had haunted it.

"Don't believe anything my parents say," he'd commanded even though she hadn't met her grandparents yet. "And don't you dare tell them we were here."

"Who are your parents?" she'd asked, but her father had slipped back into a world where she wasn't welcome, wandering along the cliff without her.

"Chloe?" Kaitlyn's voice broke through. "Are you okay?"

She blinked, lowering her hand. How could she have forgotten that afternoon with her father?

But this wasn't about her and her story. She'd already been rescued. Today was all about Emma.

"I'm sorry." Chloe shrugged back her shoulders, trying to rid herself of the searing pain. "Headache. What were you saying?"

Kaitlyn opened her purse and offered up a bottle of Tylenol.

"Thank you," she said before swallowing two tablets.

"Emma is telling stories because she wants to stay with you," Kaitlyn said. "You've been a good friend when she desperately needed one."

"She likes being on the island." Chloe looked through the window again, but Emma was ignoring them. How sad, Chloe thought, that two adults she barely knew were about to decide her fate.

"Thank you for taking such good care of her." Kaitlyn reached for the doorknob. "I was worried about her being a flight risk, but she seems to have settled in nicely."

"What happens when you or Gavin find one of her actual relatives?"

"Then we'll investigate and see if she can live with them."

Emma's birth family, if healthy, would be the best for her. "I hope you'll find someone soon."

"Me too," Kaitlyn said before returning to the room. "We'll be ready to leave after you retrieve her things."

Another breath filled Chloe's lungs as she tried to settle both body and mind, reminding her adult self, on the advice of her therapist, that she was no longer four. That her younger self could trust her now to fit together the pieces.

Her own story often came in fragments like this. Shards hidden in the tightly woven fabric of her mind. And when she stepped on one, when it pricked her memory, pain often shot through her head.

She had to get rid of the fragments before they wounded her forever. No one wanted to limp through life, wounded by the past. She wanted to run, arms open wide, ready to embrace the good in it. Stop worrying about any pieces that might trip her up along the way.

Gavin swept into the lobby, thumbing through a stack of papers at the front desk before he joined her outside the conference room. "Is there a problem?"

Chloe leaned against the wall. "Emma doesn't want to live with the foster family."

"That's because she already chose you."

Chloe glanced again through the window as Kaitlyn explained their plan. "We don't know how she ended up on Koster Isle."

"I can talk to Kaitlyn," he said. "She can stay at your house until we find her family."

"What would I do with her?" It was an honest question. One meant for a friend.

"What you've been doing for the past week. Feed and clothe her and let her borrow one of your beds."

"Beyond that, Gavin. I don't have the faintest idea how to care for a child."

One of his eyebrows slid up, and she knew what he was going to say. That she was raised by two people who hadn't a clue either. That was the downside of attending school in a small town and then returning home. Everyone knew your business.

"My grandparents had already raised a child before I arrived. They knew what to do."

"They raised a boy, and life was much different when your dad was young."

Chloe didn't want to talk about this. She'd already relived enough today. "You still haven't heard anything about a missing girl?"

He shook his head. "I'll let you know the moment I do."

She rubbed the cable knitting on her sleeves. "How can no one be missing her?"

"Perhaps her guardian thought she was staying with another relative or friend. It happens sometimes when children are passed between homes."

"It's sad to think that no one realizes she's gone."

"I'm afraid there is a lot of sad in this world."

Kaitlyn stepped back out of the room. "She's pretty upset."

"Her foster parents will help her," Chloe said, her stomach rolling.

Gavin moved forward. "Chloe—"

Instead of listening to his plea, she rushed out the door and down the steps. At the River Market, she picked out the prettiest pink suitcase she could find, one with wheels for Emma to maneuver on her own. Then she steered *Lolli* away from the marina.

It was absurd for Gavin, who knew her so well, to think that she could step in as a parent. The people who'd raised her in her first years, a term used quite loosely to describe her childhood, had failed miserably. Flower children, her parents called themselves, even though her father was fifty years old, immersed in a culture that glorified sex, drugs, and mind-altering rock 'n' roll. Neither her father nor her mother knew what to do with the girl they'd inadvertently birthed because they'd never seemed to grow up themselves. It was a miracle that she'd survived those early years.

Nana once said that Chloe's mother had tried to care for her before Philip swept his girlfriend back into the world of drugs. Then on a bumpy drive to a music festival, near a town called Woodstock, Philip had veered off the road and flipped the van into a cornfield, heroin raging through his veins, killing both of them.

Chloe didn't remember any of it, but she had the newspaper article from 1969 in her cabinet and the memory of her grandpa's tears as he told her the story later in life. Her mother's family hadn't wanted another child, but her father's parents had loved her well. And in their love, she began to heal. Perhaps because for the first time in her life, she wasn't worried about food or a safe place to sleep or clothing to keep warm.

Like Emma . . .

She swept the motorboat around Pine Island and between a series of other islets that skipped like rocks across the channel. Instead of turning right into her lagoon, she steered *Lolli* to the left, rounding the elaborate old stone boathouse that used to greet the Pendleton guests, sunrays reflecting off the tower above. And the cliff where she and her father once stood.

Had he been planning to jump? Even worse, had he intended to take her with him?

She trembled against the vinyl seat, the answer to that question one she didn't want to consider. But no decent parent, not even a distracted one, would stand on the edge of a cliff with their child, urging them to lean into the wind.

They must have left the island soon after—she didn't remember meeting her grandparents—and then they disappeared, the next three years of her life a shadowed alley of strange people and places.

Memories like this were just a glimpse of her childhood. A glimpse of Emma now. A glimpse, even, of Poppy in the decades behind them except Poppy had never been found.

Her grandparents had stepped into her life more than twenty years ago, just hours after the accident, and shared their island and their faith and their candy shop with her. They'd rescued her from the shadows.

Chloe circled west around Koster Isle, passing a thirty-foot interceptor with bright-green lettering for the US Border Patrol. The agent on board waved as she rounded the bend near Canadian waters, and that's when she saw it. In a dip between the cliffs, lying low in the cattails on her island, was the rim of a boat.

She slowed her speed and guided *Lolli* back toward the marshland. An old rowing skiff made of aluminum, splotched with brown and blue paint like Band-Aids trying to patch the holes, was tucked into the reeds.

And then she realized that Gavin might be right.

No one had brought Emma to her island on a stormy night.

For some reason, it seemed, Emma had chosen her.

# 13
# *AMELIA*

CADE CALLED AMELIA'S NAME as he stepped onto the dock, a lantern swinging in his hand.

"Did you find Penelope?" she begged.

A dismal shake of his head preceded his words. "We've looked everywhere. The entire house and the forest and ravine."

"When you came down the hill—" Her gaze swept across the dark surface, searching for the men and woman who'd been talking about Leslie. "Did you hear anyone talking from a boat?"

"No." The light swung again as he lifted the lamp. "Is someone out there?"

She scanned the waterfront again but saw nothing except the moored boats of their houseguests. And then she wondered if she'd really even heard the voices at all. Perhaps she'd imagined the men delivering opium. The woman who'd announced Leslie's preoccupation.

Her mother used to say she heard people talking when Amelia saw no one in her room, and she would not become like her mum.

In that moment, she decided the voices were for her alone.

"I must have startled a bird," she said. "Did you search the shoreline?"

"Poppy would never go near the water without an adult." Cade spoke with the authority of one who'd cared for Penelope like a father.

"The cliff . . ." Amelia rocked back on her heels, and he reached forward to steady her.

"Poppy wouldn't go near that either. She's a smart girl."

But such a young girl, on the cusp of turning five, was no match for the darkness or winds. If she'd gotten lost on her walk to the birdhouse, a single gust could have stolen her away.

"She's probably hiding in a corner of the house, sound asleep," Cade said. "She'll find us when she wakes."

Blast Leslie and his castle of passageways and hidden rooms and the tunnel that snaked down to the riverfront.

"You have to rest now, Mrs. Pendleton." Cade directed her toward the stairs. "We'll begin looking again at first light."

"I'll rest after we find her," she said, but she swayed on the second step, her head spinning with the breeze, her legs refusing to climb.

"I've got you." Cade lifted her off the ground, and she leaned against his chest as he strode up to the house, not caring what anyone thought. He laid Amelia on her bed and then opened the window so she could hear if Penelope called. "I'll fetch Rose."

"No," she said. "I want to be alone."

After he left, she mumbled words that might be prayers. She wasn't certain anymore. On the wall by the vanity, in the dull light that streamed through the window, the eyes of her parents in the portrait and her older sister's glare, even the eyes of Amelia's younger self, seemed to stare back with condemnation.

She'd failed them all.

In the morning, after they found Penelope, she would throw the portrait over a cliff. No longer would those eyes haunt her.

Someone knocked and she tugged on the chain of her electric lamp to brighten the room, hoping they had good news. "Come in."

Rose stepped inside, carrying a silver tray with a teapot. "Cade thought you might want chamomile to help you sleep."

Amelia stared at the teapot, wondering if her maid had added anything extra to the tea. She couldn't trust this woman anymore. "I asked you specifically to stay with Penelope last night."

"I know—"

"Why did you leave her again?"

The teapot slipped an inch down the tray before Rose rebalanced it. "Leslie called for me."

Amelia bristled at the sound of this woman calling her husband by his given name.

"Mr. Pendleton," she spat. "He is not Leslie to you."

"Yes, ma'am."

"Do you know what happened to Penelope?"

"No, ma'am. I wish to God that we could find her."

"But you weren't even looking. You were—" Amelia didn't finish. How could she accuse this woman of being near the boathouse when she didn't trust her own memories?

Rose placed the tray on the nightstand. "I need this job, Mrs. Pendleton."

"I want you out of my home," she said, her voice as sharp as a butcher's knife.

"I can't leave tonight."

When her maid's gaze wandered to the family portrait, Amelia switched off the lamp. "You're dismissed, Rose."

"I'll return with black tea in the morning."

A clock chimed from the lower floor. Five times to remind her that even though darkness still prevailed, tomorrow was upon them. She wanted to scour the passageways, comb every corner in the house, but her eyes were too heavy, her body drained.

If only she could turn back time, unwind to when Penelope begged her to stay in the nursery. She never should have left.

"If you can't find my daughter," Amelia said, "you're not welcome here."

A sob echoed through her chamber before Rose rushed out the door.

The moment she left, Amelia yanked the Koster family off the wall, shoving the portrait behind the vanity. It was her fault these ghosts were haunting her family. Her fault Penelope was gone.

She didn't care about the arrival of the Roosevelts or the Syracuse newspaper reporter or any of their other guests. Leslie could spend the rest of the summer here, winter too for that matter, locked away in the smoking room with Rose as his only guest. Once she found Penelope, Amelia would take her and their flock of birds on the first train home.

Koster Isle wasn't a safe place for any of them.

14

# CHLOE

"I'm Logan Danford." The man stretched his arm over the front counter as if Chloe was supposed to celebrate the intrusion.

Instead of shaking his hand, Chloe pulled a canister of gummy seashells from the shelf. Emma had slipped away from her chair behind the counter, leaving her drawing of Paddington Bear, to hide from this broad-shouldered man who looked like he might tackle anyone who unwrapped a chocolate football.

"Are you here to buy a tackle box?" Chloe asked, pretending she'd never heard his name before.

Logan lowered his arm, a grin spreading between his trimmed beard, lighting the turf green in his eyes. "I don't know much about fishing."

Chloe refused to smile back. Linebacker was his position, she guessed—shrewd and strong. And a lineup of girls were probably noted in the black notebook that he'd tucked under his arm, ready to swoon over his golden-brown hair and confident grin that made him appear more college boy than career man.

He could leave all that cockiness outside.

She pointed at the chalkboard sign overhead. "Twelve blocks in a box, twelve kinds of candy. You can fit anything from these shelves inside them, scattered like flotsam across—"

She cut off her quote of that rotten review as he eyed the open tackle box on the counter. "The blocks look like cubicles."

"I suppose," she said. "We can cram a whole lot of candy into one."

"Just like they cram a whole lot of people into the cubes at my office."

She refused to concede that she'd received his messages or succumb to a smile that, she guessed, usually opened doors. "And which office would that be?"

"The *Post-Standard*," he said. "I'm sorry. I didn't introduce myself very well. Thought you would remember my name from the messages."

She had remembered, of course, but wasn't about to tell him. There was a reason she hadn't called him back.

As Logan perused the rows of candy, Chloe scanned the espresso counter on her right until she saw the tip of Emma's head pressed back against the display window, reminding Chloe of the rowboat she'd found hidden yesterday in the marsh.

When she realized that Emma had picked her island as a safe place, she'd turned *Lolli* back in the direction of Clayton. Then she'd walked into the police station with the empty suitcase and handed it to the caseworker, Emma refusing to look her way.

"I just have to do a quick check of her things," Kaitlyn had said before opening the suitcase for good measure. Then she'd looked back at Chloe. "There's nothing in here."

"I was planning to retrieve her things for her but—"

Kaitlyn didn't say anything, just waited for Chloe to finish.

"Until we find Emma's family—" Chloe had paused, all the worry and concern flooding back, but she wasn't going to let it stop her—"I'd like to invite Emma to stay with me."

Kaitlyn gathered her stacks of papers into a neat pile. "I believe we can arrange that. What do you think, Emma?"

Instead of replying, Emma swiftly packed Fraidy in the carrier and stepped into the lobby. Chloe told Gavin and Kaitlyn about the skiff that she'd found in the marsh. They were skeptical about Emma's ability to paddle to Koster Isle, even if she'd crossed the channel before the storm, but Chloe knew the girl was strong beyond her years. They might doubt her, but Chloe suspected that Emma would continue to surprise them all.

The rowboat led to more questions, of course, between Gavin and the caseworker. Who owned it? If Emma had arrived on her own, how far had she paddled? And why had she chosen to stop at Koster Isle?

Chloe hadn't stayed for the discussion. She followed Emma down the steps, and they'd purchased elbow macaroni along with cheddar cheese, a box of bread crumbs, and a two-liter bottle of Coca-Cola at the marina store. Acting as a parent, she'd decided, was much too lofty a goal, but an aunt was supposed to spoil her niece. The role of an aunt, she could embrace.

Logan returned to the candy counter. "Did you get any of my messages?"

Instead of answering, she began filling small bags with an orange candy that tasted like Tang. She'd line them up beside the register, and they would be sold out before the end of the day.

"I left seven of them, I think."

Eight, but she wasn't going to argue. Instead she held up a bag. "Would you like to purchase some candy, Mr. Danford?"

"Call me Logan." He pulled out his wallet and dropped a five-dollar bill on the counter.

"Cade's Caramel Corn is a community favorite."

"Fill up one of those boxes with whatever candy you like best."

She glanced across the jars of candy, the canisters and displays that contained hundreds of different treats. No one had ever asked her to fill a tackle box with her favorites.

The maple stars were first, each one hand molded from pure maple sugar and stored in glass jars. She slipped three of them into a cube, and then she opened a drawer and selected French burnt peanuts, cola gummies, and sour cherries.

As she worked, Logan stepped away from the counter, limping as he walked. He probably got tackled in a football game, she thought, before scolding herself. Nana would have lectured her about spitefulness. Or bitterness.

He could ask all he wanted about the Pendleton family. She didn't have to answer.

He stopped in front of the sculpted ship, examining the sails. "This is remarkable."

"A local artist designed it for my grandfather."

He leaned down to look at the waves. "I've never seen anything like it."

"I guess that's the beauty of original art."

"How long have you owned this place?" he asked.

"Officially, for two months," she said. "But I've been working here for most of my life. My grandparents owned it for about thirty years."

People stopped buying wooden boats in the 1960s, but candy never went out of vogue. When their friends were thinking about retiring, her grandparents decided to divest themselves of Ridell Boats and launch Cade's Candy Shop to do what they did best—share their lives and gifts with others. Together they sold Grandpa Cade's homemade candies and Nana's peppermint chocolate and a host of other treats, but sales were never the priority. Grandpa Cade knew everyone's name and a piece of their story. Nana bundled up words of wisdom with every sale and then stopped to pray for anyone who asked. Sometimes the space was more chapel than candy store.

By the time Chloe joined her grandparents on the island, Cade's Candy Shop was a popular place for tourists and locals alike. The sales ultimately gave them the extra income needed to raise a child in their twilight years along with an apartment during the winter months. Grandpa Cade passed away in 1977, while Chloe was in high school. From the time Chloe graduated from college until her grandmother had to move into memory care, she and Nana had managed the shop together, sharing a bit of sunshine in Grandpa Cade's honor through their treats and friendships alike.

"It's like Willy Wonka at his finest," Logan said as he traced one of the lollipop portholes. "You have a whole lot of nostalgia packed in this place."

"The most wonderful place in the world."

He glanced up. "You're quoting Charlie Bucket?"

"An expert," Chloe said. "When times are hard, people flock to the past."

"The past is fascinating, isn't it?"

And just like that, she'd fallen straight into the trap. "I'm not talking about the Pendletons."

A smile crept across his face. "So you did get my messages."

"Most people around here have put Poppy's story to rest," she continued, resisting the urge to return his smile. "Only tourists ask about it anymore. And nosy—"

"Reporters?"

She shrugged.

"Don't you want to know what happened to her?"

Of course she wanted to know, used to ask every old-timer when she delivered their candy, but it was none of his business. He was just blowing in like a thundersquall, riling up trouble. Then he'd breeze back out and leave behind whatever mess he dumped on them.

Chloe searched for Emma along the side wall but she was no longer tucked behind the counter. "I have more pressing things on my mind."

"Cade Ridell was your grandfather," he said as if she might have forgotten.

"I'm aware of that."

"What did he tell you about the Pendletons?"

"My grandfather passed away when I was a teen. You don't want to rely on my memories." She'd asked her grandpa about the castle, about the people who'd once lived there, but his vague answers hadn't seemed important back then. Nana had been the anchor in Chloe's life, a gift when she needed it most, but the Pendleton family was a taboo topic around her.

"I'd still like to know what you remember."

She filled the last cube with Smarties. "Reporters never seem to get the facts straight."

"I'll triple-check them."

"My grandfather didn't remember much about the Pendletons. He certainly didn't know anything about Poppy's disappearance." One of Logan's eyebrows slipped up as if to counter her words, and she took the bait. "What do you want to tell me?"

"That things are not always as they seem."

She didn't need a puffed-up reporter to tell her that.

"Maybe you can give me a tour of the castle," he said. "I'll just take a few photos."

"I don't think so."

"It's definitely hard to keep my facts straight when those who have the answers won't help." Logan limped slowly to the other side of the shop, studying the colorful jars along the way, seemingly as mesmerized as her younger guests. Then he stopped beside the espresso machine. "I didn't realize you had company."

Emma's voice erupted from the floor. "I'm not company!"

He tapped one of his hands on the polished birch. "You must be the guardian of Cade's Candy."

"I'm not a guardian either." Her head popped over the countertop. "I'm Emma. Her ward."

"I see."

Chloe handed him the tackle box full of her favorite candy. "Emma is my guest."

"Okay."

"And she's off-limits to your questions."

He splayed one hand out like a shield. "I'm not the enemy."

"Actually, you are."

He opened the plastic lid and popped a sour cherry into his mouth. "How did I become your enemy?"

"If you write this story, my island is going to flood with strangers who have no regard for my property."

"I don't think so."

She stared back at his grin. Was he trying to annoy her? "Tourists thrive on a good mystery."

"Exactly. It's not so exciting, perhaps, if we solve it."

*Solve it.*

The words rang between her ears. She hadn't thought about what might happen if a reporter removed the mystique instead of feeding the monster. Was it really possible for them to find out what occurred that night on the island almost ninety years ago?

Maybe it would deter people instead of bringing them to her island. Koster Isle would no longer double as Ghost Island.

"No matter what you write, it will light a new fire under those who can't resist a ghost story. They'll swarm my island and I am somehow responsible for keeping them safe, no matter what I post about No Trespassing."

"You aren't responsible for trespassers."

"That wouldn't stop someone from trying to sue me."

"Tell you what," he said. "I'll talk to my editor. If I don't find out what happened to Poppy, the paper won't run a story."

Chloe's laugh sounded more like a cough. "Your editor's not going to approve that."

"I'm working on more than one article," he said. "And she isn't fond of running stories about past events anyway without a new angle."

"There's always a new angle."

"Or some sort of resolution," he continued. "But if I find out what happened . . ."

"You'd probably win a Pulitzer."

He shrugged.

"And sell a few papers." She began filling another tackle box to deliver to a customer on Wellesley.

"You sell candy to make people happy. We sell newspapers to keep them informed. Nothing wrong with that."

"I sell candy to keep my grandpa's legacy alive."

"Then if we work together, we can do both," he said. "A story like this will bring more customers to your store and you can tell them all about your grandfather."

An increase in guests, particularly those who enjoyed sweets, was essential to the future of her shop, and she liked the idea of honoring Grandpa Cade, but she still couldn't trust a reporter. He would elbow her to the side if she got in his way. Better for her to step aside now.

Logan opened his messenger bag and pulled out a manila folder. Then he tossed a piece of paper onto the espresso counter. "I think we can agree on at least one point."

"What point is that?" she asked as he leaned back against the counter, blocking her view of the document.

"To set the record straight for everyone involved," he said, "we need to find out where Poppy went and why."

*We?* There was no *we*.

"The speculation will never stop," he said. "Not until we find the truth. Did you know that Penelope Pendleton will turn ninety in July?"

"Poppy is no longer alive."

"How do you know that?"

"It's impossible—"

He glanced at the magical ship. "Seems like you might be a person who believes in possibilities."

A door opened behind her, signaling Jenna's imminent arrival at the counter. Her friend, whom she dearly loved, would think that almost any kind of publicity was good for Cade's Candy, especially an article that would invite more tourists to visit their store.

"I'll think about it," Chloe said.

"Perhaps you can memorialize your grandfather by sharing his story, like you do through this shop. Especially since he was one of the last people who saw Poppy alive."

What was he talking about? Grandpa Cade had never told her that he saw Poppy before she disappeared.

Then again, he'd said the aviary glass was from a broken window.

"Logan?" she called as he walked toward the door.

He turned back. "Yes?"

"Where did you find that information about my grandfather?"

He nodded toward the paper he'd left on the counter. "You can read about it there."

Smiling, he leaned toward the espresso machine. "Goodbye, Emma."

The girl squeaked out a goodbye before he left the shop.

15

# LOGAN

LOGAN PRESSED BACK the column of pain that was advancing up his quad. If only his right leg would stop aching, distracting him when he needed to focus. He should stand up, move away from the microfilm reader, and do the stretches prescribed to him, but the Syracuse library would close in a half hour and tomorrow he was driving north again to interview three other people about Poppy's story since Chloe Ridell refused to speak with him.

He scrolled to the next page of the 1910 issue of the *Post-Standard*, searching for any lingering clues as to what might have happened to Poppy Pendleton after her father's death.

Chloe knew the stories, he suspected, that the papers hadn't reported, and any lead would be nice right about now. His article was due in two weeks, and he'd crashed into a dead end.

Copies of old articles piled on the printer beside him. Before he'd shown up at Chloe's store, he'd already read through an anthology of stories about the Pendleton family, beginning in 1902 when Leslie Pendleton first purchased Koster Isle and laid the castle foundation as a surprise for his wife. He only lived in the castle for a month before his death.

A Syracuse reporter named Harry Baden had tracked the Pendleton story until he passed on in the 1950s. His initial reporting commended Mr. Pendleton for his hard work as a lad, building a successful clock company before he branched out into other enterprises, but his later articles weren't nearly as glowing in regard to Leslie Pendleton's character. A smuggler, Harry eventually called him, using the castle as a hub to deliver opium from Canadian ports into New York. He would dodge steep taxes while the drug was still legal and then profit off the sales of Poppy's Tip-Top Tonic, his opium-laced wonder syrup. Harry believed that Mr. Pendleton had overdosed after imbibing too much of his own tonic, but questions had remained over the years as to whether it was accidental or intentional. And whether his death was connected to the disappearance of his daughter or a sad twist of fate.

By all accounts, Leslie Pendleton had been a good father, doting even, although Logan questioned the man's exploitation of his daughter's name. Had Mr. Pendleton thought the poppy reference funny? As the years went on, there'd been speculation that a possible suicide might have been the outcome of his financial demise. Even as he was building a castle on Koster Isle, his own kingdom had been crumbling with new regulations on the medicinal use of opium and competition in the clock industry that he'd long monopolized.

After Poppy disappeared, reporters across New York had scrambled to locate her. While Mrs. Pendleton only gave one more interview to Harry Baden, her attorney was quoted in many of the articles, begging for the return of the Pendleton girl, offering a thousand-dollar reward to anyone who found her.

A blaze of yellow journalism followed the sparks of Harry's investigation. Stories ran in the *New York Times* and *Chicago Tribune* and newspapers across the country. Some of the reporters interviewed guests from the Pendleton party. One even quoted President Roosevelt, who said he was saddened by the tragedy, sending his condolences to Mrs. Pendleton. Most of the newspapers and magazines simply rehashed or syndicated a story that had already been told. For years, headlines were about purported sightings or the speculation of a murder.

Logan's gut turned at the thought of this woman losing both her husband and daughter in the same night.

Twenty-five years after Poppy vanished, the son of Charles and Anne Lindbergh also disappeared. Thousands of leads flowed in, some of them extravagant reports from those seeking fortune and fame. Then the body of the Lindberghs' baby was found. While there was still plenty of speculation as to what happened, they were able to grieve the loss.

Logan raked his hand through his hair as he continued scrolling through the microfilm. How could Mrs. Pendleton go through life not knowing what happened to her child?

"I still have to dig that last reel out of storage."

He glanced up to see Max, the reference librarian who was a solid decade older than Logan's thirty-two years, standing over his shoulder. The man wore a pea-green bow tie with a white dress shirt and a matching green cap. To impress the ladies, he'd once told Logan, except he was already married. A point he seemed to forget whenever he started flirting with the patrons.

But Max was a master at research, and Logan had learned to rely on him in the past six months since he'd started working at the *Post-Standard*. Max could answer most of his questions, both historically and about local events, but he hadn't uncovered anything new about the Pendleton family.

"When do you think you'll have it?" Logan asked as he turned the dial.

"Should be ready first thing in the morning. You heading up to Clayton tomorrow?"

"Around lunch."

"I'll put the reel behind the desk. Stop by whenever you'd like." Max's mouth dropped when two women in their twenties strolled into the reading room, both of them wearing snug dresses and grunge hats. His interests, it seemed, knew no bounds.

Logan clapped his hands together. "Max!"

"Sorry." The librarian refocused on their conversation. "I'm curious to see where your research leads."

"If you want, I'll let you take a look at the copy before it goes to print. You can fact-check to your heart's content."

Max stole another glance at the women. "My heart is never content."

"You have a wife, man. Love her well."

"Doing my best."

Logan snorted. "Really?"

One of the women stopped to read a magazine, and Max's eyes wandered again. "I may have a tad room to grow."

Logan returned his attention to the film. "Speaking from someone who took way too long to grow up, I'd suggest you start sooner than later."

"At least your options are open." Max pointed at the desk. "My colleagues drool in puddles every time you walk into this room."

"Limp, Max. I can't take a decent step anymore."

"Like they care about your bad leg. You could ask either one of them out, and they'd follow you and your limp right back out the door."

Logan laughed. "You should earn extra money for your dramatics on Broadway."

"It's just the truth."

He shook his head. "I'm not looking for a date."

And Max sighed as if he were royally disappointed by this news.

Logan whirled his chair around. "How long have you been married, Max?"

"Ten years," he moaned. "Ten very, very long years."

"Treasure the wife that you have," Logan said. "You won't regret it."

"I think you're crazy."

"Not crazy. Divorced and wishing I could go back a decade and mend what I broke." He swiped the articles off the printer and shoved them inside the leather bag with his laptop, voice recorder, and pocketknife.

"Sure you don't want a dinner date?" Max asked. "Make me a hero around here."

He clapped the man on the shoulder. "I'll be back for that reel."

"You've got twenty minutes until close if you want to keep reading."

"Thanks," he said before turning to read one more article on the screen. With the advent of World War I in 1914, media attention shifted to the news in Europe and then on to the flu pandemic, Depression, and Second World War. The last indexed article that Logan had found about

Poppy's disappearance was from the *Post-Standard* in 1952. Another editorial by Harry Baden, who believed the girl was still alive.

Journalism, when done right, was about justice, no matter how old the crime, and Logan was determined to see this story to the end. Not just because his editor thought it would make for a compelling feature but because he wanted to know what happened to Poppy. To honor her life and legacy for her birthday this year.

Chloe thought he was digging up this story to win some sort of prize—and he couldn't deny the shot of adrenaline over the possibility of solving this mystery—but it was also his way of righting one of the many wrongs in this world, using words instead of weapons. And a historical feature was a welcome break from his other assignment—investigating new racketeering charges against the city's former and currently imprisoned mayor. In his editor's mind, an ex-firefighter and Marine should take the hardest stories, and that was fine with him. He wanted justice for today as well as the past.

Tomorrow was the deadline for his article about the corrupt mayor. He'd finish it tonight and then return to Poppy in the morning.

Logan grabbed his messenger bag off the floor, the worn canvas blending with the browns in his bomber jacket, and said goodbye to the librarians at the front desk. None of them drooled when he shuffled by.

He was missing something in the Pendleton story, something that seemed to be dangling right in front of him, but he couldn't figure out what it was. Five years ago, he would have taken an evening run to rekindle his thoughts and begin fitting together all the puzzle pieces in his head, but he could barely manage a walk down the street now and it hardly cleared his mind.

The streetlights guided him to his apartment near the university, and he climbed to the second floor. Maybe one day he would buy a house again, settle down. The first time he'd tried, he and Nicole had been much too young and way too idealistic in their thinking of what a happy marriage between two nineteen-year-olds would look like, playing house together in a trailer on her parents' farm.

Nicole had been a good mama, the best, in the few months that God had given them a son. They'd prayed desperately for Shiloh's life, but God hadn't granted them the answer they wanted. Shiloh's heart had failed after four months, in Nicole's arms, and then their marriage quickly unraveled. Some hardships brought couples closer together, but this loss quaked the foundation of their fleeting time together.

Nicole had three more kids after Shiloh, all born in rapid succession with the man she'd married while Logan was out saving other families from harm. He had mourned the failure of his marriage, even as he grieved the loss of his son, but he didn't blame Nicole one bit for leaving him. She'd needed a husband fully engaged to return her love.

Not a day went by when he didn't think about Shiloh.

Not a day went by that he didn't thank God for the days, as few as they were, that he had with his son.

With his mind caught up in the past, Logan tripped on a curb and fell toward a newsstand, landing on the sidewalk. An elderly woman, out walking her poodle, offered her gloved hand, and he took it.

Humble pie—that's what his grandma used to say he needed to eat in mounds after he and his team tromped all over their opponents on the football field. Now he was eating plenty of it. A double portion on days like this.

It wasn't until much later that evening, after he had bandaged his arm and eaten two orders of chow mein, after he'd finished the article about the former mayor and settled into bed, that it struck him what he might be missing about Poppy's story.

A good mother fought for her kids, but he'd also seen Nicole collapse inward after their son's death, barely a ghost of the woman he'd married. Not that he judged her for it. He didn't recognize himself either in those years.

But if Shiloh had disappeared from their home instead of lost the battle with his faulty heart, what would she have done? His former wife, he felt certain, would never have let the story die. She would have spent the rest of her life using every resource available, talking to reporters, searching for answers, fighting for her family even if the rest of the world was at war.

But after Harry Baden's second article, Mrs. Pendleton was never quoted again in any newspaper that he'd read. Almost like she'd disappeared as well.

He stared up at the haze of street light that spread across his ceiling. What happened to Poppy's mother after her family was gone?

# PART 2

*Be like the bird who pauses in flight*
*on a branch that bends beneath her,*
*yet still she sings,*
*knowing she has wings.*

ADAPTED FROM *Songs of Dusk* (1836)
BY VICTOR HUGO

16

# *AMELIA*

NEW YORK CITY

SEPTEMBER 1911

Months had passed before Amelia realized that President Roosevelt and the First Lady never arrived on Koster Isle. Months that turned into years before she realized much at all.

A mockingbird flew by her bench this morning, and Amelia felt the shimmer of breeze from its wings. Four whole years had slipped by since the gala, each day spinning around her like a branch caught in a whirlpool, twirling in circles but never going anywhere.

Birds were the only thing left that still made her hollow heart sing.

The faintest of lines on her paper, the last ones to complete the sketch of Minnie, the scarlet macaw perched across the narrow path, and Amelia lowered her pencil. She could almost hear the falling of time with it, piling up the hours and days and years of her life. Like an endless drip of sand through an hourglass. Meaningless, as the teacher in Ecclesiastes so dutifully noted. Chasing after the wind.

Instead of remembering the sweet memories from her daughter's life, Penelope haunted her like one of the ghosts who shadowed Ebenezer Scrooge, taunting her at every turn about what might have been, pointing out what Amelia had done wrong.

Four years might have passed, but the night of Penelope's disappearance was forever etched in her mind. And from that terrible memory hung the rope of each new day, sweeping back and forth like a pendulum with the rhythm of life, slowly circling every sunrise and sunset, every breath that forced itself in and out of her lungs.

The steadiness kept her upright. The constant sway in clearly defined bounds.

Amelia glanced up at the leaves above the glass aviary, the colors singed with yellow and orange. Death was coming, and the leaves didn't even know it. They kept struggling, eking life out of the branches that could no longer sustain them.

Soon all the life would fall from the trees along Fifth Avenue, but it would continue on inside the glass house. Sometimes the birds banged against the windows as if they sought freedom on the other side, but she'd never let them out into the world. The cruelty on the streets would kill them. The loneliness and despair.

*Alone.*

The word rolled around Amelia's head like a marble seeking a rail. Something to stop the racing. She'd spent a decade before Leslie's death ensuring that she had people around her—family—and now she was left with no one on this continent who cared for her beyond their monthly wage.

After leaving Koster Isle, she'd cloistered herself in the Manhattan mansion and aviary, thinking she might find some sort of satisfaction here, but nothing filled the empty space inside her. She could no longer stomach the petty fighting and jostling in order to be throned by the gilded royalty of New York or all the conjecture in the papers, including the many articles speculating about what happened to her husband and daughter.

Whenever she closed her eyes, she could still see the fireworks above the St. Lawrence. Smell the Scotch on Leslie's breath. Hear the whispers from the river and the screams early the next morning when one of the servants had found Leslie on the sofa, no breath left in him.

Harry Baden had returned to their castle, determined to find the truth, along with a host of officials from the mainland. Police, detectives, and Mr. Haynes—her husband's lawyer and business manager.

The investigators had taken away Leslie's bottle of tonic, but in those hours when she was supposed to be celebrating her daughter's fifth birthday, those hours when she could barely get out of bed, she'd wished for the syrup that had swept him away.

Instead, she'd spent days answering endless questions, as if she'd been the one to add the opium to Leslie's drink and hide Penelope from them all. They asked her about Leslie's money, questioned her motives, wondered where she had been in the early morning hours. Mr. Haynes helped search for Penelope, and even he never seemed to believe her innocence.

They'd all suspected her then, and some of them still did.

Ultimately, she'd inherited what remained of the Pendleton estate, but her money wasn't old or new in the eyes of society. It was blood money. Even if she wanted to attend the luncheons and balls, no one wanted blood in their homes.

She erased the edge of Minnie's wing on her sketchbook and redrew it.

Long ago, she'd decided she would rather be with her birds than a roomful of those perched on limbs of their own making, critiquing her levity, belittling her grief, touting the feats of their children. Sometimes she even dreamed about returning to England. Her father hadn't written in years nor had her sister. Not that Amelia was speaking to either of them, but the news must have reached England about Penelope's disappearance. Neither of them offered their condolences.

Having one less girl in his family might be more of a benefit than a tragedy to her father. She didn't want to think what her sister might say at the news.

If her mother were still alive and in her right mind, she would have been worried. But Lady Koster had lost touch with the realities around her long before she died. She never knew about her husband's affairs when she was at home or the mistress that replaced her after she left.

She was content enough in her room at Holloway Sanatorium, referring to the grand building and grounds as Windsor, commanding the staff around as if they were her servants. Lady Koster had reigned as queen over all of England from her castle.

Amelia had visited the sanatorium once a week until her mother died. How she missed her mum.

After most of his property and his mistress were gone, her father remarried a woman who'd wanted to visit America. Then he swept the Koster girls onto a ship for a tumultuous ride across the Atlantic, arriving at the port of New York in 1894 for an extended stay. Long enough to marry off his younger daughter to Leslie Pendleton and return to Holloway with the oldest.

Amelia dropped her pencil again and wrapped both arms over her stomach as if she could fold herself in half. Or perhaps stitch back together the pieces that she'd become. In hindsight, she'd longed to be honest with herself and those around her. Honest, even, with Leslie.

But the truth of her story would have ruined them all.

She was two different people, on two continents. Even though she'd tried to keep the branches of her American life separated from her British roots, her freedom was long gone.

Four years ago, after she'd locked out the world, after she'd retreated to the glass aviary behind her city house, Cade had tried delivering all her birds to Manhattan, turning a Pullman train car into a temporary birdhouse. Sadly, Fred had flown off after his cage door jostled loose. Nothing Cade had said could coax Fred back inside when an infinite sky awaited him over the river.

Amelia liked to think he was keeping Penelope company, wherever she'd gone.

With the exception of Minnie, Fred's mate, the birds fluttered freely in this new space, oblivious to the pain outside. Snow might tumble across the glass, canopying them with white on the coldest days, but her birds were warm enough. And it was the only place where Amelia felt moderately warm as well. Even in the summer, the tomb of her mansion was cold. Instead of shivering inside, she and Minnie would sit here together, mourning what might have been.

Another bird flew past her before settling onto the branch of a dogwood, a melody on its lips. Reminding her that she was still alive.

After delivering the birds, Cade had returned to Koster Isle. Then he'd stayed through the winter months to care for the castle even as he waited for Penelope's return. Every week, he mailed reports about his work and sometimes sent Amelia pressed petals from the flowers she had planted long ago, describing the change of each season, remembering Penelope's love of the water and birds.

He had asked for her permission to begin building boats, when he wasn't working on the property, and she'd promptly replied that she cared not what he did in his free time. It seemed that boat building was as good as any enterprise to keep oneself occupied on an island.

While she didn't care about the upkeep of the castle, Cade's kindness meant the world. He was the only member of her original staff who'd remained, and sometimes, after reading one of his letters, she felt a twinge in her chest, the slightest of longings, to return to her long-forgotten gardens and island aviary as she waited for news about her daughter.

But she never wanted to go back inside the castle.

The door opened, but she didn't turn.

"I've brought you tea," Fiona, an older woman with impeccable taste, said as she placed a fancy tray on the table. The teapot was accompanied by the requisite cream and sugar cubes, blueberry scones, bowl of red grapes, and another plate filled with sliced cucumbers and tomatoes. Two delicate teacups were arranged on saucers painted with birds as if Amelia might share her tea with Minnie.

The staff was working hard to sustain her life.

"Thank you," Amelia said. "You may go."

Some days she wished she could lose herself in the busyness of household chores. The staff had little time to think about what they'd lost when the planning of days pressed in on them, the sands in their lives pouring steadily through the glass.

Amelia, on the other hand, had nothing to distract her when questions crowded the corridors of her mind. Not even her sketching relieved the wondering of what happened to Penelope and the reliving of that horrific night.

She'd missed something, and she couldn't seem to find it in her scrapyard of memories.

When she looked back up, Fiona still stood beside her. "I don't need any assistance with my meal."

Fiona lifted the teapot, acting more like a mother to her than a servant. "You have company."

"I don't want to see anyone."

"Mr. Haynes said he must speak with you."

Her husband's business manager rarely stopped by the house, and when he did, it usually wasn't as the bearer of good news. Leslie hadn't shared with her the unfortunate turn in his clock business before he died or the demise of his stock. It was the reason some even speculated that his death had been suicide. But optimism was Leslie's constant refrain. A decrease in one business only meant an opportunity in another.

Amelia had no use for Poppy's Tip-Top Tonic, but she had needed an income. Weeks after Leslie's death, Mr. Ingram purchased the factory that bottled the syrup, promising to replace the opium content with a milder version of laudanum more suitable for children. Then Mr. Haynes used the equity to purchase certificates in a number of railroad, telegraph, and telephone companies along with an interest in a motorcar company called Packard. The stock market crashed near the end of 1907 and many of her investments collapsed on the exchange, but the dividends from her portfolio had still been enough to provide for her household and birds.

"Mr. Haynes will have to come here," she told Fiona.

"Of course."

Fiona dropped a cube of sugar into Amelia's teacup and then drowned it in black tea. After Mr. Haynes left, Amelia would spend her day sipping tea and feeding scones to the birds.

Her business manager sat on the bench across from her, fidgeting with his hat, two pieces of pomade-drenched hair standing on end.

She shook her head. "You don't need to say it."

For four years, he'd been offering his apologies. Four years of clumsiness between them.

"I'm still sorry all the same. For your loss. Leslie was—"

She interrupted him. "Penelope was my only loss."

A flutter of bird's wings in the silence. While Leslie's wealth continued to provide for both her and Mr. Haynes, he didn't miss her husband much either.

She lifted the teacup to her lips, a drop slipping down her throat. "You must be here for a reason."

"I'm afraid your income is suffering again."

"It's not the only thing suffering."

"You should get out of this house, Mrs. Pendleton. Move into someplace smaller and much warmer for the winter."

"I have no place to go." Besides that dreadful castle.

People would think her ungrateful for Leslie's gift if she said aloud how much she didn't like the island, but the truth was that Leslie had built the castle for himself. He'd only used the excuse of her visiting with family in England that year to move ahead with the work.

Mr. Haynes shuffled through a stack of papers in his lap. "I'm afraid you might not have a choice."

Drops of tea spilled over the saucer when she replaced the cup. Until that moment, with the plummet in her chest, she didn't realize she had any feeling left inside.

He glanced up. "Not that you are destitute."

"I should hope not."

"But you cannot afford this house and your castle for another year."

"I'll sell Koster Isle," she said.

He scanned the windows of her regal mansion. "You only use two of the fifty rooms in this place."

"You shouldn't be talking to my servants, Mr. Haynes."

"Someone must pay their wages."

Of course, he must speak to them. She hadn't managed anything in her household for years.

"Thank you," she said slowly before filling the second teacup. "For all that you've done for me."

She crossed the path to offer him the cup, and they sipped their tea as the birds serenaded on both sides.

"I think you should visit the castle in the spring," he said before handing her a piece of paper. "Here is the latest report from the caretaker. The grounds and house, he says, are in good condition."

The shake of her head was so strong, it flung a coating of tea across her skirt. "I want to sell it."

"I've made some inquiries on your behalf." His face looked pained. "No one wants to buy a mansion in the North Country right now, especially not one where . . ."

He didn't have to finish. No one wanted to live in a cursed castle, including her.

"But someone will buy this house?'

"Plenty of people want to live on Fifth Avenue."

The children of the Astors, she imagined, were probably counting the hours until she left Manhattan. Then they could vie for her home.

"You don't have to live in the whole castle," he said. "Just open up a few rooms and spend your free time outside."

"I'd be snowed in for the winter."

"I'll purchase a fashionable brownstone off Riverside so you can winter here."

"What about my birds?"

He considered her question. "Perhaps Mr. Ridell can watch over them during the winter months."

The house looming beside her could go—she had no need of it—but to separate from her birds for the winter?

"A letter arrived yesterday." He dug an envelope out of his coat pocket. "From Ottawa."

He didn't have to explain. They had received hundreds of letters in the days after Penelope's disappearance with return addresses from Boston to San Francisco and plenty from Canada, all from people who'd sworn they saw her daughter, anxious for their reward. Once she'd even received a letter from a woman in Calcutta who was certain that she had seen the Pendleton girl.

Other letters were demands for ransom, saying they would hold Penelope hostage until Amelia sent the designated funds. Or that her daughter was already gone, inquiring about a trade. Money for information about what happened to her.

A small fortune had been spent in the futile search. The detectives that Mr. Haynes hired had followed every lead, but none brought Penelope home. As the months passed, the number of letters fell to dozens until it became a slow trickle of inquiries. They hadn't received a letter in at least a month.

A glimmer of interest pricked Amelia's heart, seeping into her veins, and she quickly stifled it.

"Amelia?"

"It would be a miracle if someone located her now."

"But it's possible," he said.

She snapped back to the chirping in the birdhouse. "Forward it to the detectives."

"Shall I read it to you first?"

"There's really no need . . ."

*Dear Mrs. Pendleton,*

*I've read about your unfortunate circumstances over the years, but I have good news. I believe I've seen your daughter near Montreal. This girl, at least, is similar in appearance with longer hair and less fancy attire than the photograph in the papers. Goes by a different name but I'm fairly certain it's her.*

*I feel it prudent to reach an agreement to the amount of the reward prior to providing more information. Contact me at—*

"Stop!" The warning from Amelia's lips sounded like the caw of a bird.

Mr. Haynes looked up. "The man has more information."

"For money."

"Of course he wants money."

How she hated these people who saw Penelope as an opportunity for their personal gain. Like she was a chip in a poker game as they gambled for the win.

"Give the letter to the agency."

He tucked it back into his pocket. "I'm sure Mr. Gagné will contact you again."

"Then the detectives should follow up with him." They'd tracked down every lead and not a single one had guided them to Penelope. "This summer she would have turned nine . . ."

"I know."

"I miss her so."

He glanced around the glass walls. "You are locked inside this place as if it were an institution. I know you've needed time to grieve, but the whole of society thinks you have lost your mind."

No one in New York knew about her mother's final years in Holloway. No one knew what happened to her sister in the same sanatorium. And yet, she feared that society was right. She was turning into the person she'd run from.

"I will visit the castle in May." The words slipped from her mouth, surprising her, but the moment she said it, she knew that she needed to return. "We will celebrate Penelope's next birthday there."

"That's a good idea," he said. "Don't lose hope."

But hope was a dangerous endeavor, she thought.

Hope could destroy one's heart and mind.

17

# BIRDIE

EVEN THOUGH IT WAS STILL DARK, the harbor gloomy, Birdie could hear the sweet song of a bird along the shore. Most of the songbirds had migrated south, Mummy said, but a few remained in their nests, singing in the coziness of feathers and twigs, leaves and laughter.

Could birds really laugh?

She'd have to ask Olivia when she and Pierre paddled out this morning.

While Mummy loved her, Olivia was the one who brought books and read to Birdie almost every afternoon on the upper deck while Mummy rested below.

Birdie's other friends were the winged ones who visited her on the deck of the *Adonis* whenever she snuck a piece of bread from the kitchen to share the crumbs. And she had book friends, of course. Those were stacked on the top berth in her cabin.

*Books are the best of friends.*

Olivia said that often, and with her help, Birdie had learned how to read all the stories on her own, more times now than she could count.

Not that she could count far. No one had taught her much about numbers.

Wind gusted over the deck, the houseboat groaning as it rocked and tugged against its mooring. Birdie rolled over on the cot and drew the scratchy blanket close to her ears. She never pulled it over her head unless the fog began to leak. She didn't even mind the rain until it puddled around her shoulders or threaded ice through her hair.

Whenever Olivia found Birdie asleep on the deck, she yelled at Mummy. It was dangerous, she said, for any girl to wake up with ice around her head. Mummy said the blanket and socks and woolen pajamas kept Birdie plenty warm, but Mummy didn't understand. She always slept in the stately room below, whether or not the man was here.

Whenever the man came, Birdie had to sleep outside.

Nights were scary sometimes, but on the warmer ones, Birdie preferred the open deck to her tiny berth. The smell of salt. The canopy of stars. The flap of wings against water and the call of birds. When the river started to freeze, the man would tug the *Adonis* into a house built for boats, and she and Mummy would stay in a hotel.

The hotels were her favorite. When Mummy and the man were in the room, she could roam the grounds. Even though she wasn't supposed to speak with anyone, Mummy never said she couldn't watch them. People intrigued her, almost as much as birds.

Another songbird joined the chorus, reminding her that she wasn't alone. And her mind began to wander. What would it be like to migrate to the beautiful home in her dreams? A castle with grand rooms and a grand tower and best of all, a glass house filled with birds. In her dream, the birds flew up to her hands or perched on her shoulders. Welcoming her home.

The castle in her dreams never rocked in the storms. It had the thickest of blankets and softest of beds and sweetest of treats. And a blaze inside to warm her hands and face.

She'd give just about anything this morning for a fire.

Birdie tucked the damp blanket under her shoulders and pretended it was the magic cloak from *Queen Zixi of Ix*. She liked to pretend she was Meg, a pauper who turned into a princess when she wore the fairy coat. Except Birdie would rather use the magic cloak to sneak off this boat and find her castle.

A light flickered through the fog. It didn't matter if it was a star or the lights from another boat. The glimmer offered a shot of warmth in these early hours.

Soon Mummy would call her belowdecks for breakfast with the man. Birdie didn't like him much and he didn't like her either. They simply tolerated each other for Mummy's sake.

The boat rocked gently, wooing her back to sleep.

Mummy always looked different in the dreams. Her face was softer, her hair the color of the night sky instead of the golden curls the man liked so much. Mummy once told the man that she was going to cut her hair. He said if she did, she'd have to find another place to live. After he left, Birdie had offered her a pair of scissors, but Mummy just laughed.

Mummy kept her curls, and the man kept coming back.

Birdie was floating now in her dream. Or was she flying? She could see the castle on an island shimmering gold, a flock of birds swirling around her, tangling her hair and tickling her skin.

When Mummy was happy, she'd make up stories about a birdhouse and stone castle and a little girl named Poppy who played in a field of the bright red flowers by the same name. The same girl who smiled back from the bottle of tonic that Mummy gave to her every night, no matter where Birdie slept.

None of the people in Birdie's dream saw her hovering near the clouds, but she could hear their laughter, the tinkle of glass. She could see sparkly dresses on the women and another man with a chimney-like hat, a man nothing like the one who visited the *Adonis*. He brought Birdie toys and sweets when Mummy wasn't watching.

She wished she could stay in the clouds forever, but she fell instead, tumbling toward a wall of rocks. Instead of a golden blue, the water had turned a fierce black, rolling in the wind, folding her inside. Even though she knew it wasn't real, she floundered with her arms, trying to breathe, wishing she could swim. But the water was always, always in control.

She was nothing in its wake.

Birdie screamed in the night, gasping for air. Then she woke with a start.

Wood groaned and creaked under her, fog closing in like the water. And Mummy was beside her in a nightgown, her real Mummy, a lantern in hand. "What is it?"

The fog burned yellow in her light, mixing with the lemony smell of Mummy's perfume, but neither stopped the hammering in Birdie's chest. "I was drowning."

"It's a dream, love. Olivia must have piled too many blankets on you."

Olivia was gone before Birdie settled onto the cot last night—she usually left before the man arrived—and she only had one blanket anyway. But the truth didn't matter. Birdie's teeth chattered when Mummy rolled back the damp cover, the night air seeping under her pajamas, icing her skin. But she was safe now. She wouldn't drown on the deck.

"You frightened me, Birdie." A sigh fell from her lips, heavy with disappointment over her daughter's failing. "I thought you fell overboard."

She'd thought so too. Was it possible to stop herself from screaming while she slept? "I didn't mean to scare you."

"You mustn't wake anyone else."

The man, Mummy meant. Or the people on shore. Birdie was supposed to be invisible under the blanket. No one else except Olivia and Pierre was supposed to know she lived on the man's boat.

"I love you more than anyone else in this world." Mummy leaned closer. "I won't let anyone hurt you."

"I'll be quiet." Birdie pulled the blanket to her shoulders again. No one could hurt an invisible girl.

Mummy brushed her fingers across Birdie's hair. "Are you cold?"

Her teeth chattered again. "A little."

Mummy stepped to the railing with her lantern and looked across the harbor before she returned to the cot. "Come with me."

Birdie didn't argue. Bundling up the blanket, she followed Mummy down the steps to the hallway below the deck, to the cabin with two berths—one for sleeping and one for her books. She couldn't see the stars through the porthole or hear the birds, but the bottom berth was warm and she was still sleepy.

"Let me tell you another story about Poppy," Mummy said as Birdie settled under a dry blanket. And they dreamed together about an elegant carriage with white horses, riding down city streets. A little girl who loved to pet the horses and wear the prettiest dresses and visit a famous toy bazaar called FAO. Birdie's imagination took wings again and she could almost hear the hooves on cobblestone, their steady rhythm keeping time.

She rested in that place as Mummy's voice receded, sleeping peacefully until something shuffled beside her bed and she smelled smoke and whiskey. Her eyes sprang open, and in the sunlight, she saw ten toes pointing at her like cannons from the polished floor.

Instead of Mummy, the man was in her room.

"I'll go upstairs," she said, her voice trembling. One thing Birdie knew for certain: the man didn't want her on the boat.

"Don't leave." His dark eyes fixed on her face as he stepped forward. "You don't have to be afraid."

But she was afraid. Very much. This man, she knew, wasn't her friend.

"I won't hurt you, Birdie," he said as he closed the door.

*I don't believe you.*

That's what Meg had said in the Queen Zixi book, when the witch lied to her, but Birdie wasn't that brave. If only she had a magic cloak, she could disappear.

The man leaned down to lift one of her curls, a strange smile rattling across his lips like the snake in one of her picture books. "You look just like your mother."

She froze under the bedcover, drowning in fear. She couldn't breathe in this space.

"So pretty," he said.

"I'll cut it," she whispered, remembering her mother's words, but instead of getting angry, he laughed like Mummy, the sound echoing across her bed.

The door shot open, and Mummy was in the room. "Leave her alone."

The man laughed again, and Birdie wished she could push him through the porthole. Never again would he touch her or her mother's hair.

Slowly, he lowered the curl. "In a year or two."

"Go home," Mummy said. As she shooed him into the hallway, he swatted her backside as if they were playing a game.

Mummy glanced back at her, but instead of concern, she looked mad.

What had she done wrong?

"Thank you," Birdie whispered, hoping to make Mummy happy again, but her mother just shook her head before closing the door.

Birdie inched close to the porthole, her face on the glass as she watched the quilt of sunlight resting across the water, chasing away the fog. She might be angry, but Mummy wouldn't let anyone hurt her.

Not even the man.

18

# CHLOE

A GRAY TUFT OF FUR curled up beside Chloe on the sofa, perfectly content in the warmth of the fireplace. She and Emma had visited the vet this afternoon to check on both the sparrow and Fraidy. The sparrow's wing was healing, thankfully, and while the vet was vaccinating Emma's kitten, he informed them that little Fraidy was actually a girl.

Emma scratched Sugar's belly, laughing as the dog teeter-tottered from side to side. Her stay was only temporary, of course, but if Chloe's dogs had their way, they would never let Emma leave.

"You want anything else to eat?" Chloe asked.

Emma shook her head, leaning back against the wall in her pink nightgown. "I'm stuffed through the gills."

"Me too." And they still had enough mac and cheese to feed half of Clayton.

When Emma began coloring between the lines of Strawberry Shortcake's puppy, Chloe reached for her tote and removed the article that Logan had left for her to read.

*Double Tragedy on Koster Isle.*

Chloe glanced up at the date above the headline. The article was written in July 1907 and the accompanying picture was of a properly attired Mr. and Mrs. Pendleton in the dining room of their castle. A photograph that she'd seen before in the folder of newspaper and magazine articles that Joe Lindley, one of Grandpa Cade's friends, had collected over the years.

*Leslie Pendleton, the esteemed owner of the Pendleton Clock Company and creator of Poppy's Tip-Top Tonic, met his demise on Thursday after a dinner party at the family's private island in the Thousand Islands of New York. Police are currently investigating the cause of his death. Several guests noted that Mr. Pendleton seemed in superb health during the gala.*

*Sadly, Penelope Pendleton, the heiress to the family's vast fortune, disappeared from the island the same night as her father's death. She would have turned five years old yesterday and was, by all accounts, an endearing child with green eyes and blonde curls. She was last seen sleeping inside the Pendleton Castle.*

*"We searched all night and won't stop looking for her," said Mr. Ridell, the caretaker of the Pendleton house and island.*

Chloe blinked before reading that sentence again. And she could almost hear the sound of Grandpa Cade's voice, reciting those words.

Her grandfather had told her that he became caretaker on Koster Isle after Penelope disappeared, but here, in Logan's paper, it said that Grandpa Cade had looked all night for the girl.

He wasn't just mistaken about the memory. He had lied to her.

She rested her hand on Fraidy's furry side, and the kitten scooted closer as Chloe tried to process another diversion of truth from a man who'd always seemed to be honest. Why would her grandfather pretend the aviary glass was from a castle window and then mislead her about his time on the island? It was like he was trying to rewrite history. Or revise it.

*While the Pendleton girl's first name is officially Penelope, many know her as Poppy. Mr. Ridell said Poppy had never run away from home and had no reason to leave now. She is loved by her parents and everyone who has had the privilege of meeting her.*

*More than a hundred of society's elite were attending the evening gala at the Pendleton Castle and the police will be interviewing all who were at the affair. President and Mrs. Roosevelt had planned to attend the event but sent their regrets during the party.*

*Mr. Ridell told officials that he had seen Poppy a few hours before the staff realized that she was missing. Poppy's nursemaid was unavailable to answer this reporter's questions.*

*Mrs. Pendleton is offering a reward to any individual who provides information to find her daughter. Her attorney also issued a stern warning.*

*"Anyone who harms Poppy," Mr. Haynes said, "will wish he were already dead."*

*No one has contacted the family or the police with a ransom offer, but I have no doubt that Mrs. Pendleton and local officials will search for Poppy until they uncover the truth.*

Chloe slowly lowered the article. Not only had Grandpa Cade been on the island during the Pendleton party, he had seen Poppy before she disappeared. Did Joe know about this? Her grandfather's friend had told her many stories about fishing with Grandpa Cade and the laughter they'd shared while working on their boats, but he never told her that Cade had experienced this tragedy with the Pendletons.

She took a deep breath. Something about the Poppy story had rattled her grandparents. She'd realized that soon after she came to live with them, when she'd asked what happened to the family of the missing girl. The question had shocked them, a glance of a thousand unspoken words bolting across the kitchen table. Then Grandpa Cade told her they didn't know much about the people who'd lived on this island before them.

They didn't answer her questions, but the schoolchildren in Clayton had quizzed her intently about ghosts—no, she'd never seen one—and the Pendleton child—no, she didn't know what happened to Poppy—and the castle—no, she'd never been inside. And since she never would go inside, according to her grandma, the children had grown bored.

But the story still haunted her. While there were plenty of old houses in the Thousand Islands, no one else's island or castle had the legend of a murdered millionaire and his missing daughter.

The kitten shifted, placing a paw on Chloe's lap, and she stared at Fraidy for a moment before brushing a hand across her back. She'd always been much more of a dog person, but this fuzzy creature was changing her mind.

"I don't think you're really a fraidy-cat," she whispered, rubbing under the kitten's chin. "I think you are a most courageous cat for making the journey to Koster Isle. What do you think, Emma?"

When she looked up, she realized she'd been left alone with three animals in the living room. "Emma?"

Chloe checked the bathroom and bedrooms before stepping outside on the patio, calling into the trees, fear rippling through her skin. The caseworker had said Emma might be a flight risk, but she wouldn't run again, would she? Certainly not without her cat.

Emma could take care of herself, but she was still scared for the girl.

If Kaitlyn found the perfect foster family, one that also wanted a cat, Chloe would be a mixed bag of emotions but she'd be happy for Emma. Finding a foster family was one thing though. Leaving without even a hug goodbye was quite another. While Emma might not be her biological niece, she'd begun to feel like family.

If she ran, where would she go next?

"Emma!" she shouted again.

This time, she heard a shuffle behind her, a sound louder than thunder in that moment, followed by a flutter of pink as Emma stepped back into the living room, the bird scrapbook tucked under her arm. Chloe took a deep breath, clearing her mind. Jenna would scold her for jumping to conclusions, but in her experience, people did leave sometimes. Suddenly, even.

Sometimes people walked right out the door and never returned.

But not Emma. This time, at least.

"Where did you go?" Chloe asked as Emma collapsed down beside the kitten.

"I had to get something from the shed."

Chloe glanced at the scrapbook. "Were you hiding that?"

"I want to keep it safe."

"We'll find a good hiding place for it inside the house."

Emma hopped onto the couch beside her and straightened her nightgown. Chloe had offered to purchase a new set of pajamas in town, ones without holes, but Emma just shook her head. These were special jammies, she'd said.

How could one argue with special jammies?

Emma opened the scrapbook and brushed her hand over the plastic sleeve protecting the poem about fire. Chloe didn't move in her seat, afraid she might startle the girl.

"A special woman wrote this," Emma said.

Chloe held her breath as Emma turned the page, studying the birds, whispering some of the words that had been written in calligraphy.

"I wonder why she wrote it," Chloe said quietly, her attention returning to the kitten. Emma might act strong, but she was more scared than Fraidy. She wouldn't be honest, Chloe suspected, until she knew her words wouldn't be ignored or used against her.

Emma traced her finger over the words on the last page. "I think she must have missed Penelope."

"Just like someone must miss you."

"No one misses me," Emma said firmly, a barrier growing with every word.

Instead of trying to reason, Chloe simply smiled. "You are the nicest, most capable ten-year-old I know. I'm glad to be your friend."

A hint of a smile before Emma returned to the front of the album, her attention focused on the pictures as if she were looking at them for the first time. How often had Emma examined these birds? Had she ever wondered if she could fly away from wherever she lived?

"I found a rowboat on the other side of the island." Fraidy rolled on her back like one of the dogs, and Chloe rubbed her belly. "It was tucked back in the weeds."

Emma flipped the page. "I tried to hide it."

"Why did you come to Koster Isle?" Chloe asked.

"I was looking for Poppy's Castle."

So Emma had come to this island for a reason. "And you paddled here in the storm?"

She shook her head, her eyes on the page. "I came before it rained."

"That was very courageous of you." Chloe tucked her legs under her, leaning her head back on the sofa as she tried to piece the story together. "And then when you got here, you said you knew me from the candy store."

"I saw your picture in a magazine."

"Ah," Chloe said, "the story about my washed-up shop."

Emma looked confused. "It said you had lots of candy on your shelves."

"I suppose it did." *Like flotsam along a forgotten shore.*

"My friend said she'd been there before."

"Could you tell me the name of your friend?"

Emma tilted her head, squinting her eyes. "I don't want to talk about her."

"Fair enough," Chloe said. "It sounds like she loves you very much."

"Loved," Emma said sadly, and Chloe felt the sadness with her.

"I will help you," Chloe promised, although she wasn't sure exactly what was helpful and what caused more harm. "With whatever you need."

Emma's curls bobbed over her shoulders with her nod. "It's good for Fraidy to have a friend."

"Indeed," Chloe said as she petted the kitten again. "I will take good care of her too."

Emma fell asleep on the couch, the album in her arms and the dogs resting on the floor. Chloe placed Fraidy on a fleece blanket in her carrier and then retrieved a separate blanket for Emma.

A flash in her mind, and Chloe remembered her grandmother tucking blankets over her when she was a child. Had her mother tucked her in as well? It all blurred together, but there was a feeling attached to the tucking. A memory of being safe. Warm. Someone, in that moment, caring for her.

If nothing else, she wanted Emma to know she was safe on Koster Isle.

After turning off the lights, Chloe slipped back onto the patio. The cordless phone in one hand, the article Logan had left for her in the other. She couldn't see much beyond the forest, but up on the cliff, blushing behind the veil of trees, was the moonlit castle.

Emma was safe in the cottage, but she wondered again what happened to Poppy. Had she thought she was safe in the castle?

Most old-timers believed Poppy had drowned, but no one ever found her body. And then so many people swore over the years that they saw her. Even if she'd survived, she was probably gone now, like Chloe's grandparents, but an unfinished story like hers never really died.

Maybe Logan was right. If they were able to find the truth about Poppy, it might bring the mystique of her disappearance to an end. The boats could pass by, tell the story if they'd like, but it would stop the amateur sleuths from snooping around her island.

And what if, somehow, Poppy's story, the mystery of this scrapbook, could help them uncover Emma's story as well?

*We can't talk about the Pendletons,* Grandpa Cade had said.

Chloe had been more focused on other things as a child to really consider his diversion, but why couldn't they talk about the family who'd once owned this island?.

The connection between her and Poppy hadn't even occurred to her until high school when a transplanted kid had drawn the final line between dots.

"You're the chick from Ghost Island, aren't you?" he'd said, dressed in white pants and a disco shirt of many colors as he slid his cafeteria tray onto her table.

She hadn't liked him from the start, but she learned early in life not to cower. "My name's Chloe, and it's Koster Isle."

He took a bite of his hot dog and a string of mustard hung from his mustache before dripping onto his pants.

Strange, the workings of one's mind as it remembered.

"I heard a whole lot of drug dealing went down in your castle a few years back."

"That's ridiculous."

"And then you were abandoned like that other girl."

"Her name was Poppy," Chloe had said as she picked up her tray. "And we weren't abandoned."

He'd shrugged as if he didn't care what had happened to either her or Poppy, but Chloe cared, perhaps too deeply at the time, about her grandpa and about the girl who had gone before her. Finding hope in Poppy's story had given her hope for her own life.

Her curiosity remained, but she was no longer desperate for answers about Poppy. Emma, however, needed answers right now.

In the porch light, she eyed the phone number that Logan Danford had written at the top of the article. Perhaps they could work together after all—if he was willing to make a trade. She'd leave a message on his voicemail tonight.

The phone rang twice before she heard a voice. "This is Logan."

She hesitated.

"Hello?" he prompted.

"I'm sorry. I wasn't expecting you to be in the office."

"Who is this?"

She drummed her hand on the chair. "Chloe Ridell from the candy shop."

"Ah," he said. "I gave you my home number."

Good thing she hadn't decided to call at midnight. "You didn't think I'd phone, did you?"

"I was hoping you would give me a second chance." She could hear the smile in his voice. He might be bold, but he wasn't like the mean boy in her high school. He was a professional trying to find out what happened to Poppy as well.

"Could you stop by the candy store the next time you're in town?"

"How about tomorrow?"

She hesitated again, wanting to make sure he understood her guidelines before she agreed to speak with him. "My grandfather didn't do anything wrong."

Except bending the truth, perhaps, but that wasn't pertinent to Logan's story.

"I'm fairly certain that at some point in his life, he must have done something not quite right."

"This story isn't about him." She paced the length of the patio and returned the opposite direction. "I want to be clear."

"Unless he kidnapped Poppy, I'm not interested in writing about him."

"My grandfather wouldn't intentionally hurt anyone." Of that, she was certain.

"I could be in Clayton by ten tomorrow."

She sat on the wicker chair. "Eleven works better for me."

"I'll be there by eleven then."

She hung up the phone and closed her eyes, savoring this quiet moment.

Maybe she and Logan together could uncover the stories of two girls who hadn't returned home.

19

# *BIRDIE*

NOVEMBER 1911

Two strangers—a man and a woman—paddled a skiff toward the houseboat before the veil of night hid the autumn sky. Mummy hushed Birdie, telling her to be as quiet as a mouse, before nudging her into the upper salon.

She and Mummy were on a new boat now. In a different harbor. A different man owned it, but he rarely visited. Instead, his friends came to see Mummy in the late hours.

How her stomach ached whenever they pounded on the door.

Birdie inched open the window, listening as the strangers greeted Mummy from the water, but her mother didn't invite them onto the boat. She didn't even offer a rope to tie their skiff.

"We're looking for a man named Pierre Gagné," a woman said. "Someone in town said we might find him here."

"I don't know anyone by that name."

Why did Mummy say that? Pierre was Olivia's husband, and he'd return to fetch Olivia tonight. He was much nicer than any of the other men who visited the boat, painting and fixing all the broken parts.

"Are you certain you don't know Pierre?" the stranger asked.

"Of course I'm certain," Mummy replied.

"Do you live alone on this boat?"

"I have a servant."

*And me,* Birdie wanted to say.

"We are looking for a girl who has gone missing," the woman explained. "Her name is Poppy."

The word churned in Birdie's head like foam on the river. How did these people know about the girl on the tonic bottle?

The man spoke this time. "She's been gone for more than four years."

"I hope you find her," Mummy said.

"So do we. There's a steep reward for anyone with information."

"What kind of reward?" Mummy asked, her dress blowing in the wind.

"A thousand dollars."

*Who would pay so much money for an imaginary girl?*

Birdie waited quietly, wishing that Mummy would ask why they were looking for the girl from the bottle.

If only someone was looking for her too.

Mummy leaned toward the railing. "Her mother must really miss her."

"She's wracked with grief."

"I'm sure she is." Only Birdie could see Mummy's smile as she turned away from the railing. Strange how she seemed to delight in a mother's sorrow.

Mummy didn't instruct Birdie in whether she should stay in her hiding place, but after the strangers left, Birdie trailed her toward the kitchen, remaining at the door between the kitchen and dining room, one of the boat's two fireplaces crackling behind her.

"Who was that?" Olivia asked as she dried her hands on a towel.

Mummy flitted past her to the window. "We have to move the boat."

Olivia snorted. "Tell that rat of a man who owns it."

"He's not coming until the end of the week," Mummy said.

"Then Pierre will hire a tug for us tomorrow."

"We need to leave tonight."

Olivia shrugged. "Swim to shore then and ask someone else to move us."

Birdie crept under the dining table, her eyes squeezed shut as her mind wandered back to the canopy of colorful birds from her dreams. Mummy and Olivia might be arguing again, but she could pretend she was playing with her birds. Flying south for the winter.

"I hate this boat!" Mummy shouted.

"This is one of the finest boats on the river."

"I still hate it."

"That's because you are occupying yourself with monsters instead of settling down with a gentleman."

Mummy's laugh sounded mean. "A lot of good settling down has done you."

"Pierre is a good man," Olivia said. "He loves me."

"Right."

Olivia banged two pans together, the sound clattering through the dining room. "Don't you dare try and sweet-talk my husband."

"What would I want with him?"

"What you seem to want from all men, Ellie. No one feels sorry for you."

"They should. This dreary boat will be my demise."

Both women were standing beside the table when Birdie opened her eyes. Mummy with her golden locks, always curled, waiting for her next guest to arrive. Olivia with the familiar kerchief over her graying hair, the material colored the purples of dawn. The women had fought about Pierre before, the mistakes that he made when he tried to varnish or fix the boat, the long seasons he was gone. Mummy had said she was only keeping him employed because of Olivia since the two of them, Olivia had said, came as one.

Olivia began setting the table. "Pierre should have been here by now—"

"He probably took off," Mummy said. "Men tend to do that."

"Maybe in your experience."

"We are better off without him."

"My husband isn't yours!" Olivia screamed, and Birdie jumped, hitting her head on the table when a plate shattered.

"You're better off without him."

"You can't possibility know that," Olivia said as she plucked a piece of the broken china off the floor. "I'm not going to live on this boat forever."

Mummy laughed again. "You'll stay because of the money."

"I'll stay because of Birdie. Someone needs to watch over that girl."

"I watch over her just fine. She's my daughter."

"Then you need to act like a mum," Olivia said. "Keep her away from those vile men."

"Those vile men pay you too."

"Don't remind me . . ."

Birdie pulled her knees to her chest after Mummy left, but she didn't crawl out of her hiding place. Pierre read Birdie stories on the deck sometimes, when he was between jobs. Sometimes he even let her hold his fishing pole as they waited for dinner to bite. So different than Mummy's men. Then he would disappear whenever Mummy's guests came, and Birdie missed him while he was gone.

Pierre was a threat, Mummy once said, but Birdie didn't understand. When she'd asked Olivia about it later, her friend said Mummy thought most people were a threat. That's why she rarely left the boat.

Shoes shuffled through the dining room, and Olivia swept Birdie off the floor like the broken plate. "You don't belong here."

That was the problem. These days, she didn't feel as if she belonged anywhere.

Olivia carried her all the way to bed and pulled the covers over her. "You need to sleep, little one."

But she didn't like to sleep after dark. Mummy didn't require her to stay on the deck in the colder months, but she never knew who might be in the hallway or open her door by accident, thinking it was the latrine.

Sometimes it felt like Mummy didn't even remember Birdie was there.

"God loves you, child." Olivia kissed her forehead. "You may not know it yet since the people that He created to care for you have been so cruel, but His love is as wide as this river and just as deep. Sink into it, Birdie."

She shook her head, not wanting to be disagreeable, but sinking was scary, especially when she didn't know how to swim.

"I can't breathe underwater."

"This is special water," Olivia said softly, her brown eyes as sweet as honey. "More like falling into a mound of feathers. You can take a deep breath and rest for a while."

"I'll drown in the feathers."

"You won't drown," Olivia said, clutching her hand. "Just fall straight into the warmth of His love."

Love meant someone cared for you an awful lot. She'd read about it in her books. How mummies and daddies were supposed to love their children. Like Olivia loved her.

Olivia, she thought, was an angel.

Another man came after Olivia left; Birdie could hear him down the narrow hall. The visitors spent most of their time in Mummy's bedroom at the front of the boat, the room with the windows that looked away from town. Birdie had a room on the other end, next to the one for Olivia and Pierre on the nights they stayed. Except Pierre hadn't come to the boat tonight like Olivia had said. Instead, her friend had returned home alone.

Someone opened Birdie's door in the late hours and woke her from her sleep.

"You like candy?" the man asked.

She liked candy plenty, but she didn't like him.

"Of course you like candy," he said. "All girls do."

"Mummy!" she shouted, but this time Mummy didn't come.

*Never stay in a place when you know it's time to leave.*

Someone seemed to whisper those words in her ear, but she had no place to run here.

Her eyes tightly shut, Birdie slipped onto one of the birds in her mind, grasping the feathers between her fingers, holding on for life.

Maybe the birds were her angels instead.

"Fly," she whispered.

And the bird flew her far away from the riverboat.

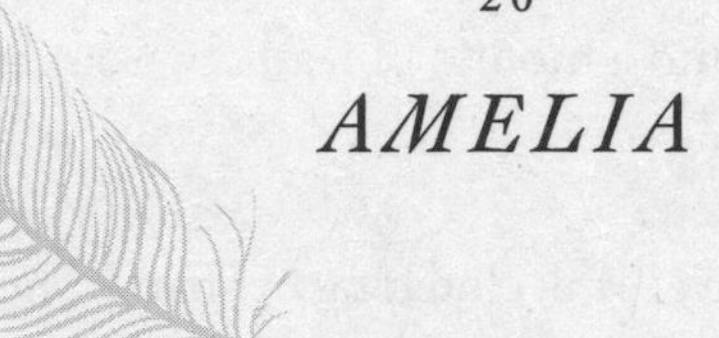

# 20
# *AMELIA*

KOSTER ISLE

MAY 1912

It started with flowers, freshly cut from the spring gardens that Cade had maintained during the past five years. He'd brought them to Amelia's room every day since she'd arrived back on the island and arranged them neatly on her vanity. Fiona was usually with her, brushing her hair when the caretaker arrived, but her maid had already left this morning to help in the kitchen.

Amelia hadn't been alone with Cade since she'd returned to the island. Hadn't been alone with him since he'd carried her up the stairs, the night that Penelope had gone missing.

Cade Ridell was just a few years her junior, eight at the most, but he no longer looked like the lad that Leslie had hired to work initially at his clock company and then as a caretaker. In fact, he'd grown into quite a handsome man with shoulders broad enough to bear the entire burden of Koster Isle.

In her grief, she'd lost the beauty of her youth, but the years alone on the island had bolstered Cade into manhood. He must be almost thirty now. While he was employed as a servant on Koster Isle, he carried himself like the master of this estate, and in the regal morning light, he looked as if he was ready to rule the world.

Did he have any family on this continent or was he alone like her?

"Would you like anything else?" Cade asked. "Something to eat, maybe, for a late breakfast? The root cellar is full of vegetables and we have plenty of fish."

She didn't respond. Cade was supposed to care for her house and gardens and birds. Not concern himself with her meals when she wasn't the least bit hungry.

"I could take a boat into Clayton," he continued, "fetch whatever you'd like . . ."

"I'll have tea in the aviary." She inhaled the last breaths of life emanating from the brightly colored petals on her vanity, crisp and sweet. Even though the air was warm, the cold that crept through her skin kept everything frozen inside her. How she wished for a chisel to break through the ice, an anchor to keep her from floundering. Give her the opportunity to feel something outside the birdhouse.

She'd sold her monstrosity of a house on Fifth Avenue, a ready buyer in one of the Vanderbilts. The small staff who'd traveled with her had transported all eighteen of her birds back to the island. Mr. Haynes was preparing a brownstone in New York City for her, and the birds would winter on Koster Isle like they'd discussed, basking in the warmth of electric light and Cade's care.

Next spring, she'd already decided, she would return to England. She no longer needed her father's pounds or his goodwill to take her in. She'd lose herself in London's parks, visiting the birds there.

"Something is lodged behind your vanity," Cade said as he knelt on the rug beside her.

She blinked, startled at the reminder of the Koster family portrait that she'd hidden away. "I don't think—"

But he'd already dragged it out. "It's your family's picture."

"Indeed."

"It must have fallen off the hook."

She slipped onto the vanity chair, her gaze on the flowers instead of the portrait. While it didn't matter as much if her secrets were exposed now, no good would come from the truth. "I don't want it in my room."

He lifted the frame. "I'll store it then."

"Burn it please."

"It's irreplaceable," he said, shock jarring his steady cadence. The portrait tucked at his side, he studied her as if trying to solve the mystery she harbored.

"I don't want it anymore."

Weeks passed before she saw Cade alone again. The weak drum of her heart beat a little stronger when he stepped into the aviary one evening, but the moment Cade saw her, he moved back toward the door. "I'm sorry to interrupt."

This time, she didn't want him to leave. "You're not disturbing me."

"I'll return later," he said, shifting a bag of seeds between his hands.

"Please." She motioned him forward. It was the first time in years that she'd wanted anyone else in the aviary. "It's no interruption."

He took another tentative step under the glass.

"Thank you for taking such good care of Koster Isle while I was in the city," she said as he moved toward her. "And for caring for my birds."

"It's my pleasure." The birds flocked close to him as he neared her bench. Then a lovebird crossed between them, searching for her mate. A song of delight spilled out like wine when she found him. Pure joy at the sight of her beloved.

"Mrs. Pendleton—" Cade began.

"Please call me Amelia."

He shook his head. "I can't do that."

"I suppose not." She waved her fingers through the air as if she could brush the rejection away. "It was silly of me to ask."

He stood quietly beside her, gently stroking the golden crown of a kinglet that had perched on his arm.

"Did you dispose of my family's portrait?" she asked.

He glanced up from the bird, seemingly startled at question. "I have taken care of it."

"Thank you," she said. "It would only pain me to see it again."

"Why does it cause you such pain?"

She pondered his question. "My family wasn't happy before my father commissioned it, and the turmoil only grew worse in the years that followed. He eventually sent my mother to a sanatorium."

She'd said too much, the words slipping out with ease. It had been a long time since she'd allowed herself to return to those years, the curtain drawn firmly across the stage in her mind. No one had applauded after the final act of the Koster family's performance.

Cade didn't seem surprised by this revelation. "Was your mother unwell for long?"

"She thought she was a member of the royal family."

"I suppose all of us have dreams."

"It wasn't just a dream." Amelia had never talked to anyone about all that happened in her family, not even Leslie. Perhaps it was this special place, with someone who seemed to care about more than the money that kept him employed, that prompted her to confide a part of her story. "When I was twelve, my mum managed to get inside Buckingham Palace. Walked straight through the staff entrance except she didn't stop at the kitchen. She made it all the way up to Queen Victoria's rooms before she was waylaid by the palace guards."

Not a sound came from his lips, disbelief or disgust. He simply listened.

"Mum would tell the other residents at the sanatorium that her confinement was a terrible mistake. That the queen would arrive soon to take her home."

"Is she still at the sanatorium?" he asked.

"No," Amelia said. "She died within a year."

"I'm sorry."

Amelia shook her head. "My father married soon after her death. He was so relieved to be rid of her; it almost felt as if he'd planned the whole thing."

The lovebirds had retreated into the harbor of leaves, but the kinglet remained on Cade's arm. "If I may speak my mind . . ."

She didn't respond, not certain she wanted to hear his thoughts.

"I think you need a companion," he said slowly. "In addition to your birds."

Her shoulders bristled under her summer dress. "It's not your business to tell me what I need."

He looked away. "You're right, of course."

Another moment passed as she drummed her fingers on the ivory silk of her skirt. "But it's good of you to consider it."

Cade sat on the bench beside her as if he were her equal, but instead of feeling affronted, she was pleased to spend her evening with the man who'd carried her up the stairs years ago. The man who'd cared about everything important to her.

What was important to him?

She didn't dare ask this of a servant, but she couldn't help but wonder at his interests beyond caring for Koster Isle.

Cade's honey-brown hair turned golden in the fading light, his body a tower of muscle and grit. If only she could borrow some of his strength. If only he could help her carry more than his workload.

Money kept her clothed and fed and gave her prestige in the city and an island to hide. But he was right. She didn't have a single friend. Not even one person, beyond Mr. Haynes, who she trusted, and he would certainly end his employment if the money in her accounts was no longer plentiful.

"Don't you ever get stir crazy on this island?" she asked. "Especially in the winter."

"Only until the river freezes," he said. "Then I sail across it on the ice punt."

What would it feel like to sail on ice? Sail with this man at her side?

She shook her head, freeing herself from the ridiculous thought. That curtain she must close as well before either of them stepped onto the stage.

Cade leaned forward, elbows on knees, the scent of pine wafting from his skin. "May I ask you a question?"

"You may ask whatever you'd like," she said, her eyes on the electric light glowing on the other side of the path, a spark on the canvas of evening sky behind the glass.

"The night that Mr. Pendleton died . . ."

She braced herself. The police had interrogated her for hours after his death, relentless in their questions about both Leslie and Penelope, and she'd told them of the many people who were jealous of her husband's success. While she hadn't mentioned the voices she thought she heard by the boathouse or the opium that Leslie consumed, the detective found an empty bottle of Poppy's tonic beside his goblet. They knew. And still, they hadn't been able to explain what happened to her daughter.

"You don't have to be afraid of me," she said quietly. Instead of replying, Cade kept his gaze on the glass, watching the stars appear above the water. "You don't believe me?"

"I like working on this island."

"And your position is secure, no matter what you ask."

He seemed to contemplate her words before speaking again. "That night, back in 1907."

A sharp pain pressed between her ears. "I'll never forget it, Cade."

"I checked on Rose and Poppy before the party and all seemed to be well, except Poppy was asking for you. I found you talking with the reporter right here."

She remembered every detail of that evening, reliving each moment repeatedly over the years. "I rushed straight up to the nursery to see her."

"Why did you leave her there alone?"

Amelia rubbed her right temple as she leaned back against the bench, acid souring her stomach. "Penelope was never supposed to be alone. Rose left her to attend Mr. Pendleton."

"I see."

And she wondered if he did. "Rose was one of many who made themselves available to my husband."

"I'm sorry, Mrs. Pendleton." He stood beside her. "Have you been to the nursery since you returned?"

"I am never going back into that tower."

"Perhaps you will remember something," he said. "A clue the detectives missed."

Looking back, she didn't know why she went, but she followed Cade up to the third floor, staring at the narrow steps, listening to the rhythm of Leslie's clocks on the walls. The details of that night, five years past now, seemed to be chiseled in her head, but if there was any hope of a new memory, she would risk it.

Stale air flooded out when Cade opened the nursery door. She stepped tentatively inside, remembering the mound of covers that she'd thought hid Penelope. At what point had Rose gone back down to Leslie? The detectives had interviewed the maid at length, and she swore that Penelope was in the room when she left.

Was it possible that someone else could have been in Rose's bed when Amelia arrived? Or was her imagination playing games again?

She ran her fingers over the papered pattern of river with blue and green rippling across the wall, then smoothed her hand over Penelope's now neatly made bed. How she missed her daughter's laughter in this place. Their shared love for birds.

"Do you remember anything new?" he asked, his tone wistful.

"Nothing of significance."

"I've come up here often in the winter months, wondering if I missed anything when we searched."

"She's gone," Amelia said sadly. "I suppose we all must come to terms with it."

The entire Koster family, she'd decided, was cursed.

"I don't think I'll ever completely come to terms."

She looked over at him, desperate to change the course of their conversation. "You've taken good care of this place, Cade. I still don't understand how you stay here all winter, but I thank you for it."

"You might find you like the quiet when the snow begins." He gazed out the window beside her as if the endless ripples beyond the castle held answers for both of them. "It's a good place to settle one's heart."

"Perhaps."

"And when the ice freezes, it's not lonely anymore. You can sail across the ice to the mainland or stop and fish with friends."

"I'd prefer to stay by the fire."

"The fire here is always warm," he said, his voice gentle but strong.

Her heart leapt even as she caught a glimpse of herself in the mirror. The past five years had stolen her youth, her black hair threaded with gray, her cheeks shallow. But she was only thirty-four, the same age her mother had been when Amelia was born.

What would it be like to begin again? To be completely free of the Koster family and the Pendletons? Not Penelope, mind you. She would always hope and pray for a miracle. But what would it be like to be free from all the expectations that she'd borne on herself?

An ember flickered inside her, and she marveled at its warmth.

Maybe a companion, like Cade suggested, was what she needed in this season. Another woman who might understand. When she was younger, she'd had friends. Instead of attempting to play with her sister, she befriended some of the servants' children who lived on their estate. No one divided the lines of propriety in their youth. They rocked their dollies together and sang silly songs and pretended they were equals.

She'd been happy in those days.

"If I did want to find a friend," she said slowly, "where would I begin?"

"In Clayton." Cade's eyes blazed back to life. "St. Mary's has a sewing bee. Dozens of women spend their Fridays there."

Her hands twitched, craving something to keep them engaged. "What exactly does one do at a bee?"

"The ladies sew dresses and scarves for the children at an orphan asylum up in Ogdensburg."

Long ago, her governess had taught her how to use a needle and thread. Even if she was a bit clumsy at it, she could sew a scarf, couldn't she? A girl Penelope's age might wear it.

"Would you take me over in the runabout?" she asked.

His nod was rapid, clearly pleased. "Of course."

"I'll consider it."

The following week, Cade steered her and Fiona across the river, fifteen minutes to the dock in Clayton. While Amelia didn't join in the talk around her, the work kept her hands and her mind occupied. Then more rides followed as summer flowed toward fall, and she made acquaintances among several of the women. Friday mornings swiftly became the highlight of her week.

"Be careful," Fiona said one August evening after they'd returned home.

"I'm plenty safe here."

"With your heart, Mrs. Pendleton. I worry about you and Cade."

Something like rage burned through her at the implication that others thought she might care for the caretaker of her castle.

Mostly because Fiona's words were true.

"Don't concern yourself about me."

But something switched inside her like one of the electric lights Leslie had installed. She no longer had a husband or a sham of a marriage or a child to hold it all together. And she no longer cared about the protocol from her past. The gilded in New York could have their fancy parties and dresses and meals at the Waldorf-Astoria. She wanted Cade.

When summer finally ebbed into autumn, the islands ablaze with color, Amelia couldn't bear the thought of returning to the city. As she walked on the paths, sketched in the aviary, even worked in the gardens, she basked in the fragile rays of joy.

The early autumn weeks passed swiftly, the nights cooler, and the women at the bee began talking about snow. By the first of November, the staff had packed their things, leaving only a few suitcases for Cade to deliver to the train station.

She'd wanted one more night in the castle before she hibernated in her brownstone. One more night to say goodbye to her birds for the winter. One more night to say goodbye to a desire that had taken flight in her heart.

A torrent of snow fell overnight, the winds whipping up drifts around the castle. They could still slip down to the boathouse through the tunnel, take the boat across to Clayton, Cade explained as he lifted her cases from the floor of the great hall, but his voice lacked confidence.

"I want to stay," she said.

He glanced out at the turbulent river. "The weather should be better tomorrow."

"I don't want to leave tomorrow either."

He studied her cautiously as if he was trying to understand. "But the river will freeze soon."

"I know."

"You'll have to wait until it's frozen to take the ice punt across."

"I want to stay, Cade," she repeated, relishing the quiet. No one was watching them from the banisters. No one rattling in the kitchen or mopping the floor.

He set the suitcases back on the tile. "Stay for what?"

She didn't break away from the curiosity that filled his gaze. "For the winter."

"Only a handful of people winter on the islands."

She smiled. "You do."

"I'm used to it."

"And my birds," she said.

"It will be lonely until the freeze."

Why was he warning her away now, after encouraging her to stay?

She lifted her chin, breathing deep, her eyes locked again on the gray ones across from her. "I don't think I'll be lonely at all."

"Mrs. Pendleton."

"Please," she said, "call me Amelia."

"All right." He slowly lifted her suitcases again. "Amelia."

Then he took her luggage back into the house and built a fire in her room.

# 21
# LOGAN

LOGAN FOLLOWED CHLOE and her dogs up through a covered passage that connected ruins of a half-timbered boathouse with the castle. It was a slow hike with his bum leg, trailing two furry guides who clearly owned this land, sunlight crisscrossing the dirt path as it streamed through windows in the corridor.

He'd been determined not to trip. Not that it really mattered—he'd fallen plenty of times over the past five years—but he wanted to save face in front of Chloe. No sense frightening her any more than he'd already done.

"How did your grandfather end up on Koster Isle?" he asked as they neared the house.

"He worked on a ship for passage from England to New York in his early teens. Then Mr. Pendleton hired him as a janitor at his clock company."

"So Mr. Pendleton transferred him to the island?"

"I didn't know my grandpa worked here when Mr. Pendleton was still alive," she said. "I thought he came a few years later."

"I'm surprised he didn't tell you more about Poppy."

"I was only fifteen when he died," she said. "There were a lot of questions that I never thought to ask."

He couldn't imagine an age where one didn't ask questions. He'd been born asking them. "Did your grandmother work for the Pendleton family?"

"No." She wound her curly hair into a knot and clipped it. "Nana was born in one of the lost villages upstream. She didn't move to Koster Isle until after she and Grandpa Cade married."

"What do you mean by *lost*?"

"Washed away, really. Or sunken. It was flooded to create the St. Lawrence Seaway. She moved to Clayton when she was about eighteen and met my grandfather at a church bazaar."

"You must miss her," he said.

She swept her hand over a lichen-stained stone on the surrounding wall as if she could siphon its strength. "Terribly."

"How many children did they have?"

"Just my father." Something shifted in her face when she glanced back, a shadow whisking across it. "He's no longer alive."

"I'm sorry . . ."

She fastened her jaw like stone, trying to press back the sadness.

"What happened to him?"

"I'm not like Poppy," she said, her focus back on the wall. "My story is private."

"I understand." Her story was her story. The details weren't any of his business.

They were under the house now, facing a locked door that probably led into a basement. He scanned the walls for cracks. The doorframes for gaps. While the structure seemed sound, standing underneath this monstrosity of a house brought back a plethora of memories that he didn't want to entertain.

He needed to find a way inside today, take photographs, and then locate someone who could help him understand what might have happened to Poppy.

"This way." Chloe directed him through an open arch, onto a weed-ridden lawn, and he whistled when he looked up at the gray castle that mimicked a medieval fortress from Germany or France. The Pendletons had poured themselves and probably most of their money into this house.

"Thank you for bringing me here," he said as he searched the castle windows, dozens of them lodged between stone. If only he could walk the halls inside where Poppy was last seen.

"I'm doing this to help Emma."

"I know." Chloe had agreed to work with him in hopes that they might discover a connection between the scrapbook dedicated to Penelope and Emma's family.

She petted the dark-brown Lab that she'd called Maple. "I'm afraid we won't find much."

"Perhaps together we can coax these walls to talk."

He slipped a Nikon camera from his rucksack and adjusted the aperture before shooting several pictures of the tower. Then he eyed the concrete balustrade and steps to the patio. The pain meds he'd taken back in Clayton weren't doing much good after their walk up from the river, but he wasn't going to stop now.

Chloe and one of her dogs followed his slow climb to the veranda as if they might catch his fall, and a new scenario played through his head. The balustrade crumbling and him tumbling and taking Chloe to the bottom. Even if she stopped his fall, it would be mortifying for them both.

"You doing okay?" she asked.

"Stellar," he said. "Practicing for a tortoise race."

She laughed at his rotten joke, and it diffused some of the awkwardness. "I'm certain you would win."

He returned her laugh. "It's a pretty stiff competition."

"At least second place then."

He straightened his shoulders. "That would make my parents proud."

They crested the balcony, and he stopped to take a breath as they looked over the brush that must have been a manicured garden a hundred years past. The property reminded him of an estate near his childhood home, the mansion built by a canning jar tycoon. Logan had spent several high school summers landscaping the former Ball family grounds. With a little toil and the proper tools, he thought, Koster Isle could be revived as well.

"Where do your parents live?" Chloe asked.

"Muncie, Indiana. Most of my family is there."

"Did you grow up in Indiana?"

"Born and bred. My parents raised me, four brothers, and almost five hundred acres of corn."

"Sounds like they would qualify for sainthood."

And then some. "I'd nominate them both if I could."

"It'll be dark in an hour or so," she said, petting the yellow Lab. "You want to walk around the castle?"

"I want to go inside."

"If I had the key, I'd let you in."

The conversation was a repeat from their short boat ride over. She'd never stepped inside the castle, and he was incredulous at the thought.

An ornately carved set of doors barred them like a portcullis from entering the first floor. It wouldn't have surprised him if the Pendletons had built a bridge and moat around this place to rival the estates of their neighbors, ruling as king and queen of Koster. During the Middle Ages, they would have had archers in the siege tower to defend their land.

Normally a doorknob wasn't a point of fascination for him, but he stared at the brass knob and its ordinary keyhole, wishing he had a bobby pin. It was possible that his skill of picking the back door lock on his parents' farmhouse might come in handy.

Persistence was the key, he thought. Sort of like working on this article. There was always a way to uncover the truth, even if something happened almost ninety years ago. He just had to keep searching. "Locked doors don't bother you much, do they?"

"Clearly not as much as they bother you." Her eyes focused on the sliver of river between the trees. Even though they'd just left the water, it seemed she was longing to return.

He studied the door again and the windows along the veranda. In spite of Chloe's insistence that he wouldn't be able to get inside, he still verified that it was locked. "Why don't you want to go into the castle?"

She tucked a flyaway hair back into its clip. "That has nothing to do with your story."

"You're right." But he suspected her story was intertwined with the Pendletons.

"You are welcome to look around the grounds and take pictures," she said. "But I can't imagine any sort of evidence would remain. The police would have scoured every inch of this estate."

"Did your grandfather tell you anything about their search?"

Instead of answering, she prompted him forward. "Do you want to see the other side of the house?"

"You're avoiding my question."

"It's hard to keep up when you're interrogating me."

"Interviewing," he said, "not interrogating."

"Feels like the same thing."

"I'm trying to jog your memories."

She started walking. "My grandpa took care of Koster Isle for most of his life, but he really didn't like to talk about the past."

"Mrs. Pendleton left the island to him?"

Chloe nodded. "She didn't have any other children after Poppy to inherit her property. I suppose it made sense to give him the cottage that he'd built and the rest of the land."

"Or she was buying his silence."

She twitched as if she'd never thought about that possibility. "Why would she need his silence?"

"That's what I'm trying to figure out."

"My grandfather wasn't hiding anything." But even as she said the words, her confident tone faded.

"Maybe Cade knew something she was trying to keep secret."

If he had a football, he'd toss it up and catch it a few times as he waited for her to speak. But instead of responding, Chloe continued walking around the veranda.

He asked way too many questions. That's what his parents used to say, and Nicole agreed. But how could one not ask? Not wonder? Especially if the questions meant finding the truth and ultimately justice. The questions that now came with his job, dogging him until he found answers.

Even if he couldn't uncover all the answers, that didn't mean he should stop asking. Wondering and searching for the truth.

As they rounded the balcony, he scanned the right side of the house, covered partially in the trees. "Where are the other doors?"

"There's a side door closer to the cliff." Chloe pointed toward the trees. "It's locked as well."

"I'm sure a locksmith in Clayton would have access to a boat."

Her eyes shifted toward the river again as if she were taking a sip with her gaze. "My grandmother always thought it was too dangerous to go inside."

He eyed the structure again, and while the stone walls were covered with lichen, they looked sound. "Someone has kept it in good order."

"Grandpa Cade looked after the castle along with the rest of the property," she said. "I only stayed away for my grandmother's sake."

"And now?" he asked as they wandered around the house.

"I'll go inside when I'm ready," she said. "Why are you so intent on digging up this story about Poppy?"

"My editor gave me several options for an upcoming feature."

"And you chose the hardest one?'

"I'm trying to right a few of the wrongs in this world."

"With your pen?"

"More like my computer, but yes, by whatever means I can."

As they neared the trees, Logan saw a short door that stood as high as his waist, like the bottom half of a stable door. He pushed it, hoping the door would open into the house, but it was locked from the inside.

First lesson learned in the fire academy—breaking a window only amplifies a fire. But this house wasn't on fire. In fact, it probably could use a little fresh air.

"I could take out a window." He smiled at Chloe. "We could crawl inside."

"Right." She rolled her eyes. "Only if you repair the glass."

"Considering it . . ."

A few more steps through the weeds, the dogs sniffing the land around them, and they found a taller door built, he guessed, for the kitchen and garden staff. A corridor where mud could smear across the floor and food could spill on the ground before they served their guests.

Even though the door didn't have a keyhole like the one on the veranda, he still reached out to see if it would turn.

The door was barred shut, but along the trim, a few inches above his shoulder, was a small brass knob, much like the one on the former estate that he used to mow. The family had never changed the original side door on their carriage house or the knob that pulled a chain on the other side.

The carriage house was on private property, guarded around the clock, but when the door was locked, none of the workers ever needed to search for a key.

Logan began turning the knob on the Pendleton door, and he heard the chain cranking on the other side. "How about we go inside the house today?"

She checked her watch. "It's too late to get a locksmith over here this afternoon."

He stopped turning. "If I can get us inside, can I look around for a bit?"

"As long as you don't break a window."

Another turn and the axle yanked the remaining slack of its chain, lifting the iron bar from its socket, and with a loud click, Logan pushed open the door.

## 22

# CHLOE

CHLOE STARED INTO THE DARKNESS as if a dungeon awaited them in the corridor. "I thought you were joking."

Logan grinned at her like he'd pulled the key out of a top hat. "Nope."

"How in the world did you figure that out?"

"Sometimes we just need to look at things from a different angle."

She glanced up at the small knob hidden in the trim. "I'd never have thought to look there."

"Some builders installed these in older houses to keep their owners from being locked out," he said. "Makes good sense if you live on an island."

That must have been how Grandpa Cade had entered the house without a key. He was probably afraid to tell her. Afraid, like Nana, that she might get hurt inside.

She stepped back. "I hope you take some good pictures."

"Will you go with me?" he asked.

A shiver snaked its way up from her toes until she shuddered. "No, thank you."

He leaned against the doorframe and crossed his arms like she was a conundrum in need of resolution. "I think you're curious."

"I think you're crazy!"

"I can't believe you don't want to explore this place."

"It's not that I don't want to—"

"What is it then?"

This was the question that had haunted her for most of her life. Something, beyond her grandparents' warnings, that kept her from entering the castle. She wasn't afraid of ghosts, was she? That was ridiculous. Nothing lived in here except perhaps mice. "I don't know."

A gust made the branches overhead tick like an old clock, the wind taking her back to an earlier day when Nana warned her about the dangers inside the abandoned walls.

"My grandmother kept me out of here by telling stories about the falling roof and flying bats and ghost that haunted the rooms."

"The ghost of Leslie Pendleton?"

"She never mentioned his name."

Logan waved her inside. "We'll ward off any ghosts together."

Her teeth chattered, and she wondered at the arctic breeze that drifted over her. Where had it come from on this sunny spring day?

Rubbing her arms, weaponry to ward off the chill, she tried to remind herself that she was no longer that kid who was afraid of the dark. No longer afraid of falling or fast vehicles or being alone.

She'd been conquering her fears one at a time over the years. Perhaps it was time to conquer this last monster in her mind.

"Sugar and Maple have to go with us," she said.

"Of course."

"But I'm not sure that we'll go far." Instead of leading the way, her dogs attached themselves firmly to her heels as she stepped into the hallway.

Logan grinned. "We can just walk until we see the ghosts."

She ran her hand over the peeling wallpaper, between several clocks on the wall, wishing she'd brought her flashlight from the boat. "I don't believe in ghosts."

They crossed through a mudroom with wooden pegs on the walls, the sunlight marking a path through the clock-adorned walls, dust instead of dirt covering the wooden floor. Almost a hundred years ago, servants would have bustled through here to the kitchen gardens and to care for the birds in the aviary. They would have prepared meals and polished silver and stored the china when the Pendleton family returned to New York.

The house must have looked pristine during the Gilded Age, but what had been happening among its people?

She and Logan moved into the sunlight that streamed through the kitchen's leaded glass windows. With only an hour of daylight left, they couldn't linger. She didn't have any problem taking the boat back over to Clayton in the dark, but they'd need every ray of light to retrace their path through the tunnel.

The longer they walked, the more pronounced Logan's limp became. He might have overwhelmed her a bit in his tenacity to contact her, but he'd proven himself to be kind to Emma in the shop and gracious to her today. So much for the pompous stereotype she'd concocted in her mind.

"Are you doing okay?" she asked.

"I'm in my element." He stopped, glancing back at her. "How are you?"

Her nose twitched. "It smells like a dumpster in here."

"Probably not what the Pendletons envisioned for their castle."

"Sometimes life doesn't go the way we envision, I guess."

"But when it doesn't, we can keep pressing in a new direction," he said, "for as many days as God gifts us on this earth."

She let his words sink in even as she pondered the days and gifts of God. She'd spent much of her life trying to keep her grandfather's legacy alive on this island and through the candy shop. And she wondered again if God had something else in store for her.

His neck arched back, Logan stared at a crack in the plaster ceiling. "I wonder where Mrs. Pendleton went after her family was gone."

"I've never heard anyone talk about her after she left the island."

Ahead of them was a butler's pantry with electric lights dangling from the ceiling and a long built-in hutch with columns of dinner plates and saucers and cups. When she opened a heavy drawer, she realized it still contained silverware with the letter *P* engraved on each piece.

"Those must be worth a fortune," he said.

She carefully pushed the drawer back in and looked at the clock on the wall. The hands had stopped at 5:56. "The whole place is like a time capsule."

He eyed her curiously as if her inch of imagination were a mile. "I hope so."

They moved into the dining room with its walnut panels and long dust-coated table surrounded by more than twenty upholstered chairs. Grime clouded all the windows. "Perhaps you can find something with the clarity of hindsight."

"I'm a bit of an expert on hindsight," he said before turning toward an archway.

Outside the dining room, an enormous marble-floored hall climbed four stories. A grand piano melded into one corner of the entry, the worn walls filled with artwork and dozens of clocks. She could imagine them calling out their cadence decades ago, a steady march of ticks and tocks in their rhythm of time.

For a glimpse of a moment, it felt like she'd actually been here before.

She hadn't wanted Logan to unearth this story. Hadn't wanted the publicity or to confront the past. But now the ghosts in Poppy's life seemed to be intersecting with her life and Emma's as well.

A grand staircase was the centerpiece of this elegant hall, its carpet dusted with plaster from the ceiling. A dozen doorways circled the staircase, leading into different rooms, and each floor above was caged with railings.

The Pendleton family probably thought they would spend dozens of summers at this castle before passing it along to their children and grandchildren to continue their legacy, like Nana and Grandpa Cade had done with the cottage. Mr. and Mrs. Pendleton would have hired the best stonemasons to build a structure to withstand the storms.

It would take more than her and Logan puttering through, she prayed, to bring down the roof.

Her dogs sniffed the wainscotting along the perimeter, their tails wagging. They could probably smell life teeming inside the old walls.

Chloe turned back to the staircase and flushed when she realized Logan was watching her.

"What is it?" she asked.

He stuck his hands in his pockets. "I'm still wondering what you aren't telling me."

"I wish my grandparents had talked more about the Pendletons." She brushed her hands back over her hair. "But it was almost like they wanted me to forget the family ever lived here. Like my grandpa was afraid . . ."

She'd said too much. These were her doubts, her own fears talking. Her grandparents were the strongest people she'd ever known.

His smile flatlined, his green eyes pooled with concern. "What are you afraid of?"

And her heart seemed to fold, pressing against her ribs. It felt as if Logan had lifted her out of a soapy bucket of emotion and was trying to wring her dry. "I don't want to discuss my fears, Logan."

"Fair enough," he said. "Was your nana afraid of the Pendleton family too?"

She turned swiftly from him and his questions to circle this great room, looking at the dramatic paintings of waterfalls and thunderstorms and a placid one of sheep surrounding a shepherd's hut.

This was the kind of digging that she'd feared most. The kind that set her mind to wondering again. Her grandma had told her plenty of stories about her family in the old country. The past, in Nana's mind, was something to be celebrated, but still Nana was afraid of the Pendleton story as well. Or of this castle, at least. And Chloe didn't understand.

She stopped at the next painting, this one a solemn portrait of Mr. Pendleton with his perfectly combed mustache and eyes that spoke more of authority than kindness and Mrs. Pendleton with her dark curls dangling over her ears, a pearl necklace resting across her thin neck and the collar of a lavender-and-white gown.

Poppy sat between them, equally as stoic in posture, but the artist had captured the hint of a smile, perfectly framed between a cascade of blonde curls.

Chloe wasn't angry at her grandparents for withholding the story of the Pendletons. Just confused. They'd been nothing except loving and kind to her, providing money and the education for her to succeed, rescuing her after her father—

A glimpse of his face emerged again from the shadows of her mind, like someone had swept away ashes from a relic abandoned in a fire. He had a scraggly beard and hollow cheeks, a cigarette dangling like a fishing lure at the corner of his mouth, greasy hair that fell to his shoulders.

She'd seen only a few pictures of him as a child, taken with Grandpa Cade on the river, and then one photo of her parents together. They'd never married, Nana told her, living apart for most of Chloe's life. But they'd gotten back together in the late sixties, just in time for Woodstock. Her mother had died instantly in the same wreck that took her father's life.

It was a miracle that the child sleeping in the back of the van, buried under blankets, had survived.

So many details eluded Chloe's memory. The accident. Talking to the police. Traveling to Clayton. Until she remembered walking with her father along the cliff, her life had seemed to begin at the age of six when she joined her grandparents on Koster Isle.

"Chloe?" Logan called, and she turned toward the stairs. "We don't have much time left before it gets dark."

Light slowly receded down the hallway. "We should head back to the boat."

"Can we climb up to the tower first?" When Logan nudged the banister, it rolled gently but held tight to its stakes. "Take a few pictures of the nursery?"

"If you hurry."

"Will you go with me?" he asked.

"No more questions about my family." He had to respect that or this was the end of their journey.

He studied her for a moment, then gave a brisk nod. "Okay."

She commanded her dogs to stay at the bottom of the staircase, and while they whined about her instruction, they obeyed.

Logan snapped photographs as they climbed, and when they stopped on the third floor, she watched him scan the hallway as if he could see Poppy.

"You're thinking through that night in your head, aren't you?"

"I'm imagining the possibilities."

"What do you see?" she asked.

He took another picture and then lowered his camera. "Someone Poppy loved, leading her out of the house while everyone else was distracted."

"You think Mr. or Mrs. Pendleton kidnapped her?"

"When a society woman, poised to inherit a sizeable amount of money, loses both her husband and her heir in one night, a lot of questions should be asked."

"I'm sure the police asked them."

"But they never uncovered the truth."

"I hope you find resolution to this, Logan, but I suspect the scheme won't be as grand as the one you've concocted in your head."

He ran his hand over the railing as he scanned the hall below. "Poppy couldn't have gone far on her own."

Chloe blinked, wishing she could pull the memories from her own childhood out of her head. What had she been doing when she was Poppy's age? Somehow she had survived what had become a dangerous situation, but she didn't know how. "Kids can be quite resourceful."

"I know," Logan said. "But if Poppy wandered from the nursery by herself, in a house filled with people, someone must have seen her."

*Not if she went through the walls.*

Chloe blinked again, wondering at her thought. Where had that come from?

Instead of revealing answers, her mind was taunting her again. Hinting at the past but refusing to color in the details. If only she could remember . . .

She refocused on Logan's hypothesis. If Mrs. Pendleton had killed her husband and escorted Poppy from the nursery, where had she taken her? Perhaps there had been an accident, like what happened to Chloe when she was a girl. Perhaps Mrs. Pendleton couldn't recover her daughter.

She shook her head, not wanting to entertain any similarities in their stories. They were two very different people, separated by a generation. Two kids lost and only one of them found. And now with Emma—

She wasn't certain whether Emma was lost or found.

"Chloe?"

She spun toward him, forgetting for a moment where she was. "Sorry."

"I found the steps to the tower."

Spiral stairs wound up to the crown of the castle, a time capsule with the most exquisite panorama on the circular wall, an artistic masterpiece in a thousand colors. Birds nested in a jungle of painted leaves, some of them perched on branches, others with their wings wide as if they were about to soar through the gallery of windows on the far side.

Chloe's head tilted back as her gaze swept across the ceiling, the air smelling like mildew. The vast blue made it look as if the tower had no roof, as if the painter wanted the children who played here to imagine a world with no bounds. A world where they could fly with the birds.

"Amazing," she whispered.

As the word escaped her lips, she had the strangest sense again, like she'd had in the great hall, that she'd been here before.

Long shadows crossed over two beds, one near the door and the other closer to a window, the floral bedcoverings neatly made. Between the beds stood an armoire and a carved chest that she didn't dare open for fear the room would be overrun by a swarm of critters who'd nested inside.

But Logan slipped out a dresser drawer and rummaged through the contents. "Look at these."

Colorful cards had been stacked inside, each one displaying illustrations of a mother snuggling with a toddler in a long nightgown, the girl's hair a tousle of blonde curls. *Poppy's Tip-Top Tonic* had been printed beside each picture in a blue and yellow ink that faded with time, a different phrase on every card advertising the syrup.

*Soothe your baby to sleep.*

*Cures every ache and pain.*

*Safe and gentle for all ages.*

*The tastiest tonic for the fussiest of kids.*

*Healthy baby. Happy mom.*

"I bet it was tasty," Logan said, staring at the illustrated mother watching over her child in bed, a picture book on the bedcover, a blue bottle and silver spoon in her hands. "And it would have put any child right to sleep. No one knows how many babies died from opium overdose back then."

She breathed deep, inhaling too much of the moldy air. How sad that something seemingly good at first, medicine for parents to help their children, could go awry.

He stared at the trading card. "Do you think that is a portrait of the actual Poppy?"

She picked up another card, one of a woman in an apron, smiling as she gazed down at a happy toddler. The girl with wide eyes and blonde hair looked very similar to the portrait downstairs. "I believe it is."

"The Pendletons seemed to make a fortune on their syrup," he said as he slipped the cards back into the drawer.

"Enough to build a castle."

A shuffle nearby and the noise shot a bolt up Chloe's spine. It was just a mouse, she told herself. Or maybe a bird. Alive, not one flying on the walls.

But the shadows crept across the goose bumps on her arms and climbed her neck, into the clefts of her memory, fighting for control.

"Chloe?"

She walked toward the fading light at the window, leaving Logan behind in a hazy cloud.

*Poppy*, another voice said, calling to her from the glass.

"Daddy?"

"Yes, Poppy."

She hadn't understood why he'd laughed, but she had laughed with him. "I'm not a poppy."

He cranked open one of the windows and leaned outside, so far that she thought he might fall, like he'd pretended to do when he'd leaned over the cliffs.

"Come with me." He held out his hand. "We can fly."

"I don't want to fly."

"C'mon, Poppy."

"Chloe," she said, confused. Why wouldn't he call her the right name? It wasn't funny anymore.

All above her were birds. On the ceiling and the walls. Birds fluttering in her chest and her mind. Pounding in her head.

Turning from the windows, she knew she had to run.

Daddy grabbed her arm and tried to force her to the window, but she struggled against him.

"I can't fly," she cried.

"Yes, you can. We can fly together."

She was only five, but she knew the truth. Daddy was lying to her.

"I can't fly," she said again, a whisper now.

"Leave her alone, Philip." Nana stood in the doorway. Nana's face but a voice Chloe didn't recognize. Her grandmother yelled at Philip until he climbed back into the window and left the room. Then she'd held Chloe until her tears dried.

Nana, her angel, had rescued her.

Chloe stepped back from the windows and collapsed on the narrow bed, trying to mop up the dark stains from the shadows.

*Nothing good ever happened in this castle.*

That's what Nana had said before she carried Chloe down the stairs.

Lips moving, Chloe prayed tonight for peace in her heart. For calm in her mind. Like Nana used to do when she was afraid.

A shuffle next to her, but this time Chloe realized it wasn't an animal. Logan was searching her face like he was trying to find the answer to his mystery there.

"What's going on?" he asked quietly as if afraid he might frighten her.

"I'm not sure."

"It's getting dark," he said, and she could see the pink hues of sky through the window, a hint of fire on the sharpest of blues. "I'm afraid I can't carry you down those steps."

"I know," she said, her voice as wobbly as her knees.

"But I can walk beside you. Help you if you need it."

She wanted to tell him *no*; she didn't need it. That she could walk down those steps alone. But it simply wasn't true.

He took her arm, and she slowly began to stand, her mind as crippled as his leg.

"What did you see, Chloe?" he asked.

She looked up at the birds, over at the windows, and knew now the castle was indeed haunted.

"Ghosts," she whispered.

23

# *AMELIA*

The St. Lawrence froze during the winter of 1912, temperatures from an arctic blast creating pillars of ice where water once flowed. As snow mounded outside the castle's door, a pressure crack began chiseling away the ice around Amelia's heart. It expanded inside her with every fire that Cade built in the sitting room, every book he read to her in the late hours, every treat he baked for them in the empty kitchen.

The birds were her companions most mornings while Cade fixed all the broken pieces around the castle. And in the afternoon hours, she learned to cook, her hands busy preparing the foods stored in the icehouse or what Cade hunted or fetched when he was able to cross into Clayton.

As the months passed, Cade Ridell split her frozen heart open like the icebreaker each spring that cleared the river channel, a brackish surge of grief and happiness pouring out in a flood. She no longer wanted to return to England. Didn't even want to visit her new brownstone in Manhattan.

Instead of a place of exile, Koster Isle had become home.

In those winter months, Amelia smothered any signal of danger. The nights she and Cade spent near the fire, pretending they were husband and wife, was a mockery of the institution—she knew that—but her marriage to Leslie had been a mockery of the institution as well. After this long season of loneliness, love was what she wanted.

No one would take it from her.

A meager staff of six returned to Koster Isle in May to restore order to the house, opening doors that had been closed for months, properly tending to the kitchen and lawn. Upon their arrival, Cade promptly returned to his cottage on the other side of trees.

There were plenty of whispers in the corridors, speculation about the winter months. Amelia could hear the servants talk, but she didn't care. For the first time in many years, she wanted to live. As long as she could be with Cade.

She filled her spring with stitching and gardening, not caring what anyone, including Fiona, thought when she dug in the dirt alone. She stayed near the path where she might catch a glimpse, exchange a word even, with the man who'd stolen her heart. Twice a week, he took her and Fiona into Clayton—on Sundays to attend Mass, on Fridays to the sewing bee. She no longer cared about such things as propriety, but Cade refused to escort her anywhere alone.

A dozen ladies made summer clothes for the orphans at the Ogdensburg City Hospital and Orphan Asylum, founded by the Grey Nuns of the Cross, and they stitched baby clothing for the maternity home built beside the orphanage, a quiet place for women from brothels or other unfortunate situations to birth their babies. Once a month, an envoy from the church took a fifty-mile train ride upriver to deliver the clothing.

A new idea began brewing inside Amelia as she sewed a baby's gown. While she had no desire to host another party for the elite of New York, what if she brought the orphans from Ogdensburg to Koster Isle? The children could spend the night in the castle's lower rooms, feast on the ices that she and the cook prepared, wade in the lagoon near Cade's cottage. They could play croquet in the garden and, maybe, the quiet ones could visit her birds.

Penelope wasn't coming home, Amelia was sure of it now, but she would like to entertain these children.

"We must alter some of your clothing," Fiona said near the end of August as she struggled to secure the buttons on Amelia's dress.

Amelia brushed her hand across the swelling in her abdomen. "I ate too much over the winter."

"Indeed."

"Chocolate soufflé and such."

Fiona mumbled something, but Amelia didn't press her. The woman sometimes said things that Amelia didn't want to hear.

She glanced at herself in the vanity mirror and saw the red in her cheeks, flushed from her neglect in wearing a hat when she gardened. She'd thought the rise in her stomach was from the extra cream sauces, the fresh meat and sweet desserts she indulged in now that her appetite had returned, but then her body had begun to change in other ways. Like it was preparing for an uninvited guest.

"Call for a seamstress in the morning."

Amelia hadn't believed it possible to grow a baby in her womb, after all those barren years between her and Leslie. She'd thought her body had stopped them from having children.

Yet now she had life growing in her; she could no longer deny it. While she could commission new dresses, repaint the nursery, sequester herself once she could no longer contain this secret, what was she to do with a child born of her and her caretaker?

When the seamstress arrived, Amelia was surprised to see her former maid walk into her dressing room. Instead of speaking, Rose eyed Amelia's swollen stomach under her shift. "I see that you have been occupied."

"I need a new wardrobe," Amelia said, a winter blast chilling her words. "Not a judge or jury."

"And I need the work."

"I will pay you well for the clothing."

Rose unrolled her tape measure and began to make notes on a pad.

"Cade's the father, isn't he?" Rose asked as she measured Amelia's waistline. But she wouldn't discuss what happened during the winter months, especially not with the woman who she suspected had been carrying on her own affair years ago.

"I'll pay you for the clothing and your silence."

"I never slept with your husband," Rose said as she inched around her.

"It doesn't matter now."

"I was only trying to keep my job."

"I'm sorry that it ended so poorly." If she could turn back time, she would never have left Poppy in the nursery. Never would have argued with Leslie. Never would have slapped the woman who stood beside her now.

"Have you told Cade about the baby?" Rose asked as she wound the measuring tape.

"It's too soon."

"I fear it might be too late."

"He's a good man," Amelia said, her mind wandering back to the nights in his arms, his kiss on her lips.

"Aye," Rose replied. "You must tell him. He will do the right thing."

But Amelia didn't want Cade to simply do what was right. She wanted him to love her like he'd done over the winter. No obligations. When he simply wanted to be with her alone.

"Don't speak of this to anyone," she warned as she paid Rose for her new wardrobe.

In all their time together, Cade had never spoken of marriage, and she secretly feared that the thought of it would ruin everything between them. But she and Cade were meant to be together. Soon they would be a family of three.

She smoothed her hand over her gown and wondered about their future. While she hadn't minded the winter on the island, the cold days spent inside by the fire or exploring together on the snowshoes that Cade wove, the snowy months would be different with a child. Cade would have to move to the city with her, and she'd hire someone else to care for the castle and birds until they returned in the spring.

Once they married, Cade would never have to work again.

By September, the staff was all aflutter as they readied the castle for the Ogdensburg orphans. They'd prepared a buffet of food and installed thirty cots for the children and accompanying nuns, but all Amelia could think about was the child growing inside her.

She told Fiona she was going to the aviary for the afternoon, and as she walked along the path, she imagined the pleasure on Cade's face at her proposal. She didn't care what anyone else thought. From now on, they could be together.

"Hello," she said quietly like a shy schoolgirl when she found him in the chapel, hammering a nail into the wall. "Have you been avoiding me?"

"Amelia—" He stumbled over the word. "I have to stay away from you."

"What do you mean?" she asked, folding her hands over the billowy chiffon in her new skirt.

"I—you don't want them to know about us."

Her chest fell, and she struggled to catch a breath. "You're ashamed of me?"

"Not of you." He brushed his grease-smeared forearm over a drop of sweat that pooled on his forehead. The look on his face was not one of pleasure. It was one of distress as the seconds passed between them. And she hadn't even told him about the baby. "I am only ashamed at what I have done."

"Loved me?"

"No," he said. "I would never be ashamed of that. Only what I have taken from you."

"You have cared for me, Cade, like no one else ever has."

He pounded the nail again as if he could pound away her words.

"I don't want to spend my winters alone anymore." Couldn't he see? She needed him more than anything else in this world. More than her birds or the Pendleton money or any care from society.

"We'd have to marry," he said.

She bristled at his tone. "You don't want to marry me?"

"It's not that."

"What is it?" she begged.

"The newspapers, Amelia—can you imagine? We'd be the sport of society. And it would be the death of you."

"I was already dead," she said. "And you brought me back to life."

He took her in his arms then. Engulfed her in his strength. "You are my greatest weakness."

"It's not weak to love."

"You would tire of the North Country," he said as he stepped away. "The winters will grow longer as the years go by."

How she wished for the return of his smile that washed away any fear. How she wished they could slip unnoticed into the house and right their world again.

"We'll go someplace else," she said. "A much smaller home so you don't have to work."

"I want to work."

Her shoulders crept forward, the burden heavy. "You love your work, I fear, more than you love me."

"We would never last, Amelia," he said slowly as if it ached to speak. "Not for the long haul."

The room swirled as she struggled to hold her bearing. What was wrong with her? Leslie wouldn't stay faithful and now Cade didn't want her either. Another man, approved by society, might marry her for her income, like Leslie had done for the lingering whiffs of British prestige. But even if she could buy a father for her child, she didn't want to marry anyone except Cade.

If only she could turn back all the clocks in the house. Return them to April when she and Cade had been happy.

"It was a facade," she whispered. Perhaps like her bird that escaped from his cage, she needed to set him free, but she didn't think she could bear to see him go.

"Not a facade, Amelia." The familiar smile crept back on his face when he looked down on her, his brown eyes warm. "I loved you with all my heart."

*Loved*—the word echoed between her ears.

"But you won't marry me."

"It would ruin you," he said.

Not that she cared any longer about her social standing. She was already ruined.

Her mind spun, not knowing what to do. She'd thrived in Cade's gentle care over the winter, and she desperately craved his love now. But she wouldn't beg, wouldn't force him to marry her, not out of obligation.

There must be another way.

"I will always love you," she said, her hand cradling the life that she held.

A servant called for Cade outside, and he stepped quickly through the door, leaving her and their baby alone.

# 24
# CHLOE

The blast startled Chloe from her sleep as if a steamer were about to crash through her bedroom window. But it was only a foghorn, echoing across the dark river, far beyond the trees. One blast meant a ship wanted to pass on the starboard side of another, two blasts for the port.

It was part warning, part invitation for captains to work together to keep their ships afloat and on course through the fog. Every dance was with a different partner but the steps were still the same. As long as the captains followed the rules of the river, the passengers and cargo stayed safe.

With her window cracked open, she held her breath as she listened for the echo of a horn. The signal that the other ship heard and all would be well. That they could pass each other safely in the night.

She smoothed her hands over the blanket as she waited. While she'd never heard the crunch of one ship biting into another, it happened occasionally, even in good weather. Plenty of boats, captained by competent men, littered the depths of the St. Lawrence.

The return horn billowed across the channel, and Chloe breathed deep of the pine-scented air. Now both ships and the surrounding islands knew—the captains were alert and prepared to share the breadth of river.

So much had changed in their world and yet some things on the river never changed. Her grandparents would have heard the ships' horns, and Poppy would have heard them too. It was these familiar rituals that bound all the islanders together, both past and present. Rituals just as reliable today as they had been decades ago.

She scooted up in bed, but she couldn't see behind the trees. On a clear night, the lantern on Rock Island swept light across the river, a beacon for boats to gain their bearings and illuminate any obstacles in their path, but tonight the fog obscured the beacon.

As the warning sound faded, Chloe closed her eyes. The ships were probably passing each other now. In seconds, they would be on their separate ways. Lakers and salties were what locals called these great cargo vessels. One traveling to Lake Ontario. The other to the Atlantic.

Her hand hanging over the side of the bed, Chloe scratched Maple behind the ears. While the lighthouse offered a measure of comfort on a clear night, fog like this hid the dangers, blinding the captain and crew from the obstacles around them. Erasing the sight of any danger in their way.

It was all an illusion, of course. The fog only offered a blanket of protection, like the one draped over her as she tried to sleep. The moment a ship hit another boat or ran aground, the illusion disappeared.

That's what the fog in her mind had done for her. The thin blanket had protected her for many years, kept her from remembering what her father tried to do. Just yesterday, she hadn't remembered why the castle had frightened her, and now, she would never forget. Would her father really have jumped with her? Perhaps, in a drug-induced fog, he was trying to play the hero and rescue her. Or Poppy.

But that was crazy.

No wonder Nana didn't want her to return to the castle. The memory of what almost happened, the danger, probably haunted her for the rest of her life.

Until yesterday, Chloe hadn't remembered being with her father in the castle, and in the hours after she'd taken Logan back to Clayton and brought Emma home, she'd tried to remember more. Those were the lost years of her life, like the lost villages where Nana had lived on the river. Water had covered her memories over time, and she was struggling to make out the pieces from the surface.

Perhaps it was finally time for her to dive deeper and excavate this shipwreck inside her.

Chloe shivered under the covers. She'd been five when her father brought her to the castle, around Poppy's age when she disappeared. And he'd been obsessed with finding Poppy; she remembered that now.

He must have rented a boat in Clayton or maybe he'd borrowed one from a friend. She'd been scared to ride with him across the river—she remembered that as well—afraid they would overturn in the waves. In hindsight, it was a miracle they'd made it to the island without capsizing.

She didn't remember what happened after Nana had shouted at her son in the tower, but he probably took Chloe away again. She didn't remember being back on the island until she returned to live with her grandparents for good.

Nana must have been so worried for her only grandchild in those years even as she mourned the loss of her son to the drugs that, in turn, stole his mind and any affection for those who loved him.

Why had her father been obsessed with Poppy's story? He'd been out of control that night in the nursery, his mind strung out. She, on the other hand, was trying to process it all at once in these early morning hours.

Logan had apologized repeatedly as he'd coached her down the steps and then steered the boat back to Clayton. But it wasn't his fault. The memories would have returned eventually, and this time, she was glad she wasn't alone. She never would have made it down those steps without his help.

The ships would have passed by now, gone their separate ways to the lake and ocean. She listened for a moment to the quietness in her house. Emma, it seemed, was still asleep along with the kitten and dogs. All was well at the moment in her little cottage.

How she missed her grandparents on peaceful mornings like this. Grandpa Cade's laughter that enveloped all those around him. Nana's kindness in pouring mugs of cocoa and blessing upon blessing with her words.

But there'd been brokenness beneath the laughter and blessings and Cade's famous candies. Sadness over the loss of their son.

No one knew what went on sometimes in families. The good and the bad. No one could possibly understand except those who had lived through it.

Logan had questioned her desire to keep the Ridell legacy alive, but she owed her life to her grandparents in more ways than one. For the life of her father first and then for rescuing her from him.

She owed them everything.

Her hand swept across Maple's silky fur, and she snuggled back against her pillow. Through the veil of fog, she saw a faint orange light sweep through the trees, blinking back at her. *Watch me*, the lighthouse seemed to whisper when it flashed its warning. *Fix your eyes on me, and I'll keep you away from the shoals.*

Hours later, she woke to the smell of Nana's hot cocoa, and Emma beside her, sliding a bright pink mug, one with kitten eyes and whiskers, onto the nightstand.

"You were making funny noises in your sleep."

She cringed, afraid of what she might have said. "I had weird dreams."

"I'll say."

Chloe took a long sip of the creamy, warm drink. "Thanks for the cocoa."

Emma smiled. "It makes things better."

"It really does." Any drink made and delivered by someone who cared patched up a world of wounds. "Jenna invited you over for lunch today on the farm."

The smile flooded her face. "I'll go!"

Emma and Jenna had become fast friends. Emma loved to visit the playground that stood empty all summer, waiting for the autumn rush. She petted goats and fed the chickens and sometimes rode the pony in Jenna's stable. Jenna and her husband had renovated their farm so they could welcome families each fall with a pumpkin patch and hayrides even as they dreamed of having their own children one day to enjoy the swings and slides.

"Will you come to the farm?" Emma asked.

"Not today," she said. "I have to take care of the shop, but by the end of next week, we'll have more people working. I can get away then."

A crisp sky, layered like ice above the water, welcomed the morning as their boat rounded the granite skirt on Picton Island and crossed the open channel to Clayton. When they walked into the store, Jenna waved at them as she answered the ringing phone.

"Chloe's right here," Jenna said before planting the cordless phone on her hip. "It's that cute newsboy."

"Give that to me." Chloe snatched the phone away from her and moved toward the office door, Jenna's laughter echoing behind her. "Hi, Logan."

"Is Jenna laughing at me?"

She glanced back. "Jenna mainly laughs at herself. She thinks she's hilarious."

Logan cleared his throat. "What time should I be there tomorrow?"

She'd volunteered to take Logan over to Grindstone Island on Friday to meet Joe Lindley and look through the man's vault of local history, but after what happened to her at the castle—and now that he'd seen the tower—she figured he would drop both her and her stonewalling to interview any remaining sources on his own.

She closed the door behind her. "You still want me to take you to Joe's?"

"Why wouldn't I?"

She could think of multiple reasons, most of them involving instability on her part, but she didn't want to rehash the disaster at the castle with him. "How about one o'clock?"

"Perfect."

She glanced back at the glass window on the door. Jenna stood on the other side, a silly smile on her face. What was this, third grade? "Bring a pair of wellies if you have them."

"I have no idea what a wellie is."

"Mud boots."

"Where exactly does Mr. Lindley live?" he asked.

"You'll see."

Jenna was still grinning when Chloe returned the telephone to its base.

"Stop it."

"Why?" Jenna brushed crumbs off the counter. "Just talking to that newsboy makes you glow."

"Logan isn't a newsboy. He's a full-fledged reporter."

"I hope he tells your family's story."

"Not my story," Chloe said. "The Pendletons'."

"I'm pretty sure the two are one." Jenna lit the Open sign. "Are you going to the credit union today?"

Chloe's stomach rolled. "Maybe."

"You have to finalize the estate soon."

"I know."

Jenna hugged her. "It's hard."

"Very."

Seconds later, the door chimed, and with each chime came a steady stream of customers who left with bags of sweets and smiles on their faces, just like they would have fifteen years ago when her grandparents ran this place together. Chloe didn't know how much longer the shop could stay open, but she was determined to make each day a happy one for every guest who walked through their doors.

Emma helped fill a stack of tackle boxes before heading out to the farm with Jenna. While she'd become streetwise long before most children, it was good for her to enjoy a few hours as simply a kid.

Chloe steamed a small pitcher of milk until it doubled and then poured it over two shots of espresso to fuel herself after a short night of sleep.

The door chimed again, and Chloe glanced downward like she always did to greet the children first and then their parents. But no child accompanied the man in a dark-green uniform.

Her gaze quickly rose to the yellow patch identifying this man as an agent with the US Border Patrol.

She'd never had a customs officer visit the store and her mind rapidly paced through all the things that she might have done wrong but came up empty. While Clayton was near the border, her shop was firmly in Gavin's jurisdiction.

She reached for a metal scoop and dug into a canister of spiced gumdrops. "How can I help you?"

The agent brushed one hand over his dark, trimmed hair and then slipped off his sunglasses, dropping them inside his front pocket. But he didn't take his eyes off her. "I'm looking for a missing child."

The scoop tipped in her hand, all the candies sliding back into the bin. "A missing child?"

She dropped the scoop on the counter and hid her twitchy hands in the folds of her sweater.

"A girl," he said as the metal clanged against wood. "Name of Emma."

Chloe didn't say anything, stunned. Why was a border agent searching for her?

It didn't feel right, and Nana always said when in doubt, go with your gut.

The man pulled a photograph out of his other pocket and inched the picture across the counter. It was a snapshot of her Emma with the river in the background, any smile erased from her face.

"I'm sorry to hear this." She'd speak with Gavin before she'd give any information to this man, no matter what sort of patch he wore on his sleeve.

"We have to find her," the man said. "She could be in danger."

Chloe blinked at the intensity of his stare. "Danger of what?"

"I'm afraid I can't say." He glanced around the shop as if just now seeing candy-filled shelves. "But I thought she might have stopped by for something sweet."

"I'll keep my eyes open," she said. "Do you have some sort of flyer that I can hang on the door?"

"I'm afraid this is a private investigation."

"I see."

"I'll give you my number." He slid Emma's picture back into his pocket. "Please call me if she shows up."

Chloe picked up a pen and scratched his phone number across her message pad. "I'm sorry, I didn't catch your name."

"Mitch," he said. "Agent Mitch Yancey."

She picked up the scoop instead of shaking his offered hand.

Then, seconds after he left, she bypassed the credit union and went straight to the police.

25

# *BIRDIE*

MARCH 1914

Mummy said she was done with boats. They'd found a new man to take care of them, much older than the others. He smelled like caribou instead of cologne, and his hair was an oily gray, his stomach bulging like a robin's breast. This man lived alone in the woods, not far from the river, trapping creatures from the forest for fur and food.

Once spring began thawing the ice, Birdie rushed out each morning to watch the cormorants playing hide-and-seek in the river, the osprey gliding overhead. How she wished the St. Lawrence would take her far away from here.

Sometimes, she would lean her head against a rock and dream about the castle in her mind. A tower where she could hide. Mummy sometimes whispered about taking her back to the castles in England. When she asked if they had birds in England, Mummy just laughed. Olivia was the only other person who had cared about birds.

But Olivia was gone now, taking most of Birdie's books and all the joy with her. Mummy said that Olivia didn't love them anymore, but Birdie knew the truth. More than a year ago, after the strangers inquired about Poppy, Olivia's husband had returned to the houseboat. Pierre had been whistling on the front deck, fixing a railing that she'd watched Mummy loosen.

Birdie was inside the upper lounge, huddled on the settee with one of her books, the door open as she waited for Olivia to come back from town. Pierre hadn't seen her and neither had Mummy.

Her mother hadn't yelled at Pierre that morning, but she'd been plenty angry. It was the quiet that Birdie feared most.

"Did you get your money?" Mummy asked calmly, looking down as he leaned away from the boat, hammering the rail.

"What do you mean?" he'd stuttered in return.

Mummy didn't move. "The money for Poppy."

He tossed his hammer back on deck, pulling himself toward the platform. "She is Poppy, isn't she?"

Mummy blocked him. "Where is the money?"

"They wouldn't pay me a cent."

"What did you tell them?"

"The truth." His fingers curled around the broken wood. "Someone had to."

"You imbecile."

He didn't speak again and neither did Mummy. Instead, she grabbed the hammer and pounded Pierre Gagné like he was a nail.

Birdie had dropped the book in her lap, horrified as Pierre tipped backward. His scream—a terrible, awful noise—and then a splash. Birdie couldn't get either sound out of her head.

Mummy turned from the balcony, her heels ticking like a clock. Then her gaze had swept across the windows, pausing on Birdie in the sitting room. A warning in her stare.

After she left, Birdie leapt from her seat and rushed to the railing, searching the water as if she might be able to rescue Pierre. Then she'd thrown over a rope ladder in hopes that he could still cling to it, but the river had swallowed him. And she'd wished the water would swallow her too.

Instead of jumping, she hid in her room and then she wept for hiding, ashamed like the Cowardly Lion in *The Wonderful Wizard of Oz.* If only she could breathe of the poppies like Dorothy, fall asleep in the meadow, escape with the birds in her dreams. The flowers could be deadly, she knew—they almost killed the Lion—but the Scarecrow and Tin Woodman carried Dorothy and Toto to the river shore.

If only she had someone to carry her too.

She never knew what happened to Olivia. The skiff that she'd taken into town had been retied to the houseboat after Pierre died, and Mummy rowed Birdie to shore for the last time.

Tonight she warmed her hands over the stove and then picked up a towel to dry the tin dinner plates and cast-iron pan. The man's shack didn't have electricity nor did it have an indoor toilet or running water. She didn't mind the outhouse most months—she preferred being outside—but the winter had been bitter cold. Her hands and feet had grown numb when the snow and ice arrived, and it burned to thaw them whenever she returned to the shack.

How she longed for her woolen blanket from the houseboat. Her books. Her birds.

Her one real friend.

She blinked back tears before Mummy saw them. More than anything else, her mother hated tears.

For weeks after Pierre drowned, Mummy was nice to her. She would read like Olivia had once done. Tell her stories about England and the elegant steamer that had transported them across the Atlantic. Birdie couldn't remember traveling on the steamer, but Mummy said she was much too young for those kinds of memories.

How she would love to sail away on a steamer now.

Sometimes Mummy was still nice, but not on the days when she and the man drank moonshine from muddied bottles. He brewed his own whiskey in a still, built right next to a pile of bones from moose and wolves and salmon. And all sorts of vermin. They'd drink and then Mummy and the man would make fun of Birdie's short dresses and her curly hair that was ratty enough for birds to nest inside. Once the man asked if he could nest there too.

The man had come after her then, laughing as he chased her out the door. Birdie had spent that night wandering in the icy forest, taking comfort in the stars and the call of the birds come morning. After hours of wandering, her stomach had growled like a bear. When she found her way back, the man and Mummy were still asleep, but the next day Mummy cut Birdie's hair, saying the men in England wouldn't care about her now.

Birdie was more worried about the men in Canada.

It was too cold for her to go outside this evening. The three of them were in the main room, Birdie stacking the dry dishes after their meal, Mummy and the man drinking their moonshine. Soon, Mummy and the man would go into their room while Birdie pulled her straw mattress under the table, a place that she could escape on any side.

Mummy was angry at the man tonight, telling him to mind his own business, and Birdie wondered if Mummy was going to hammer him too. She wouldn't have minded if Mummy got rid of the caribou.

His gaze slithered like a rattlesnake toward Birdie, watching her like she was a slab of bacon straight off the griddle. "It's time."

"Not yet."

The man groaned at Mummy, the sound working its way into a growl, and Birdie eyed the door on the other side of him. If she tried to escape . . . how fast could he run tonight?

"Why do you protect her?" He was talking to Mummy, but his dark eyes had locked on Birdie.

Mummy stood up, a barricade between them. "She's my daughter!"

"And it's time she earn her keep." The man slammed something on the table. "I'm tired of paying for you both."

"You're barely paying for me," Mummy spat. "We're used to luxury, not this squalor. I'm worth a whole lot more on my own."

"Worthless, more like. You're the only one around here who thinks you're royalty. Like you're raising some sort of princess. She needs to do more than the dishes."

"In due time." Mummy took another sip as if the battle was already won. "She's not yet twelve."

"Eleven is plenty old."

"I'll find her a husband then. A rich one. Certainly not an old fool like you."

*A husband.* Birdie's stomach twisted. The only husband she knew belonged to Olivia, and Pierre was already gone.

"We're taking a ship back to England," Mummy said.

The man's laughter echoed around the room. "How are you going to get money for that?"

"I'll find a way."

"You'll need at least a hundred dollars just to make it to Liverpool."

"We'll leave here this spring." Mummy scanned the forest outside their lone window. "There's money to be had in Montreal."

"Good riddance," he said. "You'll find plenty of men willing to part with their cash for a favor or two."

"Except you."

The man stood and took a clumsy step forward. "You leave the girl with me, and I'll buy you a ticket to China."

Birdie turned the pan in her hands. She would never stay here alone with that man.

# 26

# *AMELIA*

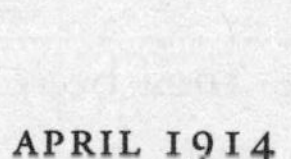

APRIL 1914

Amelia stepped carefully from the boat transport, cradling a beautiful boy as the porter placed one trunk and then her valise on the dock. "Would you like me to take these up to the house?"

As they stood in the shadow of Pendleton Castle, he must have a hundred questions about her lack of staff and the introduction of a baby. He prudently kept the questions to himself but stared down at Philip until Amelia covered her son's face with the blanket she'd crocheted.

"The caretaker will help with my luggage," she said.

The porter's gaze didn't break. "There are rumors about this island. That it's not safe for children."

"It's safe enough for us."

"I hate to leave you and your baby alone."

"We won't be alone for long." She slipped a coin out of her purse and pressed it into his palm, thanking him for his assistance before he motored away.

Last September, she and Fiona had accompanied their young guests back to the orphanage in Ogdensburg, and Amelia had spent the winter in the maternity home next door. Those months had been good for her. Not only had she kept her hands quite busy, she'd lost herself in the work.

Originally, Fiona had intended to return to the castle, but she'd decided to remain at Ogdensburg orphanage to help the nuns with the children. Amelia's former maid even talked of taking the vows of poverty, chastity, and obedience to become a nun herself. After Philip was born, Fiona and the nuns encouraged Amelia to return to Cade, saying no boy should grow up without a father and that Cade should be given the opportunity to care for his child.

The truth was, Amelia's heart ached for Cade, more than it ever had for any other. She'd longed to see him again, hold him close, but she hadn't dared to send him a letter. Hadn't wanted him to take pity on her.

She'd been overwrought the last time they spoke. Then she'd left the island abruptly without being honest about her heart and their child. Without even speaking to him again. And in her absence, she hoped his love, like hers, had grown.

She wished she had come back earlier. Weeks, even, after their baby was born. But the ice flowed late this year, making it difficult to cross, and she was afraid of losing their son. He was four months old now, and she knew that Cade would love him and her well. For a lifetime.

In these past months—years, really—she'd begun to value a simpler life. With the sale of her house in the city and the investments and properties managed by Mr. Haynes, she had enough income to provide well for her and Cade and Philip. They could stay in this castle for the rest of their lives if they wanted, so Cade could work on his boats. While she would protect her son's reputation, she didn't care what anyone thought of her. She only wanted the three of them to be a family.

She nuzzled her nose to her baby's forehead and smiled. Everything was about to change for both of them.

"You'll be happy here," she whispered.

As she scanned the shore and cliff, she could see pictures of a boy who would fish and swim and hike the paths of this island with his father, a man whose life circled around others instead of demanding they orbit around him. Their new life was about to begin, and she would crumble the expectations of those who lived to criticize, continuing to feed her child from her own breast and marrying the man her heart loved.

As she waited on the dock, she heard a familiar whistle in the trees, and her heart leapt as she pulled Philip close. After all her imaginings over the past months, all of her wondering, it was finally time for him to meet his papa.

Cade stepped out of the trees, onto the platform, and then he froze, staring at her as if she were an apparition.

"Hello, Cade," she said quietly.

His gaze dropped to the baby in her arms. "You've returned."

"Yes."

His eyes didn't leave Philip. "With a child."

"Indeed."

The single word hung between them like drapery. She wanted to pull back the heavy curtain, expose the light.

He took a small step forward. "Is he—"

"Cade?" A woman called from the top of the hill, sunshine in her voice, but Amelia felt no warmth. Instead, a cold wind blew across her heart.

"I almost forgot . . ." The younger woman's voice faded as she stared at Amelia, her eyes swelling in alarm.

"You remember Miriam, don't you?" Cade said. "She was in your sewing circle."

Amelia nodded slowly as Miriam handed him a thermos. She remembered this Scottish girl well, her ease with the needle, her willingness to help Amelia and other newcomers, her enviable youth. She wasn't proper like the women who took their lunches at the Thousand Island Yacht Club but pretty in her shirtwaist and colorful kerchief tied like a ribbon around her hair. A simple beauty.

But why was she here on the island?

Working, that must be it. Cade had hired her to prepare the house for . . .

But who was supposed to arrive while Amelia was gone?

Miriam stepped forward. "You have a baby."

"My son," she said simply, brandishing him as if he were a shield. Or a sword.

"Miriam and I married last month," Cade explained.

A blast shot up the river, swirling the water around her, threatening to steal her away. She'd thought Cade would be waiting for her on the island, pining even, over the winter and spring, remembering their time together. Longing for her as she had done for him.

Instead, he'd been courting another.

Perhaps that was the reason he'd suggested the sewing bee to Amelia long ago. Perhaps he'd actually wanted to visit this woman in Clayton. A woman with little means but much prettier and younger than Amelia.

How long had he loved her?

"You've married again?" Miriam asked with the confidence of an equal.

"I have not."

Something switched in the younger woman's face. Her voice remained calm when she spoke again, but there was an edge to it, as if she needed to carve out the truth. "What is your baby's name?"

"Philip," Amelia replied slowly. "Philip Pendleton."

He would never take on the name of Ridell now, and she didn't want him to have the hauntings of Koster either.

"Mr. Ridell, could you please start a fire in my sitting room? And take the luggage upstairs." She and Philip would both need the warmth until the boilers began to heat the dormant space.

Cade tipped his cap. "Of course."

"Mr. Haynes has sold my house in the city and released the servants. I am quite capable of caring for most of my needs, but I will need a small staff for the summer."

"I will inquire in Clayton," he said.

"Thank you." How she hated the formality in her voice, the propriety of their discussion. This was nothing like she'd envisioned for her welcome home.

Cade lifted her valise. "I will return for your trunk after I build the fire."

"I'll take the valise now so you can carry the trunk," Miriam insisted, removing it from his hand. "We'll work together."

He flashed her the brilliant smile that he'd once reserved for Amelia. At least, she thought he had reserved it for her. She wasn't certain of anything now.

Windows lined the passage between the boathouse and castle, sunlight splattering into puddles on the rough ground. Cade didn't turn on the electric lights, and she didn't ask him to. While Amelia unpacked her trunk, Miriam worked with Cade to prepare the upstairs rooms.

Mr. Haynes had said her stocks were recovering after the crash, that she would have enough money to live on Koster Isle. She couldn't marry Cade now, but she and Philip would be safe here until she decided where they would live next.

That evening, after she'd prepared a dinner of melted cheese over Miriam's bread, she sat in the vanity chair in her dressing room, rocking the cradle. While she might obtain a nanny for the daytime hours, Philip would spend the nights in her room. He would never sleep or play in the nursery and she certainly wouldn't spoon-feed him any of Leslie's old tonic.

Her heart skipped a beat at the familiar knock on her door.

"Come in," she called.

Cade opened the door but didn't step inside. Instead he eyed the cradle. "Is he my son?"

She took a long breath. "Without a doubt."

"I wouldn't have married," he said. "I didn't know—"

She rocked their baby again. "I should have told you."

He raked both hands through his hair. "I would have taken care of you both."

"You and Miriam are better suited to be husband and wife," she said although her heart screamed otherwise.

"I will talk to her," he said, a firm line drawn between them now. "We will come to an arrangement."

"There is no need for an arrangement. I will simply raise Philip as my own. Let others say what they like. I'll tell them I adopted him from the orphanage."

"Where will you live?" he asked.

And she blinked, surprised. Did he expect her to leave her own island? "Here, of course."

For as long as they needed to stay.

"Of course," he agreed, but there was no pleasure in his words.

A cascade of hurt threatened to pour out in rage, but she stuffed it back inside, pressing to strip her voice of any care. "You may remain employed as caretaker," she said. "Does Miriam need a position?"

He shook his head. "She works at a house on Wellesley."

"Perhaps she can be persuaded to manage the kitchen and laundry here."

"I will ask her."

When he moved into the room, she braced herself. He wouldn't try to proposition her now, would he? She'd refuse him, of course. She would have to.

"I will not interfere with you and your wife," she said.

He gave her a curious look as if he would never consider her an interference. And she pretended she was glad of it.

"A woman came to the island a few weeks ago." He dug something out of his coat pocket and folded it into his hand. "She said she'd been searching for you."

"Did she leave her name?"

"No." He paused. "Her hair was light colored, but she reminded me of you."

The shiver in her chest spread through her limbs. Was it possible . . . ? "What did she want?"

"She asked me to give you this." He tossed a royal-blue pouch onto the settee.

"Did you look inside?"

"No," he said. "It's not for me to interfere in your life either."

Amelia looked at the velvet pouch, afraid to touch it. "What did you tell this woman?"

"The truth." He stepped back into the doorway. "I didn't know where you had gone and I didn't know when you would return."

"I thought you would wait for me," she said. "I thought—"

"And I thought you'd be honest with me, Amelia." His voice cracked. "Mrs. Pendleton."

She stood and straightened the sleeves on her striped shirtwaist. "From now on, we will stay out of each other's business."

He looked back at their baby in the cradle, and she thought for a moment that he might pick up Philip, but then he was gone.

*You love no one but yourself, Amelia.*

That's what Leslie had told her long ago.

But it wasn't true. She'd spent years fighting for the success of Leslie's enterprises and their daughter's well-being. Then she'd given herself to Cade, loving him like she'd thought he loved her.

She had loved Cade, hadn't she? He'd certainly made her feel good. Leslie's money, the approval of the gilded set, the love of a daughter, and the affection of her caretaker—it all made her feel like royalty.

But what had it done to everyone else?

She squeezed her arms across her chest, Leslie's words echoing again as the lamplight reflected in her mirror. And she stared at the glass. No wonder why Cade hadn't wanted her. She'd aged poorly, her face streaked between islands of skin, her lush dark hair crackling into gray. Her youthful smile had been weighed down, buried really, in years of grief.

She stood carefully, not wanting to awaken Philip. The sisters at the maternity home hadn't allowed the women to wallow. Some of their words were harsh, others kind, and yet others, confusing.

Confusion was all she felt now.

She had been thinking beyond herself, hadn't she? Thinking about Penelope and now Philip. Thinking about the Koster family's few remaining members in England, those who'd tried to hide her sister's impropriety long ago, the danger that Ellie posed to those around her when not in her rightfulness of mind. The years her sister had spent properly hospitalized in England like their mother.

Secrets benefitted all of them, not just her.

She reached for the pouch that Cade left and peeled back the velvet. Inside was a piece of wood, shaved and carved into a flower. She studied the piece in the light until she slowly realized what it was.

A poppy.

She turned it over and saw the words burned on the back.

*I know.*

And then Ellie's name, signed at the bottom.

Amelia dropped the flower, another blaze raging inside her.

How long had her sister been in New York?

And what exactly did she know about Penelope?

She was terrified to think what Ellie had done . . . or what she might be planning next.

## 27
# CHLOE

"It's like the river flows right through your veins," Logan called out as Chloe steered them around an outcropping of rocks, wind fanning out her hair. These boulders had taken down a few boats over the years, usually during a storm, but the sun was ablaze this afternoon and the lullaby of a breeze had charmed the waters into a trance. "You know exactly how to navigate all of this."

Even though she tried to suppress it, a smile broke through. *"Gie it laldy."*

"What does that mean?"

"Give it your all!" she shouted as they flew around Whiskey Island, formerly Coral Island because of the maze of shoals that protected its shoreline. The island had been aptly renamed Whiskey during Prohibition as a precarious hiding place for rumrunners and their smuggled goods. "My grandma's family was from Scotland, and Grandpa Cade liked to toss out a few Scottish phrases to make her laugh."

"Laughter can change everything."

"So can hopping waves," she said as the wake from a speedboat sprayed over them.

He slid his aviator sunglasses up on his outcropping of light-brown hair before he gripped the edge of *Lolli's* windshield, watching the red and green sidelights blink. "I think I'll stick with laughter."

She throttled back on her speed. "You get seasick?"

He cupped water in both hands and splashed it on his forehead. "I'm afraid so."

"I've got a couple of paddles if we need to go any slower."

"This is fine with me," he said as they crept ahead.

"Joe's a sailor inside and out." She glanced at Logan again, a smile still playing on her lips. "Hopefully, he'll still like you."

"He'll like me because I'm your friend."

"Colleagues, Logan. Not friends." Even though it felt like they should be more than colleagues after he'd helped her down the castle stairs. He must have thought she'd lost it, curled up like a child in Poppy's nursery as her dreams had warped into reality. Seasickness was nothing to her collapse.

But he'd respected her request to stop asking personal questions, and she appreciated his not probing any further into what felt like a panic attack.

"Maybe he'll like me," Logan said, "when I tell him how much I appreciate his help, just like I appreciate your help."

"Flattery will get you nowhere."

He leaned toward the side of the boat, looking at their clear path across the current. "Only place I'm trying to get at the moment is Grindstone Island."

"We'll be there in ten minutes." As she scanned the open waterway in front of them, someone on the radio asked for directions to moor their catamaran near Wellesley Island. She turned down the chatter as another voice began rattling off a response. "You feel better now?"

"Slightly. I no longer want to jump overboard."

She throttled up a notch. "We might get there in nine minutes if this breeze stays at our back."

"How long were your grandparents married?" he asked.

"That's a personal question."

He lifted both hands, palms facing the sky. "You were the one talking about your grandmother."

Point taken. "Sixty-three years."

"Amazing."

"Grandpa was ninety-two when he died."

Logan stretched out his right leg in the aisle between them. "What was your grandma like?"

How was she supposed to explain how much she loved her nana . . . and how frustrated her grandma had been with her only son?

"She loved to bake and sing, and she absolutely adored my grandfather. They loved each other well for all those years."

"It's rare, I think, to find love that withstands the many tests of time."

She nodded. Her grandparents' love for each other had withstood, thrived even, over the years. But the storms of life had battered their love for their son as he continually defied them. Her grandpa had loved Philip—she'd heard it in his stories, seen it in the pictures—but her father never seemed to reciprocate. It was like he preferred to loathe himself.

After Chloe went to live with her grandparents, Nana had been diligent in wiping clean every inkling of Chloe's tendencies to despise herself and her circumstances. It was much more than a *pick yourself up by your bootstraps* way of thinking. The healing tonic of Nana's wisdom was grounded in the Good Book that she read every day.

While Chloe's earthly father might have failed, Nana liked to say, her heavenly Father would never fail her. Instead of scattering the pieces of her life, God would help her mold them into something good.

Chloe had believed the woman who made her minty hot chocolate and read her stories about heroic women and tucked her under a pile of blankets before bed. The woman who'd cared for her body and her spirit. Nana had been a shield on one side, protecting her from further harm, and a healer on the other to mend her wounds.

As Chloe grew older, she sometimes wondered what Nana would think if she'd been the one who was betrayed. Abandoned. Would she still believe in a Father who truly loved her?

"I'm sorry about what happened in the tower," Chloe told the man next to her.

"You don't have to apologize."

"I went someplace else . . ." How could she explain what she saw? She'd been trying to process it ever since they'd left the castle, but she still didn't understand all the memories lodged inside her. And who was she supposed to ask now about her father? No one else except her grandma knew what happened.

"You want to tell me where you went?" he asked.

She hesitated. "It's not a story I want reported."

"I'm researching Poppy's story as a reporter." He paused. "Your personal story would be held in confidence as a friend."

"Maybe another day," she said. Trust was hard enough for her, but to trust a newspaperman? Even if he became a friend, he still might condense her trauma into a sidebar. Another tragedy on Ghost Island.

Straight ahead was Grindstone, and she steered left. Unlike Koster Isle with its sole cottage and looming castle, Grindstone was a large island populated with hundreds of houses and farms. Few people spent their winters here, but Joe both summered and wintered in his cabin, surrounded by a few hardy neighbors who didn't mind the loneliness that could creep into one's bones when snow sometimes piled up against their doors into March. They could make the long haul across the ice when the river froze, but when the spring ice melted into floes, it was precarious to cross.

Locals often said that those who wintered on Grindstone were tempting fate without an ambulance or fire engine at the ready, but some of them didn't have the income to migrate south when the geese took flight. Staying was a risk that Joe and others were willing to take to keep their property and then pass it along to their children. Joe wasn't going to sell his land or the family home where he'd lived for most of his life for the purported security of the mainland, which he didn't think was secure at all. And in his case, his daughter and her family lived on the same property so he was never lonely for long.

"A storm took Joe's dock about a decade ago," Chloe explained as she killed the engine near the shore and pulled on a pair of rubber boots. Then she tilted up the motor and climbed over the side. Her boots sank into the muck, tugging at her heels, but the riverbed never won this battle. She knotted a rope and pulled *Lolli* and her passenger to a post before tying up her boat in the shallow water.

Logan scanned the column of trees beyond the seawall and the hill above. Then he studied the strip of marsh as if a monster might rise out of the mud. "Where does Joe keep his boat now?"

"At a community boathouse around the bend."

"And you don't want to dock there because . . . ?"

"We'd have to hike up a rocky path that someone tried to civilize by calling it a street," she said. "That's why I told you to bring wellies."

"I've got them." He held up a wader boot before pulling it on.

She reached over the gunwale and dug a plastic bag from under her front seat.

"Did you bring him flowers?"

She laughed. "He'd slam the door in our faces if we brought flowers."

"Scotch, then?"

"Jelly beans."

Logan swung his legs over the side of *Lolli* and slipped into the marsh beside her, his messenger bag strapped over his shoulder. Balancing himself on the side of the boat, he took a few steps, and her stomach dropped. With the memories from the castle taking up too much space in her head, the rush to make sure Emma was safe while Gavin investigated Agent Yancey and then hurrying to make it to Joe's house long before dark, she'd forgotten about Logan's bad leg.

How terrible to make him trek through this mud.

She took a deep breath. "I'm so sorry."

"You should be." His dimpled grin spread slowly across his face, making him look more like a kid again than a grown man. "Rotten of you to help me with my story."

"I mean, about the muck." She nodded at the embankment stubbled with grass and trees. "It probably would have been easier to walk through the forest."

"I've been through worse," he said. "Of course, that was when my legs acted like they knew each other. It was a partnership I took for granted my first twenty-seven years."

Perhaps she should return his volley of questions, ask how he'd injured his leg, but with the challenge ahead, it didn't seem like the right moment.

He took another careful step in the shallow water and weeds, a smile still playing on his lips. "You gonna catch me if I fall?"

She eyed his broad frame, the bomber jacket snug from muscles that would deter most people from bothering him. Between the muscle weight and six inches that he had on her, it wouldn't be a pretty catch.

"We'd both end up in the water," she said.

"Then it's a good thing I can still swim with this leg."

"I'm afraid you won't swim far. We'd just be covered in mud." She debated offering her arm, but how awkward would that be? More like an insult, she feared.

"I've got this, Chloe," he said, releasing her from the wondering.

And he did. With his frame tilted at an angle, he trudged toward the shore, then replaced his waders with hiking shoes once they were firmly on ground.

As they slowly climbed rough slabs made from stone, a raspy voice hailed down. "Are you going to spend all day lazying around on the beach?"

"We're thinking about it," she shouted up toward Joe's cabin. "The fish are much nicer than some of the people around here."

"Hope you brought sunscreen."

Chloe laughed at the look on Logan's face, his smile fading, eyebrows raised in alarm. "He's harmless."

"Are you sure?"

"Quite tame as long as I keep feeding him these." She pulled a tackle box out of the bag, each cube filled with his favorite beans. Joe Lindley, the local Lorax who spoke on behalf of the river and trees, had never met a jelly bean he didn't like. "He actually enjoys company."

"Could have fooled me."

Joe critiqued Logan as they neared the door. "Who are you?"

He offered the man his hand. "My name's Logan Danford."

"Logan is with the Syracuse paper," she explained again like she'd done over the telephone.

Joe tugged on a worn cloth vest that barely covered his midsection. Nothing he liked better than a willing listener for his stories.

That, and jelly beans.

He shook Logan's hand and then waved them both into the living room. While the outside of his cabin appeared to be in shambles, the inside was immaculate. Joe's wife had passed away about twenty years ago, not long after Joe had retired from building houses and barns across the islands. According to Joe, he'd been born with a hammer in his hand, and he'd die holding one too. Instead of quitting, he brought his skill indoors, carving cabinets and furniture from the island's harvest of birch and cedar and pine. And a steady supply of snowshoes for anyone needing a pair.

Joe popped open the tackle box and began collecting the beans, one at a time, starting with cinnamon on the left and gradually making his way across the rainbow of colors before he offered the box to Logan.

"You can have any that you please," he offered. "Just one, mind you."

Chloe studied the older man. He was always generous with his time and stories, but she'd never known him to be generous with sweets.

Logan took his time, winning over Joe with his questions about the flavors, complimenting him on his choices. Apparently flattery would get him somewhere, because after he chose a margarita-flavored bean, Joe offered him a strawberry daiquiri one too.

Then Joe closed the lid and tucked the box on a bookshelf before turning toward her. "I heard you had a girl come live with you."

"Her name is Emma," she explained. "She's back at the shop with Jenna."

Her friend had Emma coloring in the back office in case Mitch Yancey decided to pay their shop another visit this afternoon.

Joe's weathered forehead wrinkled in concern. "She might eat all the jelly beans."

"She just might," Chloe said, caging her smile. "Good thing I know where to find more."

"I'd like some root beer ones next time."

"Yes, sir." She glanced over at Logan, perched on the edge of his chair, before looking back at the older man. "You wouldn't happen to know anyone who is missing their daughter, do you?"

He ate a few more beans from the collection in his palm. "Did Emma lose her parents?"

"Seems like it."

"I haven't heard about a child missing around here in years."

Chloe didn't probe. He could be talking about Poppy, but he could also be hinting at her past. If Logan hadn't dug up her entire story yet, she wasn't ready to volunteer.

Joe turned to Logan. "It's been decades since Syracuse ran a story on Poppy."

Logan pressed his hands together, tapping his thumbs like he was keeping time to a drumbeat in his head. "Will you tell me what you know about her family?"

"Don't know that I can add to the mounds already published, but I'm always glad to help a friend."

"I appreciate the friendship." Logan grinned at her before removing a notebook and pen from his coat pocket, and she fought the urge to roll her eyes.

"Chloe, here, knows most of the stories."

"But not all the facts," she said. "I thought you might be able to show him the articles that you've collected. One of the stories Logan found says that my grandpa was at the castle the night Poppy disappeared."

Joe eyed her curiously. "Cade never told me that."

"What did he tell you?" Logan asked.

"Why do you want to write this article?" Joe countered.

"Because I'm a reporter—"

Joe's eyes narrowed as if he were trying to find a destination on the map spread across Logan's face. "No one digs this far into the Pendleton story unless they have a good reason."

Logan's swagger faded as he leaned forward on the chair, his hands on his knees, glancing at her again instead of Joe. "I lost . . ." He paused before his gaze settled back on Joe. "My son died twelve years ago. There's no bringing him back."

The air rushed out of Chloe's lungs, a dozen questions pounding through her head.

Joe studied the man in front of him. "And you think you can bring back our Poppy?"

"Her birthday is coming up in July. I'd like to at least find out what happened to her before then."

Joe collapsed back in his chair with a shake of his head. "That's not an answer."

"If she has passed on, I want to put this story to rest for her memory and for any family she might have left behind." Logan's confidence returned with the tap of his pen on paper. He was genuine, it seemed, in his words and certainly persistent in his pursuit.

"All the Pendletons are gone now," Joe said.

"You don't know that for certain."

Joe took a breath, his gaze wandering to the river. "I suppose I don't."

"I only want to find out where she went."

"I'm sorry about your boy," Joe said. "I'm afraid I can't help much with your story, but I'll answer any questions that I can."

Logan pulled an audio recorder out of his bag and set it on the polished coffee table between them. "Do you mind if I record our discussion?"

Joe eyed the recorder, and Chloe saw the glint return to his eyes as he ran his hand down the front of his vest again, checking to make sure each button was in its proper place. "I can't say I mind at all."

"When did you meet Cade Ridell?" Logan asked.

Joe crossed one leg over the other, the tip of his toe sticking out of a hole in his black sock. "Cade took me under his wing when I was still in my teens, taught me and a couple other fellas how to build the custom skiffs that people once owned around here, but I can't say he liked to talk much about the Pendletons."

Logan made a note before looking up. "Why are you so interested in what happened to Poppy?"

Joe retrieved the tackle box and slipped several more jelly beans out of it, rattling them around his palm like they were spare change.

"Poppy was just a year younger than me." Joe popped the candy into his mouth. "I'll never forget the night the police scrambled onto Grindstone like a mess of sand crabs, searching for her in barns and houses and along the shore. Most people already thought she drowned, but it was the job of them fellas to look for a missing girl on land and in the water."

Logan noted something on his paper. "Do you think she drowned?"

"The St. Lawrence has sure taken its share of lives over the years, but locals grappled the shoreline around Koster Isle right after Poppy went missing. You know what grappling is?"

"I have an idea."

"They search for a drowning victim with ropes and hooks."

Chloe waved her hands. "No need to elaborate."

"If Poppy fell off a cliff or over the side of a boat," he continued, "the river would have given back her body eventually. Unless she was trapped in a vessel, of course. Then—"

"Joe!" If she didn't stop him now, he would spend the rest of the afternoon trying to impress Logan with his vast knowledge of the more gruesome river facts.

"The river almost always returns the dead," Joe said solemnly. "To bury a body on shore."

Logan beat his pen on the notepad. "You must have some sort of hypothesis."

"Everyone around here has an idea or two." Joe stood and shuffled down the hallway, returning with two manila folders stuffed full. "The papers ran regular articles about Poppy right up until the archduke in Austria was killed. Then news of that wretched war drowned out everything else in the world."

"What do you think happened to Poppy?" Logan asked.

"Leslie Pendleton was all cozy with drug runners on both sides of the border, but with his buying and selling and storing of opium, he was bound to make someone spitting mad."

"He was storing opium at the castle?"

Joe rolled his shoulders and then lowered his voice. "The tourism folk like to say he built the place for his wife but really it was to hide his cache. A bootlegger, that's what he was, long before Prohibition. Except he was running drugs instead of rum."

"And Poppy got caught in the middle." Logan tapped the edge of his paper with his ballpoint pen. Admirable self-control, Chloe thought, for him to let the conversation flow in chunky pieces instead of shooting questions at the older man.

Joe nodded. "Right smack."

"The opium," Chloe said slowly. "That's why Mr. Pendleton called his daughter Poppy."

Was it possible that the man had left opium behind? Yet another reason why her grandma wanted her to stay away from the castle. Nana probably knew about the drugs being smuggled and stored.

Joe opened the top folder. "By all accounts, Mr. Pendleton doted on his daughter, named her the highfalutin name of Penelope so she'd fit right in with all sorts of rich folk. But to nickname her Poppy and then name his tonic after her . . ."

"If Mr. Pendleton had been part of a smuggling network," Logan said, noting something with his pen, "one of his enemies might have killed him and kidnapped Poppy."

"More likely, they killed her by accident when they came for him," Joe replied. "Any other crook would have demanded a ransom."

Chloe leaned back in her chair. "What a mess." Some mysteries were simply impossible to solve, especially after all these years.

"Maybe the smugglers didn't mean to kill Poppy's dad," Logan said. "Maybe they just wanted a payment."

"I'm sure the police suspected the opium had something to do with his death." Joe spread the articles across the coffee table so Logan could read them. "Maybe even looked the other way. Companies back then didn't have to say what they were putting in their food or drugs. The government was still trying to sort out all the legalities."

"Like Coca-Cola," Chloe said, remembering what Grandpa Cade had told her when she'd started working with him at the candy shop. "Cocaine used to be one of the main ingredients."

Joe nodded. "Back then, people could buy a drug-infused drink at the soda fountain and take home a bottle of Poppy's Tip-Top Tonic to give to their kids. I suppose, if it didn't kill ya, it might have killed anything ailing you."

Chloe glanced down at Joe's colorful tackle box, still partially filled with candy. She wanted to bring joy to people, but too much of anything could hurt. How did one enjoy the simple pleasures without being consumed?

"Perhaps Mr. Pendleton was really trying to help people with his tonic," Logan said.

"I'm pretty dern sure that Mr. Pendleton was more concerned about making money than providing any sort of medicinal value with his syrup. He was New Rich, of course. Not respected in the city of New York like all those who'd inherited their fortune instead of dirtying their hands to make it."

"Ironic," Logan said.

"New-money folk clamored up here a hundred years ago so they could snub the old money together. Did you know they nicknamed the channel from Clayton to Alexandria Bay *Fifth Avenue*?"

Logan shook his head.

"Men the likes of George Boldt and George Pullman and Frederick Bourne of the Singer sewing machines built their kingdoms here."

Logan scribbled on his notepad. "Did Mrs. Pendleton come from money?"

"Probably, a long time ago. Her family was from England, and by the time she married, I suspect they had shallow pockets and a super fancy title."

Logan looked back up. "She must have grieved deeply after she lost her husband and daughter."

"I never met her," Joe said. "She came back another summer or two after Poppy disappeared, but I don't think she returned after the fire in their birdhouse."

Chloe's gaze swept up from the papers, the tarnished sign from the aviary staked in her mind. The words from the strange poem.

*Flames whip in fury, royal embers caged in brass.*

"How did the fire start?" she asked.

"The paper said it was an electrical short." Joe switched legs and stretched out his arms. "Although, I have to tell you, the strangest thing happened that night."

She and Logan waited for him to continue.

"I wasn't but thirteen at the time." He rocked back twice in his chair, relishing the attention.

"The fire . . . ," she prompted.

He rocked again. "That same afternoon, I was cleaning up at the marina in Clayton. A woman strolled up to the dock all high and mighty with her British talk and a whole load of attitude. She offered to pay someone a dollar to transport her to Koster Isle. It was getting late and no one wanted to haul her out, but I s'pose I needed the money. Winds were good so I offered her a ride on my sailboat."

"I wonder what she wanted," Chloe said.

"I didn't give it much thought, but she said her name was Eva." Joe tapped his hands together. "No, that's not right. Esther."

Chloe glanced at Logan, and he shrugged.

"That's not right either." Joe closed his eyes. "Wait just a minute. It'll come to me."

"No rush," Chloe told him.

"Ellie! That's her name. She said she was going to the island to see her sister." Joe scanned the rows in his tackle box again before selecting a blue raspberry bean and handing it to Logan. "And I didn't find out about the fire until weeks later. I was too busy fuming about the fact that she never did pay me that dollar."

Logan ate the offered jelly bean. "Did you tell the police what happened?"

"I told my dad, and he said he would talk to them."

Another note on Logan's pad. "Did the police keep searching for Poppy in those years?"

"Can't say that I know. So much happened under the table back then."

"Why didn't you tell me about the fire?" Chloe asked.

"You never asked."

Logan leaned forward. "Do you know what happened to Mrs. Pendleton?"

"I do," Joe said as he thumbed through the papers. "Tragic end to that story."

They waited until he finished his hunt.

"The article seems to have walked away, but she died in a shipwreck on her way back to England."

Chloe fell back in her chair, surprised. Why hadn't her grandparents told her about Poppy or Mrs. Pendleton?

Joe lifted another jelly bean from the cube for himself. "She left Koster Isle to your granddaddy."

"Do you know why she left him the island?" Chloe asked.

Joe closed his eyes again as he relished the candy, and she thought for a moment that he'd fallen asleep. Then he opened them. "I guess she was still hoping that Poppy would one day return. She probably wanted someone there waiting."

"But Poppy never came," Chloe said quietly.

"Another girl did though." Joe smiled. "And Cade and Miriam couldn't have been more proud of you."

28

# *AMELIA*

"HELLO, SISTER," ELLIE SAID as she swept into the aviary. A flutter of wings raced under the glass roof, the birds frightened from their roosts. "I've missed you."

Amelia pulled Philip close to quiet his whimper. She'd been trying to lull him to sleep tonight in this place that once brought comfort to her and Penelope. A place of wings and song.

Ellie strolled past the lantern that Amelia left hanging near the door, the slit that snaked up her skirt offering anyone who might wonder a view of skin. Then she rolled her hands over a cluster of leaves, deciding, it seemed, what to do with it all.

Kingdoms rose and tumbled swiftly in her sister's world.

"You've had a baby," she said. "Just like me."

"I'm nothing like you, Ellie."

"People think I'm crazy, but you were the one who always spun the truth for your own good."

A bird shifted in the leaves, and Amelia saw a glimmer of red. Minnie had come to keep her company. "For the good of everyone in our family."

"And you continued your spinning here, it seems. Handsome fellow, that caretaker of yours. Seems like he's done his job quite well."

Had her sister heard the whisperings in town about Cade? Amelia shifted slowly on the seat even as her mind vied for words to diffuse the storm. "Why are you here?"

A cloud of perfume settled in the aviary. It distracted the boys, Ellie had told Amelia when they were younger. A scent she'd called her salvation.

The head cantor in their parish called it sin.

Ellie had aged much better than Amelia, retaining the youth of her face and slenderness in her hips, but Amelia wasn't fooled. She'd seen what happened when Ellie was enlightened or enraged. The girl in the neighboring village who'd been beaten silly when she caught the attention of one of Ellie's suitors. The kind boy who'd refused her sister's pursuit, later accused of theft. Lord Koster, their father, had convinced the magistrate of Ellie's innocence in both cases. The doctors eventually declared insanity and sent Ellie to the same sanatorium where Lady Koster once lived.

Amelia didn't think Ellie had lost her mind. She thought her sister found a strange sense of satisfaction, with perfectly clear thinking, in watching an enemy's demise.

Ellie ripped a new leaf off one of the branches and twirled it in her fingers. "The doctor said my baby was dead."

The man had whisked Penelope away after the birth, telling Lord Koster that he worried about Ellie's ability to care for a child. Before her father began making inquiries for adoption, Amelia had volunteered to take Ellie's baby to New York as her and Leslie's daughter.

"The doctor thought she should be raised outside the sanatorium." Philip began crying, and she bounced him gently in her lap, afraid her sister might try to harm him if he didn't stop.

Ellie's gaze wandered to the glass wall behind Amelia, scanning the water. "It wasn't their choice or yours to steal her."

"It was for her good," Amelia said. She'd traveled all the way to England after receiving the telegram from her father, begging her to come. In one sweep, she'd rescued Ellie's baby and her family's reputation and then her marriage as well when she'd returned home with a Pendleton heiress. Leslie might have suspected over the years, but he never knew with certainty that Penelope wasn't his.

"You did a terrible thing, Amelia."

"I did it for you, not to you."

"You took my daughter for yourself," Ellie continued, crushing the leaf in her hand. "Because you and Leslie couldn't have your own. You needed him, and he needed her."

"You don't know anything about Leslie and me."

Ellie began to laugh, a guttural sound that frightened Philip into silence. "Your husband's eyes were as big as saucers when I told him about his precious Poppy. All that time, he really thought you'd birthed him a baby."

When had her sister talked to Leslie? "Why did you—?"

"The story was much too good to keep to myself," Ellie said. "I had to approach him first, of course, that night you locked him in the smoking room. He had his purse at the ready to pay for a delivery in the harbor. I promised to keep his secret about Poppy if he paid me well."

"But you killed him instead," Amelia said slowly.

Ellie's laughter eased into a smile, the delight of her memories seeming to settle. "I hadn't been planning to kill him, but he was too curious. Then he tried to pierce me with a silly fire poker. Fortunately, his brain was as foggy as the river and his aim equally as clunky. He didn't even realize that I put a little extra tonic into his drink. Just kept sipping the whisky like it was afternoon tea."

"You are wicked, Ellie."

"No more than you. We are the same, I think. Bred from a lunatic and a liar."

Amelia's stomach tumbled. She'd taken on her father's lies and borne the weight of it, breeding more lies on her own. This baby in her arms, she was going to lie about him too. Say he was adopted from the orphanage. More lies to burden the next generation.

But she wasn't sure how to unravel it now.

"You took Leslie's money and then you took Penelope."

"I retrieved her," Ellie replied. "You can't steal what's already yours."

"What did you do with her?" The crack in Amelia's voice betrayed her utter fear.

"I got rid of Poppy a long time ago."

When Mr. Haynes told her about a man near Montreal who was convinced that he'd seen Penelope, Amelia had tried not to hope, but the smallest ember had been stoked inside her. The detectives had thought Mr. Gagné might lead them to Penelope, but then he vanished and the girl with him.

Any remaining hope of finding Penelope burst now, a storm of tears falling down Amelia's cheeks. The girl had done nothing wrong. She'd been born into a family that seemed to thrive on hurting its members. Keeping them all in their well-established places. The doctor in England had told them that her sister wasn't capable of caring for a baby, but Amelia would never be able to understand how she could kill her own daughter.

Ellie stepped closer. "Stop crying, Amelia."

How her sister hated tears.

Amelia wiped her cheeks even as she rocked Philip. "The police will find you."

Ellie paced along the path. "No one knows that I took her, and kidnapping is a nasty charge, Amelia, on top of murder. If you get the idea in your head to go to the papers or the police, I have witnesses ready to defend my case."

"Not on this continent."

"A nurse from England will come to New York, and several people who live in these islands believe you murdered Poppy and Leslie for the money. Would swear to it even."

Even though seven years had passed, she had no doubt her sister could sweet-talk almost anyone into testifying. Once again, she'd pay for Ellie's crime.

"It won't help you much if Penelope is gone."

Ellie's eyes gleamed in the lantern light when she smiled again. "No one cares about Poppy anymore."

Amelia's insides curled, grieving the end of Penelope's life, a niece she'd raised as her own. Penelope would never return now and Cade loved another.

Her sister wouldn't hurt Amelia, not as long as she had enough money to provide for them both, but if she stayed on this island, Ellie would haunt her for the rest of her life and probably hurt Philip in the process.

She and Philip would have to leave tomorrow, at first light. They'd move to Philadelphia or Chicago or out to San Francisco where, she'd heard, they could start anew. Someplace her sister wouldn't find them.

Amelia stood. She needed to get Philip away from his aunt. "How much do you want?"

"I don't need money." Ellie held up several pieces of Amelia's jewelry and the gold Pendleton watch that Leslie had engraved. "I already borrowed these from your room."

Amelia eyed the aviary door, the lantern hanging on a hook beside it. Why was Ellie threatening her with kidnapping and murder charges if she didn't want a bribe?

The answer came like a swift kick to her ribs.

It was a game, she realized. Like the ones her sister used to play when they were in school. Taunting Amelia. Distracting her. Making her squirm when she concocted a story about Amelia stealing their mother's diamond-clustered brooch, given to her by Queen Victoria on her wedding day.

Amelia had been ten when she was whipped for her sister's thievery. And she'd never trusted Ellie again.

"You can be on your way then." Amelia waved her to the door, terrified of the dark games, once again becoming her sister's pawn. "That jewelry will provide plenty for you."

*Just like Mother's brooch.*

She almost said it but the truth would only hurt her now.

"I suppose I must go before that rat of a boy leaves me stranded." Ellie studied the bundle in Amelia's arms. "It's unfortunate. Philip really is a beautiful child."

Amelia turned and raced toward the door, but she wasn't fast enough. Ellie beat her to it, snagging the lantern on her way. Then she swiveled near the door, and Amelia froze as her sister teetered the handle, swinging it like a pendulum. As if she controlled time.

Philip wailed as firelight sprayed across the leaves and glass.

"Put it down," Amelia begged, the flames of fear raging inside her. "I have more money, more jewels, inside the house. You can have it all."

Everything she owned except her baby.

"I don't want your money," Ellie said.

The lantern cracked when it hit the stone walk, and a moment later Amelia heard the click of a lock. The bolt meant to keep the birds safe had turned their home into a prison.

Orange trickled up the path, leaping into a tree, and Amelia watched as it consumed the branches, the leaves. Her chest pounding, she looked back at the entrance and saw her sister's face on the other side of the door, grinning through the glass.

This was no game.

Ellie wanted her dead.

## 29
# LOGAN

*Shipwrecked Sister.*

The bold headline was splashed across the front page of the *Post-Standard* on May 30, 1914.

While the article was slim on details, the facts probably conveyed via telegram, an elegant passenger ship called *Empress of Ireland* had slipped under the St. Lawrence the night before the story ran. Even though they weren't official sister ships, the reporter referred to the *Titanic* and *Empress of Ireland* as siblings, both succumbing to the same fate. Except the *Empress* sank before it ever reached the Atlantic, with almost fifteen hundred people on board.

Logan skimmed through the microfilm until he found more information. The ship departed Quebec City about ten hours before fog settled over the frigid river, disorienting the *Empress* crew and the captain on a Norwegian coal-carrying ship called *Storstad* that was traveling the opposite direction.

Two years had passed since the sinking of the *Titanic* and a number of precautions had been implemented to prevent a similar disaster, including fifty-six lifeboats stocked on the *Empress*'s decks, if needed, to save everyone on board. But most of the passengers were asleep when the *Storstad* carved a hole in the ship's side, the impact more like a knock than a crack according to those who were awake. They didn't even realize they were in trouble until the floor began to slant.

Fourteen minutes after the *Empress* was struck, most of the passengers were plunged more than a hundred feet below the surface.

Logan shivered. Was this where the tragic story of the Pendleton family ended, all of their lives stolen along the river?

His heart wrenched as he studied the pictures of the children who died in the wreckage and those who had been orphaned. A lifetime had passed, almost eighty years, since the ship went down, but still the sadness was profound. The sorrow over losing a loved one.

It was a weakness of his, this taking on of another's pain, and if he wasn't careful, he would feel it all.

Afternoon light played on the brick building across the street, his mind racing back to the flames of a house fire in Indiana, a tragedy that took the lives of a young mom and her four-year-old son trapped inside.

He'd found them in the smoke, tried to rescue them, but it was too late to give them the gift of life. Seven years before that fire, he had lost his son, and when that woman and her child died, when the burning rafter knocked him down, everything changed for him.

Before the accident, he didn't care much if he lived or died—he'd already lost his son and his marriage—but in those hours after a comrade pulled him out of the building, the anger pent-up inside spilled out. In his renewed quest to live, his quest to understand, he'd screamed at the God of the universe. Looking back, it was more of a call for help, but at the time, he'd ranted about justice, making demands as if he knew how to run this world.

He'd seen plenty of evil in the past decade, whether it was his time fighting in the unpopular Contra War or trying to extinguish flames from arson-induced destruction across Indiana. During the surgeries to repair his leg, as he spouted off accusations against God, he'd begun to realize that God had given him a choice to bring either good or evil into this world.

He thought of the doctors and nurses who'd saved his leg. The military men and women who stopped crimes against humanity. The writers who exposed corruption and infused both hope and truth into the dark world. The police and caseworkers who were trying to find children like Emma a loving home.

They were all planting seeds of God's Kingdom, he thought, in their weary land. And a harvest of good could grow each time a community—a family—chose to do what was right. When together they embraced shalom.

He was still a fighter, that much would never change, but since the accident, he wanted to fight fire with words.

He turned the reader knob until he found the roster of those who'd been lost the night the *Empress of Ireland* sank, listed alphabetically by their last name. He scrolled until he found the surnames beginning with the letter *P*.

Amelia Pendleton was there, like Joe thought, a ticketed passenger who'd gone missing in the wreck. A sad confirmation about Poppy's mother.

Why was she returning to England? And who was she traveling with?

No one had ever found Mrs. Pendleton's body, he discovered, but more than a thousand people died in the wreck, most of them never recovered.

His eyes were on the screen even as his mind wandered to the nursery tower. He'd thought Chloe was just being difficult when she refused to go inside the castle, and he had pushed when he shouldn't have, pushed until she agreed to climb the staircase with him. But something had frightened her in that room. Taken her back in time.

For a few moments, he'd been afraid that he wouldn't be able to coax her back down the steps. Thankfully, they'd left the castle without another flashback, Chloe harboring the kind of memory that sprang without notice or welcome, ensnaring anyone who tried to hold it back.

"The *Empress of Ireland*, huh?"

He flinched at the interruption before turning to see Max peering over his shoulder, the man's bow tie dotted red and white. "I just learned about it."

Max leaned against a rack. "It was the deadliest shipwreck ever in Canadian waters."

Logan swiped the copy of the ship's manifest off the printer.

"You should write an article about it," the librarian said. "Only a few people survived, and most of their stories have been lost over time."

"I wonder why."

"World War I began two months after she sank, and then thousands of soldiers began dying overseas. No one cared anymore about a shipwreck."

After he finished writing the Pendleton story, maybe he could focus on *Empress of Ireland*. Amelia Pendleton might have died that night, but what had happened to those who survived? It would make a fascinating article. Right a few more wrongs in this broken world. "I'll think about it."

"Let me know if you need anything else." Max glanced at his watch. "I'm off in fifteen."

"You're leaving early?" Logan asked.

Max's face flushed. "Taking my wife out to dinner."

"Good for you," he said. "You won't regret it."

Max looked back at the article on the screen. "One man swam four miles to shore after the *Empress* went down. No one knows how, with all that freezing water. And another guy survived this shipwreck and the sinking of the *Titanic*. He said waiting around for the *Titanic* to sink was agony, but the *Empress* didn't wait at all. She just rolled over like a hog in a ditch." Max glanced at his watch again. "You have dinner plans?"

His mind was still on the hog.

"I haven't really thought about dinner."

Max grinned. "Maybe we can go on a double date? I know a couple of—"

"I'm actually heading up to Clayton within the hour." He'd planned to call Chloe to tell her that he'd found Mrs. Pendleton's name on the roster, but he'd much rather see her tonight than have dinner with a stranger. And, in all honesty, he wanted to see her again whether or not they talked about this story.

Maybe he'd book a hotel room, stay in Clayton until the end of the week.

"You must be almost done with that Pendleton story."

"I hope to be finished soon," Logan said.

"Your editor is sure giving you plenty of time."

"I'm covering high school sports on the weekends and whatever else she needs me to do in between, but Poppy's story is a priority for her too."

"I'll see if we have anything else on the Pendleton family," Max said. "And if I can uncover more information about the *Empress* passengers."

"I'll read anything you find."

Logan drove the hour and a half through farmland and waterways until he reached the St. Lawrence. The surface was placid this afternoon, but he could imagine the fog draped over the shoreline like a cloak. Impossible to see.

He found Chloe inside the shop, barricaded behind the counter from a crowd of tourists as she measured, mixed, and served up treats like a bartender. Her lips pressed together in determination as she worked, a clear fighter under her worn sweater and hat, both of them knitted with a dove-gray yarn. Chloe seemed to thrive in sprinkling joy with her maple candies and lemon drops, her blue eyes sparking with delight as she helped both adults and children.

It might need a little updating, but he liked the nostalgia in her shop. And he could see the possibilities as well. Candy-striped wallpaper. Glittering light fixtures. A sparkling new ship in the center with a pool of water underneath.

Logan waited by the old sculpture, scanning the room until he found Emma sitting on a beanbag, hidden between the espresso counter and a dozen drawers on the far wall. He had talked to his editor, asked if she'd heard of anyone looking for a missing girl that matched Emma's description, but no leads yet.

He hadn't wanted to alarm Chloe, but since he joined the *Post-Standard*, he'd heard too many stories about other children who had slipped through the system. He didn't want to think about what Emma had seen in her life, but he could understand why she might not want to return home.

"I'll be a few minutes," Chloe told him when the front counter cleared, her eyes focused on a family perusing shelves on the other side of the shop.

"You mind if I talk to Emma?"

"Please do." She turned to him as she lowered her voice. "Have you found anything about her family?"

"Not yet."

"I'm waiting to hear back from Gavin too."

The door chimed behind him, and another group crowded into the shop.

"Hey, kiddo." Logan eased onto the tile floor beside Emma. "You doing okay?"

She petted the carrier as if the canvas top doubled for the kitten nesting inside. When she looked at him, he saw a glint of steel. Determination maybe. A stubbornness that had surely bolstered her survival.

"Totally fine for you to say no," he said.

Silence.

"How's Fraidy?"

"Hungry."

"Ah, we should remedy that soon."

The glint in her eyes softened, ever so slightly, but he could see it begin to fade.

The kitten shifted inside the carrier, secure on one hand and yet longing to be free on the other. Sort of like the girl beside him.

"Could I ask you a few questions?"

Emma wrapped her arms firmly over her chest. "I don't like questions."

"Me either." He grimaced as a spasm raced up his leg. "Actually I don't like answering questions. I really like to ask them."

She repositioned the carrier. "What did you do to your leg?"

She might not be forthcoming with her own story, but he admired her gumption. "Hurt it in a fire."

"Anyone else get hurt?"

"A few people," he said slowly.

She put the carrier on her lap and folded herself over it. "No one's going to hurt Fraidy and me."

"Not on my watch, that's for sure." He leaned back against the counter and crossed his bum leg over the good one. "I'm trying to help Chloe find your family."

"Why does everyone want to find my family?"

"So they can decide what's next for your life. Unless you're ready, of course, to get your own apartment and a job and all that."

Her eyes flashed again. "Fraidy and I could live together."

"One day, for sure, but until you're eighteen, you probably need to live with an adult. I suspect wherever you lived last didn't have a decent friend or relative to care for you."

Chloe had told him pieces of Emma's story. About a scrapbook with an inscription to Penelope, filled with sketches of birds and hand-scripted poetry. A border agent named Mitch who scared her. An unnamed woman who had been kind. And a rowboat that she managed to paddle to Koster Isle.

"I don't want to talk about it," she said.

He studied her briefly before looking back at the counter. Chloe didn't seem to realize it, but she and Emma were actually a lot alike. Both independent. Both stubborn. Both of them sporting the same curly brown hair. And both of them trying not to drown.

"Did you live with your mom or dad before you came to Chloe's?"

"No one is listening to me!"

"We're only trying to help," he said.

She ran her hands over the carrier. "I never met my dad, and my mom left me. All I have is Fraidy."

"And now Chloe."

When she glanced up, he watched that thought chisel away some of the hardness in her eyes. "It's good to have someone," she said quietly.

"Very good, indeed," he replied. "Chloe wants what's best for you, and so does the caseworker."

"It's best for me to stay on the island."

He wanted to say he hoped she was right, that Emma more than anyone knew what was best for herself. "What about the woman who was helping you?"

"She's gone too."

And he felt her sadness deeply. "I'm sorry, Emma."

"What did you find in the library?" Chloe was standing over them, the shop cleared.

He inched his way up beside her, nodding at the stack of paperwork that he'd placed on the counter. "Joe was right about Mrs. Pendleton. She seems to have passed away on the ship, but I found something el—"

A back door opened and Chloe's colleague, Jenna, walked into the room.

"Well, well." The woman glanced between him and Chloe. "It's our newsboy."

"Journalist," Chloe said, returning to the register.

"I thought you were about finished with your interviews."

"I found more information," Logan said.

"You two can't talk about that in here." If Jenna was trying to hide her matchmaking grin, she was failing. "Emma can come over to my house for dinner. You should take Chloe someplace else for the interview."

"I'm not going to leave you here alone," Chloe said.

Jenna scanned the empty shop. "I think I can handle it."

"There might be another rush."

"Right," Jenna said before turning back to him. "You like prime rib?"

"Meddling," Chloe warned.

"I heard the inn is serving prime rib tonight."

Logan smiled as he tucked the papers back into his messenger bag. "I never met a steak I didn't like."

"For that matter," Jenna continued, clearly enjoying the awkward state of her friend, "Emma and I have been talking about a slumber party. She can spend the night out at the farm so you two can stay out as late as—"

Chloe stopped her. "I'll pick Emma up before eight."

Two hours, according to the clock.

"Fair enough," Jenna said.

Chloe retrieved her purse from under the counter. "I'm not sure *fair* is the right word."

Jenna winked at him. "Everything seems quite right to me."

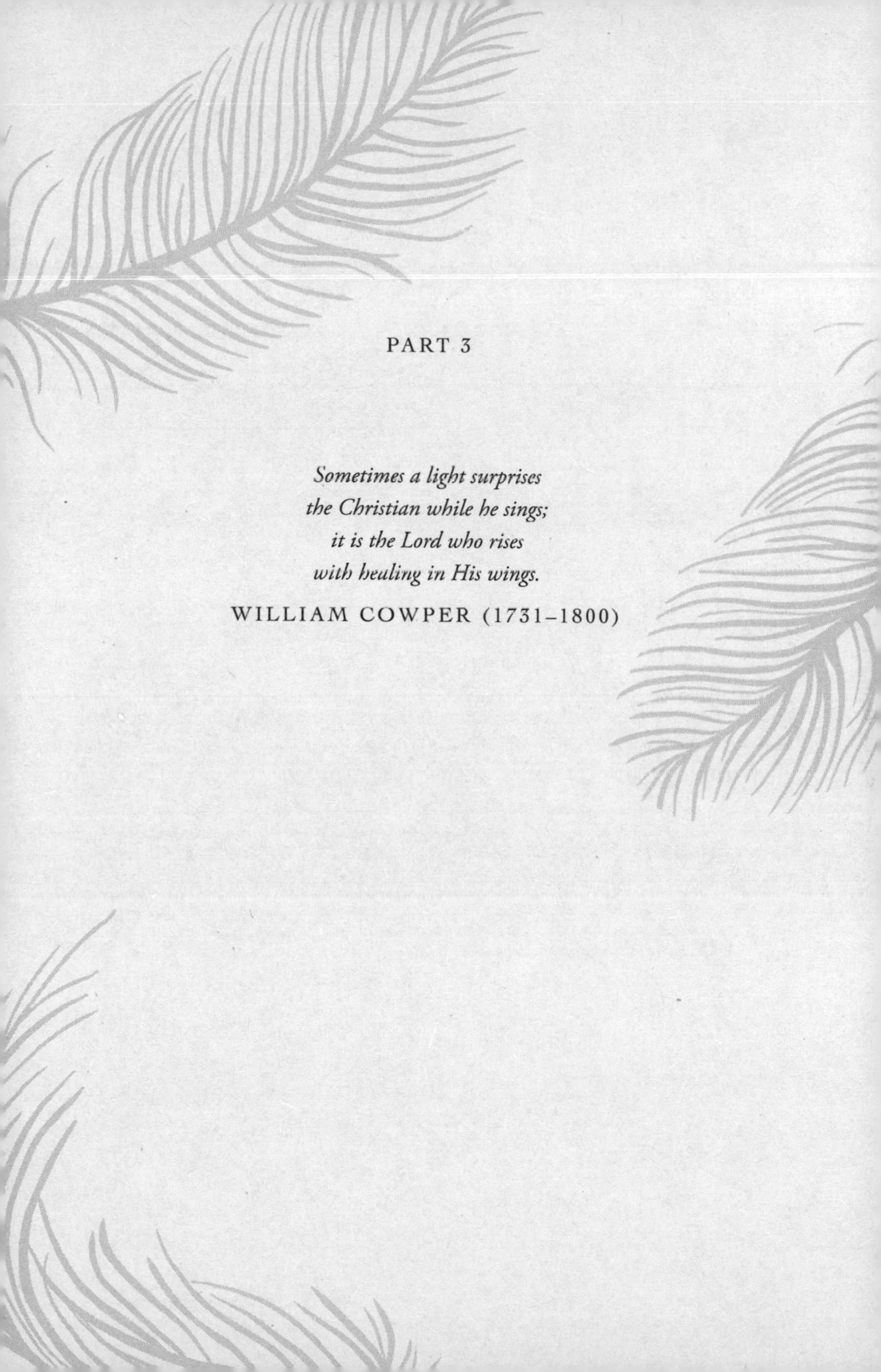

# PART 3

*Sometimes a light surprises*
*the Christian while he sings;*
*it is the Lord who rises*
*with healing in His wings.*

WILLIAM COWPER (1731–1800)

30

# *BIRDIE*

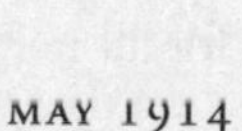

MAY 1914

Birdie dreamt of a sparrow roosting on her pillow, nudging her awake. She was back on a boat, but not one with Mummy's men. This was an ocean liner named *Empress* with paneled hallways and uniformed bell-hops and silver platters of food. A ship strewn with marble fireplaces to ward off the cold as they steamed from Quebec City to Liverpool.

She and Mummy shared a stateroom on the main deck. No more moldy shacks, Mummy had promised. Another man, one with a fine house, was waiting for them in England. A man with a son.

Birdie didn't want to think about England or the son. She wanted to breathe in the night air and watch the stars except no one could see the stars tonight. Everything on the St. Lawrence was steeped in fog.

The man left the shack in April to hunt caribou. Then Mummy had left Birdie alone in the woods. She'd been so afraid that the man would return and demand a payment, but her mother came back first.

They'd taken a train east, and after Mummy purchased them fancy dresses and shoes, they'd rented a room in a grand hotel. Birdie had been mesmerized by all the horses and carriages and crowds of people who spoke a language she didn't understand.

They didn't stay in the city for long. Mummy bought them both tickets, second class, on the next ship leaving for England.

As the ship steamed away from the harbor, just hours ago, a band had entertained passengers on the upper deck. Salvation Army, they were called. All the members dressed in uniforms like they were about to march into war.

Birdie liked sailing with an army.

Someone knocked on the door, and she held her breath. She'd thought the men were gone now.

"Mummy?" she whispered to the bottom berth.

"Answer it," her mother commanded as she tied her silky robe.

Birdie wrapped a soft blanket over her nightgown and unlocked the cabin door.

The man outside wore a cap that tipped like a teapot, a cigarette sagging between his lips.

"Come in," Mummy said with the velvety voice she used for all her visitors.

But not for Birdie. Mummy shoved her out the door. "Don't come back until breakfast."

The last thing Birdie wanted was for Mummy to be angry. She might take her back to Canada and leave her with the caribou man. And she didn't mind breathing the night air, even with the fog.

The hallway was lit with electricity, and she followed the corridor to the staircase, climbing two flights onto the promenade. No one else was outside, which was plenty fine with her. She could hear the shriek of a gull on a midnight flight, the squeak of steel as rowboats wrestled against ropes that tethered them to the deck.

With the blanket wrapped around her, she settled onto a bench, a rowboat suspended overhead, the sheen of silver glowing in the electric light. A bell clanged across the river, and she searched the horizon for life beyond their boat, for another ship that must be passing by, but she couldn't see beyond the drapery of fog.

It all seemed like a dream.

Closing her eyes, she drifted to sleep again until another nudge from her sparrow friend pushed her out of the nest. She wasn't sure if she was awake or asleep with the lapping of waves below and the chill that swept across the deck.

A bell clanged again, but this time it sounded like it was just inches beyond the rail. Then a flash of white light. Pierce of a whistle. Someone shouting in the fog and then screaming for them to get off the boat.

Birdie leapt from the bench, and when she turned toward the stairs, the ship jolted forward, the *Empress* hurtling across the river as if trying to outrun the light.

Birdie rushed to the staircase to find Mummy, but she slipped on the top step, tumbling into a puddle, her blanket falling to the bottom.

The stairs weren't supposed to be wet.

Another bell began to chime, and she was alert now, stunned by the water cascading down the staircase, freezing her toes. Passengers pressed her against the wall as they scrambled toward the promenade. Confused, frantic, most wearing nightclothes like her.

How was she supposed to find Mummy when she couldn't squeeze between the crowd?

The floor shifted and then the entire staircase leaned as the ship bowed to the river.

"Mummy!" she yelled as the steps disappeared under her feet, her shoulder banging into the wall.

Someone grabbed her arm. A bellhop, the same boy who'd helped Mummy with their trunk when they'd boarded this afternoon.

"This way," he said, pulling her toward the deck.

She wrestled against him. "I have to find my mum."

"She'll meet you outside."

The lights flickered and she grabbed for the banister, flailing against the rush of water, her heart pounding as the staircase went black.

"Please," the boy begged. He wasn't like the man. He was trying to help, not hurt her.

She reached for him then and he yanked her to the top of the staircase.

The whistle was blasting now, the ship stalled, the deck slipping farther to the right. Then the fog inched back, and she could see another ship looming in the distance but no land.

What happened to the shore?

"We're sinking," someone shouted, and Birdie closed her eyes like she used to do on the houseboat. The macaw waited for her in the branches of her mind, and she climbed onto its back.

The bellhop shook her arm. "What are you doing?"

"Flying."

"That won't do you any good. Where's your life belt?"

She glanced at the cork looped around his chest. "In the room."

He yanked his belt off. "Take mine."

"No—"

But he'd already dropped it over her head.

Something crashed on the deck as he tied the belt, one of the rowboats falling from its hold. Then the roof began caving over them. Wood and glass, pouring like rain.

*Never stay in a place when you know it's time to leave.*

But where was she supposed to go?

The *Empress* peaked like a mountain, and she thought of Pierre and his fall. Of the river that swallowed him and the woman who'd looked the other way.

"We have to jump," the boy said as they climbed to the railing.

"I can't swim."

"The life belt will keep you afloat."

She glanced behind them. "My mother . . ."

He took her hand. "If we don't jump, you'll never see her again."

But they didn't get to jump. The ship tossed them overboard, and it seemed they hung forever in the air before crashing into a wave, her mouth flooding with the bitter tang of salt and fish and steel.

In that moment, she was back on the deck of the houseboat, huddled under the icy covers, praying for the warmth of morning. No matter what happened, she wouldn't succumb to the cold.

"Paddle," the boy said, his voice faint as waves poured over them.

Another scream, the splash of oars. Then the river coughed, and she'd never forget the sloshing sound, the loud spatter, of its throat as it swallowed the ship.

Seconds later, everything was still. Eerily, bitterly, stunningly still as if the river were holding its breath. Birdie didn't have to paddle now. The life belt kept her head above the surface.

In the quiet, she tugged on the boy's hand, the current brushing over them as she floated with the cork.

"We'll paddle together," she said, her teeth chattering.

The boy was quiet now, floating on his back. She shook him, but he didn't look at her.

"Come with me," she said, her eyes focusing on a light that blinked ahead.

He pushed her away. "Swim to shore."

"I can't—"

"Swim," he said before the current swept him away.

*Grace is flowing like a river . . .*

The army of God had sung about a mighty wave that healed the sting, a sea where sins and sorrows go. A grace strong enough to make them whole and a love that filled their soul.

*Like a wave I feel it roll.*

She closed her eyes and let the words roll over her with the water.

God's grace was enough for the army.

His grace, she prayed, was strong enough for her and the boy too.

31

# CHLOE

The Thousand Islands Inn overlooked the mirror of river reflecting the sunlight, placid until a laker cruised by their window and broke the calm.

Tonight Chloe longed for calm. Sometimes she wished things would simply stay the same along the river so she could breathe in the delight of it before everything shifted again.

Logan sat across the booth from her, pulling a mountain of papers from his worn canvas bag. She hadn't been sure whether to hug Jenna when she practically shoved her and Logan out the door or hurl all sorts of choice words her way.

Now wasn't the time to be thinking about Logan beyond their partnership to find Poppy and help Emma. What to do with the shop at the end of this season was pressing enough, but what to do with Emma topped her list, especially with the border agent searching for her. Emma needed a home on the mainland by summer's end so she could start school, but even more than a house, Emma needed a family.

The server placed a bowl of fish chowder in front of her, and Chloe stirred it slowly, the steam a barrier between her and Logan.

Logan grinned. "Newsboy, huh?"

"Jenna's just being her goofy self."

"Seems like she's cutting me down to size."

"Jenna keeps all of us grounded, but she's the best of friends and an expert manager. And she's helping me take care of Emma."

"She's a good friend to both of you," Logan said.

Chloe nodded. "It's going to be hard on all of us when it's time for Emma to leave."

He took a bite of the pan-fried walleye that he'd ordered in lieu of prime rib, probably caught just a few hours ago off the shore. "Have you heard anything else about Mitch Yancey?"

"No, but the police are looking into it."

"I keep wondering why he said she's in danger."

"I don't know." She took a sip of her seltzer water. "But Emma is terrified of him."

"The caseworker won't let her go home with someone who'd hurt her."

She glanced out the window again. "Kaitlyn can't possibly know what happens behind closed doors."

"I'll keep searching for information about him."

"Thank you."

"I did find something else today." He dug a folder out of his messenger bag and placed it on the table. "Passenger lists for a shipwreck called the *Empress of Ireland*."

"Was Mrs. Pendleton on it?"

"Yes and someone else—"

She lowered her spoon, curiosity warring with her nerves. "I can't help thinking that everything is about to change."

"And you don't like change . . ."

"Not particularly," she replied as she eyed the folder.

"Which is why you're still working at your grandparents' candy shop instead of pursuing your own dreams."

She cringed at his words, her eyes narrowing. "I think you just crossed a line."

"Shifting sands, Chloe. The line keeps moving."

"When are you returning to Syracuse?" she asked.

"In a few days." He took another bite. "I want to finish this story first."

She stirred the chowder, desperately wanting to shift the sands away from her. "What made you decide to become a writer?"

"I like words."

She glanced back at him. "So do professors and librarians and preachers, for that matter."

He placed his fork on the edge of his plate and leaned back in his chair. "My mom wanted me to be a preacher."

"I could see that."

"I have the highest esteem for the mysteries of God, but—"

"You prefer to explore these mysteries another way?"

"I want to find the truth and report it," he said.

"Like Luke."

He grinned. "You know your Bible."

"A bit."

"You ever think about becoming a preacher?"

She almost spit out her seltzer. "Girls aren't allowed to preach."

"They should be."

"I wouldn't be any good at it," she said. "My wandering mind could never stick to the sermon points."

"We have that in common then. I like words and stories and uncovering the mysteries in this life, whether made by man or God Himself."

She wasn't sure that she wanted to have anything else in common with this man.

"How long have you been working for the Syracuse paper?"

"Only a few months."

"And before that?"

"I was a reporter for two years with the *Indianapolis Star*, and . . ."

She waited.

"In the Marines for four years, most of that in Central America, and then a firefighter. It was my dream job at the time."

"That's how you hurt your leg." She'd been such a dunce, assuming it was a sports injury. Even if he had hurt it playing football, there was nothing wrong with that.

Something was wrong with her instead.

"I only fought fires for a year." He sipped from his water glass as he seemed to be reliving a few memories. "Had an accident on the job, so I found a new one in public affairs while I finished my degree in journalism. I may not be able to save anyone from a fire these days, but I can fight off the devil with my pen."

"Do you see the devil in Poppy's story?"

"I see the devil when any child disappears."

"How many people have you interviewed about Poppy?" she asked.

"More than a dozen in both the States and Canada. A handful of them said that someone in their family swore they saw her after she left Koster Isle."

The sunlight faded to black outside the window until all they could see were the lights from another passing ship. Part of her wished she was tucked into her cottage by herself, away from the confusion in this world, but she was no longer alone.

"Here's one of the rosters from the *Empress*." He inched a list of names across the table, and when his fingers brushed her hand, a bolt of electricity seemed to radiate up her skin.

She pulled back but he didn't seem to notice.

"Amelia Pendleton," he said, pointing at the top paper. "She went missing the night the ship sunk."

Chloe read the woman's name and the weight of it pressed against her. "I wonder where she was traveling."

"Home to England, I suspect. So many bad things had happened to her here." Logan flipped through the pages of passengers who'd either gone missing from the ship or were confirmed dead. "But here's the kicker."

His finger traced the page until he stopped on the letter *K*.

*Ellie Koster.*

Mrs. Pendleton's sister, according to Joe.

"They must have been traveling back to England together," she said. "Perhaps that's why she came to the island."

The door opened at the opposite end of the restaurant, and Gavin McLean stepped into the room, dressed in full uniform. Seconds later, he pulled up a chair like he'd been invited to their table. "Jenna said I'd find you here."

Chloe pushed the papers away. "Is something wrong?"

"I have some news."

She pressed her hands together on the tabletop. "Logan, this is Officer McLean, one of our finest here in the North Country."

"Call me Gavin." He looked back and forth between her and Logan as if he was just now realizing she might be on a date. "Sorry, I'm interrupting."

"Logan is a reporter from Syracuse. He's interviewing locals for an article about Poppy Pendleton."

Gavin studied him. "Seems like you'd be more interested in tracking down the story of a child who lost her family today."

"I'll do whatever I can to help Emma."

Chloe leaned forward. "Did you find any information about Agent Yancey?"

"I sure did." Gavin pulled a notebook from his pocket. "He's been placed on administrative leave with Border Patrol. I haven't been able to find out why, but I went over to Wellesley and knocked on his front door. No one answered."

"Does he have children?" she asked.

"I talked to one of his neighbors, but the man didn't know anything about Yancey's family. It's curious, though . . ."

"What?" she prodded.

"The neighbor said he never sees the agent, but someone is always at his home."

Chloe sipped her water. "I suppose it isn't a crime to have company."

"True, but considering how many people are running an assortment of substances across the channel and the fact that he's looking for a child who isn't his, I'm going to do a little more sniffing around."

"What kind of substances?" Logan asked.

"Mostly cigarettes heading into Canada to avoid taxes. That's a multimillion dollar enterprise alone without the harder stuff."

Chloe cringed at the thought of boats running any sort of drugs past her island.

"Is Mitch a local?" she asked.

"I don't think so, but someone on Wellesley thought he had family around here."

"Maybe we can find them," she said.

"I'll keep looking, but you and Emma should stay at Jenna's farm for a few days," Gavin told her. "Just until we can sort this out."

Chloe pushed her fingers against the side of her head. "You think Mitch is dangerous?"

"I think everyone has the potential of being dangerous."

"But he's a border agent."

"Most agents want to stop crime, but every once in a while, criminals hide under a cloak of goodwill."

"The truth always comes out," Logan said, "in the end."

"Perhaps in your line of work." Gavin snapped his notebook shut before standing. "Mine, not so much."

"Maybe there's not always justice, but the truth tends to edge its way through the lies."

Gavin picked up the chair and returned it to the neighboring table. "We'll get justice in this case."

Logan nodded. "Justice for Emma and Poppy."

She took a deep breath. Maybe it wasn't too late to find answers for all of them.

32

# *AMELIA*

Amelia hid in an alcove near the towering staircase of the ship's elegant dining saloon and curled her empty arms into her chest as if she might rock Philip to sleep. Then she dropped her hands to her sides, a fresh wave of despair flooding over her.

Captain Kendall had already made the rounds, reminding them of tomorrow's drill on the promenade. It would only take an hour, he'd said, when someone groaned. Each passenger, no matter what class, would learn all they needed to know about his lifeboats.

Amelia wasn't worried about the *Empress* going down. She'd already lost everything, everyone, that mattered to her.

The rugged shore was in the distance; she could see it through the window, the sun exploding in a kaleidoscope of pink and orange. She blinked in the blaze of color, so like the fire in the aviary two weeks past.

Ellie had tried to kill her and Philip in the birdhouse, the flames of her fury almost consuming them. If Cade hadn't decided to check on the boats, if he hadn't been racing up the path when Ellie threw the lantern, she and Philip would have died.

But Cade had seen the flames and broken through the glass wall, not even realizing in that moment that she and Philip were inside. He'd simply been trying to save their birds.

Thankfully the birds had escaped. She'd watched them fly away as she crawled with Philip through the shattered glass.

"Let me have him," Cade had said when they emerged. Then he'd taken a screaming Philip from her arms and clung to him like a good father who wanted only the best for his son.

Tears had gushed down his face as the glass roof collapsed. And she'd just stood there, stunned by the blaze.

Cade kissed Philip's head until their son began to calm. His shirt became a blanket, wrapped tightly around Philip, then he found a grassy place for their baby to rest, far from the fire.

Minnie had lingered on a tree branch as if to make certain that Amelia and Philip were safe. Then she'd flown away in a cloud of scarlet. Maybe she would finally be reunited with Fred. Maybe their love would last a lifetime.

Minutes later, Miriam joined them, and they worked together to pump river water through the fire hose, dousing the flames. The castle could burn down for all Amelia cared, but then again, it would draw reporters and the police back to her house en masse. She didn't need the scrutiny or the questions about her baby. Instead, she'd wanted to get as far away from the island as possible.

A wave sprayed the alcove window, and she leaned back against the cushions, listening to the dinner music.

After they'd extinguished the fire, Cade lifted Philip from his soft cradle, and her heart had stilled.

What would have happened if she'd returned to the island before Cade and Miriam were wed? Once he knew about the child, Cade would have married her, but would they have been happy? Or would their love have staled like any care between her and Leslie?

She'd never know about their love, but if they had married, Ellie, she was certain, would have haunted them for the rest of their lives.

She'd seen the looks that passed between Cade and Miriam. The fear. And the longing in Cade's eyes as he held his son.

They were right to be concerned. How was she supposed to protect Philip? Once Ellie realized she'd failed this round, she'd pursue Amelia all the way to England if she must to finish what she'd started. Ellie was motivated plenty by money, but nothing caused the flames inside her sister to rage more than the thought of being wronged. Until her anger had been satisfied, her life would be consumed by revenge.

The morning after the fire, Amelia had dressed Philip in his finest clothes and clutched him to her breast. She knew she had to save him from Ellie, build a lifeboat for him in the raging sea of her life, but the thought of saying goodbye had torn her apart.

She'd asked Miriam to watch him for the afternoon, and the woman hadn't a choice really, living in Amelia's cottage, her husband the sole employee on the island. Then Amelia had filled the purse that hung around her neck with money and some of the jewels that Ellie hadn't stolen. The rest, she hid in the walls.

Amelia had arranged transport with a fishing guide who came to the island an hour later to retrieve her and her trunk, delivering them to the train station in Canada where Amelia had mailed two letters. One to Cade and one to Mr. Haynes.

It was the right thing to do but still it shattered her.

Miriam would care well for Philip, and Amelia would know he was safe. Even if Ellie followed Amelia to England, she wouldn't find her nephew. And if she killed Amelia, like she'd done with Penelope, Ellie wouldn't care what happened to Philip. Her main mission was to torment her sister. After Amelia's death, all gratification would be gone.

Amelia booked the next passenger ship leaving the Port of Quebec, but before she embarked on the *Empress*, Mr. Haynes made all the arrangements to provide for Philip. Cade would have the castle and the island and the necessary provisions immediately to raise their son as long as he and Miriam adopted Philip. That was her one requirement. For Philip and his descendants to escape the cursed legacy of the Koster and Pendleton families.

Philip would be raised as an industrious Ridell, and then, upon her death, he would inherit her stake in a portfolio of investments to manage as he pleased.

Leslie had been right about one thing: Amelia had been living her life solely for her own good. But no more. Fiona had remained in Ogdensburg to work at the orphanage. Perhaps, like her, Amelia could help at a children's home in England. She'd spend her remaining years doing something good in this world for someone else, like Fiona and the sisters in Ogdensburg had done for her. The women had little and yet, in their service, they had poured out joy.

Passengers chattered at the tables nearby, adorned in their finest attire. Laurence Irving, an English actor, was on board along with Mabel Hackney, his equally famous wife. At the table next to her was a millionaire from Montreal with his bride, talking with a socialite from the city of Quebec.

Amelia left the dining saloon before dessert, wanting to escape the feigned prestige of old and new money. Second- and third-class passengers strolled around the promenade as the sun set, enjoying the last glimpses of river before the ship broke out onto the open sea. She pulled her shawl close to her shoulders and opted to take a turn as well.

How she missed her baby boy. And the girl who had become her daughter.

How she longed to make something good from the mess of her life.

Amelia patted her neck and felt the purse hidden under fabric, the funds to begin her new life. Once she settled, Mr. Haynes would wire additional funds to her new residence. Even as the bulk of her estate would go to the Ridells, she had enough to provide modestly for herself.

As she rounded the promenade, she saw a girl, about twelve, with golden-blonde hair. It was cut short, near her shoulders, curled in ringlets.

Amelia stopped, stunned at the sight. Her mouth formed Penelope's name, but no sound passed through her lips.

The girl glanced back, not seeing Amelia really, her eyes on a heron that had joined them on the railing. It couldn't be Penelope, she told herself. It was simply a girl who looked like the child Amelia had raised long ago.

But she must be certain.

As the girl rounded the stern, Amelia rushed after her, the music from a string quartet stealing into the corridor, but the girl wasn't in the crowded music room or the quiet library or the dining room.

Ellie had said Penelope was no more, but her sister couldn't be trusted. It was possible that she gave her daughter to someone else or—Amelia shivered—after Ellie's visit to Koster Isle, she might have purchased tickets for herself and Penelope like Amelia had done for the next ship traveling across the sea.

Amelia leaned against the railing, her gaze on the gray mist that was approaching the ship, preparing to veil the *Empress* with gloom.

The girl only resembled Penelope. Surely. In her desperation, her sadness, she was seeing things. But even if it was Penelope, Amelia had no right to her. Love for her sister's child did not mean she was her mother.

Amelia took one more turn around the promenade and then slipped into her stateroom. The other passengers could spend their first night consuming music and drinks but that life was no longer for her. She locked her door and readied herself for bed, sleeping with the pouch of money under her nightclothes.

Would Penelope and Philip both haunt her for the rest of her life? She might not be able to care for either of them, but it would do her heart good to know that Penelope was still alive.

Sleep came quickly, but it didn't last. The blast of the ship's whistle shot through her room in the dark hours, and she rushed out to the promenade, her kimono robe draped loosely over her nightgown.

"Get in," a sailor shouted to her as he unfurled the rope to a lifeboat.

It was a dream, a nightmare—she would swear to it as he lowered her with a dozen others into the river. The maddening waves crashed against them, people screaming from the deck, the searchlight from another boat sweeping across them.

Then people began jumping into the river.

How could the ship be sinking? They'd only just left port.

Surely, Amelia would awaken at any moment and find herself in her warm stateroom bed.

A song rang across the water. A canary, it sounded like, but a canary wouldn't be flying along the river on this cold night.

Another salty splash. Another spray of ice. And then the white head of a whale—a beluga—emerged from the river, calling into the night.

In its wake, she saw the blonde hair of the girl from the promenade with her head tilted back, the water her pillow, a life belt keeping her afloat.

Amelia reached for the girl's shoulder.

"She's already gone," a woman behind her said.

"She's not."

"We don't have room."

"I'll make room." Amelia tried to stand, but a wave knocked her down.

Another hand reached out and pulled the still girl into their boat, spreading her across Amelia's lap. She couldn't tell if the girl was breathing, but she wasn't going to let her go now.

The boat struck another wave, tipping them into the river, and her heart capsized with it.

Moments later, a crew member on the coal ship fished her out, laying her on the deck, covering her with a blanket.

"We'll get you to shore," he said.

"Penelope," she whispered, pointing at the river.

But the sailor only shook his head.

A miracle was what it would take to find the girl now.

33

# CHLOE

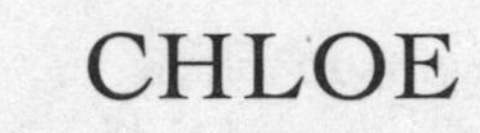

"DID YOU HEAR ME?" Chloe asked as she and Logan stood on the floating dock in Clayton.

He flicked a kamikaze bug off his jacket before taking another step toward her boat. "It would be impossible not to hear. You're practically shouting at me."

"I really don't need you to escort me to the island."

Logan grinned. "I know that."

"I've spent almost every summer of my life there. I will be perfectly fine on my own." After Gavin's warning to stay in town, Jenna happily agreed to keep Emma for the night so Chloe could retrieve her dogs and some extra clothes. She'd spend her night in the apartment over the candy store.

"Two are always better than one." He scanned the channel. "Especially when something is going on that we don't understand."

"We can't possibly understand everything."

"Please, Chloe," he pleaded as she climbed into the boat. "I need to make sure that you're safe."

How could she argue with that? She might not need an escort, but after he'd lost his son and then a woman and her child in the fire, she could understand his fear. And if she was honest, she had no desire to be alone if Mitch Yancey knocked on her cottage door.

"Come on." She waved him forward, and Logan quickly took the seat beside her.

As she steered *Lolli* into the channel, the setting sun cast a pink sheen across the water and the stone tower that rose on Calumet Island to their left. A wave hashed toward them, and Chloe shoved the throttle forward, *Lolli*'s bow cruising smoothly over it before the water calmed again.

Logan nodded toward the tower. "What's the story behind it?"

"How do you know there's a story?"

He smiled again as he zipped his jacket. "There's always a story."

A light blinked in the abandoned tower, now used as a beacon for ships and a continual reminder of those who'd flocked to the islands before them, summering in clusters to escape the sweltering heat of the city and pair their children with the right match.

"Charles Emery built a castle there about a hundred years ago," she said. "It was the first castle on the river."

"That's impressive."

"He made most of his money in tobacco and owned a hotel up the river called the New Frontenac. The hotel burned down when someone dropped their cigarette in a trash can."

"Ironic."

"Exactly. His hotel had become the gathering place for all those society members who were isolated on their islands. It was like cutting off an artery to the heart of the islands' golden age." She steered to the right of Grindstone. "The castle on Calumet burned down in 1956, but no one knows how that fire started."

Locals called it the Lost Castle now.

Poppy's Castle was ahead, and it would have been lost to the elements if Cade hadn't worked so hard to preserve it. She didn't care about society, but she loved the wildness of Koster Isle, the good memories mixed in with the bad.

"So many mysteries from the past," he said wistfully, as if he wished he could solve every one of them.

"Starting with the Native Americans, all the way through both world wars."

"Did your grandfather fight in either war?" he asked.

"No, but he used to deliver supplies over to Leek Island during the first war when it was used as a military hospital." She paused. "My father actually fought during World War II. He was fifty when I was born."

Another wave ahead, and she tweaked the throttle, the wind running through her hair. Logan and others might think she had lost herself in trying to preserve a legacy, but the truth was, she loved these islands as much as her grandparents had loved them, the sight of Poppy's Castle a consistent beacon for her way home.

"You doing okay?" she asked.

"Much better this time, thank you," he said as they cruised into the lagoon, the sunlight fading away. "What happened to your dad?"

"This isn't for your article, Logan."

"I know."

She hesitated. How she wanted to trust him as a colleague and as a friend. But it was a risk, sharing this part of her story with anyone, especially someone who could use it for his own gain.

Jenna would shake her silly. Tell her that Logan asked questions because he cared. And that was so much better than having a friend who never asked.

In that moment, she decided to dive into deeper water and excavate for him a small remnant of her wreck. "My parents both died when I was six. We were all in a van, headed to Woodstock, when my father attempted a detour through a cornfield."

"You remember it?"

"No, but I remember riding with Grandpa Cade across the channel after it happened. He told me years later about the accident."

"I'm sorry, Chloe," he said quietly as they motored into the lagoon. "No one should lose their parents like that."

"I won't say it was God's plan, but He has sure used it to redeem my life."

Logan smiled. "He is good like that."

She tied up *Lolli* and flipped on her flashlight, her dogs greeting them as they climbed the path. She leaned over to pet Maple, laughing as the dog licked her cheek.

Sugar, however, had planted herself beside Logan.

"I think your dog has a crush on me."

Chloe laughed again, relieved to emerge unscathed from the dive. "Sugar likes pretty much everyone."

"She's jealous," Logan said, pretending to confide in the dog as he scratched between her ears. "You and I are just friends, aren't we?"

Chloe trekked over a branch, ignoring his comment about jealousy. "Emma might fight you for that friendship."

"I think we can all be friends," Logan said, a few steps behind her.

"Perhaps you guys can."

"That includes you, Chloe."

Of course it did. Why did she position herself as an outsider?

Sugar let out a low growl as if she'd spotted something in the trees.

"Stay," Chloe commanded.

"I guess she doesn't like everyone."

"She's not particularly fond of squirrels."

He scanned the woods. "At least I'm in the clear."

Chloe brushed her hand across the dog who hadn't left her side. Both animals had been faithful companions to her grandmother, and she relied on them for protection too.

"These dogs wouldn't let anyone hurt you. Still . . ." Logan scanned the brush, the river a shimmering silver in the starlight. "Don't you worry about staying here by yourself?"

"Sometimes," she said, opting for candor.

"And yet you still do."

Sugar didn't growl again, but she began sniffing in circles around them.

"This spring is the first time that I've actually stayed here alone." Chloe swept a branch off the ground and tossed it up the path. *"Gie it laldy!"* she called and the dog ran past her to fetch it.

"Your dogs know Scottish?"

She smiled. "Nana taught them a little. I think it reminded her of my grandpa."

"What did she teach you?"

Chloe flipped through a mental scrapbook that she'd collected over her years, much happier to speak about those memories than relics better left in the sand. "She used to say that only a seed of courage is needed to overcome fear. A strong trunk can grow from the roots of that seed, followed by sturdy branches and beautiful flowers to face off a storm."

"You are one of the most courageous people that I know."

She looked away so he couldn't see the heat in her cheeks. "You don't know me very well."

"If you'd let me, it would only solidify what I already think."

All evening, Logan had been steering their conversation in different directions, and she felt a little dizzy. "You're here to research Poppy's story."

"Right . . ."

She turned back slowly, the beam of light settling on their feet. "I need you to stay focused on Poppy."

He cleared his throat, the lilt of his voice deepening as if he were mining the broken places in her heart. "If that's what you want."

"It's what I need."

"Maybe later . . ." He hesitated, his voice quieter, like he was trying to search for words he hadn't used in a while. "Maybe I can convince you to change your mind."

A warm breath surged through her lungs, and she twirled on her heels to cool the heat that burned inside her. She'd known it wasn't a good idea for Logan to join her on the island. Not that she worried about him harming her physically, but he was going to wreak havoc on her heart. "I have to get my things."

"Chloe," he whispered.

"I don't want to talk about it anymore."

He touched her shoulder and when a bolt shot through her again, she shook it off, stepping up the path.

"Please, Chloe."

This time she stopped, worried about the urgency in his tone. "What is it?"

He reached for her hand, covering it with his as he switched off the flashlight. "Look."

She followed his gaze up the side of Poppy's Castle, to the circle of windows above. While she hoped, at first, that starlight was reflecting off the glass, it was no reflection. A single light, like the beam of her flashlight, moved behind the window.

Logan's fingers threaded through hers, and she didn't wrestle them away.

"Let's get out of here," he said.

34

# *BIRDIE*

"MUMMY?" The word pressed through the fog of her mind, trying to find a spark of light. Her body was warmer now, a woolen blanket scratching her skin, the pounding of waves subsided. Instead of salt water, she smelled iodine.

"This one's coming around!" someone called, and she wondered what he meant about Mummy coming. Then she wondered why another man was in their room.

Feet shuffled in the darkness. A click of heels on the stone floor. Then something metal, cold and round, pressed against her chest. She gasped for breath as she remembered the cruelty of the river. The sinking lifeboat. The bellhop who'd tied his life belt around her.

The boy had saved her life, but where had he gone?

The life belt had been meant for him. It had kept her afloat while he . . .

She reached her hand up, her eyes too heavy to open. The life belt was gone now, swept away in the fog.

Birdie pressed herself up on her elbows, and the tiniest crack of light pushed through when she tried to open her eyes, pain raining down. She quickly shut out the piercing shower of stars, embracing the darkness, but her ears focused on the sounds pinging around her. Someone was shouting. Others whispering. So many voices.

"Steady now," a new man said, his hand pressed against her shoulder as she fell back on a cushion. "You're still recovering."

Her voice capsized into a whisper. "Mummy?"

"I'm sorry, dear girl."

Why was he sorry?

"We'll find help for you," he said.

Squinting again, she saw the man's white coat in the stale light, rows of beds behind him. Were they on another boat?

"Penelope?" a woman said softly, her head draped in a black shawl.

Who was Penelope?

The stranger spoke again, another name on her lips. "Are you Poppy?"

How did this woman know the girl from the tonic bottle?

Birdie struggled to understand, to answer the question, but every thought was cloaked in fear. "I'm Birdie," she finally said.

The woman gently pushed Birdie's curls away from her face. "What is your last name?"

"Just Birdie," she repeated. It was the only name she had.

"I'm—" The woman choked, seeming confused about her name too. "I'm a friend."

The doctor stepped up. "May I have a word with you, Sister Sarah?"

"Of course."

Even though they'd stepped away, Birdie could hear them speak.

"Where is her mother?" Sarah asked.

"She's missing. Presumed dead."

The words tangled in Birdie's mind, her fingers curled around the edge of the blanket. What was she going to do without her mum?

"Is there any chance her mother might still be alive?" Sarah asked.

"It's unlikely," the doctor replied. "All the survivors have been brought here, and we have already matched family members with their loved ones."

A rustling around her as she tried to imagine life without Mummy and her men.

"I know of a place where Birdie can recover," Sarah said. "The sisters will nurse her back to health."

"Will you have to travel by boat?" he asked.

Black waves towered over Birdie as she strained to hear the answer, their icy fingers lashing her skin. She would never step on a boat again.

"It's in New York," Sarah told him. "We can take the train."

The doctor glanced back at the bed. "She should be ready to travel by week's end."

Birdie closed her eyes as she sank back into the pillows. Relief was all she felt at the thought of her mother being gone and then she hated herself for it. How terrible to wish one's own mother dead.

Yet, without her mother, there would be no more men. Not in England or Canada or New York.

But where would she live now? She had no other family. No place to sleep.

Another shuffle, and she opened her eyes again when Sister Sarah sat beside her. One of the woman's cheeks was bruised, her hair pinned back under a black habit. The woman reminded her a little of Mummy except there was kindness in the way she fidgeted with Birdie's coverings, making sure she was warm.

"I'm sorry you lost your mother."

But she didn't want to talk about her mum. "A bellhop rescued me from the boat," she said. "Do you know if he lived?"

"I don't know." The sadness in the woman's voice matched the sadness in Birdie's heart. "Not many people survived."

If she'd jumped when the boy asked, would he still be alive? If he hadn't given her his life belt, he surely would be.

The boy had given his life for her, and she had nothing to offer back.

A nurse leaned over the bed with a clipboard and pencil. A red cross was stitched to the front of her white uniform, a white cap pinned to her hair. "How old are you, Birdie?"

"I don't know." No one had ever told her how old she was, and it had never occurred to her to ask.

The nurse studied her face and scribbled something on the clipboard. "You must have hit your head."

Then she remembered the discussion that Mummy had with the caribou man, when he'd said she was old enough. "Eleven," she told the woman. "Almost twelve."

"What is your surname?"

"I don't—" She paused. They needed to pin a last name, it seemed, on her. "Gagné. Birdie Gagné."

Pierre and Olivia might be gone now, but even if they weren't, they wouldn't mind if she borrowed their name.

Her response seemed to satisfy the nurse because she and her clipboard moved to the next bed.

Sarah spent hours at her bedside. At first Birdie wasn't sure what to do with the attention, but Sarah began reading a book by an Englishman named John Bunyan. Birdie rested as she listened to the journey of a pilgrim named Christian.

Sarah retrieved food for her when she was hungry, garnered extra blankets when the night grew cold, and helped her to an indoor toilet at all hours. No one had ever cared for her like this, not even Olivia, who had to leave most evenings to return home. While she didn't ask, Birdie had begun to wonder if Sarah had lost someone too.

No matter how often she thought about Mummy, she still couldn't muster any sadness over the loss. She was ready for a new journey, like the pilgrim in Sarah's book, except she had no Celestial City ahead.

She wished the nurses would let her stay here after she recovered, but the hospital needed her bed. Not for any other survivors of the *Empress*—the doctor said no one else would be found—but for those who lived in town.

A week later, a train transported her and Sarah to a new home along the river. For the first time, she wasn't living on a boat or in a hotel or a shack in the woods. The house in Ogdensburg was built of bricks and the walls inside were painted a bright blue. She had a bed of her very own, in a room with five other girls. None of the children had parents and while a few missed their mother and father, Birdie did not. She never complained about her orphan status or the chores, and as she worked, her mind wandered with the birds outside.

She didn't complain about school either. In class, she read the books she loved and learned how to make numbers work. While her lessons began with the smaller children, she quickly caught up to her class.

As the months went by, Sister Sarah was never far. She lived in a dormitory between the orphanage and the hospital and she was going to school like Birdie except she was training to become a nurse. One day, Birdie had already decided, she was going to be a nurse as well.

A year passed and then two, children arriving and then leaving the orphanage, some of them adopted, others able to obtain work on a local farm. Some of the boys were being sent overseas to fight against the Germans.

Sometimes she and Sarah strolled on the shore below the hospital and orphanage, gazing out at the river as they remembered all the lives lost the night of the wreck. And Birdie prayed quietly for the bellhop, that God had spared his life. He was an archangel in her mind, rescuing her from harm. So different from her mother, who had seemed to enjoy the pain that befell any who dared care for her.

"The first time I met you," Birdie said when she was fourteen, on a long walk with Sarah near the waterfront, "you called me Poppy."

Sarah wore a white uniform now with a cross draped around her neck, similar to the nurses in Rimouski. "That was so long ago."

"I'll never forget it." Birdie picked up a stone and tossed it into the river. "When I was little, I heard stories about a girl named Poppy. I thought you might know who she is."

"What did you hear?" Sarah asked, the breeze batting her skirt and habit.

Birdie told her about the girl from the tonic bottle, the stories about Poppy's life in a tower, the birds who swirled around her head and played in her dreams.

Sarah said she'd heard about the beautiful girl with magical wings, but Poppy didn't just live in a tower. She lived in a castle above a field of flowers and a gentle strip of river where ships never sank and men were always kind and women never lost or left their children.

Poppy's mother was different than other moms, Sarah told her. Some days she was extra nice but other days she was cruel to everyone around her.

"Just like my mum," Birdie said.

Sarah blinked, seemingly surprised to hear Birdie speak about her mother. "Do you miss her?"

Birdie thought for a moment. "Is it wrong to say no?"

"It's wrong to lie."

"I don't miss her at all." She folded her arms into her chest. "But I miss having family."

A slow smile, both timid and kind, drifted across Sarah's face. "You will always have me."

Birdie considered her words before daring to ask the question that had been stirring in her heart. "Could I call you aunt instead of sister?"

Sarah's worn eyes filled with tears. "I'd like that very much."

"Aunt Sarah," Birdie said softly, reaching for the woman's hand.

As the years went by, no one asked again about Birdie's mum.

And as the years went by, Birdie stopped thinking about her too.

# 35
# CHLOE

All Chloe could think about was the light in the castle. Who had been inside it and why? Neither she nor Logan had the answer as they convened in the candy shop, waiting in the office for Gavin and the two officers he'd taken to Koster Isle.

Emma was still at Jenna's farm along with Fraidy and now Sugar and Maple. Originally Chloe had planned to sleep in the rooms over her store, but she took Jenna up on the offer to borrow her basement couch until the police found Mitch Yancey and whoever was trespassing on her island.

The espresso machine steamed as she frothed milk for two cappuccinos. Then she sprinkled them both with Nana's peppermint cocoa powder and handed one to Logan.

"We may be here for a while." She sipped the warm drink, imagining the creamy espresso dripping down to warm her toes.

He unzipped his messenger bag and pulled out a small stack of papers. "You ever have anyone trespass before?"

"Kids ride their boats over sometimes to explore the island or build a bonfire on the shore."

"But no one inside the castle?"

"Not that I know of, but it's impossible to say. Someone else might know about the lock that you found."

"It's odd timing," he said as he tapped the side of his cup. "Emma arrives on your island and then someone else shows up at the castle."

"It's certainly suspect."

Logan emptied his cappuccino before flipping through the papers as if he might be able to resolve the mystery of Poppy's disappearance right here. It seemed, though, that they weren't the only ones searching for something related to the Pendleton family. Or had Mitch Yancey figured out where Emma went? Perhaps he thought that she and Emma were staying in the castle instead of the cottage.

Chloe stared at the ship's manifest, her mind spinning as she traced back through the list of people who'd gone missing until she found the letter *K* again. The listing for Mrs. Pendleton's sister.

Then she looked back up. "There's another Koster recorded here."

He looked over her shoulder and read the name. "Birdie."

"She was eleven." Chloe's eyes rose slowly.

"Wait—"

"Poppy," she said as she met his gaze. "And then Birdie."

Same age. Similar names.

"Do you think it's possible?" He stared back at her, the question swelling between them.

"Perhaps."

If it was Poppy, where had her journey taken her after she left the castle? And why had she been traveling to England with her mother and her aunt?

"That would mean she was alive when she left the castle."

"And then a shipwreck—"

"I was really hoping she might still be alive," he said sadly.

"Me too." She looked at the list again. "I think I've seen Ellie's name before. In my grandfather's papers."

The wooden filing cabinet in the corner had been built decades ago and was bulging with all manner of personal and business paperwork.

She'd given up on it entirely last year and bought herself a shiny metal cabinet to put beside her desk.

As Logan read through his other papers, she rummaged through the old files, past tax forms and receipts and a host of invoices, until she reached the folder containing her grandparents' will. It had been a fairly simple document. They'd left everything—the cottage, the candy shop, the castle and its island, and all their personal accounts—to her.

She didn't want to settle their estate, but even if she hated final, it was time for her to finish this. Tomorrow she would close their last account. Then she would work and pray and wonder what God had next.

She opened the file on the table and slipped out a short handwritten letter addressed to Mr. Ridell, tossing it on top of Logan's materials. "Look at this."

He scanned it before reading aloud. "'Philip will be provided for well in my will, but as much as I have tried, I cannot protect him from my sister. Take great care that Ellie is not allowed back on the island. If she returns, I fear she will destroy your family.'"

Logan lowered the paper, but he didn't return it to her. "Who is Philip?"

"My father."

"Apparently things did not go well between the Koster sisters after all."

"Apparently not," she said. "But why would this woman want to harm my father?"

He considered her question. "Maybe she was jealous of the baby."

"First Mrs. Pendleton leaves the island to my grandfather and now she is trying to protect the caretaker's son?"

"It is strange," Logan agreed. "Joe said that Mrs. Pendleton gave the island to Cade in case Poppy returned, but it still would have been scandalous, even if he was a likeable and dedicated man, to leave a fortune to one of your servants. She must have had a favorite charity, at the very least, that would have watched for Poppy and then welcomed the profit made from selling the island."

"If Poppy was with her aunt, Mrs. Pendleton must have known where she was all along." Chloe took the last sip of her cappuccino. "There are too many layers here."

"We'll unravel every one." He placed the letter on his stack and straightened the angles as if this very act would align all the questions they had and spit out an answer.

She glanced across the table at the man who'd once fought for freedom as a Marine before he started fighting fires. A man who now fought against injustice in New York. "I believe we just might."

Logan flashed her the most brilliant grin. Heart-melting, Nana would have said. Warm enough to take out their entire inventory of chocolate.

She'd have to steer away from that smile before it melted her too.

"What's next?" she asked, ready for a distraction from castle lights and melting of hearts. It was already after ten, and she hoped Gavin would return soon. That whatever he'd found was easily diffused.

Logan nodded toward the computer near the back window in her office. "Can I borrow that?"

"Of course."

After she powered it on, the modem dialed until it connected to a bulletin board. He switched to her office chair, and she scooted her chair beside him as he began typing a message to fellow journalists online. "What are you looking for?"

"To see if I can find anything else about Ellie Koster."

Logan didn't get far in his search. Minutes later, someone tapped on the front door, and he answered it.

"Whoever was inside the castle is gone." Gavin removed his cap, his thin hair wet from the mist. "We didn't see any lights on the island either."

"You want something hot to drink?" she asked.

He followed her to the counter and placed his hat beside him when he sat on a stool. "A double, please."

"Someone was there," she said as she pulled the shots.

"I don't doubt you, Chloe, but the intruder either left on a boat or is still there. We're not searching your woods in the dark."

"I don't blame you for that."

Gavin glanced at Logan and then back at her. "You sure you didn't see another boat around the island?"

"I'm positive." She handed him a cappuccino with sprinkles on top and he gulped it down. "You were supposed to sip that, Gavin."

"I don't have time for sipping."

"What should we do now?" Logan asked.

"You staying in town?"

He nodded. "At the inn."

"Good. Keep an eye out for Chloe, would you?"

"I'm planning on it."

She didn't need either of them looking out for her, but she rested her defense. It was nice in that moment to have them team up in this way. Jenna would have approved.

"And where will you be staying?" Gavin asked her.

"At Jenna's tonight. Then I'll head back over to Koster in the morning."

"Chloe—"

"Okay, I'll wait a day or two."

"I'll tell you when you can go home," Gavin said.

"You can't tell me that!"

"I don't need another missing person added to my load. You'll be just fine working from here."

"And you'd be just fine sipping your cappuccino."

He didn't even smile.

"I'm not worried about me," she said. "Just Emma."

"I know that, Chloe. You make me do the worrying for you."

Logan cleared his throat. "I'll keep an eye out for both her and Emma until you find out what's happening on the island."

36

# *AMELIA*

JULY 1918

LEEK ISLAND

A strand of waves rocked the incoming ferry as Amelia and Birdie worked together to unfold chairs on the narrow strip of grass that they'd transformed into a beach for convalescing soldiers. Almost everything was makeshift on this island, but their staff made do. With fifteen nurses, two doctors, and three assistants, they had created a respite for dozens of Canadian soldiers returning from the front in France.

After the tragedy on the St. Lawrence, Amelia embraced the name Sarah and her new roles as a nursing nun and an aunt to her sweet niece. It was the supreme grace of God, she thought. A gift for Him to return this beautiful girl whom she loved like a daughter.

The rest of the world thought Amelia Pendleton dead. In her mind, she had been dead and then brought back to a new life that resembled nothing of her early years.

Long ago, she'd condemned Ellie for her sins and then she'd done the same thing, giving herself to a man outside the bounds of marriage as if that could satisfy the deep longing of her heart. But she was no longer that woman. God, in His great mercy, had forgiven her every sin.

Sometimes, in the early hours, shame still clouded her mind but she refused to live under its weight. Her desire was to serve God now and those He brought along her path.

The Pendleton fortune was no longer hers. Mr. Haynes would have done his job efficiently by now, selling all that she'd owned except Koster Isle. Part of her estate would go to Cade and Miriam. The rest would be set aside in a trust for Philip, in a discreet fund at her request. Miriam would raise him well, but in a small part, Sarah liked to think, she was still caring for her son from afar.

"Thank you, Sister," a soldier, still in his twenties, said before sitting on one of the folding chairs. Then he twisted his cane into the grass like he was staking a claim.

"You are quite welcome," she replied before nodding at the ferry. "Sunshine and a show for you this afternoon."

"Do you know who's arriving?"

"Two new patients."

Another soldier waited in a wheelchair beside her. A farmer who'd grown a beard since he'd returned from France, his hair more gray than brown. Three children, he said, were waiting outside Toronto for what was left of their daddy to come home.

Both men were recovering from wounds sustained in the war. The younger soldier had suffered a fever that stole most of his memories while the elder recalled details from France with flourish, but his right arm had stayed behind in the trenches.

Birdie stepped up beside the older man's wheelchair as he tried to maneuver into a folding chair like his comrade. "I'll help you," she said.

He tried one more time and then fell back, his left arm not quite ready to support the weight. "Are you going to carry me out of here?"

"I just might try if you don't cooperate." Without the slightest sign of repulsion or frustration, Birdie slid her shoulder under his right stump to help him relocate to the beach chair. Then she removed his shoes and socks.

"You are a treasure, Birdie," he said as he raked his toes through the grass.

"No more than anyone else."

"Just like my oldest daughter. Course, my girl is probably married by now."

"Sixteen is much too young to marry," Sarah said from the other side of the beach.

"That's how old my wife was when we married."

"I'm never going to marry," Birdie told him, resolute.

"Then you're bound to break an army of hearts around here."

Birdie patted his good shoulder before moving on to help another man who'd called. The soldier really didn't need assistance but most of their patients couldn't resist a few minutes talking with the prettiest girl on Leek Island.

Getting herself and Birdie onto this remote island had been a feat as they were both still terrified of the river, but hand in hand, they'd made it. And they'd been here three months now, working with the hospital staff who'd arrived from New Jersey.

The ferry was closer now, all the men watching it, curious to know who would be joining them. Dozens of wounded soldiers were recovering in the island's manor house turned hospital, and when Sarah heard about their need for more nurses, she went straight to the hospital administrator in Ogdensburg and asked if she could help care for the patients on Leek and take Birdie as her assistant.

It was a blessing of God's alone, Sarah knew well, for them to be together, and the bond between them had grown even deeper in this place. While Birdie still seemed to be afraid of some of the men, she was more confident now. In the past four years, Sarah had never heard her mention Ellie or what happened in those years after Koster Isle.

Then again, Sarah never spoke about her past either. Those memories had sunk with the ship, disappearing forever under the surface.

The men flirted with Sarah sometimes, and she laughed with them. She'd turn forty-one this year and had taken her own vow of celibacy. When her work here finished, she planned to relocate to a hospital near Birdie so she could catch her niece if she fell again.

Not that Birdie needed it. She'd grown into a striking young woman, a competent nurse in training and quite ready to run her own household if she decided to marry. The soldiers here never flirted with Birdie. They were simply in awe of her bright spirit that made friends with everyone on the island. Her beautiful blonde curls and eyes that matched the turquoise hue of the river basking in the sunlight.

The lie of Poppy Pendleton had been erased, and a new reality had been born. She'd never tell Birdie what happened back in England or on Koster Isle. Instead, Birdie would live free from any worry of becoming like her mother and grandmother or Sarah, for that matter. And neither of them would have to worry if Ellie defied the registrar after the accident, like Sarah had done, and was searching for them both.

Birdie was free now from the anxiety and expectations of being a Koster or Pendleton. Here she could dream about a future without any confines or the stench of new money to repel the good people from her life.

She wanted to teach Birdie to fly on her own.

While Birdie didn't know it, Sarah had enough money to send her to college if she chose to go. Even without a nurse's salary, Sarah had enough left from her purse to provide for both of their needs. They were free now, and she wanted Birdie to soar in any direction that she chose. No one from society or the Koster or Pendleton family would bring her down.

The ferry bumped against the dock, and someone tossed a rope over the side. Rhoda, the head nurse, tied it to a cleat, and then Sarah stepped onto the platform to welcome their new patients as they were wheeled off the boat.

Sarah glanced at her watch, a plain silver one that she kept in her pocket, before looking back at Birdie. None of the soldiers had caused the nursing staff any harm, but still she always left Birdie in the care of a fellow nurse.

"Will you help Rhoda wheel our guests to the house?"

"Of course."

"The doctor will look in on them once they've settled."

She never could have anticipated who was arriving on Leek Island that day.

Fate, it seemed, had found her sweet Birdie again.

37

# CHLOE

"I'M HERE TO CLOSE my grandparents' savings account," Chloe told the manager of Seaway Credit Union.

Emma sat in an office chair beside her this morning, facing Steve as he scanned a computer screen on his desk. The bank didn't allow any animals in their lobby, but she'd agreed to let Fraidy nap at the candy store so they could visit the credit union and then the sparrow with its slowly healing wing.

Jenna, she knew, would watch over her kitten.

Steve pushed his wire-rimmed glasses up his nose. Chloe didn't know him well, but he'd graduated from Thousand Islands High School a few years after her. "We were really sorry to hear about Mrs. Ridell," he said. "She's been a valuable customer for decades."

"I know she appreciated working with you."

"Are you certain you want to close her account?"

"My lawyer says we need to finalize the rest of her estate," she said. "I'm not sure what else to do."

A smile slipped up his tawny face. "My colleagues and I were hoping you might transfer the balance into yours."

A switch inside her flipped from dread to curiosity. Why was his team discussing her grandmother's account?

"That would be fine." She handed Steve the necessary paperwork—Nana's death certificate and a copy of the will naming her as the sole beneficiary.

He didn't even glance at the papers. "The account is listed as a POD."

"What's POD?" she asked.

"Payable on death," he explained. "And you're already named as the beneficiary. It won't take me long to transfer the money."

"We're not in a rush."

"Are you planning to keep the safety deposit box as well?"

She blinked. "I'm sorry?"

"The safety deposit box." He looked back at the computer screen. "Looks like Mr. Ridell began renting one about twenty years ago."

"I didn't know—"

Steve kept reading the note on his screen. "It sounds like you were supposed to access it when you closed their account. You can keep the box, if you'd like, or remove the contents. The fee is waived for our most loyal customers."

She sure didn't feel like a great customer. "I don't have a key."

"I can call Diebold right now to drill it, but—" he glanced at Emma—"I'm afraid you and the technician are the only ones allowed in the vault."

"I can't leave her alone."

"Then perhaps you could come back tomorrow."

"I'll be fine," Emma said, but she didn't know Mitch was looking for her.

Chloe checked her watch before standing up. "I'll return in an hour."

They stepped out of the bank, the door facing the waterfront. Two divers surfaced about twenty yards offshore, and one of them lifted his hand to wave before disappearing again. Logan was supposed to interview the owner of the local dive shop this morning, and she suspected that he'd talked the man into taking him on a dive. The reporter might frustrate her with all his questions, especially the ones that pierced her insecurities, but she admired his tenacity. He kept pushing for answers even when there seemed to be none.

She turned to Emma. "You doing okay?"

"I like it here," Emma said, her eyes on the river.

"I'm really glad."

"You shouldn't worry so much about me."

Chloe placed her hands on Emma's shoulders. "I just want you to be safe."

Emma met her eye again. "Thank you."

"Tell you what," Chloe said as she rechecked her watch. "I have a friend with two kids who lives down the street. They're a couple years younger than you, but if they're home, I bet they'd like to play for an hour or so."

Instead of a smile, Emma's eyes filled with fear.

"What's wrong?" Chloe asked.

Emma didn't respond, but Chloe slowly understood. If Emma hadn't attended school, she had probably never had a playdate in her life either. No trips to the playground or local pool. Few or even no opportunities to let down her guard and have fun with other children.

"They'll love you," she said.

"But what do I say to them?"

"Tell them about Fraidy."

Emma seemed to consider this. "I could tell them about Maple and Sugar too and the sparrow."

Chloe draped one arm over Emma's shoulder. "They'll want to hear every story."

"Why can't I just sit in the lobby?" Emma asked.

"Because it would break my heart if something bad happened to you."

Belle McLean was home when Chloe knocked, and she welcomed Emma with open arms. While it was the job of her husband to enforce the law, Belle didn't care much about protocol. And no one was going to bother Emma at the home of the local deputy.

"I just need an hour to finish up some paperwork," Chloe explained.

Belle waved her away. "Take all the time you need."

When she returned to the bank, the technician was ready to open her box. A blast of cold hit her when Steve unlocked the vault, and she wondered at the columns of drawers on the walls. All the mementos stored inside.

What had Grandpa Cade stored in the one for her?

Minutes later, the technician had drilled through the nose of a small drawer, and the men looked away as she reached inside. Two items were grouped together at the base. One was a key on a small chain—for the castle door, she assumed. The other item was an ivory envelope with her name written on the outside.

"Can I take these with me?" she asked Steve.

"Do whatever you'd like." He closed the drawer. "They're yours."

She hugged the letter to her chest. "I'd like to read this outside while you finish transferring the account."

He nodded. "I'll find you when I'm done."

She passed through a tunnel of bushes until she found a wooden bench that offered locals a respite from the summer crowds. As she slid her finger under the crisp glue, she breathed a prayer. Of gratefulness, more than anything, for another moment with her grandfather. And perhaps some clarity.

*If you are reading this letter, dear Chloe, it means that both Miriam and I are gone. So much has happened in your fifteen years, I don't know how to explain it all here, but Miriam and I tried our best to protect you from harm. Perhaps I was wrong in keeping some of my past mistakes from you, but I wanted you to grow in your youth without anything weighing you down. And I wanted to fix your broken heart.*

*I spent much of my life trying to fix broken things until I finally realized in this thick skull of mine that I couldn't fix anything on my own.*

*"He heals the brokenhearted and bandages their wounds."*

*That psalm sums it up best. I couldn't make things better in our family, but I prayed consistently that our Lord would bandage the many wounds from our past. Especially the ones that I caused.*

*Your father had a hard go at life after World War II. This isn't an excuse for his neglect. Only an explanation for the reality.*

*Miriam and I also had regrets. Perhaps all parents do. I should have disciplined Philip more in his earlier years, and Miriam would say that she should have disciplined him less.*

*Philip was a Pendleton by birth—my child with Amelia Pendleton—but Miriam, the kindest soul I've ever known, loved him like her own. The money in our account is what remains from the trust that Amelia set up for him. It is yours now. May you use it for good.*

*Love those around you well, Chloe, and let others love you in your successes and in your brokenness. With God's help, I pray you can forgive me. And I pray you spend your life fixing some of the broken wings in this world.*

*Your loving grandpa, Cade*

*PS: Take care of Lolli when I'm gone. She'll be good to you.*

Chloe slowly read the words again about Amelia and her grandfather and then her father, trying to process what happened in the past. This revelation explained so much. The secrets and some of her strange memories and why Nana had no use for the castle. Those walls must have held nothing but painful memories for her.

And if her father was a Pendleton, that meant, for better or worse, Chloe was a Pendleton as well. A Pendleton and a Ridell.

Her father had spent much of his adult life angry at both Miriam and Cade. Emotions, she'd always thought, that were a result of the war, but what if it was more? Like the flycatcher birds, foster parent for the cow buntings who abandoned their chicks, Miriam had willingly taken another's baby into her nest. Then she'd done her best to raise Philip after Amelia was gone.

But what if Philip had been mad at Miriam for taking him as her own?

Grandpa Cade had asked her forgiveness, and she quickly forgave the lies that he'd told her to cover up his affair. Nothing else, in her mind, needed to be forgiven.

Perhaps now true healing could begin. Perhaps, with this needle of truth, God could stitch together the brokenness that had passed down into Chloe's heart. Continue molding the pieces, like Nana once said, into something good.

Steve found her on the bench, tears streaming down her face.

"Here's your deposit slip," he said, handing it over to her.

She stared at the number. Numbers.

With a swipe over her waterlogged eyes, she tried to clear her vision. She'd never seen so many digits on a receipt. "There must be an error."

He glanced at the paper. "There's no error."

"I thought their account was empty. Memory care alone—"

"Your grandparents invested well over the years."

"I'll say."

"I'm glad you're staying with the credit union."

"I'm staying, Steve, but I'll be spending a chunk of this."

His smile didn't even dim when she said goodbye.

Chloe's gaze fell to the slip again, marveling at it. She had enough to keep her cottage and the candy shop and the entire island. Best of all, she had enough to care for Emma as long as the girl needed a place to stay.

Nana was right. God, it seemed, had something really good in store.

She hurried to the McLean home and found Emma laughing with Belle's kids, her feet dangling in the water.

"Let's go check on our sparrow," Chloe said, and the vet greeted them with a cloth carrier in hand.

The sparrow was ready, her wing healed, and Emma transported her like she had done so often with Fraidy, balancing the cage carefully until they reached the park. Then she gently placed the carrier on the ground and looked through the mesh opening.

"You stay safe," she whispered. "It would hurt my heart if something bad happened to you."

Emma unzipped the mesh and stepped back before taking Chloe's hand. The bird hopped out on the dirt and lifted her gaze to the sky. Then she spread her wings, and Emma and Chloe squealed with delight when the sparrow flew.

## 38

# *BIRDIE*

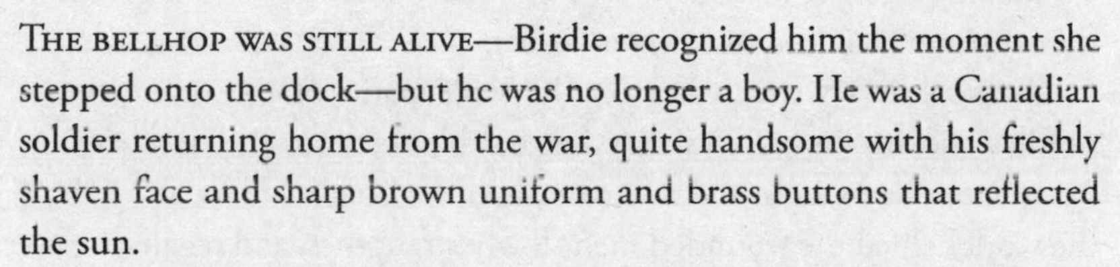

The bellhop was still alive—Birdie recognized him the moment she stepped onto the dock—but he was no longer a boy. He was a Canadian soldier returning home from the war, quite handsome with his freshly shaven face and sharp brown uniform and brass buttons that reflected the sun.

Relief flooded Birdie's heart at the sight, surging through her entire body and erupting across her face in a smile. But the man didn't smile back. He didn't even speak to her. Instead he slumped in the wheelchair, his lips locked like a vault with a thousand secrets trapped inside.

This man had saved her life four years ago when he'd given her his life belt. Convinced her to climb back up the sagging stairs. She'd hoped for a miracle, prayed for one on those nights in the orphanage when his kind eyes would watch over her in the darkness. When he would press through the nightmares about sinking boats and wicked men and take her hand in his.

The man before her didn't realize what he'd done, didn't even see her with his vacant eyes, but he'd been with her, tucked away in her heart, since the *Empress of Ireland* disappeared.

But she never dared to dream that he might really be alive. How could he be when almost everyone from the wreck lost their life? She'd certainly never imagined that she would find him here.

Birdie swept behind his chair quickly lest he blink and recognize her, not wanting to talk about it on the dock. Then she chided herself for her childishness. She'd only been a girl on the ship, barely dressed in a nightgown, a silhouette in the fog. He might remember—she hoped he remembered—giving her the life belt, but he wouldn't recognize her today.

"I'll take you to the house," she said.

"Thank you."

Those were the only words he spoke as Birdie rolled the wheelchair onto the dirt path, following Rhoda and the other wounded soldier up to the manor. She didn't know what else to say to this angel of a man, but her heart hammered like it used to do when she slept on the deck of the *Adonis*, watching the stars. Like the woodpecker in the distance as it pounded against a tree.

How she wished the light that reflected off the man's brass buttons would leap straight into his eyes. How she wished she could give him the same gift that he'd once given to her.

Two soldiers were sitting on the wide patio of the main house, needles clicking in hand as they knitted blankets for the new arrivals. Aunt Sarah had taught them to knit, and the doctors marveled at how the work helped the wounded men slowly strengthen and regain the use of their fingers and hands. Everyone could contribute something, Aunt Sarah liked to say.

Birdie prayed the soldier in front of her would reawaken to life again soon. And perhaps, one day, he would remember her, as she had remembered him.

*William.*

Rhoda posted his name, written in block letters, over his bed, one of twelve in the music room. He didn't speak to the staff or the soldiers around him. As head nurse, Rhoda took over his care, but Birdie sat beside him whenever she could, like Aunt Sarah once did for her.

William was a man now, but she wasn't afraid of him. At least, not like the men her mother once entertained. He'd saved her life and she would do everything in her power to save him too.

In his first weeks on the island, William rarely opened his eyes, and when he did, they were focused on the patterns in the pressed tin as if the ceiling's scrollwork held the answers to some mystery in his mind. As if he could see things that she did not.

Birdie wished she could step into his head and help him find the path back to shore, but she didn't know exactly what to say. So she offered this passage through the writing of others. Beginning with the Gospel of Luke. The writer of that book, she'd learned in school, was a physician and follower of a God-man named Jesus who understood the power of healing on one's body and mind. She read the verses at William's bedside whenever the nursing staff didn't need her help. And it seemed to her that Aunt Sarah and the other nurses began requiring less of her assistance after William arrived.

Whether or not he was listening, the other bedridden soldiers were quite intent on her words. William only opened his eyes when she finished. Then he'd thank her again. Day after day those simple words linking them together. A quiet bond, she liked to think.

*There's nothing wrong with him.*

The nurses whispered about William over their meals, but Birdie never criticized him. Almost every other soldier on Leek Island was missing a limb or recovering from a gunshot wound or fractured bone or bout of infection, but William's body was whole. It was his mind that had broken.

How did one fix a broken mind? More than anything, she wanted to give life back to the man who'd given it so freely to her.

When Birdie finished reading Luke, she began borrowing other books from the manor's library. *Pilgrim's Progress*, she read next, and *The Call of the Wild*, and then she began reading the beautiful poetry of Henry van Dyke.

"I think it's time for you to move outside," Rhoda told William on a clear, warm day in August, a month after he arrived.

He didn't argue as Rhoda and Aunt Sarah helped him into a chair, but his eyes were closed as Rhoda wheeled him to the door.

Aunt Sarah waved at her. "Come along."

Birdie followed the nurses to a grassy ledge above the river, a breeze rustling the boughs of pine around them.

Aunt Sarah unfolded two lounge chairs and then handed her the book of poetry. "Read," she whispered, "for as long as you need."

Then they left her and William alone.

Birdie looked over at his handsome eyes fixed on the endless mirror of water below. While he wore a plain white shirt and trousers instead of his uniform, he was as alert as any soldier who faced an enemy.

What had those somber eyes seen on the battlefield? And what had they locked away?

She knew how one's thinking could freeze into place for a long season, and then how a mind could repeat the same events over and over as if trying to change the course of time. The battle to find goodness in the midst.

Glimpses from her childhood often repeated in her head. Her mother's wicked laughter when Birdie asked to cut her hair. The man who touched her in places he should not. The memory of cold water and screams from the sinking *Empress*. The splash of Pierre's body when her mother pushed him overboard.

She didn't know if she would ever be free of those memories, but she was trying to replace them with better ones, steering her lumbering mind to memories that made her smile. The grasp of William's hand when he helped her on the ship, the sailor who'd fished her out of the river, Aunt Sarah embracing her at the hospital and never letting her go.

Under the cathedral of sunlight, she began to read another poem by Henry van Dyke. One about a man's search for God. Instead of being confined in a chapel, the poet had found God on mountain heights and in the valley, among depths of water and the expanse of a starry night.

*Thou who hast taken to thyself the wings*
*Of morning, to abide*
*Upon the secret places of the sea,*
*And on far islands, where the tide*
*Visits the beauty of untrodden shores . . .*
*To thee I turn, to thee I make my prayer,*
*God of the open air.*

A prayer lingered on Birdie's lips as she looked across the channel again with its cluster of islands in the distance and breathed deeply of air shared by all who lived along the river.

God was in this great place, above the river that had tried and failed to drown her and William. God was above the war that continued battling in William's mind.

But why hadn't God stopped the war or the shipwreck or the man?

She didn't know the answer, but God hadn't looked away in their distress either; she was certain of it. If God was in the secret places and the wide-open ones too, His presence could be found in the midst of a battle and depths of a river and confines of a cabin.

Perhaps that's why His presence could be found more easily in the open. People couldn't muddle it up so easily out here.

Soon they'd be able to see the starry sky that van Dyke had mentioned. Soon the screams of that cold night long ago would return.

She should probably take William back to the house before the sunlight was gone, but this moment seemed sacred. Aunt Sarah had said they could stay here as long as they needed.

She and William were together in this crisis of mind. Not hand in hand. Not even looking at each other. But side by side.

For tonight, it was enough.

"God is here," she said, not knowing if William heard. "In this open place."

He hadn't forsaken either of them.

She felt a shift beside her, the hint of an awakening. And her heart leapt at the possibilities.

She turned slowly, afraid of frightening him. Terrified at what she might see.

When William finally emerged from the fog, when he was forced to face the threatening waves of this life, would he be able to swim like he'd done after the shipwreck? Or would he sink further into himself? The sorrows that he'd experienced in battle, she feared, would drown him.

William studied her face in the golden frame of dusk as if he was trying to figure out where she fit into the framework of his mind.

"You were on the *Empress*," he said slowly.

"I was." She wiped back a tear, afraid she would frighten him if the joy that welled inside gushed down her cheeks.

"We were . . ." He was searching again, trying to make sense of the world around him. She waited as the sun flared into orange. Waited for him to find his words.

Then his eyes widened and she could see the emerald green of Ireland in them, pure wonder leaping from his gaze like firelight as he broke free. "You were the girl on deck with me."

She smoothed her hands over her skirt. "I'm not a girl anymore."

"I thought you'd drowned."

"I thought the same of you." She brushed away another tear. "I would have died if you hadn't given me your life belt."

He searched the river as if he might see the crest of their sinking ship, and in that moment, she was flung back into the frigid water, grasping for the boy who'd saved her life, wondering what happened to her mother. Fear mixed with a peculiar hope. While she'd been desperate for warmth, she hadn't wanted to travel to England or return to the caribou man.

She'd fallen asleep in the river long ago, and when she woke again, she was in the hospital, ready to embark on the journey that her heart longed for.

"How did you get out of the water?" she asked.

"Someone pulled me onto the *Storstad*. Once I'd dried out, the shipping company put me right back to work."

She closed the cover of the poetry book. "You didn't have time to recover."

"My hands were aching for something to do." He rubbed them together as if they were in urgent need of another task. "I searched the papers for news of you, but so many died. I didn't even know your name."

She tucked the poetry beside her. "I'm Birdie."

"Birdie." He reached for her hand now, like he'd done in her dreams, and held it in silence as the last of the evening colors began to fade. "I'm William," he said. "Will Townsend."

"You saved my life, Will Townsend." She grasped his hand tighter, never wanting to let it go. "I'm forever grateful."

His hand grew heavy in hers, and she watched as his eyes faded like the sunlight, slipping back to gray.

"William," she whispered. "Please don't leave."

She couldn't lose him again.

His hand dropped back into his lap and a shiver swept up her spine. Then he closed his eyes as he returned to the depths, leaving her on the shore.

But this time Birdie wouldn't let him drown.

"Please," she begged, like he had once begged of her. "Swim."

Instead of taking his hand again, Birdie did the unthinkable. Leaning forward, she kissed his cheek, and when he still didn't look at her, she brushed her fingers over his face, his hair, as if she could brush away whatever had blinded him from the beauty left in this world.

"Please, Will."

He blinked, his gaze slowly focusing again on her face, fear raging through his eyes. Whether he'd felt her lips on his skin, she didn't know, but he knew she was there, stepping into his fear.

"Swim with me," she whispered.

He blinked again.

"We have to swim."

He shuffled in the chair, the slightest of movements that sounded like thunder.

"Don't leave me," he said.

She smiled softly as she threaded her fingers back through his, her heart hammering fresh in her chest. She hadn't lost him. "Never again."

A star flickered on the canvas above, God lighting the night sky, she thought. A beacon if they lost their way.

"Birdie?"

"I'm right here."

Sighing, he rested his head on her shoulder.

Will's mind might be crippled, but he wasn't broken.

He just needed a beacon to find his way back home.

## 39
# CHLOE

"I KNEW BIRDIE."

Chloe turned and stared at the girl who'd sauntered into the basement in Jenna's farmhouse and then snuggled up in a big chair beside Logan and Chloe, her curly hair tied back with a teal ribbon.

Logan dropped the article in his hands, the one that announced a marriage between Birdie Gagné and a man named William Townsend—two *Empress of Ireland* survivors. She and Logan had searched the ship's manifest for a Gagné, but the only Birdie they found had the last name of Koster.

"What do you mean that you knew Birdie?" Logan asked.

"On Wellesley Island. She . . ."

Fraidy crawled onto Emma's lap and nudged her hand until she began petting her.

Poppy. Birdie. Emma. All the pieces seemed to be there, Chloe just wasn't sure how to fit them together. "Birdie was the one who gave you the scrapbook."

A shock of lightning flashed outside the sliding glass door, followed by a rumble of thunder, as another storm moved in this evening, the pounding rain predicted to last all night.

"She didn't actually give it to me," Emma said.

Chloe pulled her legs close, crisscross on the couch. "What do you mean?"

Emma looked at the window. Maple's nose was pressed against the glass while poor Sugar hid behind the couch as if ignoring the storm would make it blow away.

Logan wanted to pester Emma with questions. Chloe could tell by the way he rocked his pen between his fingers, focusing all his nervous energy into balancing what must be a hundred thoughts colliding in his head.

This afternoon, after she and Emma released the sparrow, she'd met up with Logan to tell him about the letter. Between his interview, subsequent dive, and a library contact in Syracuse, he'd uncovered more information as well. Jenna had spoiled the three of them with a dinner of grilled steak and roasted vegetables from her garden, and then Logan and Chloe had spread an assortment of papers across the basement floor and coffee table, hunting for answers.

While neither of the Koster sisters appeared to survive the *Empress of Ireland*, Logan's contact found a brief mention of a young woman named Birdie who was eleven when the ship sank. Logan had called two county clerks' offices, asking about a death certificate for Birdie Townsend, but they had no record for her.

Chloe picked up the announcement that Logan just read, faxed from the library, and skimmed it again. Birdie had married William Townsend of Ottawa on June 18, 1922, both of them survivors of the shipwreck. That alone, Chloe thought, deserved an entire article.

William fought in World War I and was working as a boat builder when they married. Birdie was a recent graduate of the Hepburn School of Nursing in Ogdensburg. William had several family members listed in their wedding announcement, but no family was listed for Birdie.

If Birdie Townsend was Poppy, how did she end up in Ogdensburg and where did she go after they married? Logan's colleague was still searching for an obituary or other information about her.

Chloe draped her legs over the edge of her seat, the article in hand. "This is important, Emma."

The girl shook her head. "It doesn't matter anymore."

"It actually matters a lot." Emma could help them find Birdie, but even more important, Birdie's story could help set Emma free.

She didn't want to scare the girl, but maybe she needed to be afraid. Better fear, Chloe thought, than having Mitch take her away. A little fear, maybe, would have kept Chloe off the cliffs all those years ago.

"Emma . . ." She breathed the jasmine scent from a candle. "A man stopped by the store last week when you were with Jenna." She glanced at Logan and saw his eyebrows partially raised. He knew what she was going to say but made no attempt to stop her. "Said his name was Mitch."

Emma pulled Fraidy to her chest. "What did he want?"

"He was looking for you."

A shudder wracked through Emma's body, and Chloe wished she hadn't been quite so direct.

"What did you tell him?"

"Nothing important. You already told me he was a nobody."

Emma pumped her head.

"But we need your help," Chloe continued. "We know Mitch lives on Wellesley Island, but we don't know where you lived or how he knows you. You can't spend the rest of your life afraid of him."

"I'm afraid of more people than just him!"

Logan wrung his hands together. "Who are these people?"

"Birdie helped me," Emma said. "Gave me a safe place to hide."

"Then why did you come to Koster Isle?"

Tears now, streaming down Emma's cheeks and soaking Fraidy's fur. "Birdie left the island last month."

"Where did she go?"

"To the hospital." She sniffed. "Then she died, and Mitch said he was going to send me away too."

Chloe joined her tears. "So you ran."

"Birdie told me, if I was ever scared, to paddle to her son's house in Alexandria Bay, but the winds were blowing the other way."

A reel rolled in Chloe's head. When Emma's friend, her protector, passed on, Emma took her scrapbook and left Wellesley.

She glanced over at Logan. He'd been so close to finding Poppy, right before her birthday, and the hope of being this close, actually meeting her, must have been exhilarating for him. Then to learn that she had just died . . .

But Logan was fully intent on Emma. "Where was Mitch planning to send you?"

"On a saltie," she said. "To be with the sailors."

Chloe's back pounded the couch, her stomach churning. No wonder why Emma wouldn't talk. She could only imagine one reason to send a ten-year-old girl on a ship.

Adults should be protecting children, not exploiting them. And it seemed that no one except Birdie had been trying to help her.

So much was wrong with their world.

She met Logan's gaze and saw his sorrow and rage. "We're going to take care of this, Emma," he said. "You don't have to be afraid."

"Why did you come to my island?" Chloe asked.

"Mitch sometimes talks about Poppy's Castle."

Her words sent shivers up Chloe's spine. "I wouldn't think you'd listen to Mitch Yancey."

"It pays to listen to him."

"I suppose it does."

"He didn't know that Birdie used to tell me stories about a girl named Poppy. Someone had rescued her, and I thought just maybe . . ."

"Someone would rescue you too." The words came out as a whisper—Chloe hadn't meant to say them aloud—but the truth settled over both of them. When Emma was afraid, she'd traveled to Poppy's Castle for help.

Koster Isle might frighten some people, but it had been a place of refuge for both of them.

She checked her watch—it was a quarter till seven. Another glance at Logan, and she knew they were on the same page.

"Jenna!" she called, and her friend came rushing down the steps.

"What's up?"

"Could Emma help you feed the chickens tonight?"

Jenna glanced at the window, the rain still battering it. "You can't feed chickens in a st—"

Chloe interrupted. "Please?"

Jenna looked at her and then at Emma. "Of course. Come along, sweetie."

Not a single quip this time from her friend, but a smile emerged on Emma's face. "Chickens still need to eat in a storm."

"Exactly."

"And you and your boyfriend need to talk about all the stuff that you don't want me to hear."

A blast of heat warmed Chloe's cheeks. "We're not—Logan is not my boyfriend."

Instead of laughing, Logan winked at the girl. "Nice try."

Emma and her cat rushed up the steps, but Jenna lingered by the couch.

"I've got her tonight," she said. "You two do whatever you need to do to get the truth."

Chloe smiled at her friend. "Thank you."

"Nothing can stay secret forever," Jenna said.

"I wish that was true."

Logan eyed the telephone on the side table. "If it wasn't so late, I'd call the municipal clerk's office up in Ontario to see if someone recorded Birdie's death there."

"I'm sorry that your Poppy Pendleton story seems to end here," Chloe said.

His eyebrows arched. "Why are you sorry?"

"It seems you were close to finding her alive, and if you'd been able to interview her, you would have won a boatload of awards."

"The person I'm most concerned about at the moment is Emma."

She studied him. "Are you certain?"

"This must be very hard for her."

And she saw nothing except sincerity in his face. "You are a good man, Logan Danford."

"I'm not—"

"I've known good and bad, and I promise, you qualify as one of the good guys."

"God is good," he said, his eyes on the rain-soaked window. "I'm just trying to partner with Him."

That's what she wanted as well, to be a partner in God's goodness. To bring all things lovely back into this world. Not so people could escape. So they could explore.

As she leaned to pet Sugar, still cowering behind the couch, Logan turned back to her. "Chloe—"

"Yes?"

"Why would a US border agent be talking to someone about Koster Isle?"

# 40
# *BIRDIE*

MAY 1923

"I can't do this."

"Please, Birdie." Will looked at her so earnestly, this gift greater than any she could ever imagine from the man she'd married eleven months ago. "I built her. Just for us."

Birdie eyed the small houseboat that he'd berthed on a private dock near Alexandria Bay. *Open Air* was what he'd named her, from the poem that Birdie had read to him five years past. When everything changed for both of them.

Soon after, a private benefactor had offered her a scholarship to attend the new nursing school in Ogdensburg while Will apprenticed for a boatwright named Ridell. Aunt Sarah had suggested a meeting between the two men, and after Will made his way from Leek Island into Clayton, a new dream began to grow inside him.

Birdie was overjoyed for Will to have a new purpose for his life. Work for his hands. And she was thrilled as he spoke of one day crafting a boat on his own.

But to live on a boat?

He'd meant to surprise her with something good, but she was facing her greatest nightmare to even step on board. He knew so little about her past. Only that she'd lived in Canada before the shipwreck, and her mother had died on the *Empress*. In her mind, life began the moment that she'd stepped into the orphanage.

She wanted nothing of the years before Ogdensburg. Not even a memory.

But an army of them were pressing through the walls of her mind, and she couldn't slay them fast enough. "I'm terrified of boats."

Will took her hand, his fingers calloused from the carving and sanding. Tender and strong. "I know."

"And yet you built it."

"You helped me overcome my fears," he said. "And now I want to help you overcome yours."

It wasn't just the water. It was the man—the men—who'd lived on board. She still had nightmares about them coming to her room.

But Will loved her. From the moment they'd watched the sunset on Leek Island, as his eyes opened again to the world, she'd known his love. Even on the hardest days when he fought his own battles.

Some days it took time to return from his wanderings, but he always came back. And never once had he tried to hurt her. The battles were real, but the love in his heart conquered all.

She took the smallest of steps, inches really, over the gunwale and stared at the front deck.

"She's thirty-two feet long," he said proudly. "Eleven feet wide."

"It's beautiful." She looked into the windows and saw a sink and shelves in the galley, a table already set for two. Then she rolled her hands over the buttons on her midsection. They'd have to squeeze three chairs there soon.

"How did you build all this?"

"With these." He held up his hands, grinning now, a fire lit in his gaze. So different than the man who'd first arrived on Leek. "I had a little help."

"Is there a motor?" she asked.

He shook his head. "I'll hire a tug when it's time to move. I have a slip already arranged for the winter."

This was no pleasure boat like the ones he built for the richer set. "You want us to live on this, don't you?"

His smile fell a notch. "Only in the summers, but not if you don't want to, Birdie. We can sell it anytime. Tomorrow, even. If I keep making boats like this one, I can provide well for our family."

She kissed him then, even as she clung to a metal rail. "Don't sell it."

"Are you certain?"

"I will stay here with you." She was free now like her namesake. Free to live on a houseboat with the man she loved. Never on her own, she thought, but with Will she could do almost anything.

Hours later, Aunt Sarah arrived for a tour.

"Mr. Ridell taught you well," she said, smoothing her hand over the varnished woodwork.

"He is the best in the islands."

"How is his family?" she asked as she arranged the bouquet she'd brought in a vase. Often Birdie had wondered what happened to her aunt's family, but like Birdie, she never spoke of the past. It was as if they'd emerged from the *Empress* tragedy reborn, the old buried deep in the riverbed.

"He just has the one boy," Will said. "A fine lad. Spitting image of his father."

Aunt Sarah smiled as if she could envision the Ridell family as a happy sort. Then she turned back to the craftsmanship of Will's boat.

"It's exquisite," she said, running her hands again over the narra walls, the red wood imported from the Philippines. "Built from love."

"Indeed." Birdie could feel it in the seams, every notch and plank carpentered by the husband who surprised her each new day.

Sarah hugged her close, kissed her cheeks. "William will take good care of you."

And she knew that he would.

"This is for you." Aunt Sarah handed Birdie a scrapbook filled with pictures of birds and a collection of writings. "I want you to add to it. Make it your own."

Birdie hugged the gift to her chest. The two people who loved her expected nothing in return, and everything inside her embraced their gifts.

Turning the pages, she studied every sketch, each poem, until she reached the end. "Who is Penelope?"

"A girl who was very special to me."

"Thank you, Aunt Sarah."

"It's been the greatest of honors to have you as a niece."

When night fell, Birdie and Will crept down into the space that he'd lovingly carved into a bedroom, but she could hardly breathe in the bowels of this boat. The roof felt as if might cave in and even though they hadn't left the dock, she felt as if she might drown.

*Never stay in a place when you know it's time to leave.*

She needed to leave, but she didn't want to go far.

Reaching across the bed, she took Will's hand, her voice shaking. "Do you mind if we sleep on the deck?"

He lit the lantern and then smiled. "In the open air?"

"Yes, please."

"I don't mind at all."

Together they pulled the feather mattress and a mess of blankets up to the deck. As Will wrapped his arms around her, holding her under the stars, the fear began to subside.

"Birdie?"

She inched closer. "Yes?"

"Why do you think God saved me from the wreck on the river and the wreck in the trenches?"

She felt his chest warm against her back, strength flowing into her. "Maybe because He knew we needed to swim together."

He kissed her hair, and she sank deeply into the wonder of his love.

Hours later, she was awakened by a different sound. The sharp call of a bird. One she didn't recognize. Perched on the rail at sunrise was a redheaded macaw with feathered layers of yellow and blue, like the one she'd seen in Aunt Sarah's book. And somehow, the bird looked familiar to her. Then a blue macaw joined the red one, and it seemed in the early hours as if they were watching her.

"Will," she whispered, but by the time he woke, the parrots were gone.

The birds returned several more times, but she never got to tell her aunt about them. A week later, Aunt Sarah's heart failed. Broken, the doctor said, as she worked an overnight shift in the maternity ward.

Birdie cried for her aunt's brokenness. The secrets she'd kept.

For five sweet summers, Birdie and Will nested on their boat, and then they sold the *Open Air* as their family expanded, moving into a bigger boat that he built, raising all six of their children on the water—two whom she'd birthed and four orphans from Ogdensburg who needed homes.

And she cherished the scraps of pictures and poetry that Aunt Sarah gave her, not adding a single page to her treasure of a book.

41

# LOGAN

"Let's see if we can find Gavin," Chloe said, donning her rain jacket as if she were Clark Kent. She'd already tried the police station three times, but no one answered the phone.

Logan took a sip of the coffee that Jenna had delivered downstairs. "Or we could call 911 like most people."

Everything within him said to move, but he was no longer a first responder. Now he had to step out of the way of those employed to save lives and then report on the events.

Chloe stepped to the dark window, only flashes of lightning now in the distance. "This situation hardly equates to normal."

He didn't say the words, but he wanted to beat Yancey to a pulp for threatening to harm any girl. Beating up the man, he knew, would only deflect from what the agent had planned, but still . . .

They needed law enforcement involved.

"First thing in the morning," he said, "we'll go to the police station."

She shook her head. "We have to go tonight."

A second draw of caffeine warmed his throat. "How do you know?"

She hesitated before speaking. "Sometimes I hear things."

"What sort of things?" he asked, trying to placate his concern.

She paced around the table once before looking back out the glass.

"Chloe?" he persisted.

"It's usually a quiet voice," she said. "Something inside that tells me when I need to move."

"You have good intuition."

"Nana used to call it *God whispers*. Except tonight, it's no whisper."

Another crash of thunder rocked the house. "You want to cruise around town until we find the police?"

"No." She strapped her purse over her shoulder. "I want to knock on Gavin's front door and tell him what Emma said."

It was after eight when Chloe drove them down a dirt lane to a cluster of houses near the water's edge. A woman answered the door—Gavin's wife, he assumed—wearing a dark T-shirt and white carpenter jeans, her feet bare at this late hour. Then she gave Chloe a hug before inviting them into the foyer.

"This is Logan Danford," Chloe said. "The reporter from the *Post-Standard*."

"Solving our local mystery about Poppy, I'm told."

Logan shook her hand. "Chloe's helping me."

"I'm Belle, Gavin's wife. I'm so glad you're here. I was worried sick about you two."

Chloe glanced at him, but he didn't know what Belle was referring to.

"Gavin and Bret left right for Koster Isle when they got your call."

"Who did you say called them?" Chloe asked, the concern in her eyes mirroring his.

Now Belle looked confused. "Gavin said that you did. He was pretty upset that you went back to the island."

"We've been at Jenna's house," Chloe said. "I tried to contact him on his mobile phone but the call wouldn't go through."

Belle's eyes widened with alarm. "Why would someone else call my husband from Koster?"

Gavin had been asking too many questions, Logan suspected. Questions that were downright dangerous.

"Something's wrong," Belle said, and he agreed.

"How long ago did he leave?" Logan asked.

"About an hour ago."

"Now we should call 911," Chloe replied.

Belle was halfway down the hall before she called back. "I'm calling the police chief first."

He knew that Chloe wouldn't wait for the police chief or the scramble of officers. "Let's go," he said, pointing toward the door.

"You sure you want to come?"

"Nope, but I'm not letting you go alone." Every instinct within him wanted to take care of her, whether or not she needed it. Thankfully, she didn't fight him.

The patches of lightning were gone when they reached the Clayton Marina, only a sprinkle of rain remaining. No guarantee, of course, that the storm wouldn't return, but Chloe didn't seem to care one whit about the weather. And he admired her for it. If a ship was sinking, he'd want her at the helm.

She unlocked the storage bin on *Lolli* and tossed him a life jacket. Then she turned on her radio and sped quickly across the channel, the waves jostling them like dice in a plastic cup, the parkas draped over their life jackets doing little to stop the wind or rain.

An entire force of police from Clayton, he hoped, was close behind.

Halfway across the river, he lost his dinner over the side, but if Chloe noticed, she didn't comment. Nor did she slow the boat. She was focused on the dark island ahead, whizzing around other landmasses and shoals as if she were dodging potholes on the highway. He could turn off the red and green sidelights, he suspected—blindfold her, even—and she and *Lolli* could find their way home.

As long as no one got in their way.

He'd spent half his day with Tyler, a man who dove the *Empress of Ireland* last year. After the interview, Tyler asked if Logan wanted to take a dive near the shore so he could see a glimpse of the riverbed. Logan had readily agreed. The river was a dangerous place, Tyler explained as they swam away from the shore, especially where the *Empress* had sunk.

The currents were strong in that wide section of the river, water freezing, visibility nil. And the *Empress* lay a full 140 feet down in its bed.

Few had tried to explore it, Tyler said, mainly because it had claimed the lives of two divers along with the 1,012 who drowned when it first went down. Most of the passengers had never been found.

Years ago, someone had discovered a gold watch on the shoreline near the wreck, *Pendleton Clocks* engraved on the case. And he wondered, sadly, if Mrs. Pendleton was wearing it at the end.

As they neared the lagoon, Chloe shut off the lights, the engine idling. With the cloud cover and blur of rain, visibility was low. No one on the island should be able to see them.

"What do you think?" he whispered, his stomach recovered from the nausea.

"I think Gavin should know better than to come out here on a night like this," she replied, worry threaded through her voice.

"Pretty sure he'd do just about anything to help you, Chloe."

"His boat should be here!" She retrieved a floodlight and swept it across the surface. If the policemen were trying to be covert, she'd ruined their cover, but it seemed like they'd all stepped into desperate-measure status now.

Nothing but the dock and a forest of reeds showed up in the glare.

"We have to check the castle," she said.

He squinted, trying to see the path, but everything beyond the dock was draped in shadows and mist. "We can't use a flashlight on the island."

"We have to use it to hike up the path."

"Then we'll be a beacon for the wrong kind of people."

She turned the boat around. "Let's try the old boathouse."

The rain stopped as they motored to the other side, the clouds parting. Moonlight cast a sheen over the river. Chloe killed the engine when they drew close to the dilapidated boathouse, the three remaining peaks pointed like missiles in the air, and turned off the radio so no one would accidentally announce their arrival.

They saw no light. Heard no other sound beyond the lap of water against the cliff. Perhaps Belle was wrong. Gavin and Bret might have answered a call on another island.

"Gavin isn't here," he whispered.

"He's close." Chloe lifted a paddle from the space between her chair and the hull, steering the boat quietly along the shore.

"You got another one of those?"

She handed him a second paddle, and together they trolled around the boathouse.

"Look at that," she said. An inflatable powerboat was roped to a piling on the other side.

He stopped paddling. "What kind of boat does the Clayton police force use?"

"Aluminum."

"The police chief will be here soon," he said, plunging his paddle back into the water to push them away from shore. "We'll let him do his job."

Right now, Logan's job was to make sure Chloe made it back safely to the mainland.

"We can wait in the channel." She started the engine again, pointing *Lolli*'s nose back toward Clayton, but they didn't go far before he saw something floating on the river. Driftwood, he hoped, but his instincts screamed otherwise.

He ripped off his parka. "Where's the floodlight?"

She handed it over to him, and when he flipped the switch, light illuminated the surface. Logan swore when he saw someone, facedown, in the water. He might no longer be a first responder by title, but he and Chloe were the only ones out here.

He tossed his shoes by the parka and heard Chloe shout his name before he plunged into the river, ice water smacking him in the face. His leg might deter him on land, but at least he could still swim and the life jacket would keep him afloat.

A life jacket wouldn't do anything, though, to fight hypothermia, and he didn't have long before the cold set in.

Chloe steered after him as his arms pumped overhead, and when he reached the officer in the river, she quickly hung a ladder over the side.

How they got Gavin on board, Logan wasn't certain, but he and Chloe managed to haul him into the boat. Then he performed mouth-to-mouth while Chloe called for help on the radio.

Seconds later, Gavin coughed up water and then life breathed back into him.

"Bret!" the deputy called as he inched himself up against the hull. Logan sat right beside him.

Chloe spoke to another officer on the radio until the lights of two police boats swept around the island. One of them fished Bret out of the water where he'd been floating on his back, thankfully still breathing.

Neither officer knew exactly what happened on Koster Isle. They'd both been hit on the head, it seemed, on their hike up to the castle and then dumped out in the frigid water. Someone sank their patrol boat about thirty feet from the boathouse.

Logan's stay at the hospital in Alexandria Bay was short. Once the nurse checked his vitals and the doctor approved, he and Chloe traveled to the second floor via elevator to visit Gavin.

"I'm grateful," the deputy said, a rerun of *Magnum, P.I.* blaring on the TV. "To both of you."

"Whoever did this should be hung," Chloe told him. "Mitch Yancey, I suspect."

"I don't know that we'll ever prove it." Gavin clicked off *Magnum* with his remote. "We didn't see a single person on the island, and the inflatable boat was gone by the time the investigator arrived. If it was Yancey, I'm sure he hightailed it out of New York."

Logan glanced out the window at the St. Lawrence. They had to work together to keep Emma safe until they found this man.

"Emma said she was afraid he would send her away on a ship," Chloe said.

Gavin's face blanched. "On a ship?"

Logan shifted in the metal chair, any sign of fatigue vanishing. "Are children being sold on the river?"

"No one has proven it."

"Gavin?" Chloe pressed.

"I've only heard rumors. Not a bit of evidence." Gavin homed in on Logan. "But if I was an investigative reporter, I'd dig a little deeper. You don't have to stick with jurisdictions."

"I'll start digging," Logan said. "Emma told us that a woman named

Birdie Townsend helped her on Wellesley. She said Birdie passed last month."

"Passed across the channel, maybe."

Chloe almost hopped out of her chair. "What?"

"I'm well acquainted with Mrs. Townsend," Gavin said. "She had surgery a couple weeks ago on her wrist and ended up needing some work on her hip too. Thankfully, she hasn't passed on, on."

Logan tugged on his ear as if he hadn't heard the man quite right. Was he saying . . . ?

"Where is Birdie?" Chloe asked.

Gavin smiled at both of them before he looked at the ceiling. "Upstairs."

42

# BIRDIE

WELLESLEY ISLAND
JULY 1992

Birdie kissed her palm and pressed it against the cold stone that marked the place where her darling Will had been laid to rest, in the sweetest of company beside their third child, a little girl who'd been born still.

How she missed this dear man who had sailed through most of life with her. How she missed his gentle presence and wonder at what he could engineer. His love for her and their children and the river. She'd never quite gotten over her fear of the water, but he eventually helped her see the St. Lawrence as an ally. After he learned to build boats, Will had taught her to swim.

Birdie threaded her fingers together as if she could, just one more time, hold her husband's hand and watch the blaze of sun rise over the river together.

Beside the grave was a box their oldest grandson, Daniel, had carved from cedar, Will's initials engraved on the top beside a sail. Birdie opened the box on this cool morning and wiped her fingers over the silver Military Cross kept inside. Her husband had fought for everything he loved. His beloved country. Their six children. Her future alongside him.

The governor general of Canada had decorated him for heroism on the battlefield, but Will Townsend was, most of all, a hero in her heart.

About thirty years ago, when Will had grown too weak to raise another anchor or dive to repair a hull or shaft, their four sons worked with him to build a waterfront cottage on ten acres of wooded property they'd purchased on Wellesley, the only island with a bridge stretching into Canada and then another wing spanning over to the mainland of New York. They'd settled along the water that glued their two countries together and loved their children and all the birds and animals who chose to make their land home.

Over the years, a loving God brought boys and girls like Emma straight to her door. And she'd asked Him to bring more.

The fog of the past still blurred her thoughts at times, like Will when his mind was trapped in the trenches, but she hadn't lived her life as a prisoner to them. She'd jumped into the waters next to Will and swum, trying to rescue as many others as she could along the way. Instead of hurting people like Ellie had done, she'd wanted to be like Aunt Sarah and then Florence Nightingale, another British nurse who'd saved many lives, caring for those who needed a new set of wings. And that's what her children and grandchildren were doing too. Rescuing and reforming in their own way. Crusaders, every one of them, bringing healing around the world.

Seven years ago, Will had slipped into the next life with a beading plane in his hand, working alongside three of their grandchildren as they built a new Townsend boat. The family finished the boat a year after Will's ruptured aneurysm and named it *Going Home*.

Birdie turned slowly with the help of her cane and glanced at the small crowd that had gathered among the hickory trees and deerberry shrubs, giving her plenty of space to have a moment with Will. An even bigger crowd, she was told, would be joining them at the house.

Ninety years—that's how long she'd lived on this earth. And today all these loved ones wanted to celebrate with her.

Her gaze swept across the stream of smiles. Five of her children were here and at least half of her twenty grands and all their babies. Eight at last count. Then there was Chloe Ridell, sweet Emma, and Logan Danford, a reporter from Syracuse. He was writing a feature story, of all things, about her life.

Gale, her oldest daughter, had stayed back at the house to greet their guests, but she and Birdie would return to the meadow after the party to say good night to the daddy she'd adored.

Daniel stepped forward, so handsome in his finest suit to honor her and his grandpa. He traveled the world now with a medical team, but he'd flown home last night for her birthday. "You okay, Grandma?"

"Just another moment."

He helped her to a bench beside the graves and then kissed her cheek before retreating. They were so good to her. Letting her sit like this.

Her gaze wandered beyond the tombstones now, out to the river. People had been looking for her—or at least, Poppy Pendleton—for years. She had seen the castle often from the river and enjoyed the time, many years ago, that she and Will spent with the Ridells. She'd heard the stories about Leslie Pendleton and his only daughter, but she never suspected that she was the lost girl.

She didn't remember much about her life as Penelope, but Poppy's magical story had been tucked away in her heart since she was a child. Thank God a reporter hadn't located her until now. The reality of becoming a Pendleton, the onslaught of an investigation, would have changed everything for her and Will and their kids.

Since Chloe and her reporter friend found her, the remaining Townsend family had conferred, and after much deliberation, the majority thought she needed to tell her story. She'd agreed to an interview with Logan and shared the scraps of memories from her childhood, how she'd longed for a magic cloak when she was a girl, how a shipwreck had become her salvation. She avoided any mention of the men who visited Ellie's houseboat, but she told the reporter about what seemed to be happening in Mitch Yancey's house, across the creek from the Townsend land. That's what they all should be focused on right now.

Birdie turned again, this time to the wooden structure in the distance. The agent had built a dock at the mouth of the creek, but his house was tucked back in the cedar trees. He was a charmer; that much was certain. Birdie had never crossed the creek to Mitch's house, but he came often to hers, bringing bouquets of roses to her door. One of her sons had asked him to stop, but he kept leaving flowers on her stoop. A reminder, it seemed to her, to mind her own business when she saw the many women he paddled up the creek and when children like Emma waded across to play in her meadow.

She invited all of these kids into her home. Sometimes they would share a piece of their life, but more often, when they visited, they would simply eat her cookies and listen to her stories and then, like Emma, they would be gone. Birdie had called the police multiple times, voicing her concern, but no one else had shared her suspicions about the border agent until now.

Logan wouldn't run the story in the *Post-Standard* until the authorities apprehended Mitch, but he'd answered a few questions for her. Amelia Pendleton, her biological mother it seemed, had died with the *Empress of Ireland* along with her aunt—the hard-hearted woman whom she'd called Mummy. The woman who had stolen her from the castle. No one, least of all her, understood why Ellie had done it. The woman clearly didn't enjoy being a mum.

While she had a houseful of beautiful children, Birdie had never had a niece. Chloe was the granddaughter of Amelia Pendleton and Cade Ridell, the man who'd rescued her husband and helped them start a new life. Now Chloe was family, and Emma was safe.

Her blessings overflowed.

She'd barely stood from the bench when Daniel was beside her again, this time with a wheelchair that he'd custom-built to cushion her body from the many bumps along the path. So like Will. And the whole crowd paraded her back to the house, their chatter filling the forest like a flock of birds. And filling her heart with joy.

"I'm sorry, Grandma," Daniel said when the wheelchair hit a rut.

She patted his hand over her shoulder. "I'm just fine."

Emma stepped up and took her hand as they neared the house. The girl had made her way into Birdie's home and her heart. How happy she was that Emma was with Cade's granddaughter, but it must have cost her a lot today to step back into the shadow of her prison.

"Thank you for coming," Birdie said.

"I'm sorry for taking your book."

Birdie still didn't understand why Aunt Sarah had collected the pictures of birds and poetry into a scrapbook, dedicated it to Penelope, and then given it to her. Still the poetry about the flames had fascinated her. The words about secrets, whispered in the storm, had resonated deep within. The secrets she so boldly sang.

*But no one hears her voice, they only see her wings.*

Had Aunt Sarah known she was Penelope?

If she hadn't died so soon after giving Birdie the book, perhaps she would have explained the secrets that she held through the storms.

Birdie squeezed Emma's hand. "That scrapbook was meant to be shared among family."

Emma had tried to return it while Birdie was still in the hospital, but she wouldn't take it. Not only did Emma prize the book, Birdie thought she needed it. And Sarah's memories would live on through her.

"I'm not family," Emma said.

"Oh, sweet girl," Birdie replied. "You'll always be part of my family."

When Emma smiled at her, Birdie leaned closer before nodding toward Mitch's place. "And you are free of him."

The Townsend house was full when they returned, family and friends spilling out to the patio and lounging under white tents that Gale had rented for the day. Even if ninety years were worth celebrating, the catered food and sparkling lights were too much fuss in her mind. But it brought the entire Townsend family together again. That gift was the greatest one.

The day was filled with food and pictures and stories, and by evening, her children had begun spreading out in rooms around her home, many of them spending the night.

"Are you ready?" Gale asked as she readied the wheelchair.

Birdie scanned the faces who remained. Emma. Chloe. Several friends from church and her years working at the hospital. Logan Danford. She suspected that she would see more of him in days to come, even after he finished his article.

"Perhaps we should wait another hour," Birdie said.

"The fireworks will be starting in an hour."

"Fireworks?"

Gale blanched. "I wasn't supposed to say anything."

Her children. They were trying to re-create, she suspected, a celebration extraordinaire to redeem what had been lost on her fifth birthday. Except there was nothing to redeem. The years with Ellie and her host of men, she would wholly admit, were vile, but redemption had already taken place.

Still, she would celebrate with them.

Gale, so like her father, had rigged a flashlight on the wheelchair handle so they could find their way back through the hickory trees.

"I miss him so much," Gale said as they moved toward the cemetery.

"Me too."

"I wonder what he would have thought if he knew about the Pendletons."

"He would think he wasn't good enough to marry a Pendleton," Birdie said slowly. "When he was the perfect man for me."

"I worry about you, Mama, being here alone."

Birdie smiled. "I'm hardly ever alone."

"But Mitch—"

"The police say he wouldn't dare return to the islands, not after what happened to Gavin and Bret."

"I hope they find him soon, wherever he is."

As they neared the meadow, Birdie heard the song of a whip-poor-will, keeping the forest alive with music through the night. How she loved it out here with her birds.

"Do you remember," Gale said, "when you lived at Pendleton Castle?"

"I have vague recollections, but I don't know which memories were true and which ones were reconstructed from Ellie's stories. She had to do something, it seems, to make me believe my earliest memories were a fabrication."

Gale turned off the flashlight when they reached Will's grave and starlight rained over them. When Birdie was younger, she'd had a nightmare of a woman stealing her from her bed. Nightmares about a man who had thrown a blanket over her head that same night and rowed her away. When she told Olivia, her friend said Birdie must be worried that someone was going to steal her from the houseboat, but Birdie never worried about that. In hindsight, one of Ellie's many men probably helped steal her away.

They only had a moment beside Will's grave when the quietness of the night was shattered by a scream.

Gale whirled toward her. "What was that?"

"An owl," she replied. One, she feared, that was being threatened.

The owl shrieked again as Birdie scanned the creek. And then she saw a light on the edge of Mitch's property, bobbing toward the creek.

Gale leaned down, her hand on Birdie's arm. "I'll take you home."

Birdie shook her head. "You have to call Gavin."

"But we don't know who that is."

"Who else would be there at this hour?" If it was Mitch, she wasn't going to let him hurt another girl.

"I'm not leaving you here," her daughter said.

"No one is going to bother an old woman like me." But Emma might be in danger. For some reason, Mitch thought he needed that girl. "Go call Gavin."

When Gale still didn't move, Birdie reached for her hand, squeezing it gently.

"Please," she said. "For Emma."

"I'll send Daniel right back."

As Gale rushed away, Birdie felt an odd press of walls around her, someone tugging her wrist. Then the walls started falling over her head, and her entire body jolted at the memory.

"Gale," she called as the details gelled in her mind.

Her daughter turned back. "What's wrong?"

"If Mitch returns to the castle . . ." She took a breath. "Tell Gavin there are tunnels behind the walls."

As she waited in the meadow, a storm of fireworks sprayed the sky red and purple and white. She might not be able to apprehend Mitch herself, but she would sit here in the firelit woods, beside her brave husband's grave, and pray that someone would stop the man.

## 43

# CHLOE

CHLOE AND EMMA DANGLED THEIR FEET off the end of Birdie's dock as the fireworks faded and the twinkling boat lights of those who'd stopped to watch continued upstream.

The display, Chloe hoped, could be seen across the islands. Thanks to Logan and his editor, the news about Poppy Pendleton wasn't known yet beyond the Townsend family, but everyone in this region, the river rats and the summer guests alike, would soon celebrate Birdie's life well-lived.

A photographer had accompanied Logan tonight, taking dozens of pictures, and Logan had lingered to watch the opening fireworks until the photographer said he was about to drive Logan's truck back to Syracuse alone. After a hug for both her and Emma, he headed home.

When Mitch was finally behind bars, the story of Poppy Pendleton would become a series, running in all the newspapers that the parent company of the *Post-Standard* owned. Logan, she had no doubt, would win the Heisman of journalism awards.

She didn't know when he would return to Clayton, but she hoped soon. Perhaps she and Emma might take a trip down to Syracuse as well.

A voice whispered in her ear, urging her to take Emma's hand, telling her to run, but she quickly dampened it. Birdie's home was a safe place, the weather still. She must have misheard tonight.

"What's that?" Emma asked, pointing at a boat.

Chloe's heart clenched as someone searched the river with a floodlight, like she and Logan had done when they were looking for Gavin.

Had someone fallen overboard?

She hopped up to scan the surface but didn't see anyone in the water. The river was calm tonight, the temperature warm. If the person was sober, if they'd donned a life jacket before their fall, they wouldn't drown.

The floodlight lifted and swept across the Townsend property. Chloe couldn't see the hull of the boat, blinded by the flood, but suddenly, a speedboat was beside them, bumping into the dock.

The light was relentless, burning her eyes, stealing her sight. But like a mama bird knows the cry of her chick, Chloe knew the moment Emma was gone. Then she flew, both arms spread across the water, right into the back of the boat.

A man swore as he twisted Chloe's arms behind her, but she didn't dare speak, not until she understood what was happening.

With her hands bound, she couldn't reach out, but Emma's hand found her as the boat sped west. The men, it seemed, hadn't tied her arms.

Once they lost sight of Birdie's house, the men extinguished the floodlight along with every light on the boat. Chloe's eyes slowly adjusted until she could see Mitch Yancey at the wheel, a burly man in a black turtleneck seated beside him. She tried to waylay her fears, cut them adrift like Nana would have said, but they kept crashing back into her.

What was Logan going to think when he realized both she and Emma had disappeared? He was already trying to recover from the death of his son and marriage and then those he'd lost in the fire. He'd worked hard to keep her and Emma safe and now . . .

She should have listened to that whisper on the dock when He told her to run. Now, God help her, she would have to keep Emma safe on her own.

Chloe leaned forward. "Did you come to celebrate with Birdie?"

Mitch glanced back at her as they roared across the river. "You think this is a joke?"

"Not at all."

"I should dump you out here."

Chloe scanned the surface. If he tossed her overboard without a life jacket, like he'd probably done with the deputies, it was doubtful that she'd survive the night.

"But you've given me a different idea," he said. "A better one."

With his words, a tremor raced through her skin, the memory of her father slamming back into her mind again. The edge of the cliff and then the tower window.

She didn't want to find out what Mitch was thinking.

They wove between the dark islands, past Flatiron and Sargent and Big Gull, until she saw her castle in the stars. One of the doors in the crumbling boathouse was unlocked, and Mitch steered the speedboat inside, docking by a lantern. Another man closed the door.

How many people were on her island?

"C'mon," Mitch said after he tied up the boat.

She could hardly see in the dim light, but Mitch had one hand on her shoulder and the other on the nape of Emma's neck, pushing them across the broken planks.

"It's going to be okay," Chloe said to the girl.

"It certainly is." Mitch shoved her forward so hard that she almost tripped. How deep was the water inside the boathouse? At least fifteen feet, she thought, for the Pendleton yacht.

Chloe glanced over at Emma. "We're not afraid of nobodies."

"That's a harsh word for a friend," Mitch said. They were in the passage now leading up to the house. His colleagues, it seemed, were staying behind.

"You're not our friend," Chloe told him.

"Maybe not, but our grandparents used to be," he said. "At least your grandfather and my grandma were friendly enough. Your grandmother, not so much."

She bristled. "Miriam was kind to everyone."

"That's rich," he said, mocking her. "You don't know, do you?"

Was he talking about Amelia? She certainly didn't think about that woman as her grandmother. But if so, how did he know about the affair?

"Most of my family thought my grandma was crazy, but I listened to her. She told me all sorts of things about this castle."

When she didn't take the bait, Mitch volunteered. "Your saint of a granddaddy had a few downfalls including a little fling with Amelia Pendleton that ended up with a baby boy."

"It doesn't matter to me," she said. "Miriam is still my grandma."

"And our grandparents," he continued, "helped Mr. Pendleton distribute his opium stash to the world."

She flinched. The promise of money could unravel anyone, she supposed, but she couldn't fathom her grandpa smuggling drugs. He wanted to bring joy into people's lives, that much was certain, but not for the money.

Was Mitch trying to make her angry? Or distract her with what might have happened back then instead of what could happen right now.

"Seems like you might be the one smuggling," she said. "Not my grandfather."

"I don't smuggle," he said. "Just help a bit with storage."

Emma glanced back. "You have tons of cocaine at your house."

"Shut up."

"I'll go to the castle with you," Chloe said, dragging her feet along the path. "But you don't need Emma."

"She's mine," he said, and the smallest of sounds, like a yelp, escaped from the girl's lips.

"No, she's not."

"Her mama sold her to me over the winter."

A bout of nausea crashed through her. She'd heard of such things, but she didn't want to believe it was true. Not today. "Where is her mother now?"

"No idea," he said. "She took a bus to Atlanta months ago."

Another soft cry from Emma's lips, and Chloe wished she could engulf her in a hug. She'd been abandoned by the person who was supposed to protect her from men like Mitch. "You can't buy people."

"You can in my world." They were under the castle now, and he flipped on a flashlight, his other hand clutching Chloe's arm so she wouldn't run.

"It's an evil world you live in."

He snorted. "And a lucrative one."

"We won't help you with any of your work." Chloe glanced over at Emma and saw strength growing again in the girl's eyes. They might lose the battle, but neither of them was going to leave this castle willingly with Mitch or his friends.

"You are going to help me tonight." He jabbed her forward again. "Both of you."

They passed by one of the arches that led out to the overgrown yard, Mitch's light falling across both of them and onto the dirt path. He probably had a weapon tucked in his jacket, but he only had two hands, both of which were in use.

"It seems to me that you're scared," Chloe told him.

"I'm not scared."

"Scared of a ten-year-old girl at that."

His voice hardened. "I'm not afraid of anyone."

*A flight risk,* the caseworker had said. And she dearly hoped Emma remembered how to fly.

Chloe nudged Emma with her foot. "A ten-year-old who is pretty darn good at running."

The smallest of cues, softest of words, but they hit like a cannonball. Emma might have felt beaten by his cruelty, but she took off like a champ, straight toward the archway.

Mitch swore as his flashlight swung to the right, the beam illuminating the corridor, light that Emma needed to escape. Then he turned back and belted Chloe's shoulder, cursing her with an artillery of words, but his anger only amplified her resolve.

He shoved her ahead. "My colleagues will retrieve her."

But he didn't know about the skiff hidden in the folds of Koster Isle.

"You are willing to risk everything for her," she said slowly as she realized why he needed Emma. "Risking everything because you've already sold her to someone else."

"You don't know anything about the risk."

If he didn't deliver, it might cost him his life.

Chloe refused to move another step until Mitch pushed her back into a brick tunnel. Displayed on the wall was an old Pendleton clock, its rim rusted from the weather. He tipped the clock to the side, and underneath was a brass knob like the one that Logan had found.

A door opened in the brick, and Mitch yanked her inside. Then he directed her into a room near the entrance, beside a pallet stacked with white bricks. Dozens of them encased in plastic wrap, bound together with rope.

"You are smuggling cocaine."

He borrowed one of the ropes and tied Chloe to a metal chair, her arm and shoulder pounding.

"I'm only storing the bricks," he repeated as if that was a more virtuous enterprise than the actual smuggling. "It's a viable business."

"Not when you're keeping your drugs on my property."

"I'm just the middleman," he said. "For whatever needs distribution."

People and drugs.

Mitch reached for a clipboard. "And it's been a pleasure doing business with you."

"I have nothing to do with your business."

"That's not what Gavin and the others are going to think when you and Emma disappear."

She winced but her voice held strong. "They won't believe it."

"A friend is coming to pick these up tonight," he said, sweeping his hand over the bricks. "And you're both going along for the ride."

The chair squeaked when she moved. "Emma and I will find our own ride back to Clayton."

Hopefully Emma was paddling away from the island right now.

If only she'd listened to that voice back at Birdie's house than neither of them would be in danger.

If only God would speak again—this time she wouldn't ignore His voice.

Mitch started checking things off his list. Inventory, she supposed, for the underbelly of this industry.

"Is it worth it?" she asked.

He looked up. "What do you mean?"

"Selling your soul."

"I'm giving people what they want. Nobody cares about my soul."

She heard another noise along with the creaking of her chair, like the whine from a storm, but it hadn't been windy when they arrived. Perhaps one of Mitch's colleagues was patrolling the tunnel.

She prayed he hadn't found Emma.

Then another sound jolted her. Not a whisper this time, but the bark of a dog, and she coughed to cover it up.

"You think this dust is bad?" Mitch snapped. "Wait until you smell what's in a ship's hold."

Chloe shuffled in her seat again, the creaking sound echoing across the room, and he glared at her. "Stop doing that."

"The chair squeaks whenever I move," she said, her voice louder than before.

"It's maddening."

Wishful thinking, perhaps, but she thought she heard another bark. And it seemed to be near the door.

She coughed again, praying that, even though she'd failed to listen the first time, God wouldn't abandon her now.

"I'll kill you right—" His words were cut off when Maple bounded inside the room, rushing to Chloe's side, and she wished she could wrap her arms around her dog.

Instead she nodded at Mitch as she belted the command. *"Gie it laldy."*

Seconds later, Maple took him down.

Logan and Sugar were right behind, and Logan quickly secured Mitch with the remaining rope.

"He has more friends on the island," Chloe told him. "They'll find us."

"The police are close by," Logan said, her chair creaking one last time as he carved through the rope with his pocketknife. "They already apprehended a boat down by the docks."

"And Emma . . . ?"

The girl popped her head into the door. "I'm right here."

"Thank God." Chloe sighed with relief.

"She was cruising toward Clayton for help."

Emma smiled before thumbing toward the man on the ground. "On his boat."

Mitch was swearing at Emma, at all of them, but no one was paying attention.

Logan wrapped his arms around both Emma and Chloe, pulling them close.

"How did you know we were here?" Chloe asked.

"Birdie's daughter called Gavin. Told him we needed to take down the man."

She nodded at Mitch. "You did."

"And she told us about the tunnels," he said. "I didn't think you'd mind if I retrieved Maple and Sugar to help."

She petted her dogs and hugged Emma again and then kissed the man who'd rescued her in the castle walls.

# 44
# CHLOE

OCTOBER 1992

"The hot water heater is off," Logan shouted from inside the cottage. "All I have to do is drain the water lines."

Even though the air had cooled, the winter guard marching in, she didn't move from her seat on the back patio. Instead she'd pulled the blanket that Miriam had knitted for Philip closer to her chest, trying to embrace another change.

The flames of autumn lit her forest. Fire-red sumac. Candy-orange maple. Golden teardrops that dripped from her birch trees.

It was like they were all grieving this goodbye together.

Logan's first article about Poppy had been published a month ago, after Gavin arrested Mitch and several of his so-called friends. Then he'd found Emma's mother in Atlanta. The woman, strung out on drugs, relinquished her rights to her daughter.

Logan's story hadn't mentioned Emma by name, but the exposé, they'd all decided, would strike fear in anyone who wanted to kidnap another child in these islands.

In Mitch's boredom, perhaps, or his quest for an inkling of fame, he'd decided to talk to Logan from the visiting room at the federal correctional facility in Ray Brook. His grandmother was Rose Yancey, he'd explained, a seamstress who'd been privy to many of the Pendleton secrets. And Logan began digging from there.

When the Syracuse editor realized the breadth of Birdie's journey, she'd flown Logan to England in search of the birth records for one Penelope Pendleton. Instead, he discovered that Eleanor Koster—known as Ellie—had actually birthed Penelope when she was staying, quite unwillingly, at a mental health institution. According to the paperwork, Ellie's mind was unsound, and the doctors had taken the baby away.

Her sister had raised Penelope as a Pendleton until Ellie was released from the sanatorium. Then she traveled to New York to claim what was hers.

Chloe shared her own story with him then, every bit of it, and gave him permission to run whatever he wanted. She'd do about anything to protect her grandpa's legacy, but she wouldn't cover up the truth.

Logan had sifted through all the broken pieces, honoring her childhood while sharing the realities of her family's past. In his hunting, he'd found no indication that her grandpa was ever involved in the opium business, even when it was a legal substance, or that he'd received a windfall of money beyond the trust that Mrs. Pendleton left for their son.

Grandpa Cade had moved soundly from hero to human in Chloe's mind, and she'd decided that was a good place for him to land. He'd made tough choices in his life, wrong ones at times, but he'd worked to restore where he'd failed and love well those who God brought his way.

As she and Emma both stepped onto a new path, God had begun melding their brokenness into something beautiful like only a good Father could do. She was no longer afraid of her past or Poppy's tower or being left alone. In fact, the entire Townsend clan had adopted her and Emma into their fold.

More articles followed in the Syracuse paper, and in the midst, Logan had written about the candy shop, calling it *vintage* instead of *washed-up*. Customers had poured in through September to buy sweets and ask questions and taste the peppermint cocoa that Logan had touted as a treat. They also wanted to meet Chloe Ridell, the Pendleton heir.

The door squeaked open, and Logan stepped onto the patio, offering her a mug of cocoa.

"Thank you," she said, taking a sip.

He sat down beside her. "You'll be back in a few months."

"I still hate saying goodbye." How she'd miss this little cottage that embodied everything good in her world.

"We'll bring out an iceboat soon to check on things."

She glanced at him. "It can be a pretty bumpy ride over."

"I'll still come with you."

And she loved him for it.

They could visit once the river had frozen, but in the spring, it would be much too dangerous to cross with the floes. She'd have to wait until the ice melted to return.

The telephone rang and she stepped inside to answer it.

"Glad I caught you," Gavin said as she finished the warm drink.

"Should I be glad?"

"I think so. We just arrested the last of Yancey's gang. All of them are behind bars."

She took a deep breath. Emma had already started school in Clayton, and even though the police had apprehended Mitch, Chloe had been afraid for her.

"What about other women or children being trafficked on ships?"

"That's an investigation that will last much longer," he said, and she glanced over at Logan, grateful for his tenacity to investigate this too. "We're partnering with Border Patrol."

"Is Emma safe?"

"I don't see any reason to send her away."

And she was relieved to hear it.

When she hung up the phone, Chloe looked back at the trees, the sky beyond bruised from an oncoming storm.

"What are you going to do about Emma?" Logan asked as he washed out their mugs.

She dried them with a towel although they'd be plenty dry on their own in the next three months. "I think . . . it's crazy, Logan."

"What's crazy?"

The idea rattled again in her head, like it had been doing since she'd hugged Emma in the basement of the castle. In that moment, she'd never wanted to let her go. "I'd like to adopt her."

He smiled. "I don't think that's crazy."

"If she'll have me, of course."

"I don't think there is any doubt."

She looked back at the living room where she'd gathered last night with Emma, Fraidy, and the dogs. A whole crowd in this small space. "I don't know anything about motherhood, really. Especially not a preteen."

Logan looked like he was about to say something to disband her theory, but he eyed the dark sky upstream. "We better go. It's supposed to start sleeting in an hour."

She strapped the last bag over her shoulder and locked the storm door.

"Will you come home with me?" Logan asked as they climbed into *Lolli*.

She tilted her head. "I've already been to Syracuse."

"Not there." He stalled for a moment. "To Indiana."

She lowered herself into the captain's chair but didn't start the motor. "Why would I go to Indiana?"

"To meet my family," he said. "I think you'd like it there."

A picture washed through her mind of meeting his parents and then walking through the cornfield to the little cemetery that he'd described. Placing a flower on Shiloh's grave.

The sky grew darker as they lingered in the lagoon.

"Emma could stay with Jenna and Kyle for a few days."

"You've already asked—"

"Please, Chloe." He stroked his hand across his beard, his eyes intent on her. "Come with me."

In the past six months, he'd journeyed with her through the onslaught of memories, through the maze of good and bad, the beacon of truth flickering in the darkness.

And she couldn't imagine life without him in the months ahead.

"I'll go," she said, and he smiled at her.

It was time, she thought, to step into his story.

45

# LOGAN

APRIL 1993

*The Good Ship* was still the centerpiece of Chloe's Candy & Coffee, but the hull and her lollipop portholes had been recrafted from alabaster, a sculpted pool of turquoise underneath. Like the rest of the remodeled shop, the sculpture sparkled afresh under glittering light fixtures blown to look like wings.

Through the display window, Logan could see the store walls striped like candy, and the sweet smells—the rich scents of chocolate and caramel and all the flavors of Chloe's new confections—were wafting into the street. Behind the espresso counter, he saw a red-painted sign that read *Joe's Jellies* and a wall below filled with candy-packed chambers.

Spring tourists streamed past Logan at the entrance, rushing around him like he was a boulder blocking the tide. Jenna was at the front counter when he finally stepped inside, ringing up sales for their modified menu of frozen drinks on this warm day. Candy itself, Chloe had told him, wouldn't keep their store profitable, but she thought there was money to be had in coffee.

He was immensely proud of how hard they'd worked over the winter.

Jenna didn't want her name on the sign, but the women were equal partners now. They had redesigned the space with glass counters to make the aisles look like a jewelry boutique. Edible necklaces. Bracelets. Ring Pops in red and blue.

He tapped the small box in his pocket.

"Newsboy!" Jenna shrieked before running around the counter to give him a hug. "We didn't think you were ever coming home."

*Home.*

He liked the sound of that.

"I've been continent hopping. Three of them in the past month."

"I heard. Did you track down the interviews you needed?"

"Yep. And a ring of traffickers has officially been stung."

"Well done," Jenna said. "They hired the right reporter when they snagged you."

Over the winter, the *Post-Standard*'s parent company had reassigned him to a national news desk. He would be traveling on assignment—hunting down bad guys, if he must—but he could do the actual writing, the fighting for justice, from anywhere.

"I don't suppose you're here to see me," Jenna quipped.

"What do you mean?" He grinned. "It's lovely to see you."

"Chloe's escorting Emma home after school. Since the weather's nice, they'll probably stop at the park to take a deep breath before the weekend craziness begins."

A group of kids pressed against the display window, and he could hear their laughter through the glass. "Looks like the weekend has already started."

"Business has been fabulous, thanks to your story—and the magic-making confectioner that Chloe hired to turn her ideas into fancy treats. Birdie stops in about once a week to buy a box of sea salt truffles, and the crowds go absolutely wild whenever she flies through the door. We really should put her on payroll."

"Has she been to visit the castle yet?" he asked.

"Not yet." Jenna tapped her fingernail on her cheek and then pointed it at him. "I think she's waiting for a wedding."

He grinned. "I wonder who's getting married."

"For someone who likes to ask a lot of questions, you're sure taking your sweet time."

"I'm still formulating."

"Formulate faster," she said, her hand falling to her stomach.

"I hear congratulations are in order."

She smiled. "Kyle and I will be hiring Emma as a babysitter next year."

"I'm happy for you."

He had other questions, but more than the asking, he wanted to see Chloe. She'd already stolen his heart last year before they went to Indiana, and after a week with his family, his mom told him to snatch her up before Christmas. But he'd begun listening closer, like Chloe, to the God whispers. While he might have been ready to move ahead, Chloe was not.

But now . . . just maybe.

He found Emma and Chloe laughing at the park as they swung side by side. Emma leapt from her swing when he stepped through the gate and bolted toward him.

"Hey, kiddo." In one swoop, he picked her up, wishing he could twirl her around with two good legs, but she seemed satisfied with his hug.

Then Chloe was beside him, her sundress dancing in the breeze. "You've come back."

"Of course." He wasn't sure if he should kiss her in front of Emma, but she kissed him first.

Emma giggled, and then Chloe laughed again with her. And he knew it was time to ask her the question that was about to pop out of his head.

They walked Emma to the shop, both of them holding one of her hands, and then Jenna shooed them away. "Go find someplace to just *be* for tonight. Emma and I are fine."

This time Chloe didn't argue.

She escorted him to a bench along the river's edge as a ship passed the shore. It would be a long time, he hoped, before smugglers of any kind returned to the St. Lawrence.

"Surprised?" he asked as he stretched his arm around her.

"Pleasantly."

He grinned. "Good."

They'd talked just yesterday when he was in Panama, minutes before he stepped on the plane.

"The shop looks amazing," he said as she rested her head on his shoulder, settling into the nook of his arm.

"I was hoping you'd like it."

"And Emma seems quite content."

Chloe watched a saltie pass by. "I guess I have news of my own."

He braced himself, not sure whether or not the news would impact what he wanted to ask of her.

"I finally talked to her about adoption."

"What did she say?" he asked, breathing deeply again of the river air.

"That birds of a feather should always flock together."

He laughed.

"Kaitlyn already submitted the paperwork. She said a judge should sign it soon."

"I'm happy for you, Chloe. You'll be a great mom."

Silence settled over them before she spoke again. "Do you have any other questions for me?"

He cleared his throat, as nervous as the day he'd brought her to Indiana. "I never thought you'd ask me to ask a question."

"I never thought you'd stop asking them."

He glanced sideways. "I'm afraid you'll have to help me with this one."

"What do you mean?"

"If I get down on one knee, I'm afraid I won't be able to stand again." When her mouth dropped open, he grinned. "You might have to catch me."

She smiled. "I believe I've already caught you, Logan."

"Indeed."

"And you don't even have to get on one knee."

He took the ring box out of his pocket and held it out, the antique silver and crest of diamonds glistening in the light. "It's my grandmother's, but she said that she would like nothing more than to see it on your hand."

"I'd like nothing more myself," she said as she slipped it on.

"To our flock," he said.

"Our flock and our future."

"Chloe—"

Her smile started to fall. "What is it?"

"Look at that," he whispered, pulling her close.

They lingered there, watching together as a small chunk of ice, the last of the season, floated past.

EPILOGUE

# BIRDIE

AUGUST 1993

Logan and Chloe married in the island chapel they'd restored. Only a handful of guests fit inside for the wedding—Birdie, Emma, Jenna, and Logan's immediate family included. The remaining members of the Townsend and Danford families along with Joe Lindley and the McLean family and a host of Clayton friends waited in the forest for the short ceremony to end.

When the chapel doors opened, in lieu of throwing rice, each guest opened the birdcage in his or her hand. And the sight of the birds released into the woods, some walking, others flying, all of them offered a safe place to nest, warmed Birdie's heart.

The day marked the birth of Chloe and Logan's marriage and the beginnings of a bird sanctuary on Koster Isle.

"You have to see inside the castle," Chloe said, taking Birdie's arm.

While Birdie no longer needed a walker or a cane to support her hip, she always welcomed help from one of her clan.

Gale took her other hand, and they slowly walked up the stairs to the veranda door and then Birdie stepped carefully inside.

She marveled at the immensity of the atrium and the gallery of fine paintings and all the clocks that hung on the walls. But if she'd been a few years younger, she would have run the opposite direction when she saw her own portrait hanging on the wall.

How strange to see oneself in a ghost of a place.

In that moment, Birdie counted every blessing that flooded into her mind. Her children and grandchildren and her prince of a husband. If she'd stayed on Koster Isle, if she had been raised as a Pendleton, she would have missed a life of pure contentment with the love and laughter of Will and their children.

And if she'd stayed with Ellie, she suspected things would have been much worse. Chloe had told her that Ellie was her biological mother, stealing Poppy away from the woman who was actually her aunt. After living with Ellie for seven years, she could only imagine that Amelia Pendleton had been trying to protect her. She was grateful for what seemed to have been a steady few years before she was swept into chaos.

Chloe wasn't her niece, as they'd first imagined. They were cousins, it seemed. The only descendants of the Koster girls.

Birdie stepped up to another portrait near the front door, a formal one of a family dressed in stiff attire, not a single one smiling in the artist's rendition. Then Gale stepped up beside her and pointed at the girl with golden ringlets, her head circled in a bow.

"She looks like you, Mom."

Birdie studied the face whose features she mirrored. "That's Ellie."

Chloe pointed at the younger girl in the picture, the one with dark hair. "That is her sister, Amelia. The aunt who raised you."

People were gathering outside on the patio, a full spread of food waiting to be enjoyed, but Birdie wasn't ready to join them. Instead she turned back to Chloe. "Where did you find this picture?"

"In one of the tunnels."

Chloe and Logan had found other things behind the walls. Jewels and housewares and dozens of clocks that they'd shared with the Townsend clan, but Birdie hadn't heard yet about a portrait.

"I'd like a moment," she said, "if you don't mind."

Gale and Chloe exchanged a glance before they stepped away.

When they left, Birdie moved closer to the oil painting, studying the dark-haired girl. And then she looked at another portrait of Leslie, Amelia, and the girl named Poppy.

She ran her fingers across Amelia's face, her eyes sad.

"Aunt Sarah," she whispered as she pulled her hand away. "Sister Sarah from Ogdensburg."

Logan thought Amelia Pendleton had perished in the shipwreck, but she hadn't. She had found Birdie in the hospital and taken her to a safe place, then helped her find work on Leek Island and a scholarship to attend nursing school. Amelia had sat on the front pew for her and Will's small wedding and gifted them with money that, Birdie suspected, funded Will's boat so they had a place to live.

This was the woman who'd lavished Birdie with love and shared Poppy's story, in her own way, through poetry and pictures. Perhaps she would have told her the whole story eventually if she hadn't died so young. Or perhaps not. She was probably scared that Birdie might hate her for taking Ellie's baby at first and then for not protecting her once she brought Poppy home.

Instead, Amelia had watched over Birdie in those later years, and Birdie had wanted to be just like her when she finished school.

While she wouldn't judge—shouldn't judge—what had happened between the sisters, she knew for certain that Amelia Pendleton had rescued her, but she would never again think of her as Amelia. She was, forever, Aunt Sarah in her heart.

As the guests chattered outside, Birdie ran her fingers once more across the smooth oil paint that colored her aunt's face, and then she kissed her cheek.

She couldn't hear Aunt Sarah's voice anymore, but all across Koster Isle, generations to come would hear her singing in the chorus of birds and watch her strength borne on fragile wings.

KEEP AN EYE OUT FOR THE NEXT TIME-SLIP NOVEL BY

# MELANIE DOBSON

*Coming in 2024 from Tyndale House Publishers*

And follow Melanie Dobson on social media:

 *MelanieDobsonFiction*  *melbdobson*  *MelBDobson*

CP1647

# A Note from the Author

Poppy Pendleton captured my heart from the moment I began writing this novel, and she wouldn't let me go until her whole story unfolded on paper. As I wrote about Poppy's wings, it was pure joy for me to research the Gilded Age castles in New York, the many fascinating people who have lived on the St. Lawrence, and all the secrets hidden in the craggy Thousand Islands.

While the threads of river stories wove this novel together, the heart of my book was actually inspired by a baby in Ohio that my great-grandparents adopted in 1923. My aunt recently discovered a family portrait with this girl, but both my grandpa and great-uncle—her adoptive brothers—died more than thirty years ago, and no one else in my family remembered her name. Following the tragic death of my great-grandparents, my grandpa and great-uncle went to live with their aunt, and the little girl seemingly disappeared.

Last year my research-wizard stepmom and a Cleveland librarian found the name of this girl in the state records. Young Marjory Wacker was listed on the 1930 census as *friend* in another home, two hours north from where she'd spent her early years. While we still don't know exactly how she ended up with the MacKims, we have inklings of a difficult journey. Her name was eventually changed, and in 1940, the census recorded Marjorie MacKim as *daughter*.

The unknowns from Marjorie's life ignited a hundred questions in my mind. She was one of countless children who have been lost over time. One that, through story, I wanted to find.

In the middle of my search, Poppy emerged from the blaze of unknowns.

I wanted to plant Poppy in a story garden that contained both shadows of danger and shimmers of courage, along with plenty of soil to cultivate her love of birds and books and the open air. *Devyn's Dilemma* by Susan G. Mathis and *The Humming Room* by Ellen Potter were novels that had captivated me with the beauty and legends of the Thousand Islands, and I quickly discovered that this was the perfect home for my fictional world. Centuries ago, after missionaries arrived in the New World, a legend was born among the local tribes that these islands were created when a thousand flowers fell from the transfigured Garden of Eden and sprinkled across the river. As my story grew, I wanted Poppy and Amelia alike to embrace hope like this along the moody St. Lawrence, right in the midst of its storms.

Koster Isle is my own creation, but the size and topography would be equivalent to Deer Island, owned by Yale's Skull and Bones society. Multiple castles and derelict mansions inspired Poppy's Castle along with the nursery in a Gothic British estate called Tyntesfield that I had the honor of visiting with fellow writers and friends Cathy Gohlke and Carrie Turansky (Tyntesfield inspired Carrie's Highland Hall). Some of the formerly regal homes in the Thousand Islands can only be seen in books now, but I had the opportunity to explore the restored Singer Castle on Dark Island and Boldt Castle on Heart Island along with the Boldt Yacht House that sits across the channel on Wellesley. I also explored the streets of Clayton, home to the former Herald Hotel. Legend has it that more than a hundred years ago the hotel began serving Sophie's Sauce, created by the wife of a local fishing guide. You might have heard of it. According to one rendition, the diced pickles in this unique dressing were supposed to represent the region's thousand-plus islands.

The St. Lawrence, named by Jacques Cartier, funnels the world's largest reservoir of fresh water to the Atlantic, providing essential transportation, a wildlife habitat, and inspiration for poets and artists alike. The immense river divides the Canadian and American mainlands, but it also unites people on both sides as they share and preserve this binational waterway.

The historical Saint Lawrence was a Roman deacon and martyr who cared for the poor about two hundred years after the resurrection of Christ. I am constantly in search of hope flickering in the darkest of places and setting *The Wings of Poppy Pendleton* on a river named for this courageous, faithful man was particularly inspiring. While Valerian, the emperor of Rome, was murdering citizens in his quest for power and wealth, Lawrence believed that people, including the widows and orphans in his city, were the greatest treasure in God's Kingdom.

Protection of the vulnerable is a critical need in our world today. The Mann Act, passed in 1910, was the first law in America to prevent women from being trafficked, but it did not specifically protect minors. The law has changed over the years, including an amendment in 1994 to increase the protection of children. Now it's a felony to willingly transfer anyone under the age of eighteen for the purpose of prostitution.

I was stunned to discover in my research the prevalent and quite legal use of opium at the turn of the nineteenth century. *Harper's Weekly* called morphine-spiked tonics like Mrs. Winslow's Soothing Syrup "the poor child's nurse" because the popular drug would coax little ones to sleep. Sometimes, sadly, these children never woke up. By 1895, according to *Smithsonian* magazine, about one in two hundred Americans were impacted by drug addiction, but it wasn't until 1906 that Teddy Roosevelt signed the Pure Food and Drug Act requiring addictive drugs to be listed on product labels. The drug crisis continues today with more than eighty thousand Americans dying in 2021 from overdoses involving opioids.

To research this story, I spent a week exploring the North Country (photos from my trip can be found at melaniedobson.com) and then pored over a mound of books. Some of the most helpful resources included *Of Time and an Island* (John Keats), *Fool's Paradise* (Paul Malo), and *River Song* (Phil Jenkins). The most difficult portion of my research was reading the firsthand accounts of the deadliest shipwreck in Canadian waters, but *The Tragic Story of the Empress of Ireland*, written in 1914 by L. T. Myers, and *Dark Descent*, published ninety years later by Kevin F. McMurray, were vital in the building of my story. Only 4 of 138 children survived the *Empress of Ireland* with Grace Hanagan, the seven-year-old daughter of the Salvation Army bandmaster, being the youngest. Two bellboys—Charles Spencer and Samuel Baker—also survived, and an Irish seaman named William Clark was rescued from the wreckage of both the *Empress of Ireland* and *Titanic*.

Many people contributed their vast knowledge, editorial expertise, and family history to *The Wings of Poppy Pendleton*. As hard as I work to interview professionals and verify facts, I'm certain this book is not perfect. As always, the errors are mine.

A special thank-you to:

Kenny and Melody Brabant (authors of *River bRat*) for inviting me to their home in Clayton and sharing their many stories. I laughed when Ken introduced himself as a "character." While he is not Cade, he has been a caretaker on Grindstone Island for forty-plus years and told me that he begins each day with "a bowl of nuts and bolts." Melody's grandmother was a cook on *La Duchesse*, an elegant 106-foot houseboat built in 1903.

Matt Macvittie, the curator and collections manager at the Antique Boat Museum, for kindly giving me a tour of *La Duchesse* in its restored glory. The communications staff at New York's Office of Children and Family Services for answering my many questions about foster care. Thomas LaClair and the Thousand Islands Museum for use of the vintage map to build my fictional world, and Martin Debofle at the Empress of Ireland Museum for helping me with the impossible-to-find-online facts.

Tom French, author of *Wind Water Waves* and recorder of local history through riverstories.org, who gave me access to his family's oral history. Tom's detailed writing and recordings were invaluable in helping me understand the heritage across generations on the river.

Noelle McKee, the owner of Teeter Totter Sweets & Treats in Oregon, who let me pick her brain about all things candy. My daughter and I have visited her cozy shop multiple times since, under the guise of research, to sample vintage sweets and custom confections. Mike and Linda Jodoin, founders of Miss Hannah's Gourmet Popcorn, for their hospitality and sharing the heart and logistics of their family-run business along with their desire to spread joy through their amazing treats and relationships they've built with all those who visit their store. Jennifer Haessly, friend for life, for educating me on all things bank related. Jim Traut, my favorite retired firefighter, for helping me see the world through Logan's eyes.

Nicole Miller, Dawn Shipman, Tracie Heskett, and Julie Zander for your wisdom, debates, and years of friendship as we continue growing together as writers. Michele Heath, first reader and dear friend, for your insight and for brainstorming the details of this story. Kerri Weldon, gracious reader friend, for your kindness and willingness to walk alongside me as I wrote about your beautiful islands. Tosha Williams for your forever friendship along with your many notes and prayers. Each of you and so many more friends are God-gifts to me.

Natasha Kern, the gold standard of book agents, for your direction and encouragement. My colleagues at Tyndale House Publishers and our foreign publishing friends, including my amazing editors, Stephanie Broene and Kathryn Olson, along with Andrea Martin and Tyndale's top-notch marketing, distribution, and partnership teams. How grateful I am to work with you.

Readers—I cherish every one of you. Thank you for reading my stories and sharing your own and joining me here for another journey.

My husband, Jon, who abounds in encouragement and grace and superpower tech skills, an exceptional gift for this not so tech-savvy writer. Daughters Kiki—joy giver, music lover, and fellow creator of stories—and Karlyn, who is courageously serving our country in the US Navy. My parents, Jim and Lyn Beroth, for loving me well, praying over every story, and telling the world about my work.

And just so you know, I happen to have the best sisters in the world. A special thank-you to Christina Nunn, the most incredible sis a girl could ever have. We've done life together for more than fifty years, and I've been gifted with five more sisters along the way—Annalisa, Val, Laura, Tressa, and Karen. My blessings overflow with these women in my life.

A final thank-you to the Spirit of our Lord—Acts 17:28—for creativity and the legacy of story. For filling my mind with possibilities and growing my faith with every word.

# Discussion Questions

1. The main characters in this novel try to find happiness, or what some describe as joy, through various means. What is the difference between happiness and joy? How can we enjoy the simple pleasures of life without being consumed?

2. The similarities in Birdie's, Chloe's, and Emma's stories endear them to each other, creating a strong bond between three generations. How does history repeat itself in this story? And how do these characters turn a cycle of harm into healing for the next generation?

3. When Emma finds a sparrow with a broken wing, she says, "Even a fragile wing can fly again." Do you have an example from your life where a broken or seemingly hopeless situation was restored?

4. What do Amelia's birds and the aviary represent in her life? And how does Birdie's imagination give her the freedom to fly?

5. Chloe equates diving into her memories to a scuba diver searching a shipwreck, but shipwrecks like the *Empress of Ireland* are very dangerous to explore, sometimes stealing the lives of multiple divers. When is it healthy to dive more deeply into the past and when can exhuming a wreck be dangerous to our well-being? How can we balance the two?

6. While a shipwreck was ultimately Birdie's salvation, it destroyed other people's lives. As she ponders God's presence, Birdie also asks why God didn't stop the war or the shipwreck or the man. How would you answer this tough question?

7. Scottish writer George MacDonald said in his book *Phantastes*, "Past tears are present strength." How have past trials and hardships strengthened you today?

8. Several characters in the story are intent on blessing their friends and family, while others want to hurt those who love them. Then other characters in this book are conflicted about spreading joy or chaos in their world. If you were counseling Amelia or Chloe, what words of advice would you give each of them? Anything you'd like to say to another character?

9. Amelia, on the advice of the doctor and her father, believed it was in Poppy's best interest to be taken away from Ellie. How do you balance Amelia as heroic on one hand and selfish on the other? What would you do if you were asked to harbor someone else's child?

10. Logan has seen plenty of evil in his life, but he has deliberately chosen to right the wrongs in his world instead of contributing to destruction. In chapter 29, he thinks about all those who are busy planting the seeds of God's Kingdom, resulting in a harvest of good. Have you ever watched a seed of healing or peace grow into something extraordinary? And do you have a "joy giver" in your life?

# About the Author

Melanie Dobson is the award-winning author of twenty-five historical, time-slip, and romantic suspense novels. Five of her novels have won Carol Awards; *Catching the Wind* and *Memories of Glass* were nominated for a Christy Award in the historical fiction category; and *Catching the Wind* won an Audie Award in the inspirational fiction category. *The Black Cloister*, her novel about a religious cult, won the *Foreword* magazine Religious Fiction Book of the Year.

Melanie is the previous corporate publicity manager at Focus on the Family, owner of the publicity firm Dobson Media Group, and an adjunct writing professor. When she isn't working on her next novel, Melanie enjoys teaching a variety of workshops.

Melanie and her husband, Jon, have two daughters. After moving numerous times with work, the Dobson family has settled near Portland, Oregon, and they love to hike and camp in the mountains of the Pacific Northwest and along the Pacific Coast. Melanie also enjoys exploring ghost towns and abandoned homes, helping care for kids in her community, and creating stories with her girls.

Visit Melanie online at melaniedobson.com for more information about her books or to sign up for her newsletter.